DUDLEY PUBLIC LIBRARIES

The loan of this book may be renewed if not required by other readers, by contacting the library from which it was borrowed.

MUSTANG CREEK MANHUNT

JANICE KAY JOHNSON

CAVANAUGH JUSTICE: THE BABY TRAIL

MARIE FERRARELLA

MILLS & BOON

First Published in Great Britain 2022
by Mills & Boon, an imprint of HarperCollins*Publishers* Ltd
1 London Bridge Street, London, SE1 9GF

www.harpercollins.co.uk

HarperCollins*Publishers*
1st Floor, Watermarque Building,
Ringsend Road, Dublin 4, Ireland

Mustang Creek Manhunt © 2022 Janice Kay Johnson
Cavanaugh Justice: The Baby Trail © 2022 Marie Rydzynski-Ferrarella

ISBN: 978-0-263-30332-2

MUSTANG CREEK
MANHUNT

JANICE KAY JOHNSON

Mustang Creek Manhunt deals with topics some
readers might find difficult, such as sexual assault
and the PTSD that follows as a result.

Chapter One

A Boyd Chaney sighting, whether in-person or courtesy of news media, could sour any day for Melinda McIntosh. Unfortunately, those sightings had become increasingly common since he'd been elected Granger County sheriff. This morning was a perfect example. There she'd been, happily prepared to dig into her breakfast cereal, when she spread her morning newspaper on the kitchen table only to see a large photo of him, front page and above the fold.

Of course *he* wouldn't be relegated to page four. After winning the election, he'd apparently designated himself spokesperson for the sheriff's department. Local journalists ate up his every all-knowing pronouncement. Half the time, he was on the air or in the newspaper expressing opinions about other events that had taken place in this rural eastern Oregon county. Or maybe they latched on to him because he managed to look dauntingly authoritative, not to mention tall, lean and broad-shouldered, every inch the decorated former army ranger he was. Reassuring. Even his heavy-lidded eyes and almost smile came across as sexy without diminishing his air of comptence.

The voters had cast their ballots for him because, although he'd only been resident in the county for something like five years and had zero background in law enforcement, he co-owned the biggest horse and cattle ranch in these parts and had served his country overseas. He wore the dark green, sheriff's department Stetson as if he'd been born to it.

Melinda realized her hands had tightened convulsively on the steering wheel of her squad car until her knuckles ached. She was driving back toward Sadler after conducting an interview, but she'd tuned out radio traffic, and there had been some. She knew better than to let herself brood while she was on the job! *Okay, deep breath. In, out. Relax.* It could be worse. At least she hadn't seen him in person recently, and the last time had only been a glimpse when—

Her gaze focused on a black car shooting toward her in the oncoming lane on the highway. Damn, it was moving fast, almost blurring before her eyes. Not usually her business—out here beyond the city limits, she had no jurisdiction. If she'd spotted someone going ten to twenty miles over the speed limit, she'd have let them go.

This kind of driving wasn't something she could ignore.

She braked and steered to the shoulder, the right tires crunching on gravel, and was reaching for the radio when the car blew by. Two men. She thought heads turned, although it was barely a quick impression. They had to have made her vehicle as law enforcement even though it was unmarked.

She performed a U-turn and accelerated after the car, stunned by how far behind she'd already fallen. The other driver had to be going a hundred miles an hour.

Melinda identified herself to dispatch, gave her approximate location and reported, "In pursuit of a black sedan, dull matte finish. The license plate is in-state, but I couldn't get the number. Are any units in place to intercept?"

Other voices responded. One sheriff's deputy was on a paved crossroad about twenty miles to the north and was turning around to reach the highway. An Oregon state patrolman was the best bet—if the speeding car stayed on this highway.

She accelerated to a speed she'd never before attempted. If the highway had been busier, she wouldn't have dared; high-speed pursuits were discouraged for good reason. Better to set up a roadblock or even let the speeder go than be responsible for a hideous multivehicle accident involving civilians.

A voice she recognized but wouldn't expect to hear under these circumstances came on. Head of the investigative division within the Sadler Police Department, Lieutenant Edward Matson was her boss. He sounded tense.

"The Wells Fargo bank in town was just robbed. Witness descriptions of the vehicle in which the two robbers fled matches what you saw, Detective McIntosh. Dull, overall black paint job. We don't have a make and model."

"I saw two men," she said. "Didn't get a good look given the speed they were traveling."

And wouldn't you know, that was the moment when another man jumped into the discussion: Sheriff Boyd Chaney himself. Of course, his voice was deep and steady. It always was. His unrelenting control was both admirable and irritating.

"Do *not* make an individual stop," he ordered. "If the vehicle should pull over, wait for backup."

Her temper flared at the idea he thought he could tell her what to do, but this time she couldn't dispute his logic, or his right to make the decisions. This *was* his jurisdiction. Plus she assumed he wasn't speaking only to her.

"Acknowledged," the deputy agreed.

She echoed him, if a little stiffly, as did the state trooper.

"Do you still have a visual, Detective?" Chaney asked.

"Barely," Melinda admitted. "You know that Y is up ahead. I'm hoping to see which way the car goes."

"I'm now on State Route 23 waiting to intercept," he continued calmly.

He must have been monitoring the radio from his home on his large ranch. All he'd have had to do was drive out to the main road, which was the likeliest choice for fleeing bank robbers to choose. It would carry them to Highway 97, eastern Oregon's major north-south throughway. Unless they had a local bolt-hole…

If that was true, they must be panicking about now. If Melinda could see them, they could see her. If they'd imagined they could get out of Sadler, the county seat, fast enough to turn off on some dirt road to a rural property, they knew by now that the plan was in jeopardy. Boyd wasn't the man to let them race on by. If he was alone, what would he do? Shoot out the tires and precipitate a screeching, rolling, probably deadly "accident"? Or did he have one or more of his fellow retired army rangers accompanying him so they could set up a roadblock? Melinda had reason to know that Gabe Decker, the ranch co-owner, was stunningly skilled both with weapons and behind the wheel of a car. The ranch foreman, Leon Cabrera, had been a sharpshooter during his army deployments.

Yeah, but they'd end up in big trouble for getting involved in a police operation.

Despite everything going on in her head, she stayed

conscious of continuing chatter from the radio. The deputy was in place if the vehicle decided on Option #2, while the state trooper drew closer from the north. A second sheriff's deputy was joining the pursuit, but coming from well behind Melinda so not likely to be of any use.

Other state troopers had chimed in too, all prepared to watch for the car she'd described if the handful of officers closing in failed to make the stop.

Chaney asked Lieutenant Matson what weapons the bank robbers had displayed. The news wasn't good. They'd brandished both semiautomatic handguns and an assault rifle. Melinda didn't like the growing fear she felt for her nemesis, Boyd Chaney, the likeliest of them all to put himself on the line. Naturally, if *he* felt any anxiety, she couldn't hear it in his voice, which suggested he'd faced plenty of situations as ugly and emerged unscathed. Which was probably true.

Except, there'd been one time he hadn't, she knew. He'd left the army rangers after suffering catastrophic injuries that left him unable to return to active duty. To her deep regret, she'd seen his scars and the rest of his long, muscled body, too.

Had he forgotten that he was breakable, like ordinary people? Melinda asked herself in frustration.

The wail of her siren was a weird accompaniment as she kept the gas pedal to the floor. She couldn't have done it if this part of the county weren't so flat that many roads were almost ruler straight. She'd see any approaching traffic from a long distance away, too. The worst immediate disaster would be having wildlife dash right in front of her, always a possibility. Mule deer or a herd of fleet-footed pronghorns were the likeliest. Or a ranch vehicle making a slow turn onto the highway from a dirt driveway.

Although at least that would raise a cloud of dust and be moving slowly enough she could probably swerve around it without any difficulty.

"I'm gaining ground," she reported tensely. "I don't think they're slowing." Her SUV, built for law enforcement, had a more powerful engine than just about anything else on the road.

Chaney again. "A southbound semitruck just passed."

There was taut silence until she was able to report that first the speeding car and then her vehicle had flown safely past the semi. The relief went unspoken because it was so premature.

And then, "Sheriff, he's coming your way," Melinda said.

The deputy's voice crackled over the airwaves. "I'll join you."

"I think I see him," Chaney said suddenly. He must be using binoculars.

Oh, God.

"What's the plan?" she asked.

A different voice—the state trooper—said, "It just came in sight for me, too. We might be able to set up a roadblock."

"Going that fast, he could blast right through us," Chaney said. And yes, he probably knew plenty about roadblocks and both defensive and offensive driving. "Why don't you turn around? I'll pull out onto the highway right in behind him and hit the lights and siren. You can join me. Deputy Heaton, if you're ready, we'll close around him."

"You watch out," the state trooper said.

"Will do. Detective, I don't know if you can join us in time—"

She'd known that was coming. He didn't like women in law enforcement. Or maybe it was just *her* being a cop.

"The more of us there, the better."

The deputy would be bursting out of the crossroad any minute. If they could surround the speeding car, overwhelm it with their presence, they might have a chance to make the arrests without a gun battle. It was rare for bank robbers to actually kill anyone, she'd learned from her training. But these two, who knew how they'd react to stress?

DAMN, BOYD HATED that Melinda, of all people, was involved. She was a good cop, he *knew* she was, but if he had to see her shot, he didn't know how he could live with it. If they shot her, he knew damn well he wouldn't be arresting and cuffing those two with the professionalism required by a man in his job.

He also wished he and the others weren't planning a difficult move conducted at a high speed when the four of them had never worked together. His own deputy was his biggest concern; when Boyd had taken over the sheriff's department, he'd found an appalling lack of training and support. He could at least assume the trooper had been trained in these kinds of maneuvers.

Here came the black bullet. Attention split between his rearview mirror and the view ahead, he accelerated on the shoulder, determined to reach maximum speed to enable him to pull in tight behind the target. Hard to judge, but—

He looked the passenger right in the eye as the car passed and then tucked his police SUV in behind, dangerously close to the bumper in front of him. Within moments, Heaton exploded out onto the highway to close in on the driver's side. The trooper, who'd also built up speed on the shoulder, squeezed in on the right, and within minutes Melinda's unit joined Boyd to complete a pincer movement. All four of them had lights flashing and sirens screaming. Pray to God no southbound traffic appeared right now. Boyd watched for any sign those fools were going to start shooting, but after a minute brake lights flashed and the black car began slowing.

Their speed dropped to eighty, seventy, a more sane sixty miles per hour. Still no other approaching traffic. Boyd didn't take his eyes off what he could see of the two men in the vehicle ahead of him.

At his order, Heaton pulled up so he was even with the front fender of the speeding car as he gestured for it to pull over. The state trooper sped a distance ahead before swerving to block the northbound lane. He immediately leaped out and planted himself behind the bulk of his vehicle with a rifle braced to open fire.

Within moments, the car pulled onto the shoulder and came to a stop, squeezed on three sides. Heaton was out, crouched behind his vehicle, handgun held in a two-fisted grip. Melinda followed suit, staying behind her car door.

This was the most dangerous moment.

Boyd grabbed a microphone, opened his door and called, "Step out of your vehicle. *Now*. Hands up, in plain sight."

The pause seemed excruciatingly long, but probably didn't last fifteen seconds. First the driver-side door opened, then the passenger side. Boyd didn't take anything for granted until both men were lying on the pavement, cuffed and had been searched. They had guns aplenty in the car, but had been smart enough to know when to give up.

Even then, the fear that clutched Boyd's belly hadn't loosened its grip. Sweat soaked his uniform shirt beneath his arms and down his spine. He hadn't felt anything like this since his first few combat experiences in Iraq, and he knew who to blame.

Tall and slender, Melinda stood not five feet from him, her Glock held steady in her hands as she stared down at the two men who both had their heads turned away from her. Eyes that could look as richly colored as a forest glade were steely, her mouth tight.

"Let's load them," she said.

Boyd pried his clenched jaws apart enough to allow him to say, "Would you prefer to stay with the car? We can transport the prisoners for you."

Her eyes held deep suspicion. "No, I'll take one. If I can borrow Deputy Heaton to take the other, I'd appreciate that. I would prefer to keep them separated."

He bent his head in acquiescence, his neck stiff.

She hadn't been willing to give him a break, not *one*, since he'd screwed up so badly with her. He had to accept that she was a cop, a good one from what he'd seen and heard, but he hated the idea of her driving that many miles with one of these potentially violent scumbags sitting in the back of her car, filled with hate as he stared at her through the grille.

Not my business.

The state trooper cleared his throat. "I'll get on the radio and let everyone know we've wound up this incident successfully. Then I'd better get back on the road myself."

Boyd wrenched his gaze from Melinda's and held out his hand to the trooper. "Thanks. Wouldn't have gone nearly as well without you."

The guy, tall and lean, probably in his forties, grinned as he shook Boyd's hand. "Sheriff." He nodded at Heaton and Melinda. "Deputy. Ma'am."

Boyd waited for her to snap, *I'm a detective, not a ma'am*, but she smiled. "It was a pleasure." Apparently, she saved all her aggravation for him.

"Let's load 'em," Boyd growled, and bent to pull the driver to his feet.

Head down and unresisting, the bank robber stumbled to Heaton's squad car and climbed in with minimal assistance. Boyd slammed the door behind him and turned to find that Heaton and Melinda had the other prisoner up.

Tight-lipped, Boyd jerked his head toward her vehicle. "I'll wait here for a photographer and the tow truck. I assume you'll want the car delivered to your city impound?"

Still obviously wary, she said, "Yes. Thank you. I'll make the call."

Maybe he'd regain his equilibrium before the police photographer arrived. "Drive carefully."

Melinda nodded in his direction, spoke briefly to Heaton, got into her squad car and drove away without another word to Boyd. Not even a glance back in her rearview mirror, as far as he could tell.

Left alone on the side of the highway with his stomach roiling and his rib cage feeling tight, all Boyd could think was that he and Melinda had never had a chance. Given hindsight, he couldn't imagine why he'd ever dreamed they could sustain even a short-term relationship.

But she looked as enticing as ever, and a hard truth stirred the turmoil beneath his breastbone. He still wanted this woman as much as ever, even if he couldn't see himself breaking his vow.

He would never again let himself care too much about a woman who regularly put her life on the line, no matter how sexist that made him look.

As SHE DROVE, Melinda kept an eye on her prisoner, who hung his head and averted his gaze. Didn't say a word.

That left her free to kick her own ass for bristling the way she had at the least excuse. Really? She'd promised herself to be cool and completely professional the next time she and Boyd happened to encounter each other. She could only hope he hadn't noticed how she reacted to him. He hadn't done or said anything to set her off. Her mistake had been letting her guard down for him in the first place. She wished she'd never let him see the vulnerability she normally covered effectively behind her kick-ass cop persona. Which—face it—was who'd she'd become. The gut-wrenching end to her relationship with Boyd Chaney had been the final punctuation. Balancing a relationship or family and the job wasn't happening, not for her. She couldn't even let herself regret that.

Next time she had to deal with him—and there would be a next time—she'd do better.

And—damn—she'd just driven most of the way back to Sadler while, once again, allowing herself to be oblivious to other traffic and exchanges on the radio. She'd get herself or someone else killed if she couldn't keep her focus when she was on the job.

A few turns in town and she pulled in behind the jail, parking right beside Deputy Heaton's squad car. A cluster of cops and guards had been waiting for them. Three peeled off to take charge of her prisoner.

She got out and greeted them, not surprised to see that a fellow detective, Sergeant Daniel Deperro, was first to reach her. As the most experienced investigator in their department, he was something of a mentor to her. Matson had started talking about retiring, and everyone assumed that Daniel would be promoted to take his place. Melinda hoped that happened. Daniel, too, had seen plenty of active duty in the military, but unlike Chaney he never treated her any differently than he did the male members of their unit. He'd never shown any interest in her as a woman, either, but these days she was grateful for that. Respect and friendship were what mattered.

She wouldn't diminish herself for any man, and that's what she'd felt Boyd Chaney had asked of her.

Chapter Two

While she ate her lunch in the break room at the police station—leftover vegetarian chili reheated in the microwave—Melinda idly read the *Oregonian* newspaper, one of the West Coast's major dailies. This was a two-day-old edition she'd somehow missed. Bite halfway to her mouth, she lost interest in food as her gaze snapped to a headline: *Outgoing governor pardons convicted killers*.

What? Okay, it wasn't uncommon for a governor to issue some pardons on his or her way out the door. Convicts on the list might be elderly and a burden on the taxpayers, or people convicted of murders that were so personal—say, a woman who'd killed an abusive husband—they were unlikely to reoffend. Or there could well be cases where there was serious reason to question the conviction.

She was being paranoid, that's all. She'd checked on Gene Dorrance not that long ago—a couple of months, maybe?—and he'd still been in lockup at the state penitentiary in Salem in western Oregon. He hadn't been convicted of murder or even manslaughter, but even so, if he'd come up for parole, her department should have been notified so an arresting officer could attend the hearing. The threats he'd made as he'd shuffled, shackled at wrists and ankles, out of the courtroom were on record.

Still, appetite abandoning her, she set the spoon back in the bowl and kept reading, apprehensive despite herself. She never had liked the current governor; since he was being tossed out after one term, clearly the majority of voters felt the same.

She had to turn pages and refold the newspaper to continue reading the article. Now she was just scanning, looking for familiar names.

A familiar name.

It wouldn't be here. Nobody was crazy enough to let—

The name jumped out at her. *Gene Dorrance.* Melinda sat staring down at it. For how long, she didn't know, but her lungs suddenly demanded air. Her mouth must have been hanging open, too, because it was so dry she reached for her bottle of water.

And then she read the brief paragraph about the man who'd kidnapped and held two young women—one a minor—for over two years, sexually molesting them the entire time.

Melinda would see those faces in her mind's eye until her dying day. Gaunt, expressionless, eyes dulled by lack of hope. Racks of bone, their entire bodies showing years of suffering. Rescuers had had to speak to the women quietly, gently; they seemed confused by any directions, unresponsive. Melinda remembered the photos of two other young women who'd been reported missing in the same period. Neither were found at his place, but she was almost positive that at least one of them had been there. His two captives had, after a period of hospitalization, both mentioned hearing whimpering when he first dragged them into his basement.

The article didn't say why the governor would have chosen to pardon this monster, or who had recommended Dorrance for his consideration. Melinda started to reach for her phone, intending to call a guy who worked in the warden's office at the prison whom she'd gotten to know in the past, but then she thought better of it. Front section of the newspaper crushed in her hand, she left the break room, cut through the detective squad room and reached Lieutenant Matson's office. The door stood partly ajar, but she rapped on it and waited for his voice.

"I'm here."

She marched in and laid the paper in front of him. "Did you know about this?"

"This?" He was already reading. After a moment, he shoved back his chair and shot to his feet. "Of course I didn't know! Why the hell weren't we notified?"

"Because he wasn't paroled. But *this*—" She felt sick. "They still should have let us know. What were they thinking?"

He shook his head. Matson had been primary on the investigation, as horrified as she'd been. Melinda had been a patrol officer at the time. After speaking to Dorrance as a responding officer, but unable to substantiate the information in a 911 call about potential domestic violence, she'd been left with a bad feeling. A *really* bad feeling. She'd seen a couple of small things that conflicted with what Dorrance had told her. She'd gone to the lieutenant, who listened to her. Somehow, Dorrance had learned about her role in bringing him down. She'd become the focus of his greatest rage. Probably, she'd thought at the time, because he couldn't endure the idea of being bested by a woman.

Matson was already in the middle of making a call. She plopped down on a chair and waited. As angry as the lieutenant was, eavesdropping was easy.

"He was released *two days ago*?" Matson hardly ever raised his voice, but this was an exception. He'd all but rattled the glass in the window inset in the door. "Nobody paid attention to the notation that this convict's last words in the courtroom were a promise to take revenge on everyone who'd had anything to do with his arrest? And those two women—" His eyes met Melinda's. "We need to locate them immediately. I'm guessing they haven't been warned, either?"

His expression became grimmer by the minute. He didn't like anything he was hearing. Yet when he ended the call, he set down his phone almost gently. As if the alternative had been slamming it down hard enough to break it.

"Dorrance was a good boy. With no infractions on his record while he was in custody. The attempt prison officials made to throw cold water on this plan was ignored. And no, they have no idea where Dorrance is. He walked out a free man. Wasn't required to give an address or even the name of a contact."

"He's here," she said numbly. "You know he is."

"It's been, what, seven years? That first rage might have dissipated."

"He's vicious and crazy. What, you think he got rehabilitated?"

Her boss groaned, scraped a hand over his face and sank back down on his desk chair. "No. I think he's spent those seven years making detailed plans. Lovingly revising them."

"We need to inform every single person he might blame. And then we have to find Dorrance."

"I agree. Is Deperro here?"

"He was at his desk a minute ago." Melinda frowned. "He wasn't with the department back then."

"No, but he's best qualified to lead any manhunt we launch."

Her mouth opened, but Matson shook his head.

"He has experience you don't, but no matter what, paying *you* back is that madman's number one objective. We can't put you out there leading this operation."

Fear drove some of her fury. "You expect me to hide in my closet? Take a vacation? Waste more time on the question of whether we should arrest a kid for borrowing his daddy's car?"

The lieutenant winced. "You're still on that?"

"Yeah." She was all but quivering with intensity. "Along with trying to figure out who's smashing car windows at the mall so they can help themselves to whatever shoppers left in open invitation on the front seat."

He grimaced. "I'm not saying you can't be involved with this hunt. We'd never have caught him if it weren't for you. You had more insight then into who he really was than the rest of us put together. We'll need you to predict his moves. I just can't have you on public display."

What could she do but give a tight nod? She tended to get prickly when her ability to do the job was discounted, and with good reason, but in this case she did understand his decision.

"Stick your head out and call Deperro in here," he added. "Warnings to any conceivable targets have to come first."

BY THE TIME Daniel Deperro got off the call he'd been on and joined Matson and Melinda in the small office, the lieutenant had pulled up the bare-bones records.

"I don't want to miss anybody," he said. "Melinda, why don't you call Records and get them to send up everything we stored?"

Binders and boxes filled with police reports, evidence ranging from bloody garments to guns and plaster casts of footprints or tire prints, interview transcripts, photographs and more were stored in the basement. Recently, the records department had needed to expand into the basement of city hall. What she'd be requesting should still be stored in this building, though.

Melinda stepped out of the office to make that call while Matson shared Gene Dorrance's history with Deperro, explaining why they believed he'd follow through with his threats.

The lieutenant's decision to put Daniel Deperro in charge might have stung more, except Melinda respected her fellow detective and liked him. Too many cops in this conservative, rural county still didn't want to work with women. She'd had to fight hard to get where she was. Daniel had never once treated her as anything but a smart cop deservedly promoted to the detective squad. Off the job, she'd become good friends with him and his social worker wife, Lindsay. Just last weekend, she'd gone riding with them both at Daniel's small ranch, where he bred and trained quarter horses for fun.

Reentering the office, she said, "They promised to have everything up here in fifteen minutes max."

"Good," Matson said grimly. "I say we find the two women before we do anything else."

"They need to go into hiding," Daniel agreed.

Melinda had grabbed her laptop, but didn't immediately start a search. "I had a thought."

Both men waited.

"I think we should go to the press. TV, newspapers, even local bloggers. Get his face out there. Identify him as dangerous and likely armed. Ask anyone who sees him to contact us immediately."

Cops in general dodged reporters whenever they

could, so she wasn't surprised that Lieutenant Matson and Daniel stared at her in appalled silence for a minute.

Daniel was the first to nod, although he didn't look happy. "Much as I hate the idea of creating community-wide hysteria, I agree. Spreading his picture as widely as we can is the best way to hinder his movements. And as far as we know, he's not an experienced killer."

"I've always believed he is," Melinda said. She told him that the two women they'd rescued had insisted there'd been a third women in the home initially. "But it's more than that. The guy is forty-seven years old. Forty when he was convicted. These two victims were supposed to be the first he ever abducted and raped? I seriously doubt that. There could have been a long succession of them. We just didn't find the graves."

"It's also possible these were the first he kept around for a long time," Matson suggested, not for the first time. They'd had this discussion before. "He could have warmed up to it with one-time rapes and, yeah, possibly murder."

"None of the work on his house that created the lockdowns where he imprisoned the women looked recent."

Matson didn't remind her that Dorrance had held both women long enough to give the additional walls, doors and locks time to age. Melinda knew that, but she'd all but swear she'd seen a cluster of ghosts down in that basement. Or at least felt icy shivers from them breathing down her neck. Of course, she'd never told anyone that, and wouldn't now. It didn't matter, anyway; what mattered was protecting everyone Dorrance had threatened and throwing him back behind bars for the rest of his life if he made a move on anyone.

She, her lieutenant and Daniel divided up initial tasks. Matson would make immediate contact with everyone who had prosecuted Dorrance—and with the defense team, in case he was angry because his lawyers had failed to get him off. The lieutenant would also talk to the Sadler PD chief, who liked to be kept up-to-date and would need to warn the mayor before the press conference.

Daniel was to sit down with the evidence boxes, familiarizing himself with the investigation, and while he was at it, make a list of every person who'd been involved, in case Matson and Melinda had forgotten someone. He intended to search for any links Dorrance had with anyone—family or friend—who might be close enough to offer him shelter now.

Melinda was to locate and warn the two female victims, then every cop who'd had anything to do with the investigation and arrest.

"The neighbor who called 911 in the first place," she said. "If she hasn't moved…"

"Put her on the list," the lieutenant agreed.

She opened her laptop as soon as she sat down at her desk. She'd kept track of the two victims for a couple of years, but, unsurprisingly, neither wanted to stay in the area.

"If I dare go out in public, every single person who sees me will know exactly what happened to me," one of them had told Melinda. "That's all they'll see. I want a chance to not be pitiful in everyone's eyes."

Melinda had been impressed by Andrea Kudelka's strength, once she'd had a few weeks to start believing her ordeal really was over. Her eyes remained haunted, though, and anything an outsider would call real recovery was certainly years away, if it ever happened.

The two had shown no inclination to cling to each other. To the contrary. Until the rescue, they had never met face-to-face, knew each other only from screams and sobs muffled by thick cinder-block walls.

"Seeing her reminds me of what happened," Erica Warner had told Melinda in a whisper.

Her own attempt to stay in touch with both women had quickly ended. *She* reminded them of the horror they'd lived through, too.

Andrea had been a local girl living on her own, even though her parents were still resident in Sadler. Erica was from… Eugene, on the other side of the state, if Melinda remembered right. She'd been a horse-crazy kid who had been thrilled to get a job on a dude ranch. Initially, at least, she'd gone home to Eugene, but chances were everyone she'd known there had also pored over every detail made public of her hideous experience, and she'd face exactly what Andrea had already foreseen.

In fact, as Melinda began her search, it was apparent Erica's parents no longer lived in Eugene. The Kudelkas had moved away as well, but an aunt Melinda remembered seeing was still listed locally.

The question was, would their captor want to punish them for their escape before he did anything else, or would his greatest need be revenge against the people who had destroyed his life?

With a groan, she picked up her phone. Police officers first; she could reach them, or at least most of them, a lot more quickly than she could trace two women who had been determined to disappear.

As, she hoped, had the next-door neighbor, whose name was no longer listed by the phone company.

BOYD LAY ON his belly in the dirt, eye to the Leupold tactical scope attached to his Remington M24 rifle. Keeping his sniper skills sharp was probably a waste of time these days, but the attack made on the ranch a couple of years ago had convinced him that no place was safe. Besides, he liked the precision, the intense concentration he had to summon to shoot accurately over several hundred yards.

He might not have bothered building a gun range here on ranch land had it been only for him, but his partner and the ranch co-owner, Gabe Decker, was also a retired army ranger, as was their foreman, Leon Cabrera. Leon was one of the best snipers Boyd had ever seen work.

He and Gabe liked hiring former rangers, or at least giving refuge to men who needed to reintegrate into society and weren't doing so well at it. The range gave them all a chance to decompress while also reminding them of things they'd done well.

Yeah, is that what I'm doing out here today? Boyd asked himself. *Trying to convince myself I know what the hell I'm doing with my life?*

He wished he had an answer.

Wiping his mind clean, slowing his breathing, he gently pulled the trigger. Once, twice, three times, before he paused to study the target. Those had been damn good shots, would have been kill shots at five hundred yards. He still had it—whatever *it* was.

But, damn, there were things he should be doing instead of coming out here to the range by himself. Gabe was having to shoulder too much responsibility for ranch operations since Boyd had taken on a second job: county sheriff. Trouble was, this was home for the two men now, both of whom had been badly enough injured, they'd had to leave the army sooner than they'd planned. It hadn't taken long for Boyd, who settled here in Oregon first, to discover how incompetent the sheriff was and, therefore, how useless it was to call for any help from law enforcement. He'd been mad enough to decide he could do better, even if he'd never been a cop before.

Now he had to prove it, which meant he had two full-time-plus jobs.

Can't work 24/7, he told himself, grimacing as he rose from his prone position. He'd damn near lost his right leg, courtesy of an explosive that had flipped his Humvee, and the scar tissue wasn't the only reminder. He hurt more when he was on his feet than when he was on horseback, Gabe the opposite.

His phone vibrated in his pocket, which didn't thrill him. What new screwup or even disaster would he now have to deal with?

The name on the screen stunned him. Melinda McIntosh. The last thing *she'd* ever want to do again was call him. This had to be bad.

He pressed his thumb to the "accept" button and answered. "Chaney here."

"Sheriff, do you have a minute?" she asked stiffly.

Sheriff? Really? They'd made love, spent one especially memorable night in his big bed here at the ranch. That lovemaking had been so good, he wondered if it could ever be near as good with any other woman. Which was a stupid damn thing to think, but this wasn't the first time it had crossed his mind.

Irritated, he said, "For you, I have a minute. *Melinda.*"

Silence shimmered in his ear before she conceded.

"Boyd."

"What's up?"

"We have a situation. Ah, I need you to call one of your detectives, Miguel Cordova. You may know he was an SPD officer who shifted to working for the county when you had an opening for a detective."

Before Boyd had become sheriff, but he did vaguely

know Cordova's work history. The guy was sharp, unlike several deputies Boyd had been nudging toward retirement or had already let go.

"I thought this would be better coming from you," she continued, "and we'd have needed to bring you up to speed anyway."

One-handed, he snapped his rifle case closed and slid it onto the back seat of his pickup, slammed the door then got in behind the wheel. He didn't make any move to start the engine.

Her tension was contagious.

"Up to speed on what?"

She summed it up quickly: seven years ago, Sadler PD had arrested a real creep who'd kidnapped two young women and held them for years so that he could rape them repeatedly. He—Gene Dorrance—had been convicted, no problem, and gone off for a long stay at the Oregon State Penitentiary.

"I was catching up while I ate lunch today by reading a two-day-old *Oregonian*."

Hell. He never missed a day's paper. This had to be connected to the article—

"The governor pardoned a whole bunch of inmates. One of them was Dorrance. By the time we called over to the prison today, he was long gone."

Having a really bad feeling about this, Boyd asked, "Why would he come back to Sadler?"

"I was in the courthouse when he was led out. Somehow, he spotted me. He was looking me right in the eye when he said, 'I'll pay you back. Every last one of you.'"

Boyd's eyes closed and he bumped his head against the headrest. "Were you the only arresting officer in the courtroom for the verdict?"

"No, several of us were there. Actually…" There was

the tiniest hesitation. "I wasn't a detective yet, and wasn't the arresting officer, but he blamed me most of all."

This was what he'd feared when he found himself falling for a woman with a dangerous job. It had been her choice, not his, to break off the relationship, but he'd convinced himself she'd made the best choice for both of them.

So why was he as scared as he could ever remember being?

Chapter Three

Sergeant Tom Alvarez walked around the corner of the single-story, ranch-style house to meet Melinda, who had peeked in what windows she could on the north side. Two bedrooms, clearly unused, while the blinds were closed tight on what was probably the master bedroom window. Fortunately, gates on each side of the house had made their first reconnoiter easy.

She felt lucky to have been able to pull the sergeant in instead of having to bring a green patrol officer. Deperro now had more important things to do this afternoon than provide her with backup while she verified that the one cop she hadn't been able to reach was fine. Fortunately, the alarm was being taken seriously department wide. She wasn't the only cop to have heard Dorrance's threat.

"Window into the garage is covered," Alvarez reported. "Can't tell if Guy's pickup is in there or not."

Guy Jonas hadn't been answering his phone. This… welfare check, yeah, that was the best way to describe it, was a product of her paranoia. He was probably fine. Jonas was off for two days, yesterday and today. Officers were encouraged to answer their phones even when they were off duty, but that wasn't a rule set in stone. Hard to grab a call if you were riding a cutting horse in a competition, climbing Mount Baker, or were head-deep in the engine of a car you were working on. Sometimes, you just needed to turn off the ringer and pretend the job didn't exist.

That said, Melinda had left two messages on Jonas's voice mail this afternoon. She'd have expected him to check it, whatever he was up to. When she was being fair, she'd describe him as conscientious on the job. He made it hard for her to like him, because he'd let her know in subtle and not-so-subtle ways since she hired on that he thought law enforcement should be a male-only profession. Of course, half the other officers with SPD probably thought the same. They'd just shrugged as time went on and resigned themselves to being stuck with her. She'd like to think she had won over some of those.

But not Jonas.

Which had nothing to do with the fact that she and Tom Alvarez were going to have to break into a fellow officer's house.

Back door, they decided. Their entry would be less obvious to neighbors, and the pane of glass inset in the kitchen door would be easier and cheaper to replace than a larger front window.

Peering in, Melinda hammered on the door again. Nothing moved. He'd left dirty dishes piled in the sink; from here, she couldn't tell whether they were breakfast or lunch dishes or left over from the evening before. The kitchen wasn't a pit, though. He must mop occasionally, and no food had been left out on the counter. He wasn't married, she knew. As with too many other cops, he had at least one divorce in his past.

Alvarez grimaced, pulled his service weapon and reversed it in his hand so he could use the butt to break the glass. "He's going to be mad as hell," he muttered. "Jonas isn't the understanding kind."

He did have friends in the department, Melinda knew, although apparently Tom Alvarez wasn't one of them. Maybe Jonas didn't like working with someone who had darker skin than his any more than he did women.

"Do it," she ordered.

Glass splintered and fell, most inside, some onto the coir mat at their feet. She half expected to hear a roar of anger, but it didn't come. Guy Jonas either wasn't home, or—

No. I'm being paranoid, she reminded herself. Why would Dorrance have started with Jonas, who along with her had been a first responder on that domestic violence call but had hung back and made his skepticism for her theories plain? Dorrance should have *thanked* him.

Alvarez used the butt to clear enough shards so that he could reach in and unlock the door. As he opened it, he called, "We're coming in, Guy! It's the police." He kept his Glock in his hand, but at his side. Startling a cop in his own home could be dangerous and he was clearly aiming to appear as unthreatening as possible while being ready in case anyone else was in the house.

Melinda unsnapped her holster and rested her hand on the butt of her police-issue Glock as she stepped inside.

Listening hard, she also drew in a deep breath, and swore.

Tom Alvarez did the same.

After a single glance at each other, not needing words, they did a seamless sweep of the house. The smell of death didn't mean someone who was still alive couldn't still be in here.

They found Jonas sprawled on the carpeted floor right beside the bed in his room. A horrifying amount of blood had soaked into the carpet around his head and shoulders, much of it drying now. This hadn't just happened. He'd either grabbed for the bedside stand on his way down and pulled it over, or it got knocked over in a struggle. A lamp had hit the floor, the bulb breaking. The drawer was half open, a few items spilling out, including a small box of condoms.

Melinda felt a pang of pity for him. There'd be no dignity in this death. He'd have zero privacy left once the crime scene team had gone over his house and the ME took his body.

Emotions sharp—the victims of violence she saw in the course of her job were rarely anyone she knew—she still studied his position, facedown on the floor.

Without flipping him over, her best guess was that his killer had yanked back his head and sliced his throat. Jonas was—had been—on the tall side, but thin. Dorrance…wasn't as big a man as Daniel Deperro or Boyd Chaney, but tall enough and muscular besides. She wondered if he'd taken up weight lifting while he served his time. That would make sense, given his goals.

"Would Guy have had a gun safe?" She speculated aloud.

Alvarez tore his gaze from the dead man and turned his head to scan the room. "I doubt it. Lived alone, no kids. He was pretty cocky. Wouldn't have seen any need for one." His eyes settled on the drawer spilling its contents. Which did *not* include a handgun.

"He was going for his gun," Melinda said slowly.

The sergeant didn't disagree. "Ten more seconds, he might have reached it in time."

"If we're right, Dorrance just armed himself."

"Yeah. Hell."

"I don't see a phone, either. You'd think it would be here by the bed."

"It's got to be locked. Dorrance wasn't any kind of digital whiz, was he?"

"I don't think so. He was an auto mechanic." Which involved a lot more electronics than it used to. She frowned. "We can't close our mind to other possibilities. This could have nothing to do with Gene Dorrance."

"You're right," agreed the stocky cop at her side. "The timing, though…"

She let out a long breath and backed out of the room. She wouldn't quit seeing this scene any time soon, and not even a shower and change of clothes would get rid of the stench, but she blanked her mind to it, took out her phone and called Deperro.

"He's dead," she said flatly. "I could be wrong, but it didn't just happen. I'm thinking last night. He's barefoot, wearing sweatpants and a white T-shirt." Well, it had started out white.

She told him the rest of their guesses. Daniel said he'd call CSI and would be out to the house to see the scene for himself. He'd let Lieutenant Matson know, too.

However reluctant she felt, Melinda knew she should call Boyd as well. The sheriff's department would be fully involved in the upcoming manhunt, and they had to keep him informed. She wasn't coward enough to ask someone else to be Boyd's contact.

"I'll go outside to make more calls," she told Alvarez.

He nodded. "Nothing more we can do right now." More softly, he said, "Why Jonas?"

"I don't know. He was an easy target, maybe. Living alone."

As she did, she couldn't help thinking. And how many others among the potential targets?

I've got to find those women.

BOYD DROVE FASTER than was justified to go look at a body that wouldn't be getting up and walking away any time soon. The patrol schedule he'd been working on could wait, though, and he felt an uncomfortable need to see Melinda. If she was upset, she'd hide it; he knew that, but there'd been something in her voice.

The victim was a man she'd known for years, had worked with. Boyd didn't like remembering the faces of men and sometimes boys he'd killed while he fought for his country's goals, but his nightmares usually centered on friends and members of his unit he'd seen go down.

Most of the city of Sadler, the county seat, was laid out logically enough he had no trouble finding the address. The house was a modest rambler with a sunbaked lawn, what might be a fruit tree in the backyard, but no flower beds or other evidence that the homeowner had been domestically inclined.

Boyd didn't recall meeting Guy Jonas, not a surprise since he only rarely had occasion to interact with rank-and-file SPD officers. All Melinda had said, quietly, was, "Jonas was a responder during our first contact with Dorrance. Not anyone I'd have expected Dorrance to start with." She'd hastened to add that they were looking at other angles, too, in case Jonas had made an enemy closer to home.

A crime scene van barricaded the driveway, and three police cars, marked and unmarked, crowded the curb. He parked half a block down and walked, keeping a sharp eye out around him. Was this Dorrance the kind to enjoy watching after the fact, savoring the uproar he'd stirred with the murder? Not much of anywhere to hide in this neighborhood, though, Boyd concluded. Most people were probably at work, so law enforcement vehicles were the only ones parked at the curb or in a driveway. Down at the corner, an older car sat on concrete blocks on a weedy strip next to a driveway, but Boyd had driven past it and was confident it wouldn't provide adequate cover for anyone to hide. Breaking into one of the houses and watching out the window would be a possibility, although he watched for movement and didn't see any.

Even so, he had a crawling sensation on the back of his neck, one he'd learned to heed. He'd thought he was done with this kind of tension when he moved to Oregon to raise cattle and horses, but no, he'd just had to throw his hat in the ring to run for sheriff.

Following the sound of voices, he walked around the side of the house and through a gate in the fence that stood open. Three people clustered on the concrete patio that otherwise held a grill and a picnic table. Boyd knew them all: Lieutenant Edward Matson, Detective Sergeant Daniel Deperro and Melinda. She wore what he'd learned was her usual plainclothes garb: black pants and a form-fitting, crisp white button-up shirt. She added a blazer when temperatures dropped.

He wondered if she had any idea how damn sexy she was in that outfit. Somehow, it emphasized the length of her slim legs and the subtle curves of her lithe body. Even her hairstyle, captured in a knot at her nape, only succeeded in emphasizing the fine bone structure of her face.

Melinda saw him first. Her chin came up, probably in reaction to whatever she'd seen on his face, and she met his eyes almost defiantly.

He paused to say, "Mind if I take a look?" Hearing no objection, he went into the house, taking a moment to sign a sheet of paper someone had laid out on the kitchen counter as a log of who had entered the premises. He needed to get a grip on himself before he rejoined her and the other detectives.

A photographer seemed to be on his way out, but a couple of white-suited people crouched beside the body. CSI, he assumed, and a woman he recognized from the medical examiner's office.

She glanced up. "Ugly one."

"So I see."

To appearances, the victim hadn't gone to bed yet, but might have been on his way. Coming from the bathroom when he heard an unexpected sound and, instead of confronting an intruder unarmed, leaped for the drawer where he kept his sidearm? Mostly satisfied by that scenario, Boyd backed away.

He wished he'd asked about the phone. They would have looked for it, wouldn't they? Dumb question; all three of them had him beat where experience on major crimes investigations went.

The house only had one bathroom, and using his elbow he bumped the half-open door wide so he could take a look. A toothbrush sat in a glass to one side of the sink, but Jonas was tidy enough by habit to have put away the toothpaste. There were no obvious signs he'd just walked out of the bathroom before he met his death. Boyd didn't suppose it mattered, although he preferred to be able to envision a victim's last minutes.

He took a quick look around the house, but mostly what he saw were the usual indications that only one person lived here. One toothbrush, for starters. Recliner in front of the TV, remote right at hand, one chair half pulled out from the small table in the kitchen. Unused rooms. Much of the living room seemed unused, too, as if Jonas went straight to his recliner then followed the same path out when he was ready for bed. Yeah, the carpet showed wear on that path.

Outside, Boyd joined the three others. "Tell me about Jonas."

Matson and Daniel did most of the talking. Guy Jonas was forty-two years old, had been a cop for almost twenty of those years. He'd applied twice for openings on the detective squad, but hadn't been selected either time.

The lieutenant hesitated. "I won't say he wasn't a solid officer, but he was also rigid and set in his beliefs. He was furious when Detective McIntosh was promoted to one of those openings instead of him."

Melinda didn't give away any reaction at all.

Boyd looked at her. "You have any run-ins with him?"

Now her eyes narrowed. "You think *I* killed him because he was an intolerant jackass?"

"No." He let her see his impatience. "Just looking for a picture. You all knew him, I didn't."

"No run-ins. Just snide remarks, and sometimes I'd turn my head and find him staring at me. There was something in his expression." She shook herself, or was that a shiver?

Daniel spoke up. "During the killing spree that involved Child Protective Services, I brought Lindsay to work with me one day and stowed her in the break room. I saw Jonas head in there and followed. He was expressing his opinion that the victims had all been scum who deserved what they got, and Lindsay said he'd stood there staring at her for a few minutes before he started sharing his opinion. Gave her the creeps, she said."

Melinda nodded. "She and I talked about it. I don't think Guy much liked women in general. His attitude wasn't all about keeping them from wearing the badge. That said…he's the victim, not a suspect."

"We do need to find out whether he's antagonized anyone lately."

"That may be hard, given how many people the average patrol officer interacts with every day, even not counting his free time." Matson sighed. "We should talk to his ex-wife first. Friends. All the usual, even if we suspect his death is really the opening move from Dorrance."

Melinda visibly swallowed. "He played such a small part. If this *was* Dorrance, we need to widen our net, make sure we've warned even the bit players."

"Everyone on the prosecutorial *and* defense sides," Daniel agreed. "Paralegals, legal secretaries. What about jail guards? How long did we hold him before he was moved to Salem?"

They threw around more ideas. Boyd offered to help make calls, and Daniel promised to email him a list with numbers. Lieutenant Matson was going to assign another detective, however shorthanded that made them, to look into this murder as potentially having a personal angle. Melinda shook her head when Boyd asked if she'd yet spoken to the two women rescued from Dorrance's house.

"They've done a good job of disappearing. I'm still working at finding them."

Understandably, given that it had been only a few hours since they'd learned about Dorrance's release.

"I didn't see Jonas's phone," Boyd commented.

"Unless it's under his body, it's not there," Daniel said flatly.

"What about a laptop? Doesn't look like he had a desktop."

"I have a call into the station," Melinda said. "He could have left it there. I don't see him using it a lot at home."

Boyd gritted his teeth. "He'd have contacts on it."

"Probably more on his phone, but…yeah." That hesitation revealed some unease. He wasn't telling her anything that hadn't already crossed her mind.

"Friends and some of his coworkers might know if he kept both devices password protected," Matson said briskly. "Let's find out. Daniel, you stay to supervise the scene. Melinda can go back to searching for people we haven't reached. Boyd, if you can help with contacts once she's found phone numbers, that would be a help. I'd like to think none of this will impact your department, but I'm not betting on it. Some of these people have to live outside the city limits."

That was safe to say.

"All right." Boyd rolled his shoulders. "I'll get out of here. I'll be close at hand at sheriff's department headquarters if anything breaks."

The building, and his official office, was right on the outskirts of Sadler, centrally located in this sprawling county with ranches, smaller towns and miles of high mountain desert.

"Let's plan a meeting at nine tomorrow morning," Matson added. "I'd be glad to have you join us, Sheriff."

"Of course," he agreed.

Resisting the temptation to ask Melinda to walk him out, he set out across the brown lawn, his military-honed sense of caution having him placing a hand on the butt of his gun in preparation for rounding the corner of the house.

He hadn't taken more than a few strides when a faint buzz reached him. Text or notification on someone's phone, but not his. Boyd didn't even know why he stopped to look back. They'd all be busy on their phones today.

But he saw that it was Melinda who held her phone in her hand, her expression shocked.

He wheeled and went back. "What is it?"

Her gaze lifted from the phone until her green-gold eyes met his. "It's *him*."

"Dorrance?"

Her head bobbed. She held out the phone so he could read the text.

One down. Now you know I keep promises. All of them.

What was it Dorrance had said in court? *I'll pay you back. Every last one of you.*

"Why the hell would he take the chance of communicating with you?" Daniel asked.

"Because it's all about her." Boyd had to look away from her face. He'd just wandered into a nightmare. A woman he…not loved, but could have loved, had a bull's-eye painted on her back. And he didn't even have to ask if she'd be smart enough to take herself out of this killer's game and let other people hunt down Gene Dorrance like the rabid dog he was. No, Melinda was constitutionally unable to admit to any vulnerability.

She wouldn't like knowing that protecting *her* had just become his priority number one.

Chapter Four

Once Melinda took one of the two remaining seats at the table in the conference room the next morning, she looked around. Only one chair was still empty, the one at the head of the table, left conspicuously open by Lieutenant Matson. As primary on this investigation, Daniel walked in on her heels and took that spot.

Melinda hadn't been able to help noticing Boyd as soon as she stepped through the doorway. His presence was enough to make her nerve endings prickle. Big and handsome, with dark hair grown out from the almost-military haircut she remembered, he had a dominant air that would be easy to resent.

Forcing herself to look away from him, she saw that he'd brought along Miguel Cordova, now a detective with the sheriff's department and, unfortunately, possibly on Dorrance's list of targets. Two additions were a younger SPD detective Melinda had worked with a few times, Emmett Yates and Tom Alvarez, the only uniformed officer at the table.

Everyone present had either a laptop or a notebook in front of them, and most had grabbed a cup of coffee on the way in. Boyd's, she saw out of the corner of her eye, was a tall hot drink of some kind from a drive-through coffee kiosk she often frequented herself.

The hand holding the cup was large, darkly tanned and, she had reason to know, calloused.

Damn it.

Daniel rapped lightly on the tabletop. "I'll get us started. I've spoken to Dr. Neale, who has already completed the autopsy on Jonas."

Nobody winced, but Melinda felt sure she wasn't the only one who didn't want to picture a man she'd worked with for years naked and cut open.

"She didn't offer any surprises. As we speculated, the cause of death was the deep slice across his throat. Serrated blade, she says, probably a commonly found hunting knife that could have been purchased just about anywhere. I've asked one of our crime analysts to check on local sources, although Dorrance likely purchased the knife before he got to Sadler."

"Do we know yet who else was in contacts in Jonas's phone and/or his laptop?" Boyd asked.

Didn't it figure he'd zero in on that. She'd seen how disturbed he'd been by that text, probably because it came to her. Although why he'd care now, she didn't know.

"No." Daniel sounded grim. "At this point, we need to assume the worst for those law enforcement personnel involved however tangentially in Dorrance's arrest. On the positive side, although Jonas may well have had me and Officer Alvarez listed in his phone, neither of us was involved in bringing down Dorrance. Also positive, I can't think of any reason Jonas would have had any contact info for the two original victims or anyone on the prosecutorial or defense teams. Still, they don't have as much reason to protect their names and addresses as law enforcement officers do. That also leaves the lieutenant and other members of our department unless they've had reason to change their numbers. Lieutenant?"

"Nothing has changed," he said tersely.

"Detective Cordova, what about you?"

Miguel Cordova was in his midthirties, Melinda guessed, not more than five foot eight or nine, with a stocky build and a likable face. He shook his head now. "I've had the same number since I took the job with SPD twelve years ago. I did move when I got married two years ago."

Although everyone here probably knew her answers, Melinda volunteered the information that, like Miguel, she'd retained the same phone number but also had moved.

Daniel nodded. "Good. My next point should be obvious to everyone, but I'll say it anyway. You need to be hyperalert from now on. Make sure you're not being followed when you go home."

Cordova looked alarmed, but that worry had already occurred to Melinda and probably the rest of them. It would be heightened for those who had spouses and kids at home.

"First steps," Daniel continued. "I'm sending Emmett to Salem to learn anything he can about Dorrance. The warden sounds like he'll be cooperative. They're searching their records right now to determine whether he had any visitors, for example. Counseling sessions remain confidential, but they'll allow Emmett to interview Dorrance's former cellmates. We need to know whether Dorrance had or has any friends inside the walls or outside."

"Did he have a ride waiting when he walked out?" Melinda asked.

Daniel shook his head. "Taxi. I have a call into the company to find out where he was dropped in hopes we can start tracing him from that end."

"I don't see him taking the Greyhound bus from

Salem," she said. "So what's he driving? Where did he get it?"

"That's an excellent question. Lieutenant, any chance we can get a warrant for Dorrance's bank accounts? Assuming he had a penny left after paying his attorneys, he's likely to have pulled out cash. That wouldn't help us track him down, but people do dumb things."

Yes, they did. Half the crooks arrested got caught because they'd made jaw-droppingly stupid mistakes.

"If Sheriff Chaney is making you available, Detective Cordova," Daniel continued, "trying to find out what Dorrance is driving might be something you could take on. Assuming he picked up wheels right away, did he visit a used-car lot? Check out ads online? Rent one initially? We need a vehicle make and model and, better yet, license plate number."

The detective glanced at Boyd, who nodded but said, "Dorrance presumably owned a car before his arrest. Are we sure he doesn't still own the same one?"

"Another good question—" Daniel made a note "—although would he want to drive it? His license has expired, of course, and he hasn't renewed it. His tabs would have, too. Still, if his car was nondescript enough and he stole a set of plates, that might pass unnoticed."

Melinda raised the other obvious question. "If he kept his car, where has it been all these years? If nobody was starting it regularly for him, would it even run?"

"Unlikely," Daniel agreed.

Boyd acknowledged her point with the slightest tip of his head, but shifted directions. "I don't like the fact that he directly contacted Detective McIntosh to taunt her. What if she were to change her number?"

Matson frowned. "That would likely enrage him."

"Should we be pandering to his crap?" Boyd leaned forward. "If he's cut off, that might shake him up a little."

"We can learn something from his communications." Melinda didn't let herself so much as glance at Boyd. Didn't it figure he was worried about the only woman at the table? "Any glimpse into his head is better than a vacuum."

Boyd opened his mouth again, but Daniel said, "I agree. I also think that you should consider staying with one of us since it's possible Dorrance has your address."

"How could he?" she argued. "Why would Guy have known or cared where I live?"

"He probably didn't, but it's not hard these days to pluck addresses off the internet. You know you'd be welcome to stay with Lindsay and me." His eyes, darker than the golden-brown of Boyd's, met hers.

She smiled crookedly. "Thank you, but for now I'd rather not be scared out of my own home."

Had that rough sound—a growl?—come from Boyd? Probably, although she knew darn well that most men like the ones sitting around this table were programmed to see any woman as more vulnerable than themselves.

Daniel's eyebrows rose momentarily, but he didn't let himself react otherwise. "Let's shelve that for the moment. Who have we been able to talk to, and who do we still need to reach?"

IF BOYD THOUGHT for a minute that that bullheaded woman would listen to reason were he to corner her privately, he'd find a way to take her aside after the meeting. As it was, he knew better. What he'd really like was for her to go into hiding, something they were encouraging other potential victims to consider doing. So far, none of the cops on Dorrance's kill list had agreed to do that. They were armed and dangerous, too damned sure they could defend themselves. Yeah, just like Guy Jonas had done, and him a man with twenty-plus years of experience in law enforcement.

No, he hadn't had the advantage of a warning, but how much help would that really be? If he'd had the fan running in the bathroom, it would have drowned out the sound of an intrusion. People relaxed when they were home.

Did any of them have a security system? Had any of them so much as pulled their gun on the job, never mind fired it? Practice at the gun range was fine, but given only a split second to respond, using deadly force didn't come naturally for people, even cops. He'd be more willing to bet on someone who'd done combat duty in the military, but even for seasoned soldiers, reaction times would gradually slow depending on how long it had been since the individual rejoined the civilian world. Boyd was well aware that even keeping his skills sharp the way he tried to do was no guarantee.

Shutting down his wandering thoughts, Boyd made himself focus on the meeting. He'd made a bunch of the calls himself yesterday afternoon and evening and had been able to reach almost everyone. An assistant prosecutor had taken another job and left the area several years ago. Boyd was still looking for her. The sitting judge for the trial had retired to Florida.

"He does have a security system on his home," Boyd reported now. "Says he can't imagine anyone going that far to hunt him down, but he sleeps better having it. He'll take precautions from now on, until we let him know we've nailed Dorrance."

"Good." Daniel shifted his gaze. "Melinda?"

"I spoke to Andrea Kudelka's mother. She and her husband relocated to Idaho." She grimaced. "They wanted to be near family."

"Just to make them easy to trace," Matson muttered.

"You'd think that would have occurred to them." When she shook her head, light shimmered on her sleek dark hair, pulled into her usual knot at her nape. "However, the mom told me that Andrea is living under another name—and no, she didn't go to court to get it changed—and isn't near her parents. The mother said it's really hard not being able to see her, but even with Dorrance in prison, Andrea didn't feel safe. Also, she was being stalked by reporters who wanted follow-up interviews. She said she wasn't about to end up on the cover of some tabloid at the checkout stand."

Good for her, Boyd thought.

"The mother will pass on the bad news and our warning. I feel more comfortable knowing she's not in the area."

There were nods all around.

"I also located Erica Warner's father—apparently her parents are now divorced—and he listened to me for about two minutes, said, 'If you'd done your damn job searching for her when she disappeared originally, she wouldn't have suffered the way she did,' and hung up on me."

There was a moment of shared silence. Every failure was a weight that burdened any cop with a conscience. As well as she hid her emotions, Boyd didn't like seeing the expression on Melinda's face.

Lieutenant Matson must have seen it, too, because he said sharply, "You're the last person he should dump on. It's only thanks to you we found Erica and Andrea at all or followed up as hard as we did to try to determine if he'd had other victims."

She lifted one shoulder. "Not like that paid off."

Matson opened his mouth, but she shook her head and he subsided.

Daniel had been watching the exchange, but now he said, "Detectives Yates and Cordova have their assignments. For the rest of us, I think we can agree that finding this scumbag is our first priority. At least we know who we're looking for. We need to identify places that would have been available to rent a few days ago, vacant buildings where he could squat, anyone camping outside designated private and public parks. Sergeant Alvarez, I'm asking you to get the word to patrol officers to keep a sharp eye out for anyplace that appears to be newly inhabited. Sheriff, I assume you'll do the same county-wide."

"I will," Boyd agreed, "but we all know how expansive this county is. It's like trying to pick out one sagebrush from another."

They agreed that bringing in volunteers wasn't an option. The county did own a helicopter, which Boyd would get up in the air doing a search pattern immediately—and keep it in the air to the extent his budget allowed.

And beyond, he vowed silently. He could afford to foot the bill for a few days. The faster they found Gene Dorrance, the sooner Boyd could let go of this painful cramping beneath his breastbone.

They decided to go ahead with a press conference, too, which would be conducted by the police chief once Matson briefed him. The lieutenant had been the lead detective investigating Dorrance, which meant keeping him out of the public eye—unless, at some point, they decided to wave the red cape to draw Dorrance's attention.

Daniel glanced around, said, "Unless anyone has

something else to say, let's get busy. We can reconvene tomorrow morning, same time."

Chairs scraped back. Most people were on their feet when Boyd said, "No reason to hold most of you up, but I have some questions for Lieutenant Matson and Detective McIntosh. Just background."

Daniel eyed him and sat back down, as he had the right to do. The younger detectives and Alvarez hustled out. Melinda narrowed her eyes but didn't protest.

Once the door had shut behind the others, the lieutenant spoke up. "What is it?"

"I want to know why Dorrance is focused on Detective McIntosh." He paused, let his voice drop to a near growl. "Most of all, I need to understand why any judge okayed the warrant to search his house."

MELINDA'S HANDS TIGHTENED, the one under the table into a tight fist. Her nails bit into her palm. Since she still held her laptop, she hoped no one else noticed her whitened knuckles on that hand.

She worked really hard to wipe her face clean of expression before looking at him. "Are you implying that the warrant was improper?"

His gaze drilled her. "Unless my copy of the file is abridged, I'm saying the evidence presented to the judge seems thin."

Almost all of that evidence had come from her observations since Guy Jonas had disputed some of it and disagreed with her conclusions.

This was a direct challenge by Boyd, and, yeah, she was taking it personally. He had—what?—a whole year and a half of law enforcement experience, and he thought he knew better than she did?

Before she could fire back, Daniel said mildly, "I

admit I wondered about the same thing. I'm not criticizing—if the investigation had stalled, I'm guessing Dorrance would have seized the chance to kill the two women and dispose of their bodies. That we were able to go in fast saved those women's lives. But I'll admit it seems as if the judge ruled in your favor based on some... impressions, rather than hard evidence." The pause was almost delicate.

Melinda suspected that Daniel wouldn't have raised this subject, or would have done so with her alone, but it worried her that he'd stumbled over the same thing Boyd had. Although why should it? The warrant was granted. They'd found the two women imprisoned in the basement of Gene Dorrance's house, Andrea in particularly bad shape after taking a recent, severe beating, and the jury hadn't hesitated to convict Dorrance.

I was right.

"What difference does it make now?" she asked, knowing she sounded frosty but not caring.

"It probably doesn't," Boyd said slowly, "although I wonder how a guy convicted of a crime this ugly ended up being recommended for the pardon." He raised his eyebrows at Matson. "Is there any way to find out?"

Feeling under attack, Melinda snapped, "Again, what difference does it make? We know he's here. We know he murdered a Sadler PD officer."

"I like to be sure my footing is solid," he shot back. "You sound defensive. That makes me nervous."

She was. Melinda tried for some deep breathing without letting it be obvious that's what she was doing. She tried to read the lieutenant's expression. Had he doubted her then? He was being awfully quiet now.

"Let's start with the 911 call," Boyd continued inexorably. "The woman heard a scream. A long, continuing one that was abruptly cut off."

Daniel looked inquiring, so she said, "That's right. By the way, I don't think I said, but I tracked her down yesterday. She and her husband moved away shortly after the arrest. She said she couldn't stand knowing what had been going on next door all that time. They're in Arizona now."

Daniel and Matson nodded. Boyd's gaze stayed steady. *You're stalling.*

"By chance, Guy and I were only a couple of blocks away. We got there really fast, talked to her before knocking on Dorrance's door. She was certain the scream had come from his house. It sounded terrified, not like teenagers playing around. She was sure it had been a woman, but the sound was muted as if by walls. She might not have heard it at all, but the houses are on average size city lots, and hers didn't have a garage, only a carport and maybe twenty feet of grass separating her kitchen from his house." She took a deep breath. "So then we rang his doorbell."

"Had you used lights or sirens?" Boyd asked.

"No. Dorrance looked both flustered and mad when he threw the door open. He also appeared...disheveled. He was breathing hard, and his shirt was missing a couple of buttons. It was half tucked in, half yanked out. I was sure I saw a deep scratch on his neck."

"I seem to remember that Jonas didn't see it," Matson commented.

Oh, *now* he had something to say, but Melinda was sure Boyd already knew that Jonas thought she was imagining things. In fact, he had claimed not to notice anything off about the guy who'd come to the door. Dorrance was home after a day at work. What did she expect, he'd be wearing a crisp white shirt and tie? During the one year she'd been stuck working with Guy, she'd especially hated partnering with him on domestic violence calls. He gave off a definite vibe that he thought a man's home was his castle, that cops had no business butting in. He'd never said it, but she assumed that in his worldview the king of the castle had the right to backhand his woman if he felt like it.

Okay, maybe that wasn't true, but his attitude had rubbed her wrong.

Deciding not to address any of that, she said calmly, "No, but he didn't have the same angle I did. He stood to one side and toward the back of the porch." The defensive position when there were two of them was standard practice. "I asked to speak to anyone else who was home."

Even all these years later, she remembered that moment vividly. Her every instinct had prickled. Dorrance had triggered all of her alarms. He'd been sweating, giving off waves of anger and violence. She'd have said he looked crazy, although she'd had experience by then with mentally ill people acting strangely, and never felt the deep-down certainty that there was something seriously *wrong* in that house.

The three men watching her waited.

Melinda stared back at them, feeling suddenly as if she was on trial—and Sheriff Boyd Chaney was the judge and maybe jury, too. Was he jumping on this now in hopes of getting her fired from the investigation?

Chapter Five

Not so much resentful as anxious, Melinda didn't see any way out of answering Boyd's questions. Both Daniel and the lieutenant outranked her.

The really uncomfortable part was the sense that she'd been thrown into a flashback. Shifting in her seat, she said, "He insisted he lived alone. There wasn't anyone else there. He was obviously furious to have to defend himself. That flake who'd called 911 must have heard the television, but when I asked what he'd been watching, he got flustered. He retreated to say, 'I didn't mean my TV. It could have been anyone's on the block.'"

She knew what they were thinking. On any other call like that, she and Jonas would have politely retreated, fearing they'd been played, not liking it, but not suspecting anything worse than an argument that had gotten out of hand.

"I guess it was just a gut feeling," she said finally. "I tried to see as much as I could past him. There were dirty dishes on a TV tray pushed away from a recliner in the living room, yet in the hall behind him, some food sat on a cookie sheet obviously being used as a tray that I suspected he'd set down when the doorbell rang."

I suspected. Yep, she'd gone out on a limb there.

"Two sandwiches on paper plates, two plastic bottles

of water. Right next to the small table, a door was a few inches ajar. I felt…a draft of cold air coming from the house."

"He could have had the air-conditioning running," Boyd said.

"He could have, but I didn't hear it." She tipped up her chin and met his implacable gaze. "I also got a whiff of something really bad, like a sewer spill, and I saw a streak of what I was sure was blood on the door molding. And then—" she swallowed "—I heard a woman crying out, or sobbing. *Really* muffled, but under the circumstances…"

"So you apologized for your intrusion, left and reported what you'd seen and heard to…"

"Me," the lieutenant said. "My then partner, who retired not that much later, and I did some research on Dorrance. You know that." He nodded at the closed laptop in front of Boyd.

"Sure. He'd been accused of rape when he lived in northern California, but was never charged."

"The investigator there told me there'd been whispers about this guy for a while. The accuser wasn't the first, but she was the most credible. Unfortunately, she'd let a few days go by after the alleged attack, showered and bathed repeatedly, so there was no physical evidence, and no witnesses. Dorrance claimed he hardly knew the woman, but said they'd had a run-in after a fender bender, which was true. When I asked questions here in Sadler, I found women universally steered clear of him. He came on to them aggressively. People were uneasy because it was obvious he liked younger women. A lot younger. Even his employer, who rated him as a competent mechanic, didn't like the guy. Felt uncomfortable around him."

Boyd leaned back in his chair. Melinda kept her gaze fixed on the pattern of the teal-and-purple-paisley sleeve holding her laptop. Matson...she couldn't tell without studying him closely.

"So you got a warrant to search the house based on a guy whose background was sketchy, but who had never so much as been arrested, and Detective McIntosh's testimony that she thought she'd seen a smear of blood—"

She lifted her head to glare at him. "I did see it!"

"That Dorrance looked as if he'd been in a tussle, that he'd made two sandwiches that he might or might not have been taking down to the basement, and that something was up with the plumbing."

"And that when we went back to talk to the neighbor, she said she was bothered by the smell almost every time she went out in her backyard. She knew Dorrance was out in his yard daily, rinsing something out."

"Uh-huh." Boyd lifted his arms, stretching. Well-honed muscles in his chest and shoulders flexed. "There'd have been a *real* stink if the cops went in and found nothing but maybe a plumbing issue down in the basement."

"We knew we were taking a risk," Matson admitted. "We also knew we'd had at least four young women—teenagers—go missing in the past few years. One witness had seen a man who met Dorrance's appearance snatch Andrea Kudelka. What she saw then didn't get investigators anywhere, but when we tied it to Melinda's description along with her suspicions..." He trailed off.

Boyd lifted one eyebrow. "What you really mean is, to Melinda's gut feeling."

Nobody said a word.

After a moment that hummed with tension, Boyd nodded. "As it happens, I have a lot of respect for gut feelings. My own and teammates' saved our lives a few times. Thanks for answering my questions."

He collected his things, pushed back his chair and left after tossing the empty coffee cup in the metal trash container. A moment later, Matson stood too, paused to squeeze Melinda's shoulder, then walked out with Daniel.

Melinda sat unmoving, feeling as if she'd just been upended and shaken. Why had Boyd started that, and once he had, why hadn't he expressed doubt in her competence?

And, God help her, how had he known which part she'd lied about?

MELINDA HAD ONLY been a cop for a few years when the judge granted that warrant based on her testimony, Boyd reflected. That said something important about her. She had to have already earned a high level of respect from the local judiciary as well as her fellow cops.

Except from Guy Jonas, Boyd suspected, reading between the lines. Clearly, Dorrance had had no idea that Jonas would have shrugged and walked away after that first door-knock if it had been left to him.

What intrigued Boyd was his suspicion that Melinda had lied in the report used to get the warrant. He would have guessed her to be a by-the-book cop. *Being* a cop meant too much to her for her to risk her job, but he had no doubt she'd done so.

That said, he and she had worked together on a serial killer investigation, and a few times she'd demonstrated something he could best call intuition. He'd actually been spooked by it once or twice. At the time, he'd told himself again that getting involved with her had been a mistake from the beginning. Boyd didn't want anyone able to see too deeply inside him. His ranger teammates—men like

Gabe Decker and Leon Cabrera—had their own night-mares. It wasn't anything they had to talk about. Sooner or later, Melinda would have expected him to answer the questions he'd seen in her eyes.

Frowning as he walked into the ugly, single-story building that housed the sheriff's department, Boyd thought, *So find yourself a pretty, shallow woman who likes sex and would enjoy living on a thriving ranch.* Too bad he couldn't work up a lot of enthusiasm. Seeing Me-linda again, and two days in a row at that, had revved up his libido, but the focus seemed to be 100 percent on her.

Damn it, they had to catch this scumbag, and fast.

Consigning his budget to hell, he made a plan with the pilot of the helicopter that would keep him in the air as long as the light lasted and sent him on his way. For-tunately, the deputy had seemed to get what Boyd was telling him, however vague it was, but until they had a make, model and color of a vehicle to watch for, there wasn't a lot to pinpoint. Places that look like they might have a squatter or a new renter or homeowner. Single man—Boyd had armed the pilot with what photos they had of Dorrance, although they hadn't yet received an updated one from the prison. Maybe someone who saw the helicopter flying low and dashed for cover.

Boyd grimaced at his memory of a time when drug traffickers here in the county had employed an unarmed helicopter in their search for a little girl in hiding be-cause she'd witnessed the massacre of her family. Boyd and probably half the other ranchers had thrown a fit be-cause their animals hadn't liked the low-flying aircraft.

This time, people would understand—but he'd just as soon mention of the helicopter didn't appear in any news story.

If only Dorrance was dumb enough to never look up.

By the next morning meeting, all Boyd could think was, *A watched pot doesn't boil.* Or should it be, *Not a creature was stirring*? Well, except for the reporters massed outside. Usually a big story meant half a dozen reporters and cameramen showed up, but today's crowd was double that, and this wasn't for a press conference. When he drove past, someone spotted him, and several ran down the sidewalk shouting questions he couldn't hear with his window rolled up. He'd been grateful to be able to pull into the parking lot behind the station, protected today by a uniformed cop.

The somewhat smaller group—lacking both Emmett Yates and Tom Alvarez—gathered around the table in the conference room at the police station, Boyd seeing that he wasn't the only one feeling increased tension.

Daniel began, tone wry. "Yesterday's press conference was a success, as you'll have noticed. We may be sorry, and I'm not talking about the fact that we may have trouble heading out without an entourage. The phones are ringing off the hook."

Boyd nodded. "Sheriff's department, too." He had a bad feeling he'd be spending a good part of his day answering the calls and evaluating tips. So far, he didn't have much of a role otherwise.

"Nothing useful to this point," Daniel added, "although most of our officers are now occupied following up on the information." Muscles bulged in his jaws. "The problem is made worse after we ordered that no one check out a possible hideout without a partner. If this goes on long, I'm thinking we need to talk about bringing in help."

Boyd nodded his agreement. He had no idea how much help—the boots on the ground kind—the FBI would bring in, versus them sending an agent or two to advise.

Or whether the FBI would be impressed by a manhunt spurred by a long-ago threat and one dead cop.

Plus the text claiming credit, of course.

"Emmett expects to be back late this afternoon," Daniel continued. "I'd have had him join us on his phone, except that so far all he's learned is that the guy had no friends. Not a single visitor. He wasn't real popular with his cellmates, either."

That wasn't unexpected, Boyd reflected. Pedophiles were probably the most despised among any prison population—well, except for cops—but someone like Dorrance who had imprisoned and brutalized two very young women over the course of years was unlikely to stir warm feelings in men who, while they'd committed crimes, quite often violent ones, nonetheless had wives or girlfriends and daughters. There was that indefinable quality, too, the one that made anyone in close quarters with Gene Dorrance "uncomfortable."

"Detective Cordova?" Daniel prompted. "Do you have anything for us?"

"Nothing very helpful yet."

Having encountered Cordova in the hall, Boyd had heard this report from his detective just before they walked into the conference room.

"Dorrance must have stashed some money at some point, or someone owed him, because he did buy a car immediately—the taxi delivered him to a home where he was able to pay cash for an old Toyota pickup on its last legs. Bright yellow," he added. "He may not have known the color and how conspicuous it would be until he set eyes on it. It was found abandoned in a mall parking lot hours later."

Matson leaned forward. "Was a car stolen from the lot…?"

Cordova shook his head. "None have been reported stolen as of now. It's not impossible—apparently the outskirt of the lot is often used as an informal park-and-ride, and possibly a place to leave cars for people who are going to be away for a few days. It's a constant hassle for mall security, I was told. It seems more likely, though, that Dorrance met someone else who was selling a vehicle privately. What if he spotted one with a 'for sale' sign in the window, for example, and arranged to meet at the mall?"

"In other words, a car that wasn't even posted on Craigslist or the like," the lieutenant said flatly.

"Right. Used-car lots had a few sales in the day and a half we're focused on, but nobody recalled seeing anyone meeting Dorrance's description. Also, that kind of sales force typically insists on seeing a driver's license and proof of insurance before allowing anyone to take a car off the lot."

"We need to get his face on the news in Salem, too," Melinda said, voice tight.

Daniel nodded. "We're already on that. I know KOIN Channel 6 and KPTV Fox 12 covered the story. We may get lucky."

There were nods all around.

"Boyd, anything?"

"The county commissioners aren't happy. Their phones are ringing off the hook, too. I assume your mayor isn't enjoying the turmoil, either."

The lieutenant was the one to answer dryly. "That's one way to put it. Chief Austin isn't thrilled either, given that we've conscripted most of the police force. Let's pray we have a brief break in typical crime."

"I've been checking in daily with all potential victims

that I made initial contact with," Boyd said. "I assume you're doing the same?"

Everyone nodded.

Boyd already knew that Dorrance had been released back then on bail to await trial. He could have used the time to stalk police officers and anyone else he blamed for his predicament. Maybe he didn't act out his revenge then because he still hoped he might not be convicted. Could be his hopes had had something to do with the warrant.

Still, that he'd killed so quickly after returning to town suggested he hadn't had to do the expected research; he already knew where Jonas lived.

Melinda had been uncharacteristically quiet thus far.

Studying her, Boyd said, "Melinda, Dorrance was arrested in the first place because of your gut feeling. So what's your gut telling you now?" He didn't like her involvement, but as long as she was being stubborn, they'd all be fools not to take advantage of her instincts. "Will he want to drag this out, enjoy watching us chase our tails? He had to have made his first kill practically the minute he hit town. Is he stalking a second victim? Looking for an easy opportunity?"

Her face appeared pinched, plainer than usual. "I do think taunting is part of his satisfaction. He needed to get our attention, so he killed Guy right away. Now? What's the hurry?" She took and released a deep breath. "This is a man who in essence engaged in long-term torture with his kidnap victims. Watching them suffer, deteriorate physically, lose hope, all had to be a big part of what gave him a charge. That…might be applicable to his campaign to pay us back."

Daniel's forehead creased. "That makes sense."

"Does he already have a place to stay? Might he have had an idea even before he got to Sadler?"

"That's possible. Any long-time resident in the area notices vacant houses and thinks things like, 'One of these years, that roof is going to fall in if no one replaces it.'"

"If he hadn't showed up in Sadler so soon, I might have suspected that he'd found a way to buy fake ID," Matson commented. "That would have allowed him to potentially rent, say from an out-of-town landlord who wouldn't hear what's going on right now. As it is…" He shrugged.

Afraid something else was going on in Melinda's head, Boyd kept watching her. Despite her efforts to look anywhere but at him, she must have been aware of his scrutiny, because she turned her head suddenly.

Her eyes fully met his, and he flinched at what he was afraid might be anguish. "I…had a thought during the night. We stole something from him seven years ago. It's the something that made him feel strong, in control and gratified him."

Oh, hell. All Boyd could think was that he should have thought of that. Now they had to pile on another worry: that a young woman was about to snatched—or already had been.

"Yes, ma'am," Melinda said into her phone. "You have a new neighbor who makes you nervous." She held her pen poised above the notepad. "Can you tell me when he moved in?"

"Well, the apartment has been rented for almost a month, but I didn't see the new resident until recently. I mean, someone was going in and out and turning the music up too loud—I've complained twice to the manager, and she hasn't done a darn thing as far as I can tell!—but this man you're looking for could have had someone else rent him a place, couldn't he? And he has been quiet this week. I just don't like the way he looks at me."

He also could have murdered a resident and taken over the lease, so to speak.

The day pretty much stunk, as they all had since that idiot governor had blithely released a man set on vengeance. Melinda had spent the day taking an endless stream of calls and wasn't at all surprised that most were so far off, they didn't even justify follow-up. Despite her passing thought, this one sounded awfully unlikely—she couldn't imagine Dorrance would choose to take over an apartment with multiple near-neighbors and poor sound-proofing. There certainly was no indication he had any-one at all who'd have rented a place in advance for him. And when had Dorrance learned he was going to be re-leased anyway? she wondered. She hadn't thought to ask.

Still, it was always worth paying attention when a woman mentioned a single guy who made her uneasy. The vague physical description of a man who could be Dorrance would have kept Melinda listening to this par-ticular caller anyway.

"When did you see this man for the first time?" she asked.

The slight hesitation gave her a clue.

"Well, it was probably ten days ago, but I wasn't sure you knew exactly when the man you're looking for might have gotten out of prison. I mean, maybe they just don't want to admit they let him go sooner than they were supposed to."

Instead of banging her head on her desk, Melinda

wrote down the woman's name, phone number and address before picking up the next call.

Daniel was doing the same not far from her, as was Emmett Yates, returned from his jaunt to Salem, along with one other detective, Lieutenant Matson and several patrol officers. Every so often Daniel would glance at her and shake his head or roll his eyes. At the moment, Emmett seemed to be trying to wrench his hair out while listening on his phone. She totally understood the impulse.

Having stayed late, Melinda finally left the station to find the sun heading down, but daylight still holding. Sunset wasn't until almost nine o'clock in early July. Parking should be secure here surrounded by high chain-link fencing behind the brick-built police station, but she still kept an eye out on the way to her Subaru. Thank goodness, the press corps seemed to have given up for the day. She still kept an eye out, but nobody followed her from the station across town to the grocery store that was closest to her house, a Thriftway. There, she scanned the parking lot, not seeing anyone just sitting in a vehicle. An aisle away, a woman was lifting a toddler out of the back seat of a minivan.

Nobody in the store looked familiar either, not even the clerks. She didn't usually shop this late.

Normally, Melinda came with a list, having planned meals she actually intended to cook from scratch, but today she just tossed whatever caught her eye into her cart. She bought lots of salad makings and a few frozen, microwaveable meals, went through the self-check station and loaded her bags in the back of her Subaru. She clicked the key fob to unlock her vehicle and slid in behind the wheel before she saw something that hadn't been here when she went into the store.

A white, business-sized envelope, fatter than it should

be if it held only a folded sheet or two of paper, lay askew on the seat.

And on the front of the envelope, her name was printed in slashing strokes that were oddly childlike.

Her hand closed convulsively on the butt of her Glock.

Chapter Six

Knowing that he was being damned unreasonable didn't keep Boyd from being furious that Melinda hadn't called him. It was Daniel who had, and by now there'd already been a fruitless canvass of shoppers coming and going at the grocery store in hopes of finding a witness who'd seen someone gaining access to her car.

Glad that when his phone rang he hadn't made it all the way home, Boyd did a U-turn in the middle of the highway and drove straight to the police station, where the envelope was to be opened by a crime scene investigator to be sure no evidence was lost by doing it carelessly.

Striding into the basement room where the limited CSI facilities were consigned, Boyd nodded at the woman he already knew. She'd likely been called in from home, too. Otherwise, Daniel, Melinda and Matson stood around a tall table. At least they hadn't opened the damn envelope yet, he saw, even though he didn't know why it mattered that they'd waited for him.

Melinda looked stoic, but she had to be feeling unsettled.

"Any idea how this creep got into Detective McIntosh's car?" he asked brusquely.

"We've fingerprinted just in case," Daniel said, "but we suspect he used a screwdriver or the like to crack open the passenger-side window. You know how quickly that can be done."

Boyd did. Cops carried a tool designed to do exactly that for citizens who'd locked their keys inside. They got plenty of practice utilizing that tool. He already knew that Melinda had been driving her Forester for ten years or so, meaning it predated some of the fancier security protections.

"We think that's what Dorrance did when he abducted Erica Warner." Melinda sounded strained, if Boyd was any judge. "We had a witness who caught sight of what was happening. He was apparently crouched behind the driver's seat of Erica's car when she got in after work. Coworkers and family said she always locked her car."

It wouldn't take more than a minute to crack the window, unlock the door, slip in and relock before crawling into the back. That's why motorists in general and women in particular were urged to scan the interior of their cars *before* they unlocked and climbed in. Melinda had presumably done that tonight, but she'd been looking for a person, not a message.

Boyd's mouth tightened.

He nodded at the envelope, lying on a sheet of heavy white paper torn off a big roll. "Let's see what we have."

The tech carefully slit the top of the envelope, commented, "It's self-stick," then cracked it open with her latex-covered fingers. "Hair," she said after a minute. I think that's all that's in there."

Boyd couldn't be the only one who stiffened.

She picked up the envelope and tilted it so that everyone could see what, indeed, appeared to be a coil of brown hair. Then she tipped it out onto the white paper.

They all gaped. It wasn't a full head of hair, but it was long enough—ten or twelve inches—to suggest the likelihood that it was a woman's hair. That wouldn't necessarily be so in more liberal western Washington, but in these parts, not many men wore theirs long enough that it could be captured in a ponytail.

"Snipped off, or shaved from a head?" Daniel asked.

Either way, the cut was clean.

"We need to check again on every woman on our list," Matson said. "And what about Kudelka and Warner?"

Melinda shook her head. "Unless this is dyed. Andrea is a blonde. Erica's hair had a tinge of red. This…" She bent forward so that her nose was almost touching the coil. "Jen, do I see some gray strands?"

The three men leaned forward, too, Boyd squinting to focus. Yeah, he saw the gray, too. This hair didn't come from a young woman.

The tech produced a magnifying glass and examined the sample more closely. "Definitely gray. No sign that the hair has been dyed."

Daniel straightened. "So not a new victim he picked up for entertainment value."

"Unless…" Melinda stepped back from the table with an abruptness that caught all their attention before drawing a deep breath and looking at her fellow cops. "I could be way off, but what if he did have in mind a house that would work for his purposes, only it wasn't vacant?"

Daniel swore. "You think he killed the occupant?"

"Maybe, but what if he knew of an older woman who didn't hold a job? Retired, maybe, a loner? Someone who wouldn't be missed if she wasn't seen regularly."

"He likes them young. Would he be interested in raping this woman?"

"What he really likes is to make women suffer." Melinda didn't sound like herself. "That may be his primary need, not actual sexual attraction to the victim. And this time around, he can kill two birds with one stone—imprison a woman, torment her and have a comfortable place to stay where no one will pay any attention to lights coming on at night, the sound of a television, maybe even the garbage can being taken out to the curb weekly."

Boyd ran through the scenario in his head and found it appalling logical. So much for the hours they'd wasted looking for the long-vacant house that showed signs of activity that shouldn't be there.

"He'd have access to this woman's car, too," he said. "Even if we're able to find out what he bought, he can garage it and drive something else."

In her astute way, Melinda suggested, "If she's housebound, she might have had groceries delivered, which would cut down on his risk."

"And let's not forget her credit cards," Daniel said grimly.

"Yet he set out in broad daylight to leave this on your car seat." Boyd looked at her. "Why? Is he trying to give you clues?"

Creases formed on her forehead. "Maybe? Or maybe this is more of an up yours. A way of saying, 'I'm smarter than all of you.' He has to know there's no way we can trace whose head this hair came from. Even if we can get DNA tested in the foreseeable future, what are the odds we'd come up with a match?"

Zero, unless this woman had sent a sample to a genealogical website.

What was wrong with the three of them, able to lay a calm veneer over a conversation about such horrific possibilities? And why was this bothering him so much when he'd seen terrible things as a soldier, not to mention the gruesome corpses left by a serial killer and worked that investigation?

But Boyd knew—*that* killer hadn't been interested in Melinda. This one was.

"He had to have followed you."

"I was watching!" Her throat worked. "I was worrying about a reporter waylaying me. I'd swear no one was behind me."

"Unless he picked you up partway," Daniel said, almost gently. "If he knows where you live…"

Boyd's greatest fear. He ground his teeth, but decided to redirect them to the woman who'd just had the haircut. He nodded toward the hair. "How did Dorrance know this person?"

Melinda looked almost grateful. "Maybe he didn't. Maybe he only knew *of* her."

"How?" Boyd fought against a need to pace. "That's what we need to figure out."

"I agree," she said briskly. "We need to learn as much as we can about his routines before his arrest. Drive the route he'd have taken between work and home. Where did he grocery shop?"

"Or did he vary that, so no one paid attention to what he was buying?" Matson suggested. "Or the quantity he was buying?"

She nodded. "Good thought." She sounded energized by the new avenue of investigation. Of course she refused to give in to fear. "He had guns. Did he practice at a local range?"

"Have a gym?" Daniel asked.

"No, there was a weight room at his house. It's not big, only a two bedroom with a full basement. The second bedroom was well-equipped for his workouts."

"Couldn't let himself be overpowered," Daniel said dryly.

"Yet somehow Andrea did knock him aside and make

it up the stairs," Melinda reminded them. "Screaming all the way. She'd reached the top before he caught her, slammed her head on the doorjamb and dragged her back down to her cell."

Matson's throat worked. "Where he beat the crap out of her."

"Andrea is a tall woman. Close to my height, as I recall. He might have enjoyed the challenge of capturing a woman who had confidence in her strength. Reducing her to nothingness would be even more satisfying."

Melinda could have been talking about herself.

There was a moment of silence. For all that they sounded more matter-of-fact than Boyd liked—he felt downright crazed—they had to outthink this SOB. Dwelling on the suffering of his victims, including a new one, wouldn't help them catch him.

As extra motivation went, though, rage worked just fine.

"What's happened to Dorrance's house?" he asked.

"I DROVE BY YESTERDAY," Melinda told him. She tried not to look at him, without being obvious about it. Something in his very stillness made her feel as if the air was charged with static electricity that might shock her if she wasn't careful. "The bank had foreclosed on it," she said with false calm. "I knew that, and I guess I assumed it had sold or been rented or something."

"With that history?" Daniel muttered. "I'd have razed the place."

Melinda had been shocked that it still stood. Did the bank officials really think anybody would buy a place with two prison cells in the basement? Would the listing include them as possible den and hobby rooms? How about the bloodstained concrete floors? She'd driven by a few times the first year, but then let it slip from her radar. After all, she knew where Dorrance was.

Until she didn't.

"I…walked around and looked in windows," she said. "Needless to say, they're seriously grimy. I couldn't get in. It didn't look like anybody had done anything to it." The hank of hair on the table drew her gaze again, a source of primal horror. "This decreases the likelihood that we'll find anything there."

"We need to get in anyway," Boyd snapped. "Unless they changed the locks—and if they did, the new ones are probably crap—what's to stop Dorrance from squatting in the basement? Keep a hostage in one space, sleep in the other himself?"

"That's too obvious," Daniel objected.

"And yet he murdered a cop two days ago, and nobody except Melinda has thought to look at his old house."

With a half-shrug, Daniel conceded the point. "I know the manager of the local bank. I'll call him now and ask for permission for us to get in." He left the room, followed by Boyd and Matson. Melinda paused briefly to talk to the tech.

Somehow, she wasn't at all surprised to find Boyd and her lieutenant waiting for her on the main floor.

"There's something we haven't addressed," Boyd said, in the kind of voice that raised her hackles. This was a man who'd spent years giving orders, and expected instant obedience. He had to know she wouldn't give him what he wanted, and yet he wasn't softening his approach.

Conscious of Lieutenant Matson's presence, she raised her eyebrows. "And that would be?"

"You, Detective McIntosh. That could have been your hair. He wasn't just saying, 'You can't catch me,' he was threatening *you*."

Yes, when she saw what was in the envelope, she'd had a moment of imagining it was hers, that the men were standing around the table talking about where Dorrance could be holding her.

She couldn't think like that. She wouldn't.

With cool poise, she said, "I'll keep doing my job, the same as you will. Dorrance's communications suggest that he won't be in any hurry to attack me. He's enjoying too much being able to contact me when and where he chooses."

The lieutenant cleared his throat. "I have to agree with Sheriff Chaney, Detective. I worry you're minimizing Dorrance's fixation on you. I think there's nothing he'd like better than to lock you in one of his cells."

Matson had never been anything but supportive since promoting her to the detective squad. This felt like a betrayal.

"What, you want me to go into hiding?"

She became suddenly aware that he'd aged a decade in the past couple of days. Even the white in his hair was more noticeable. He said heavily, "I didn't say that, but you don't like admitting any vulnerability."

"Do any of us?"

If that was a smile, it wasn't very convincing. "No. You can't do this job if you dwell too much on the risks. But Sheriff Chaney is right in this case. You've said yourself, this scum lives to torture women. He slit Guy Jonas's throat, which is ugly enough, but quick. Do you think he'd be that merciful to you if he got his hands on you?"

She wasn't a fool, but she'd worked hard to become as invulnerable as possible. How could she back down? Let herself depend too much on other people? She'd be thrown back to a time when she had no say in her life at all. She'd sworn she wouldn't let that happen to her again. Never.

"I'm a cop. I'm armed. Andrea Kudelka overpowered him once, and in doing so saved herself and Erica. You know how that must eat at him? Right now, what he needs is a captive who is weak enough to restore his ego. He's *afraid* of me, and he should be. That's what all this is about."

Boyd's gaze felt like a red-hot laser, but fortunately Daniel rejoined them before Boyd could vent.

"I have permission. Who wants to go?"

"I've seen the house before," Melinda said quickly. "I can tell if anything has changed."

"You don't need me." Lieutenant Matson stepped back. "Keep me informed."

Boyd said, "I'm going." No compromise in his hard voice.

"I want to see it, too," Daniel agreed.

"I can bring you both back here," Boyd suggested. "One vehicle would draw less attention than three."

He was repelled to think of some reporter with gleaming teeth standing in front of the house of horrors as he or she spoke dramatically to the camera.

"Sounds good." Forced into being the referee between her and Boyd in the past, Daniel gave her a look she recognized, one that said, *Play nice.*

And here she thought she'd done so well.

CREAK.

Daniel froze momentarily on the third step from the top of the stairs leading into the basement. Melinda, hovering just above him, cringed. Had that stair always squeaked? If so, it must have worked like a gunshot on the imprisoned women. Gene's way of saying, *Here I come!*

After that brief check during which his back stiffened, Daniel continued. When Melinda reached that step, she stepped well to the side and avoided the squeak. Or maybe it was just her lesser weight, because when she was halfway down, the creak came again under Boyd's foot.

Melinda had only been down here once, and under vastly different circumstances. The electricity had been on, for starters. They hadn't had to rely on flashlights and what grimy light seeped through tattered shades on the windows. There'd been a crowd, too—armored SWAT team members followed by the two detectives, Melinda entering only once Dorrance was cuffed and the scene secured. She'd been included so that a woman officer was present to reassure the two victims.

Today, the air in the house was thick and musty. The three of them had quickly glanced around the main floor, including the weight room, complete with a dust-coated bench and set of barbells. Starting down to the basement, what she breathed in was oppressive and made her want to gag. Could she still smell the feces and urine as well as blood? Or was it all in her imagination?

She didn't ask either of the men.

The half basement would have been cramped even if it hadn't been carved up to create the two cells and a room that held the furnace and hot water tank. A five-by-ten-foot aisle allowed for wall shelves and access to a door and the few concrete steps outside that led up to the backyard. From the outside, they'd seen that the single basement window had been blocked long ago.

Having a moment longer than Boyd and Melinda to look around, Daniel played his flashlight around and said a vicious word. "They didn't do a damn thing down here!"

Somehow, Boyd had covered his left hand with a latex

glove. He cautiously opened the first door, then just stood in the opening and stared.

Daniel did the same for the second cell.

Melinda hovered behind them, not sure she wanted to see. Once in a lifetime was enough, wasn't it? Except, of course, she couldn't stop herself from following when Boyd took a step inside the tiny room.

There'd never been any furnishings except a mattress on the floor that the CSI team had hauled away. Two of the four walls were concrete, as was the floor. Dorrance had constructed the other two walls of cinder blocks made permanent with masonry. The doors were steel.

Maybe, she thought, the women *hadn't* been able to hear that squeaky stair. Maybe they'd had no warning at all of his visits.

The smell…she didn't know, but the beam of her light found those rusty stains. Most were on the floor, but Andrea had said that she'd completely broken at one point and hammered and clawed at the walls until her hands were raw and fingers broken. Melinda's stomach rolled at the sight in front of her tangled with memories.

Even deeply shadowed, the expression on Boyd's face was unutterably grim. "He should have fried. If anyone had showed the governor a picture of either of the women and these cells, surely even he wouldn't have signed that pardon."

"All it would have taken was a little imagination." Melinda knew her voice sounded arid, all her emotions wanting to go into deep freeze. Aware of his eyes on her, she backed into the hall and went up the stairs. She'd seen enough. Coming along on this little expedition had been a mistake, now that she knew another woman was being held somewhere nearby in a space that might be as bleak, her circumstances as brutal and hopeless.

Without turning her head again, Melinda marched out the front door and straight to Boyd's Granger County vehicle. The two men joined her not more than a couple of minutes later. Nobody said a word.

Chapter Seven

At the station, Daniel said, "Have you even put away your groceries, Melinda? Go home and get some rest." Then he slammed the car door and headed for his pickup in the half-empty lot behind the low, brick building.

During the short drive, Boyd's gaze had flicked constantly to the rearview mirror. He couldn't forget Melinda was sitting directly behind him. Looking at him? Fixedly staring out a side window? That wouldn't surprise him.

Now that she'd gotten out, he expected her to head for her car, too, but instead she dropped in front of his driver's-side window. Boyd lowered it.

"You have another thought?"

"I'd appreciate it if you'd back off on the protect the little woman plan." Voice steady, she held his gaze. "You've undermined me in every meeting. I don't like the implication that I can't take care of myself, especially when I know where that's coming from."

Boyd's temper fired. In a way, she was right, but mostly, she was wrong.

"I have been nothing but professional. You're hearing what you expect me to do or say instead of—"

Darkness was falling, but he could see the simmering anger on her face just fine.

"Implying that I shouldn't be part of the investigation?" she fired back. "That the *men* can handle it better?"

Yeah, he'd screwed up once upon a time, but he couldn't believe she held on to a grudge enough to misread him so completely.

"I've asked questions that needed to be asked. Being granted that warrant was a minor miracle, and you know it. I also think you embroidered on your observations because you knew what you'd seen wasn't enough." When her mouth opened, he held up a hand. "That's not a criticism. You took a big risk, but it paid off. If you'd actually been listening to me these past few days, you'd have heard me say you're observant, smart and have a kind of insight most people don't. I've asked repeatedly what you thought, what were your best guesses. That's not undermining you."

Her mouth had closed, opened again and closed. Finally she said, "But you still think I should go into hiding. Because I'm a woman."

He rolled his shoulders. "You're a good cop."

"As if you're any judge," she snapped.

He raised his eyebrows and saw a flush rise in her cheeks.

"You're right. I want you out of this. You're dangling yourself out there like bait. Communications, my ass! Dorrance has already pinned his target on *you*. Because he blames you the most for his downfall? Because he resents that it was a woman who brought him down? Who knows. It doesn't even matter, because he doesn't just want to kill you. He wants you under his control, wants to rape you and hurt you. He wants to shave your head and send us your hair!" Somehow, his voice had risen to a roar. "Do you know what that would do to everyone in this department? To me?"

And, God, he shouldn't have said that, because the shock on her face morphed into astonishment.

"You?" she whispered. "There's no reason—"

"There is, and you know it." He made himself look away from her and do some deep breathing. He hadn't meant to say any of this, was angry at himself for letting it get personal.

But it was. Damn it, it *was*.

"Daniel's right," he said, having regained outward calm. "You need to get some rest. I'll follow you home."

"You don't have to—"

"I do."

She had to see he wasn't going to yield, not on this. After a moment, she gave a stiff nod and walked away.

And yeah, she inspected the inside of her Subaru carefully before she unlocked the door and got in.

Boyd just wished Dorrance *would* try to tail her tonight.

MELINDA HATED FEELING FOOLISH, and how could she not? Boyd was right—she had waited to catch him showing what a sexist jerk he could be, and she'd called him on it without justification.

Her cheeks burned in humiliation.

She hated even more having to creep through her own house, weapon drawn, flinging open closet doors expecting the monster to jump out, peering under her bed and even in the kneehole beneath her massive antique desk. Oh, and checking window locks while well aware how quickly Dorrance could tap a hole in the glass, just as Alvarez had done at Officer Jonas's house, unlock the window and jump inside.

Fine. She'd be ready to blow a hole in him by the time he reached her bedroom.

Unless—God—he somehow masked the sound of breaking glass. Taped a pane, say, before removing it. Or waited until the neighbor's irritating rooster crowed at daybreak or provided a distraction all his own. A fire-cracker out front while he went in the back, say. Set on the outskirts of town, her small house sat on almost a half acre, and some of the neighbors owned even larger lots. She'd *liked* the sense of space, but now, even when confident she was alone in her house, she felt a crawling awareness of the dark landscape outside. For the first time since she'd completed the police academy, she drew every blind and set of curtains, and turned on most of the lights, too.

Then she put away her groceries, discovered that her stomach felt hollow but that the idea of eating nauseated her, and sat down at the kitchen table with a moan.

What had she been thinking to accuse Boyd of...what? Being overprotective? Or maliciously trying to damage her standing in the department? Either of which implied that she believed he still cared about her more than two years after they'd broken off their brief relationship.

Except...*he'd* implied that he did.

She tried to shake that off. Given Dorrance's interest in her, Boyd would have insisted on following her home even if they'd been strangers when she called to drag him into this manhunt. She would have done the same for a fellow officer who was, to use Boyd's words, in Dorrance's crosshairs.

She might even be encouraging that fictional officer to go into hiding. But that other person wasn't her. Dorrance was her worst nightmare brought back to life, and she couldn't back away and still be able to live with herself.

She moaned again, her thoughts reverting to Boyd. She almost had to apologize, which meant swallowing another dose of crow. But...had he meant it, that he'd be devastated if she were attacked or even killed? And if he did... why? Had she hurt him when she walked out on him?

All she had to do was close her eyes to picture the moment he said, "This is serious. You and me."

They'd spent an astonishing night in his giant bed upstairs in his enormous log home set in the middle of thousands of acres of ranchland. After tender morning lovemaking, they'd gone down to the kitchen, both starved since they'd forgotten all about the steaks he'd been going to grill the evening before. Boyd had been cracking eggs into a bowl while she sliced a loaf of homemade bread when he looked over his shoulder and made his pronouncement.

Melinda made a sound now, as she sat in her own deserted kitchen remembering the burst of happiness. She'd never felt anything like that before. She hadn't known she *could* fall in love with a man so completely, so fast. Seeing the tenderness and heat in his eyes, she had let herself believe in the possibility of something she had never imagined happening for her. He'd coaxed her into opening up that night, to the point where she'd told him about her youth, her sister. Explained why she'd gone into law enforcement.

But that morning, her happiness hadn't even crested when he said, "Here's the thing, though. I can't deal with you being a cop," and *poof*, all that hope and belief blinked out of existence.

She'd said, "What?" Maybe whispered it. Because she could have misheard him, couldn't she? Or misunderstood what he was asking for.

Which suggested the *poof* hadn't wiped out all her foolishly unrealistic emotions quite as fast as she wanted to think it had.

But he took care of that, explaining that he couldn't have a girlfriend who carried a gun and risked being shot on an everyday basis. He had no problem with her *working*, he'd added, but not in a dangerous career like law enforcement…

She had stared at him for what felt like ages, as if she was clicking the shutter on a camera, collecting images for a future that would not include him. Then she said something like, "I'm sure you won't have any trouble finding that girlfriend. Thanks for a fun night, but I'm asking you to stay out of my way from now on," and left.

As far as she knew, he hadn't so much as moved by the time she let herself out of the ranch house. In that last mental picture, he'd still held an uncracked egg in his hand.

He didn't follow her and hadn't called after her to stay. That was one way of taking her seriously, if not how she'd imagined at the beginning of that scene.

They didn't come face-to-face again until he'd become county sheriff and they'd had to work together on the serial killer investigation. Then she'd had a hard time seeing past her hostility.

Tonight hadn't been quite as bad. Melinda was afraid she hadn't hidden everything she felt from Daniel, but he'd avoid comment unless she behaved so badly he had to intervene. Which wouldn't happen.

Her chest burned, and so did her eyes, but she wasn't about to cry. Whatever she'd felt for Boyd Chaney hadn't survived his request that she quit her job—and his obvious belief she'd be glad to give up her chosen career to please him, or at least to make sure he wasn't inconvenienced by any worry for her at all.

That she was as attracted to him as ever, hyperaware of his presence whenever he was near, of the way he walked—or was it prowled?—the timbre of his deep voice, the intensity in his golden-brown eyes, well, she'd just have to live with it.

She'd made the right decision then, and he had obviously agreed, or he would have followed her. Would have at least tried to explain. But he didn't.

Which meant he had no right to pretend he cared about her, she thought, on a spark of restorative anger.

So forget him.

Except—she was beginning to think she had misread him in some ways. So far, for example, he hadn't tried to grab the limelight. In fact, he'd slunk around as much as the rest of them, doing his best to avoid the hungry reporters and cameramen. He'd once confirmed a statement the Sadler police chief had given. That was all.

Okay, fine. *And* irrelevant.

Called back to the moment, she gave herself a lecture. To do her job, she needed both food and sleep. Whether she felt like eating or not, she'd do it. She had a bad feeling that sleep was another story.

BOYD DROVE PAST the turnoff to the log house on the ranch where his partner and his wife and adopted daughter lived. Through the sparse ponderosa pine woods, Boyd could see lights shining from downstairs windows. Gabe and Trina tended to go to bed early, especially now that she was pregnant, but they were obviously still up. Boyd suppressed the temptation to go knocking on their door. They were good friends, good listeners, but his feelings for Melinda were too raw to share. If he needed backup, that would be different, but he didn't. Boyd was usually glad to see how happy his friends were, but tonight envy might taint the moment, and he'd be ashamed of that.

His own huge house—he still didn't know why he'd

had it built so big—was dark. His housekeeper wouldn't have thought to leave lights on for him, given the long days at this time of year.

No reason he'd be a target for this psycho, but Boyd still watched his surroundings carefully for any hint of movement as he mounted the stairs and unlocked the front door, then flicked on lights. Maybe he should have had a security system installed when the house was built, but the need for one hadn't crossed his mind. Terrorists he'd battled half a world away weren't going to follow him home.

Going into law enforcement changed the picture. You arrest enough people, you made enemies.

He wished he thought Melinda had a security system in the small house that had been more isolated than he liked to see. When they knew each other, she'd been in a rental, a duplex right in town. She'd obviously decided after their split to become a homeowner. All he'd do was feel guilty if he tried to analyze why she might have made that decision, to acquire a real home on her own.

Damn.

He'd made it to the kitchen and opened the refrigerator, not surprised to see a couple of bowls with instructions on reheating taped on top of the clear wrap.

He popped two slices of garlic bread in the toaster while the convection oven and microwave both hummed, then sat down to what had undoubtedly been green beans right out of the garden and a sizable portion of excellent lasagna. *He* hadn't had to stop at the grocery store on his way home; his housekeeper took care of that chore, along with many others.

If he hadn't panicked when he fell for Melinda, she might be sitting at the table with him right now, sharing his dinner. Except, he'd probably be even more crazed than he already was about her being the target of a nutcase.

Yeah, but she'd have had him at her side, in bed and out of it, to keep her safe, instead of her being alone in that isolated house too many miles from here.

Boyd looked down at empty dishes, not remembering having eaten beyond the first bite or two and let out a growl. There was a good reason he couldn't love a woman who thought nothing of risking her life, and he shouldn't forget that.

That was when his phone rang. He'd left it on the kitchen counter, as far away as he ever let it get. Knowing any of his ranch employees would probably call Gabe or Leon first, Boyd felt a cold clutch of anxiety by the time he picked up the phone.

The name that showed was Miguel Cordova's.

Boyd caught the call just before it went to voice mail. "Detective?"

"My little girl is missing." Terror made the younger man's voice almost unrecognizable. "She's...she's three. I just turned out the lights, and Maria and I stopped on the way down the hall to check on her. Her bed's empty, glass pane is cut out of the window." He was panting by now. "Somebody took her."

Dorrance took her.

"I'm on my way. Just hold on. Even Dorrance wouldn't—" Boyd faltered.

"Wouldn't he?" his detective asked, almost unintelligibly.

"I'll bring SPD in on this," Boyd said.

As he went out the door, the first number he called was Melinda's.

MELINDA DROVE AT high speed, using her lights and siren even though getting to the Cordova house five minutes faster wouldn't make any difference.

This abduction couldn't be chance, a stray predator who'd been watching for a chance to grab a child. She didn't believe that, and could tell Boyd didn't, either. Daniel was arranging to get a CSI team out here, in the unlikely event the kidnapper had never watched television and therefore hadn't worn gloves. Or, hey, he could have dropped his wallet, complete with ID, without noticing as he climbed out the window carrying the girl.

Actually, that part would have been tricky since he presumably had needed to keep a hand over her mouth to keep her from screaming. And why would he have a wallet, given that he lacked ID or credit cards to fill it?

Cordova lived only a couple of miles outside the city limits, but the opposite direction from Melinda's own house. After killing the lights and siren, she barely slowed enough to make the turn onto a cracking concrete driveway. Boyd's big black pickup truck was the only vehicle in front of the garage. Evidently, he hadn't taken his department-issue SUV home tonight. She parked beside the pickup, circled behind his back bumper to the short walkway and stopped dead.

A tricycle sat at the foot of the porch steps. A pink tricycle, with pink ribbons that reminded Melinda of a cheerleader's pom-poms dangling from the handlebars. At the clutch of pain in her chest, she thought suddenly, Boyd was right. Why would anyone in their right mind let themselves love someone when this kind of devastation could be the result? If they never recovered Cordova's kid, or found her dead, his wife would always know this happened because of his job. How could she put someone else through this?

Compartmentalize, she ordered herself. She knew better than to let herself get too emotional when her job was to stay calm, use her head, be prepared to act on an instant's notice.

She knocked lightly, and the door swung open immediately, Boyd's big body blocking her view into the house. His face was set in hard lines but gave away some of the same horror she felt.

"Let's take a look outside first," he said tersely.

Carrying a big flashlight, he led the way. "You haven't gotten a text?"

"Not yet."

"Do you know how much I hate this guy?"

"I have never in my life hated anybody as much as Dorrance, and that's saying something."

He gave her a sidelong look, reminding her that he was the only person here in Sadler who would know what she was talking about. Mercifully, he didn't comment.

They kept their distance from the open window and the pane of glass leaning against the side. The turned soil of a flower bed right there might have given them a chance at isolating a footprint, but lawn grew right up to the concrete foundation. With the weather having been so dry, the ground was rock-hard. Still, a careless step could damage any trace evidence left by Dorrance.

Left on, the ceiling light in the bedroom illuminated a square of the grass. Melinda could see lacy white curtains pulled aside and a mobile with what she thought were unicorns.

Boyd played the flashlight beam over the window, pausing on the sill, across the siding, down to the neatly cut pane of glass. Then he muttered something under his breath and turned off the light. "I hear someone arriving."

Melinda nodded, even though he might not see her, and turned to walk back around the house. "Are they—Miguel and Maria—um, holding it together?"

"More or less. They…had already gone through some of the early phases. They ran around outside screaming Carlota's name. Knocked on neighbors' doors even though they had to know that wouldn't do any good. When I first arrived, they answered a few questions but since then… They're sitting on the sofa. Paralyzed." He was quiet long enough to have her turning her head to study his face. "They shut down," he said at last.

She nodded again, and how meaningless was that? She was glad to see the CSI van, even though she couldn't imagine they'd find anything at all.

Boyd had stepped ahead and was greeting the pair that climbed out when Melinda's phone buzzed.

Déjà vu.

He turned slowly. Melinda pulled her phone from her pocket and stared in shock at the photo: a dark-haired girl curled into a ball, her tiny hands pressed over her ears. Even so, you could see her contorted face—and her tears.

The brief line of text said, Hide and Seek.

She thrust the phone at Boyd, who stared.

"We can't let Miguel or Maria see this. It'll kill them."

"No, but…she's alive."

He lifted his head, his eyes meeting Melinda's, and she knew they were thinking the same thing.

Chapter Eight

Melinda, Boyd and the CSI tech, a twenty-something guy named Jeff Stanavitch who was apparently a computer whiz, huddled around Stanavitch's laptop, set on the Cordovas' kitchen counter. Melinda had emailed the text and photo to him so that they could study it in a larger format. Boyd was ashamed to be glad to be out of sight of the terrified parents.

Miguel's gaze had followed people as they passed through the living room, but Maria had her face pressed to his chest. He held her tight. Crumpled tissues heaped the coffee table and spilled over onto the floor.

Stanavitch spoke up. "I think she's outside. The background is blurred, but…"

Boyd leaned closer. "You're right." It was hard to make out beyond the glare of the flash. There wasn't much background visible around Carlota, anyway, most of that above her. But— "Could that be a tree trunk behind her? At first I thought it was a wall, but look at the dark line." Was that a hint of peeling around it? He always enjoyed the sight of the grove of quaking aspen growing along the creek that curved through his ranch. Not that the abducted girl would be there; it could only be accessed on horseback or ATV, which were rarely used on his property.

Intent on seeing every detail, Melinda was all but pressed against his side. "It's white." She frowned. "It could be an aspen. Their bark is really pale."

The tech mumbled to himself, then opened a new screen, typed quickly and brought up a photo of a quaking aspen. They were often found in eastern Oregon, usually along a river. Somewhere wet enough to allow them to thrive.

Boyd kept thinking about the message. Dorrance could have said something like, *Lost something?* Or *Lost and Found.* What was he saying with *Hide and Seek*?

"What if he took her as part of the game he's playing with us?" he asked. "There's no hint he's ever been interested in young children, is there?"

Melinda looked at him. "No."

"What would he want with a three-year-old?"

"The most horrible kind of revenge on Miguel? As far as we know, Guy didn't have any vulnerability like a child. What could Dorrance do but kill him?"

Stanavitch was watching both of them now, looking disturbed.

"You have a point, but...what if he did this as a vicious kind of fun?" Boyd suggested. "And a different kind of message. What if he didn't keep her? He's saying, now it's up to us to find her. He could even be watching."

Waiting to ambush them. Terrorize Miguel by stealing his kid, give him joy when he found her, then kill him.

But that thought apparently didn't cross Melinda's mind, because hope brightened her eyes. "You mean... Carlota might be close by? Is that what you're saying?"

"He could have dumped her—" He shot a glance toward the living room. Hell. He wouldn't want the kid's parents to hear him. "*Left* her anywhere," he amended. "If so, somebody else may find her. But I'm thinking this was all about saying, 'I can get into any of your houses. Take your most precious possessions. Kill you without you seeing me coming.' So why not snatch her, then leave her nearby?"

"It can't be so close she could find her way home," Stanavitch said. "Or that we could hear her crying."

"No." Damn. He shouldn't have raised anyone's hopes. Especially not Melinda's.

She hadn't blinked in so long, he couldn't remember the last time he'd seen her do it. Her eyes were stunning, making him think of a sunlit forest glade. Then, suddenly, she closed her eyes, letting out a breath, the quivering tension draining from her body. Alarmed, Boyd wrapped a supportive arm around her. She so rarely revealed her deeper emotions, but how often did she investigate a crime involving a child so young?

She didn't react to his touch, only opened her eyes and said fiercely, "We have to show this to Miguel. He might recognize the tree. If that's what this is, judging from the width of the trunk, the tree has to be an old one. I'm not that familiar with this area. I don't even know if there's water nearby. It's also possible that there could be an aspen or, I don't know, a beech that's part of somebody's landscaping."

Bright flashes were visible from the corner of Boyd's eye. The other tech was photographing the bedroom, the window and cut glass.

Melinda watched him anxiously. He was surprised she hadn't charged out to the living room and hauled Miguel by his shirt collar into the kitchen. Was she respecting the fact that this crime had been committed in his jurisdiction? Or the fact that Cordova worked for Boyd? Either way, it seemed uncharacteristic for her, especially given her dislike.

"Okay," he said reluctantly. "I'll go get him."

When Boyd stepped into the living room, Miguel turned his head as if reluctantly curious.

"Can I have a word with you?" Boyd asked quietly.

Miguel blinked a couple of times before nodding. He gently disentangled himself from his wife, stood as if he bore a two-hundred-pound pack on his shoulders and trudged to Boyd, who led him into the kitchen.

Boyd explained that Dorrance had sent a photograph of Carlota. "It's hard to look at because she's crying and probably scared."

Miguel almost leaped forward.

Boyd blocked him. "Wait. We're speculating that he could have left her somewhere for us to find. We think that's a tree in the background and are hoping it might look familiar to you."

Both Boyd and Stanavitch stepped aside to allow the detective to plant himself right in front of the laptop and stare for a long, silent moment. His throat worked; his body shook. But then he said slowly, "That's an aspen. A big one."

"That's what we thought."

"There's a stand not a quarter of a mile away, along Mustang Creek." He lunged away. "We have to go look!"

"Cordova!"

As an army officer, Boyd had perfected the art of using his voice like the crack of a whip. Even Melinda was obviously startled at the impact. Miguel stopped in his tracks, eyes wild.

"Don't say anything to Maria. If nothing comes of this, it might be worse for her."

He swallowed.

"Get a flashlight, meet us out front."

A hard nod, and he took off at a near run.

"Good try," Melinda said wryly.

Yeah, Maria would notice something was up.

Melinda got a flashlight out of her car, too, and the three set off behind the house. The day's heat lingered, and he couldn't feel any breeze. This was beginning to feel like the never-ending day.

"None of the neighbors have fences," Cordova explained, his breath coming hard as he led the way at a trot.

Once they left behind anything that could be called a backyard, this land was mostly open and dry, a few junipers scattered among the sagebrush they had to jog around. Typical of a lot of the county. But ahead, Boyd saw the dark bulk of a grove of trees. And, yeah, the air smelled damp if he wasn't imagining things.

He swept the creek with his flashlight when they reached it and saw there wasn't much to it. A sharp bend must have resulted in something of a pool here, which explained the small grove of trees.

Again, he had to physically restrain his detective. "If we're right, we've been lured here," he said, keeping his voice low. "Is there a road close by?"

"Uh…yeah." Cordova's head turned. "There's a bridge just downstream. The road's not much, but it leads to a couple of ranches."

Damn.

Boyd had driven much of the county once he became sheriff, determined to know his territory, but there were too many roads that didn't amount to much but long driveways. The post office carriers must know the names, but there often weren't signs.

His unease crystalized.

"You two start," he said, wanting to tell them both to wait until he had a look around, but too aware of what even this brief hesitation was doing to the father of the abducted child. He was shaking like a runner held too long in the starting block. "I'm going to reconnoiter, make sure there's no handy escape vehicle parked there. Be as quiet as you can. Don't yell out your daughter's name until I give the all-clear, okay?"

"Yes. Yes!" Cordova took off.

Melinda gave Boyd a look he couldn't interpret, then trotted toward the trees.

Disquieted, Boyd realized he had to take the long way around the bend to reach that bridge. Experienced at navigating in the darkness, he turned his flashlight off. He was disturbed to see that, given the scanty lower branches on the aspens and the lack of undergrowth, the other two flashlight beams were painfully visible to him, and could probably be seen from half a mile away.

He moved as fast as he could, but it wasn't fast enough.

First he heard a startled exclamation from off to his right, then a child's cry. The ensuing silence couldn't have lasted one minute before it was split by the crack of a gunshot.

Melinda.

"Carlota?"

Melinda spun when she heard Cordova's voice, breaking with anguish and hope, and then a small, whimpering, "Papa?"

The child was here. Alive. Thank God. *Thank God.*

Heart swelling with gratitude, Melinda hurried toward them. Her head turned. What if Dorrance was also out here? She'd covered most of the short distance when a movement seen out of the corner of her eye worked like a cattle prod. Even as she thought, *Boyd*, she knew better. Instinct sent her flying through the air, colliding with

Miguel's stockier body crouched over his daughter, sending them both crashing toward the ground.

The gunshot came while they were still in the air. Miguel hit hardest, a grunt escaping him. Melinda landed awkwardly in her attempt to avoid crushing the little girl, who started screaming.

A second shot had her scrambling to cover Carlota, even as she wished she'd worn her vest. What if that bullet had found Miguel? Somewhere in there, she'd dropped her flashlight and he must have, too, because two unmoving beams illuminated nothing but trees. Maybe the shooter hadn't realized the flashlights had flown some distance from them.

While she braced herself to take a bullet, she heard running footsteps. Help coming? No, the *thud, thud* was receding. Melinda stayed where she was, kneeling protectively over the girl, but her head hung in relief.

"Miguel? Are you all right?"

"Carlota!" He sounded frantic.

"She's fine. I'm fine."

A more distant gunshot sounded, followed by a second.

Terrified anew, she wondered whether Boyd was fine, too—or whether he was down, his intense life force gone, leaving only a shell. The vivid imagery shook her.

Two more shots rang out, then…was that the sound of a car engine?

She pushed herself to her feet. Boyd might be injured, at least, need help. Momentarily dizzy, she swayed. She didn't remember hitting her head.

At her feet, Miguel was cuddling his little girl close and crooning to her.

Melinda felt suddenly uncertain of directions now that

the night was so quiet. She turned in place. No, the road
had to be that way—

"Melinda!" Boyd's voice was a roar.

If she whimpered in her relief, Miguel was too occupied to hear her.

"Here!" she called back. "We're here."

Not more than a minute later, the light from Boyd's
flashlight speared between ghostly pale tree boles until
it settled on her.

"You're blinding me," she managed to say.

"Sorry." He lowered the beam and appeared from the
darkness. "He got away. Damn it, I should have handled
that differently. I *knew* better."

She had, too, Melinda realized, but had let her instincts be overruled by the idea of a distraught, possibly
injured child too frightened to move. Miguel's fear had
probably been contagious, too.

"Was that you shooting, or him?" she asked.

"Both," he said tersely. "If I'd had a better look at him,
I'd have gotten him. I was too far away to get a good shot
with a handgun. Are any of you hurt?"

"I don't think so. Miguel?" She touched his shoulder.

He lifted his face to her, his expression rapturous.
"No. No."

Boyd cupped Melinda's cheek. "You're bleeding."

"Oh." She lifted her hand to explore it. "Just dirt or a
rock or something. We went down pretty hard."

Boyd let out a hard breath. "At least he's a lousy shot.
He was waiting here. He should have gotten one of you."

"I...saw something," Melinda said. "Movement. I
tackled Miguel. The bullets may have passed right over
us."

"We'll look in daylight," Boyd said gruffly. "We may
be able to recover one."

"Which will tell us what?" She sounded like a cop again. Almost felt like one. That steadied her. "We know he has Guy Jonas's service weapon. That almost has to be what he fired."

"Yeah." Boyd sounded seriously unhappy. "I tried to call in a BOLO, but neither of my deputies on patrol tonight was anywhere near, and the only state patrolman in the county was even farther away."

"Did you see what Dorrance was driving?"

"A sedan, not a pickup or SUV. I tried to shoot out a tire, but the way he rocketed out of here, I missed."

And was really annoyed with himself, she diagnosed. He seemed to shake himself. "Let's get Carlota home."

Those were magic words. Too much had gone wrong, but this much was wonderfully right.

Seeing Miguel fumbling with his phone as they started out, Boyd took it and found "Maria." It was ringing when he handed it back.

"We found her. She's fine." He ducked his head. "Say 'Mama.'"

The little girl summoned a shaky, tear-choked, "Mama?"

They all heard the scream through the phone.

"We'll be home in a minute," Miguel said.

Nobody spoke again, although Boyd reached out once and took Melinda's arm to keep her from walking right into a clump of sagebrush. Did he think that she'd suffered a head injury she wasn't acknowledging?

Maybe he had reason, she admitted to herself. She hated to say, *I don't feel so good.*

At the house, the celebration verged on hysteria—tears, then laughter and back to sobs. Stanavitch wiped away a tear as he and his partner decamped. Melinda blinked hard a few times.

Miguel was the one to suddenly straighten and step back from his wife and child. "We need to leave. Pack up right now."

Maria gaped at him.

"I agree," Boyd said. "It's not safe to stay here until we catch that—" He visibly swallowed the word that had almost escaped. "I have plenty of room at my house. You can spend the rest of the night there."

"I need to get Maria and Carlota away, then come back. I want to do my job." Miguel sounded grimly determined. "But I won't risk them."

Melinda watched Boyd, guessing that he'd feel the same. It was true that the city and county together didn't field enough law enforcement officers to maintain normal coverage and hunt for a madman. But—

"You should go, too," Melinda said suddenly. "Dorrance is going to be furious. This was so elaborate, but he failed. I don't think he'll just move on to another target."

Maria stared at her husband in alarm. "What happened?"

"He took some shots at us, but missed," Miguel told her.

A terrible cry burst from her. "You must come with us!"

His face convulsed, but he said, "I'm a cop. This is what I do. You know that."

"Go," Boyd said. "That's an order. You need to put your family first right now."

His detective stared at him, but finally nodded. "Let's pack right now."

The entire small family took off to do just that, leaving Melinda and Boyd alone in the living room. He focused on her with that familiar intensity.

"Dorrance wants you more than he wants Miguel. Miguel wasn't part of the investigation at all."

"He was SWAT at the time. One of the first in the house. He might even have taken Dorrance down. I... don't know who did."

"Did he testify at the trial?"

She shook her head, knowing where he was going.

"He's not just going around executing people. It's going to be worse than that. And *you're* his prime target."

"We'll catch him before he gets to me." Melinda wished she sounded sturdier. More certain.

His eyes drilled into hers. "I want you off his radar."

Part of her wanted the same. To run. But she was already ashamed of the way she'd let him take over tonight. All she'd done was bob her head and defer to his decisions. None of which had been *wrong*, but...

"I can't do that," she said. "I can't live with myself if I do."

He tore his gaze from hers, kneaded the back of his neck. "Leaning on other people sometimes isn't so bad, Melinda."

Her heart cramped. "How would *you* know?"

His jaw tightened. "Will you come stay at the ranch, at least? Or with Deperro and his wife?"

"Endanger her? No."

"The ranch?"

She wanted to, desperately and for the wrong reasons. "I...can't. You know I can't. Anyway, it's not exactly Fort Knox."

She wasn't surprised by his glare. He didn't like that but couldn't deny it. Two of his ranch employees had been horrifically murdered by the serial killer last year. That was different, of course; nobody had known the killer was after anyone on the ranch. Boyd had been mad as hell when he learned that his employee screening had missed so much in Howard Haycroft's background. Now, everyone would be on edge, watching for strangers and unfamiliar vehicles. Still, he couldn't promise her complete security.

"And I can't do my job if you hem me in too much," she continued. "And that's what you'll do, given half a chance. You won't be able to help yourself."

They stared at each other, the air all but crackling with the tension. Miguel interrupted the standoff, pulling a large suitcase and carrying another as he emerged from the hall. "We're almost ready. Maria is making sure she has Carlota's favorite toys."

Melinda forced a smile. "You're going home with Boyd for the night?"

"Maybe we should just start driving. He can't be watching us now."

"He could be," Boyd said quietly. "Let's not take a chance. You'll be safe at my place, and tomorrow I can escort you to the airport. The farther away you go, the better."

"Maria has family in Mexico. On the Yucatàn. We can go there."

"Good." Boyd rolled his head as if his neck ached and said, "Let me load those for you."

Minutes later they locked up, Boyd accepting a key to the house after having promised to send a ranch hand in the morning to board up the window as a temporary measure. She saw him look at her one more time, just before she got into her Subaru to join the convoy that would take them through town and out the other side. Her head still hurt, but the dizziness had been temporary, and she had no problem driving.

She flashed her headlights just before she peeled off to go home, hating the anxiety she couldn't shake, but refusing to succumb to it.

Chapter Nine

The media crowd seemed to be mushrooming by the day, even though flashing Dorrance's face everywhere had yet to produce a verifiable sighting. Heads and cameras swiveled when Boyd slowed to turn in beside the police station, but he ignored them and parked in back. Somebody had stationed a uniform to block any attempt by a cameraman or enterprising reporter to slip through to the back of the building.

Approaching the conference room inside, Boyd spotted Melinda and a man he didn't know in the hall. For a moment, he thought they were talking, but the guy went on in and she remained where she was, a phone to her ear.

"No!" she exclaimed when he got close enough to hear. Her gaze flew to his. "Don't tell me where you are!"

Eyebrows lifting, Boyd stopped a few feet from her.

"He called your father?" What looked like intense worry crinkled her forehead and she sounded urgent when she responded. "Call him. He needs to disappear for a while. Just…go stay somewhere, where he can't be traced. You need to do the same, Erica." After a pause, she said, "No, I don't really think he'll go after you. He's…occupied here in town. He seems to be stalking some of the police officers involved in his arrest. But I don't think you should take any chance at all. If he got to your dad…"

Not a possibility Boyd wanted to think about.

Melinda's back and forth with the young woman who'd been one of the victims continued for another couple of minutes, Boyd waiting it out. Melinda never looked away from him.

The same tiredness showed on her face that he'd seen on his own in the mirror this morning—dark circles under her eyes, worry lines that were at least a decade too soon. He wanted to smooth them out but felt lucky she hadn't jerked her head to order him peremptorily into the meeting room. Instead… He might be imagining it, but he thought she was drawing some strength from him.

Ending the call at last, she said, "I keep thinking Dorrance can't get any more evil and then he does. I had to work to find the dad's phone number. It's not good that Dorrance managed without my resources."

Boyd swore, then said, "We'd better get in there. It looks like our task force has grown. No point in us talking about this when everyone will want to hear about the call."

She nodded and went ahead of him, taking a single seat on the far side of the table. Boyd pulled out a chair between Alvarez, who was back, and Lieutenant Matson.

Two people he didn't know were present, just as well since Detective Cordova had gotten on a plane earlier this morning with his wife and child. From Portland, a flight would take them to Mexico City. Cordova had said they'd stay with family well outside of the city. He didn't see how anyone could find them. He'd call every few days to find out when they could safely return home.

Daniel introduced the two new participants as an FBI special agent, Alan Cabe, and a representative from the

Oregon State Police Crime Analyst Unit, better known as CAU. Aaron Loftis was about Boyd's age and there to help how he could, he said calmly, no suggestion that he felt superior to the mere locals. Boyd hadn't yet had occasion to call on the services of the CAU. But he knew that most jurisdictions in Oregon were grateful for its help with everything from managing a major investigation when that was beyond the capability of a small police force, to helping process evidence, do data research, handle tip lines and analyze incoming data in a way most police had no experience doing. Some of that presumably overlapped what FBI special agent Cabe could do, but too much help was better than not enough, in Boyd's opinion.

The rest of the task force introduced themselves in turn, and then Melinda and Boyd brought everyone up to speed on the events of the past twenty-four hours, including the phone call she'd just taken. Boyd was still kicking himself for not getting into place last night to locate Dorrance before letting Cordova start searching for his daughter, but nobody else commented. The hunt for a child that young and vulnerable was fraught with emotion even when she wasn't the daughter of an officer who was part of the search for Dorrance.

Their discussion about going forward was less productive. They agreed that Loftis would take charge of the tip line information coming into both the county and SPD, categorizing and analyzing it in a way that just wasn't happening. They needed a geographic breakdown, for example—what if several people living in the same vicinity had claimed to see him? Even if their particular claims hadn't been convincing, the cluster would say something.

Matson surprised Boyd by wanting to ask the public to call to report any women they knew who lived alone and wouldn't normally be missed immediately.

Melinda jumped on that. "You know that no matter what we say, people will rush to check on neighbors rather than asking us to do it. We'd be putting them in danger."

A short discussion resulted in an agreement to hold off at least temporarily. Emmett Yates was assigned to talk to postal delivery employees, who might be able to identify some single women living in isolated homes.

Then Daniel interjected. "Who says the woman is single? Or should I say, *was* single? A retired couple would have done just as well. Dorrance wouldn't hesitate to kill the husband."

The more they talked, the higher rose the level of frustration.

The FBI agent spoke up. "Unless he's highly skilled at disguises, this Dorrance will be seen. He took a huge chance leaving the message in Detective McIntosh's car, for example. I gather it was still daylight?"

"It was," she agreed.

"It doesn't take long to lower the window enough to drop in the envelope, but that's also the kind of thing that would catch the eye of someone passing by, and traffic in and out of any major grocery store tends to be constant. Since he got by with it the once, he may be emboldened to believe he can do anything he wants."

"He got into Detective Cordova's house when the detective and his wife were both home," Boyd said, hearing his own grim tone. "Broke in and abducted their daughter without making a sound."

Special Agent Cabe leaned forward. "Again, high risk. Yes, he waited for darkness, but what if she'd been awake when he climbed in the window? She might have screamed. My point is that he could have snatched her during the day when an armed law enforcement officer wasn't a few feet away. He wanted to issue a challenge more than he wanted to go unseen."

"He expects to be killed," Melinda said slowly. "But he intends to take revenge on as many of us as possible first."

Cabe, midforties at a guess, nodded. "That's my take."

"What if we persuade every single person who played any role at all in his arrest and conviction to go into hiding?" Tom Alvarez asked.

Boyd couldn't help looking at Melinda, who narrowed her eyes at him in warning.

It was Cabe who said, "How many people are we talking? Including the defense team, prosecutor's office, the neighbor who reported him, all the cops tied to his ultimate arrest?"

"Too many," Daniel said flatly. "Do we include the paralegal? The receptionist at the law firm who put calls through to Dorrance's attorney—or claimed sometimes he wasn't available? We have to be talking about twenty-five, thirty people, *and* their families. Spouses and teenage kids who have jobs."

"So it's impractical." Cabe frowned. "If this guy was able to track down one of the two victims' fathers, I worry that he's willing to go to any length to find the people he blames most. Right now, we know he's here in town, or at least nearby. Our chances of cornering him here are better than they would be if he starts traveling."

Boyd agreed, but pointed out, "The traveling would present pitfalls for him, though. Has he come up with a driver's license that can pass scrutiny if he gets pulled over? Car registration? I doubt he can jump through the hoops to fly commercially. Does he expose himself by staying in motels, or go to the length he apparently has here to set up a hideout?"

"All true," the FBI agent agreed, "but with him on the move, we'd have to warn countless other law enforcement agencies, convince them how dangerous this man is. If we have to take this manhunt nationwide, that would increase the risk of him killing someone just because they stand in his way or spot him at a bad moment."

"An ambush might be feasible, except we still have too many potential targets who've refused to hide," Daniel commented.

Except they all knew Dorrance was fixated on one particular target. Boyd tensed, bracing himself for someone to point out that logical fact.

No one did. Partly, he assumed, because the SOB clearly wanted to enjoy first taking out other people he hated.

Daniel continued, "It's essential that we follow up at least daily with each and every one of them. We can't let someone drop from our radar."

For the most part, periodic contact was already happening. While it was reassuring that everyone on their list had been alive and well this morning, sooner or later one of them wouldn't answer the call. Chances were good that person would already be dead.

What Boyd hated most was that they had no good strings to pull to locate a man who sure as hell already had his next victim targeted—and Dorrance had to be enraged because he'd failed to kill Miguel Cordova.

MELINDA WISHED THE SUN wasn't reflecting off the windows as she surveyed the weather-beaten, small house beside a grove of cottonwood trees on the outskirts of Sadler. The detached garage was in a sorry state, missing shingles on the roof like a kid shedding baby teeth, the siding gray and cracking. The doors hung crookedly but were nonetheless closed. A vehicle could be hidden within.

In marginally better shape, the house obviously hadn't had a fresh coat of paint in decades, but the roof showed signs of being patched at some point. The yard was overrun with weeds, but the driveway wasn't as it might have been if the place was deserted.

She was probably wasting her time—almost certainly was—but she'd already driven several routes Dorrance could have taken between his workplace and home, then widened her search radius gradually. Boyd wouldn't approve of her so much as getting out of her car in an isolated location like this without backup, but there weren't enough of them looking to be able to double up personnel, no matter what the lieutenant had recommended. This house *could* suit a nutcase holding a woman captive, since it was far enough off the beaten track, passersby out on the road probably rarely gave it so much as a glance.

She got out, hesitated, then drew her gun before she hustled to the garage. No windows. The doors were held together by a crude padlock, rusting enough that she could tell it hadn't been recently replaced. She pushed hard to widen the gap between the doors enough to peer in. A thin band of light let her see that the space was mostly empty. Darker shapes around the edges might be a workbench, tools like a mower and Weedwacker or a pile of boxes.

She tipped her head and listened, but all she heard was a distant whine of a motorcycle engine accelerating. From this angle, the sun's reflection wasn't blinding her when she looked at the house, but several windows were covered by roller shades or curtains. She trotted up to the porch, positioned herself well to one side of the front door before knocking on it firmly.

Now the silence was complete.

Until a small *ding* came from her pocket. A text. Her heart jumped even as she knew the text was likely from Boyd or Daniel or another cop. Or even a friend. She did have some of those.

Melinda pressed her back to the house wall beside the front door as she pulled the phone from her pocket and lifted it. A photo appeared. She had to blink a couple of times to make out what she was looking at. When she succeeded, bile rose into her throat.

Oh, God, oh, God.

Daniel. She should call Daniel first, but her thumb found Boyd's name instead.

Even as she listened to the ringing, she hoped no one was home here. If someone suddenly opened that door, she might have a heart attack—or shoot before she knew who she was looking at.

SHE MET BOYD and Daniel at Mack Humrich's house. Melinda was the first there, but she waited in her car until two more vehicles arrived. Even then, she was so reluctant to get out and join the two men, she felt as if she were moving against resistance when she forced herself out of the car.

Daniel spoke first. "We can't be sure his body is here."

He didn't want to go looking either, she realized.

A fellow SPD officer, Mack had been a SWAT team member and had served on a regional task force aiming to prevent drug trafficking. He was a good cop. Melinda had known him well. They'd even dated a few times years ago, before she'd come to her senses and realized that they'd screw up a good working relationship. He hadn't seemed to disagree, and as far as she could tell, there'd been no hard feelings on either side.

She'd give a lot to be able to believe that the dead man in the photo was someone else, anyone else, but she'd known him the minute her eyes really focused.

Boyd was watching her, so she squared her shoulders and said, "Looks like the side door into the garage is standing open."

Both men nodded. Still none of them moved.

"Is he married?" Boyd asked. "Does he have kids?"

"No kids." Thank God. "He's married, but, um, I heard they've been having problems. They might be separated. I haven't seen him to talk to in several months."

Daniel sighed. "Me either. He's been on nights."

"We going to do this?" Boyd asked.

"I requested backup." Daniel turned his head at the sound of another car. "This could be another ambush."

Broad daylight, at least three cops present, Melinda doubted it. Plus, of the three of them, *she* was the only target that would interest Dorrance. Although she supposed he might not mind mowing down other, random cops at this point.

Joined by two uniformed patrol officers, they all pulled their weapons and spread out to circle the house and garage. She was able to catch a glimpse inside the garage from that open door but didn't see anyone, living or dead.

She smelled the recently dead, though, which further sickened her.

Boyd reported finding the sliding door at the back of the house unlocked. He and the two uniforms did a search while Daniel and Melinda looked at each other, then burst into the garage crying, "Police!"

No one was there except the body hanging from the rafters. Melinda went outside, ducked around to the back of the garage and lost her lunch.

She was wiping her lips, grateful to see a faucet she could use to rinse her mouth, when Boyd appeared. He was the last person she would have wanted to see her so distraught she was puking.

"Don't say anything," she told him, stony.

He looked genuinely surprised as well as concerned for her. "What would I say? I know you've seen as bad or worse than this and worked through it." A nerve twitched under his eye. "It's…harder when you know someone. Worse yet when he was a friend."

She heard a question in that. Gentle, not a demand for information, so she nodded and heard herself say, "We dated a few times, seven or eight years ago. It didn't go very far. Both of us were more focused on our careers, but—" her mouth tasted foul "—you're right. It's different than seeing the victims of that serial killer, even though he'd done such horrible things to them."

She saw nothing but kindness on his face. Even…tenderness? Surely not from Boyd Chaney!

"Better rinse out your mouth and splash some water on your face so we can get back to work."

Melinda nodded, crouched in front of the faucet and turned on the water. When she'd finished rinsing out her mouth, Boyd's big hand appeared in front of her, offering a roll of mints.

She popped two into her mouth and handed the roll back to him. Making herself rise to her feet was hard, but she did it.

Furrows had formed between Boyd's dark eyebrows. "This is a lot more barbaric than Jonas's murder."

"Because he's mad about yesterday's disaster?" she suggested.

His gaze searched her face. "Is there any way he

could know this Humrich and you were more than fellow officers?"

Just like that, she wanted to puke again. Instead, she stared at Boyd in shock. What if Mack had suffered so terribly only because Dorrance wanted to upset her?

"I don't see how," she said in a thin voice.

"Were you dating him when the raid happened?"

"I...don't remember." She closed her eyes. Yes, she did. She and Mack had exchanged a fraught glance as she descended into the basement. "Yes," she whispered. "Even so..."

"Someone at Dorrance's law firm might have found out. Thought the relationship could be used to discredit you in some way." He made a raw sound and reached for her. "Damn it, Melinda! This is *not* your fault. You know that. The guy is a sicko."

A few days before, she couldn't have imagined a circumstance that would have had her willingly leaning into this man's embrace, but right this minute, she laid her cheek against his powerful chest and tried to soak in the strength of his arms wrapped around her.

"What happened to Mack may not be my fault," she mumbled into Boyd's solid chest, "but it's because of me."

His arms tightened. The rumble she felt in his chest had to be a kind of growl. "No," he said.

"Yes."

Chapter Ten

At the end of the day, the task force members split up to go their separate ways. Nobody suggested stopping for a meal together, even though most of them probably hadn't had lunch. Melinda, for one, had zero appetite. Daniel probably just wanted to get home to Lindsay, the lieutenant to his wife. Alvarez was married, too, and probably both the FBI agent and Aaron Loftis, the guy borrowed from the Oregon State Police Crime Analysis Unit.

Boyd…didn't say anything, just nodded, got into his SUV and drove away. In fact, he was the first to go. She couldn't quite decipher his last glance at her.

Fifteen minutes later, Melinda entered her own house with her weapon drawn and did what was beginning to be a standard search before she could relax at all. Then, after removing her holster and badge, she poured herself a glass of wine. Figuring her paranoia was justified, she kept the semiautomatic close, lying on the sofa beside her.

Although the TV remote control was at hand, too, she didn't reach for it. A little later, she'd watch the local news, see what the chief had said about the latest murder and how he handled the increasingly hysterical questions, but otherwise had no interest in entertainment or national or international crises. Instead, she stared at the dark television screen and saw Mack's body. Somebody must have called his wife, she thought. Matson, maybe?

Suddenly, what she saw instead was Boyd's face when he'd followed her behind the garage. She hadn't known he could look so gentle, or that he'd understand her shock and grief.

I should have, she realized. Of course, he'd have seen good friends die in awful ways. For the first time, it occurred to her that his desire to hire ex-army rangers to work on his ranch wasn't entirely because he preferred having like-minded buddies around—or warriors ready to spring into action when called. Rather, the presence of those men might be a comfort—they had all had the same kind of experiences, they understood each other, they might even *need* each other on occasion.

She wrinkled her nose. If any of them were ever willing to expose raw emotions.

And yet he'd accepted her doing so. Because she was a woman? Melinda tried to work up some temper but failed because she truly believed he'd have acted the same if it had been Daniel who'd just lost a good friend.

Maybe she'd jumped to conclusions about Boyd that just weren't accurate.

Melinda examined that thought for a moment but didn't know where to go with it. She'd shut the door on their relationship. Since he hadn't contacted her since, there was no reason to think he might still harbor any special feelings for her. If he'd gotten married during the interval, she was sure she'd have heard, but he might well have a live-in companion. Could be that's why he'd left without a word, probably as relieved to be heading home as Daniel had to be.

She shook her head. Forget Boyd. Who she needed to

be thinking about was Dorrance. Where he was, what he was planning, how they could stop him before he destroyed any more lives.

NOT A BIG FAN of fast food, Boyd still used the drive-through at a burger joint to load up on provisions of a sort, then navigated through town to Lieutenant Edward Matson's house.

What he wanted to do—hell, not *wanted*—what he was damn near desperate to do—was stake out Melinda's house. Watch over her. But he'd had an uneasy feeling that had become needle sharp today. Then-detective Ed Matson had been primary once Melinda persuaded the department to investigate Gene Dorrance. He could have taken a cursory look and said, *Yeah, this is a waste of my time*. He didn't. Ultimately, *he* was responsible for calling in SWAT, going ahead with the raid that brought down Dorrance. *He* was a logical next target, given that the partner he'd worked with at the time had retired and moved away, placing himself out of immediate reach.

Since the beginning, everyone had watched Melinda out of the corners of their eyes—and yes, that was probably because she was female and, in their heart of hearts, deemed less able to take care of herself, and also, of course, because she was the person Dorrance had chosen to communicate with. What nobody seemed to remember was that Matson was near retirement. He did still appear fit, but Boyd had noticed a stiffness in the way he rose from chairs or got in or out of his vehicle, maybe because he didn't want anyone to know he had back problems or the like. Was he still a regular at the range? Mostly administrative now, when had he last pulled his weapon on the job?

Boyd hated the idea of Melinda having to face down Dorrance, but he had more faith in her reaction time and skill than he did in Matson's. Thus his plan for tonight. The lieutenant wouldn't like being perceived as weak any more than Melinda would, but Boyd didn't intend to be seen—unless something happened.

Never having needed a lot of sleep, he figured to find a good place to keep an eye on Matson's house and settle in for the night. His extensive combat experience meant he could snatch a little shut-eye but be awake and alert at the slightest sound or movement. Once they caught this scumbag, he'd have plenty of time to catch up on sleep.

Turned out the Matsons' house was a standard rambler on a normal size city lot. Garages were in back of the houses in this neighborhood, accessed via an alley.

Boyd drove in a slow circle around the block, automatically noting parked cars, heavy shrubbery, the two backyards enclosed by six-foot-high board fences. Fortunately, neither of those bordered Matson's backyard, which was neatly mowed and included a couple of fruit trees and some raised garden beds filled with thriving rows of plants.

If he were the one planning to penetrate the house or make an attack when the lieutenant was arriving or departing, he'd set up or approach from the back. The front was too open, and once darkness fell would be lit by streetlamps at each end of the block as well as any porch lights left on. Anybody glancing out a front window would pay attention to a man cutting across a yard, too.

One real problem: the bulk of the garage would hide an intruder coming from the opposite direction, or that someone could hide behind any of several other garages or inside the fence of the yard just behind the Matson's.

Boyd could call for someone to join him, but what was really just an uneasy feeling didn't seem to justify asking anyone else to spend the night on watch, too.

He'd parked on the cross street and walked down the alley when he saw the lieutenant's car turn in. Stepping behind a hedge, he watched as the garage door rose and Matson drove into it, not noticing Boyd. Not impressed, Boyd could only hope the guy had at least taken a good look to be sure no one was waiting inside for him before he pushed the button to close the door, shutting himself in.

There was no other movement up or down the alley. Boyd moved to a position that let him watch as the lieutenant came out of his garage, crossed his yard and let himself into his house—through a door with a big glass pane that made even a dead-bolt lock useless. The same kind Jonas had had. Boyd shook his head. These were cops. They had to know better.

He settled between the garage and a big lilac shrub to eat his dinner. Once darkness cloaked him, he began hourly circuits that took in much of the block. He did manage a few naps, and woke because he'd set an internal clock, not because he'd been startled awake.

He carried his phone, but it didn't once vibrate during the night.

Boyd decided that after he'd followed Matson into work, he'd stay in his own vehicle to make his daily checks on potential targets before going into the station himself to join the task force meeting.

When a light went on in what was likely Matson's bedroom, Boyd stretched muscles and sharpened his surveillance. He wished the lieutenant didn't have to walk across the yard to reach the garage, making himself a perfect target. Boyd was also less than happy because he couldn't be as close as he should be without being seen. He could cover one side of the garage or the other, not both. Dorrance had fired some shots the other night, which meant he was carrying Officer Jonas's gun. He probably wasn't all that accurate, but that didn't matter if he could get close enough. So far, he'd fired the Glock only four times that they knew about, leaving plenty of bullets without him needing to shop for ammunition.

The kitchen light came on. Dawn brightened the sky, bringing into focus the landscaping in the yard, the lines of the clapboard on the house and garage. Boyd heard a few car engines as he waited, natural since early birds would be heading into work. He couldn't always tell where those sounds came from.

The back door opened a lot sooner than Boyd had expected. Matson couldn't possibly have eaten breakfast. Had he even gulped a cup of coffee? He paused on the small deck, looking from one side to the other in suspicion before unsnapping his holster and resting his hand on the butt of his service weapon while taking the step down to the grass. Not completely unaware of his danger, then.

Boyd crouched behind some shrub he couldn't identify, the only spot in the yard that allowed him to watch Matson cross all the way to the back door into the garage. What he couldn't see was around the corner of the damn structure—and he'd have to hustle to get eyes on the alley when the lieutenant backed out into it.

Matson was two steps from the door, hand outstretched with keys held in it, when movement erupted beyond him. A gun barked before the lieutenant could turn or unholster his own weapon. Time seemed to slow for Boyd, until he was seeing something like a slide show.

Black-clad man with his face covered. Gun extended in a double-handed grip.

Boyd shouted. Another shot, another. Matson falling. The assailant's head turning toward him.

Boyd running and firing simultaneously. Something burned his arm. Dorrance staggering against the garage, clutching at his shoulder or chest. Whirling around the corner.

Back door of the house opening.

Boyd yelled, "Stay inside!" and tore past the fallen man to circle the garage in pursuit of the *slap, slap* of footsteps in the alley. By the time Boyd reached it, he couldn't see anyone. He ran full out but heard an engine start and tires squeal before he reached the street. A charcoal-gray sedan turned the corner and went out of sight.

Despite gasping for breath, Boyd swore creatively. He might have had a chance of catching the murdering bastard if he'd parked at this side of the block, but he hadn't.

Holstering his weapon, he jogged back the way he'd come, calling 911 as he went.

The moment the dispatcher answered, he demanded an ambulance and gave the address. "Injured man is in the backyard." He described the car, guessed at make and model and asked for all available units to watch for it.

"I'll call Sergeant Deperro myself," he said, just as he came around the garage.

The woman pressing what looked like dish towels to Matson's chest had to be his wife. Her expression distraught, she was almost screaming, "Ed. Ed! You're going to be fine. I know you are. You *have* to be." She lifted her head, her wild eyes finding Boyd and focusing on the phone he still held. "Sheriff? Please. Please! Call—"

He interrupted. "Ambulance is on the way." He

dropped to his knees beside the lieutenant. "Let me take a look."

That look wasn't reassuring. Matson still had a pulse, but given the amount of blood he was losing, he wouldn't for long.

Boyd tore his long-sleeve T-shirt over his head and applied it to one of the wounds while Mrs. Matson pressed the already saturated kitchen towels to her husband's side.

He heard one siren, then another. When the medics appeared at a run, Boyd kept his hand in place until a gloved one wielding dressings replaced it. Then he gently drew the lieutenant's wife back.

"Give them room to work."

Sobbing, she let him help her to her feet. Still, her head turned until she couldn't see her husband anymore.

Frantically, she pulled away from him. "I have to get to the hospital."

"I'll drive you. I'll meet you out in front once you've grabbed your purse or anything else you need."

She swiped at her wet face and blinked a few times. "You're hurt, too."

"What?"

"Your arm."

He glanced down dismissively, remembering the burn across his upper arm. He'd felt that before. "I'll have it checked out when we get to the hospital."

Another sob broke from her. She spun and raced into the house. Boyd went to get his SUV, hoping he'd left another T-shirt or windbreaker in it.

MELINDA MADE HERSELF slow to a walk when she reached the double glass doors into the emergency room, even though she was scared down to her core.

Daniel's call had caught her as she was leaving her

house. She'd instantly lost all sense of caution, dashing to her Subaru without taking any precautions, and broke speed limits getting to the hospital. Thank heavens there'd been one empty slot remaining for a law enforcement vehicle, saving her from having to hunt for a parking place.

She immediately saw Daniel talking to a man in a green scrub top. The two stood near the doors leading to the back. Her gaze locked on the guy in scrubs. Boyd. A thick bandage wrapped his powerful upper arm.

So close, she thought, almost numbly. He could have been killed. Freaked beyond common sense—he was right there in front of her, for Pete's sake, *alive*—she fought to hide a reaction that was totally out of proportion.

As she walked toward them, both men turned. Boyd's gaze was penetrating.

"How's Lieutenant Matson?" she asked.

"In surgery. We were just waiting for you. Let's go on up," Daniel said.

She nodded, holding back any other questions until they were in an elevator that they had to themselves.

"He shot you."

Boyd grimaced. "Not much more than a graze. Cut through some muscle, that's all."

That's all.

Melinda swallowed. "Will you tell me—" The elevator doors opened.

They found the lieutenant's wife in a waiting room. She was surrounded by family and friends. Melinda had met Matson's son before but not his daughter and exchanged nods with him. Then the three cops retreated to another, small waiting room where they could speak freely.

Boyd told her what happened more tersely than she'd

have liked, but she could fill in the blanks. He was mad at himself, she realized, feeling as if he should have prevented the attack or killed or captured Dorrance.

Frowning, she asked, "What were you doing there?"

Daniel said, "Took the words out of my mouth."

"Just seemed logical the lieutenant could be a next target." Seeing Melinda's mouth open, Boyd said, "Yeah, I know he's a cop, but it's my impression he mostly rides a desk these days. I wondered if he'd react quick enough to a threat."

"And he didn't," she said bleakly.

"He didn't get much warning. He had his hand on his gun but didn't get a chance to draw it. I was too far away."

There was that tone again. Yep, he believed he'd screwed up.

"Lieutenant Matson would be dead for sure if you hadn't been there," she reminded him.

A stark look in his golden-brown eyes, he met her gaze. "He took three bullets. He lost a lot of blood."

Chilled, she couldn't mistake what he was saying: Matson was in critical condition. He might not make it through the surgery.

"You think you wounded Dorrance?"

"I hit him in the left shoulder." He touched the spot on his own body. "Couldn't have done a lot of damage, though, or he wouldn't have been able to run so fast."

He scrolled through photographs that showed car makes from the rear, and finally shook his head. "Older Camry is my best guess, but I'm not sure."

Daniel had already notified not only the ER here at the hospital, but also urgent care clinics and other hospitals in this and neighboring counties.

"Doubt he'd dare try to get medical care," Daniel said,

"but you might have done more damage than you think you did. Adrenaline can disguise symptoms for a while."

The men exchanged a look, and Melinda knew they'd both experienced the phenomenon while in combat.

An hour passed, then another. They took turns making calls and also checking on Mrs. Matson. Otherwise, silence prevailed. Melinda's gaze strayed frequently to Boyd. This time, he was leaning forward in the chair, elbows braced on his knees, head hanging. Did he hurt worse than he'd admit to? she couldn't help wondering.

"I hear voices." She popped to her feet.

The men rose too, and followed her down the short hall to the larger waiting room. A surgeon with his mask pulled below his chin was indeed there.

"...next hours," Melinda heard him say.

As he retreated, Daniel stopped him in the hall for a repeat of what he'd told the family. Judging from what she'd heard from Boyd, nothing about what the surgeon said was a surprise. Melinda had the impression he was being more honest with them than he'd been with the family. That the lieutenant had made it through the surgery was a positive, but he was still at high risk of dying.

As her gaze followed the surgeon walking away, Melinda clenched her teeth. "I want to kill Gene Dorrance," she heard herself blurt.

Blistering anger showed on Daniel's face. "You're not alone. I've never hoped before that I had to shoot someone," he growled.

Boyd's expression gave nothing away, even though he was the only one of them who'd actually had a chance to bring down Dorrance.

He only said, "He's a monster, but the right tip will come in. Someone is going to spot him. Sooner or later, it has to happen."

Melinda wanted to think the same, but so far Dorrance had appeared and disappeared with remarkable ease, leaving them falling on their faces in his wake.

An emotion deeper, more despairing, accompanied the anger. Feeling it swell in her chest until it all but choked her, she turned her back to the men. "The lieutenant has been really good to me. If he doesn't make it—" She couldn't finish.

A big hand squeezed her shoulder. Boyd's hand, the touch speaking for him.

Chapter Eleven

Two days later—days during which Dorrance made no move, calls to the tip lines declined and Ed Matson remained in critical condition—Boyd struggled to rein in his frustration. In the past week, he hadn't had time to so much as saddle a horse, much less actually take a ride. If his partner, Gabe Decker, hadn't accepted medical retirement from the rangers and stepped in here on the ranch, Boyd knew he couldn't possibly have run for sheriff. Truthfully, guilt still surfaced even though he was consumed by current events and his fear for Melinda, a woman who'd never admit to being afraid for herself. But, damn, he'd never realized how much he'd have to dump on Gabe.

Not that Gabe was complaining. He and his psychologist wife, Trina, had had dinner with Boyd last night. Their five-year-old adoptive daughter was away for a week, staying with her grandmother. Boyd had a bad feeling that Gabe saw right through him and knew what a big part Melinda played in his turmoil.

And maybe not just Gabe, Boyd thought uneasily. Trina was unnervingly perceptive, enough to have scared the hell out of Gabe when they first met. Boyd suspected that she was now intrigued by his own all-too-visible tension, a contrast to his usual laid-back style.

Gabe told him, "You had sole responsibility for the ranch for three years before I joined you. You did fine. I'll do fine, too. If I could help you find that piece of—" He'd glanced at his wife. "You have to know I'd be on board."

All of which was true.

Still brooding, Boyd shouldered his way into the sheriff's department headquarters, nodded at the receptionist and stalked toward his office.

He hadn't reached it when his newest hire—and the first female deputy in this county—leaned out of the squad room.

"Sheriff?" She sounded urgent. "Jerry—" She flushed. "I mean, Deputy Miller says he has a woman on the line he thinks you should talk to."

He'd like to feel hopeful, but a lot of ultimately useless callers had been forwarded to him, and undoubtedly the same was true over at the Sadler PD. Hell, the FBI, the Oregon State Police and, who knew, maybe the police departments on the other side of the state were probably all fielding equally useless calls. Still, a minute later he was at his desk and picking up his phone.

"Ma'am, this is Sheriff Chaney. I hate to ask you to start all over, but I'm afraid I need to."

She introduced herself as Sherry Williams and told him her husband had had a stroke and died four months before. "He was only fifty-four." Quiet for a minute she resumed. "One of our neighbors is a retired nurse. Maybe sixty years old? We always smiled and said hello at the mailbox—you know what that's like—but for most of that time she was still working, too, and not at all the same hours as I was. Neither of us suggested getting together for so much as coffee. But after Ron died, she brought over a casserole and sat down to talk to me. Her husband died ten years ago, you see, and suddenly, like Ron did.

I don't know if it would be better to have some warning, or not— Oh, I'm getting off track. Anyway, I found out that a lot of my friends didn't know what to say to me, but Kristina did."

"Kristina?"

"Morgan. Kristina Morgan."

Boyd jotted it on a notepad. This story was pushing all the right buttons.

"Well, my sister came to stay and I saw less of Kristina, and then I had to go back to work…" She trailed off. "I feel awful about it now, but we haven't talked in, oh, at least a couple of weeks. I've left several recent messages, and she hasn't called back. I thought she might be away, or maybe not interested in a long-term friendship—it seemed like she didn't go out much or have people over. You know."

In other words, a loner.

"I haven't seen her either, not even to wave to. I guess that's why I thought she might be away. And I can't see her house from mine. Ron and I—" She swallowed. "I have a couple of acres, and I'm pretty sure Kristina does, too. The land is scrubby, with a bunch of junipers."

When she didn't continue, Boyd asked, "What prompted you to call now?"

"Oh! I should have said! Well, to start with, I just didn't follow the news after I lost Ron. It's all so bad! I felt low enough without immersing myself in everybody else's tragedies. But the other day, I heard some people talking at work, so I did watch the local news. I kept thinking how unlikely it is that the police chief could have been talking about Kristina, but then, well, this morning I saw an unfamiliar man pulling out of her driveway."

"What was he driving?"

"Kristina's Camry. That's what was so strange."

"Did he see you?" Boyd asked with some urgency.

"I don't think so."

"Please don't make any further attempt to contact Ms. Morgan until we can do a welfare check," he said sternly.

"You'll do it soon?"

"We will. I promise."

He extracted a promise from her that she'd stay away from the neighbor's property.

He also learned that, while she hadn't gotten a good look at the man, what she saw could be a match for the photos Boyd had seen of Dorrance.

She'd called the sheriff's department because her home and Kristina Morgan's were outside the Sadler city limits. Once he had her address and the address for her neighbor, he promised to keep Mrs. Williams informed.

Then he called Daniel, wishing he could keep Melinda out of what was almost certain to be a raid.

MELINDA HUDDLED with Daniel, Emmett Yates, FBI special agent Alan Cabe and Alex Reyes, the SWAT lieutenant near what they'd guessed to be the property line. The rest of the team waited behind them in silence. Boyd had secured a warrant based on Sherry Williams's testimony, and now he'd slipped through the thicket of junipers to do the initial reconnaissance on the neighboring house.

She'd never particularly hankered to join SWAT, but Melinda stewed nonetheless because both Boyd and Daniel planned to go in with them despite not currently being members of the team. She'd vaguely known that Daniel had been SWAT in Portland, Oregon, while Boyd had certainly served on the military equivalent.

Boyd materialized through the scratchy foliage. "Can't see a car," he reported. "There's a detached double-car garage, but I can't get close enough to look in it without taking the risk of being seen."

Daniel's face was set in hard lines. "Damn, I hope he's there."

He and the group of six other men waited while Boyd donned some body armor, and then they forged ahead through the low-growing, scraggly trees. Tom Alvarez, Cabe, Emmett and Melinda trailed behind, stopping where they were just concealed from a white-painted, two-story farmhouse. A pair of deputies had parked out on the road so that those going into the house would have a warning should Dorrance drive up.

The SWAT team with their two temporary members broke into a trot that carried them across the short distance to the house in barely a minute or two. Their approach didn't seem to have incited any movement inside or outside the house.

Their backs flattened against the wall, they exchanged hand signals and split up, rounding the corners to the front and back. Melinda lost sight of the group that went to the back, which included Boyd. Daniel led the group to the front, waving two men to check the far side of the house. Shaking their heads, they rejoined him.

He hammered on the door. "Open the door! Police!"

Following a brief moment of waiting, he tried the door-knob, then stepped back and allowed one of the others to kick it open. He would have signaled Boyd's team to go in the back simultaneously, she assumed.

Tension high, Melinda hated not being able to do anything but wait and listen for gunfire. She wanted to pace, but couldn't without going out in the open. She wasn't alone; Cabe, who had ditched his usual dark suit for flexible boots, black T-shirt and cargo pants, watched with a hard cast to his face that she hadn't seen before.

She looked down at the face of her phone. A minute passed. Another. Windows all seemed to be covered, as they'd been in Dorrance's own house. Team members would have split up, some charging upstairs, others searching the ground floor as well as for an entrance to a potential basement. She had no idea whether a house of that era was likely to have one.

Suddenly Daniel, who'd removed his helmet, came out onto the porch and gestured for them to join him.

Melinda broke into a run. When she reached the foot of the steps, she saw his face, deeply lined, his jaw set grimly.

"This is the right house," he said. "Unfortunately, Dorrance isn't here."

"The owner?"

"She is." He scrubbed a hand roughly over his face. "We need you, Melinda. I think having another woman here will help."

Dear God.

She rushed up the steps and past Daniel. Looking bleaker than she'd ever seen him, Boyd waited in the entry. He thrust what looked like a bathrobe at her.

"This way."

Taking the robe, she asked, "Is...there a basement?"

"Yes."

They reached a door that stood open. She peered down the exceptionally steep staircase, closed her eyes for an instant and took a few deep breaths, then nodded at him and took the first step. All the way down, she was conscious of him behind her even as cold, dank air that stank of human waste and despair enveloped her.

The feeling of déjà vu was overwhelming.

Melinda passed a washer and dryer to join two SWAT officers who stood outside an open door. Shock and helplessness radiated from them despite the body armor that made them seem bigger than they really were, more intimidating. She was glad they had the sensitivity to stay back.

When she entered the tiny room, she was hardly aware of anything but the woman curled into a ball in one corner, yet she still saw the stark concrete walls and floor and the bare light bulb on the ceiling. Just as at Dorrance's house, a mattress lay on the floor. A stinking bucket sat by the doorway.

Feeling sick, Melinda went to Kristina Morgan and lowered herself to her knees within touching distance.

"Kristina?" she said gently. "My name is Melinda. I'm a police officer. I know those men frightened you, but we're here to take you out of this place. I promise. Let me help you into your robe."

After a long moment, Kristina lifted her head enough to look at Melinda. Her eyes… Color didn't matter. They might have been Erica's eyes, or Andrea's. Dead, and yet filled with horror at the same time.

Hoarse voice just audible, she whispered, "Okay," and held out an arm.

Melinda slipped the sleeve of the robe over the arm, then wrapped it around her until she straightened enough to get her second arm through the other sleeve. She was painfully thin—must have been a slender woman to start with—and now bruised. From the swelling and extreme discoloration, Melinda suspected her right cheekbone and some ribs were broken. Her head had been shaved, and her lips were dry enough to crack.

Melinda had been aware of sirens outside. "Can you walk?" she asked. "An ambulance will take you to the hospital. The EMTs can carry you up—"

The woman shook her head with determination. "No. I can make it."

Melinda smiled at her. "I'll be with you all the way."

Those eyes fastened desperately on her. "To the hospital, too? I...don't have family."

"I'll stay with you," she promised. "We're here because your neighbor got worried about you. I'll bet she'll want to come, too."

"Sherry?"

"That's right."

The first tears trickled down Kristina's cheeks.

"RIDE WITH HER," Boyd said in a low voice. "I'll bring you back out here to pick up your car later."

Melinda offered him a tremulous smile before hurrying to climb into the back of the ambulance.

He couldn't seem to move until it receded down the driveway and disappeared from sight. Then he looked at Daniel, who stood beside him.

"I heard you on the phone."

Daniel swore. "That SOB saw the patrol car and took off at high speed. They pursued but lost him. The officers still don't know how. My gut says Dorrance had figured out a way to get off-road and out of sight in case anything like this ever happened."

Boyd was considerably more profane than Daniel. "He's lost his bolt-hole. He's going to be madder than ever."

"What scares the hell out of me is that he's already identified backup options."

Boyd's blood ran cold at the idea. "We have to issue a general warning. Immediately."

"Would you rather do it, or shall I ask Chief Austin to go ahead?"

"Call him. Public and press both are comfortable with him." Jurisdiction didn't matter.

Daniel made the call, keeping it terse. The tension on his face never relented.

Stowing his phone, he said, "Done. Let's walk through."

"CSI on the way?" City and county, with their limited budgets, shared the same unit.

"Van's coming up the driveway."

Boyd glanced. Sure enough.

Neither spoke more than a few words as they studied first the living room, where the remote control sat on the coffee table beside two empty beer cans, then the kitchen. Dirty dishes and pans filled the sink. Daniel did put on latex gloves and opened the cupboard beneath the sink to allow them both to see a full trash receptacle. Meat bones, empty cans and plastic containers lay on top.

"No pizza boxes or fast food," Boyd commented.

"Lucky for him, Kristina must have had a well-stocked kitchen."

Or, as someone—Melinda?—had speculated, he'd been able to order groceries to be delivered. Left on the front porch, undoubtedly.

Boyd rolled his head to loosen aching muscles. Like Melinda, he'd already hated this guy. That hate had sharpened into a lethal edge.

Daniel still had his eyes on the trash. "Plenty of DNA."

Boyd grunted in acknowledgment. The kitchen was rife with fingerprints, too, for what use they were when they already knew the perpetrator's identity.

The one bedroom on the first floor was likely Kristina's, but the bloody sweatshirt and T-shirt on the floor weren't. Boyd wanted to pick up the sweatshirt to see where the bullet hole or holes were, but really, what difference did it make? Despite setting himself up to guard Matson, he hadn't succeeded in taking down this monster.

Somewhere, Dorrance had found first aid supplies. Discarded dressings soaked with now-dry blood filled the bathroom trash can.

Kristina's purse lay on top of the dresser, where it had been rifled. Every compartment was open, unsnapped or unzipped. A small package of tissues, lip gloss, hairbrush, a somewhat tattered paperback book with a bent cover and a price sticker from a thrift store all spilled out. A wallet lay open, stripped of any bills or credit cards.

At least now they could put a stop on the bank cards.

Yeah, and Dorrance would know they'd do it.

Boyd said, "It's probably already too late, but see if you can station officers near drive-through bank machines. If he's using his head, he'll want to get as much money out as he can from any cards Ms. Morgan had."

Daniel got on the phone again.

Nothing appeared to have been touched upstairs. Probably the scumbag had opened bureau drawers and closets to be sure they were empty of anything of value, but Boyd doubted Kristina came up here for more than a cursory cleaning. The house was a lot bigger than she needed. He wondered if she'd be able to bring herself to live here again. Go down those steps into the basement to put in a load of laundry.

Boyd kept remembering the expression on Melinda's face as she'd ushered that poor woman out of the small basement room and, one slow step after another, up the stairs. A cramping ache took up residence beneath his breastbone at the memory of the patience and tenderness she'd displayed. Her heart was a lot softer than she wanted to admit.

SWAT decamped, as did Daniel and Boyd at last. They had to reorganize their manhunt and catch this creep before he got his hands on another woman—or killed another cop he blamed for his downfall.

Heading for the hospital, Boyd discovered he was gripping the steering wheel so tight, his knuckles showed white. He deliberately relaxed his hands.

He guessed he'd known for a while that he was in love with Melinda again. No—still in love with her. More in love with her.

When mortar fire penetrated the theoretically safe compound in Afghanistan, he'd lost the only other woman he'd ever loved Guarding himself thereafter had seemed smart. He'd clung to that belief, even though now he saw that all he'd done was lose Melinda anyway, albeit not to death. If he hadn't been such a damn fool...

Yet he hated as much as ever knowing she had a dangerous job. How could he live with that?

Pulling into one of the parking slots reserved for law enforcement, close to the emergency room entrance, he grimaced.

He already was living with the knowledge that a killer had a target on Melinda, wasn't he? And, damn it, he *knew* this wasn't anything like conditions in a war zone. A rural county in Oregon like his should be relatively peaceful. Trouble was, he'd met Melinda in the middle of a local war zone, when drug traffickers were desperate enough to get into the murder business and even target a little girl who endangered their profits. Yeah, he'd had reason to be nervous about Melinda being a cop.

Then, city and county law enforcement had had to catch a serial killer last year, and now there was this sick bastard.

A part of Boyd wanted Melinda to be safely tucked

up at the ranch, instead of central to this manhunt. But if she was willing to do that, she wouldn't be the woman he increasingly feared he loved till death do they part, would she?

With a groan, he climbed out of his SUV, used the fob to lock the doors and headed into the ER for the second time in a matter of days. As long as he was here, he could stop by intensive care and check on Ed Matson.

Chapter Twelve

Melinda stared straight ahead through the windshield but saw only the face of Gene Dorrance's most recent victim. "Nobody should ever have to suffer through what she did."

Boyd glanced at her. Okay, she wasn't blind to all of her surroundings. She was never not conscious of his presence.

"No," he agreed.

After displaying surprising patience, he'd persuaded her to leave the hospital at last. Sedated, Kristina hadn't been in any shape to be questioned. He'd been right; there wasn't anything more Melinda could do. Thank heavens for Sherry Williams, the neighbor, who had become fiercely protective of Kristina and clearly had no intention of leaving her alone.

"She was there when I needed her," she told Melinda privately. "If I have to take more time off from my job, I will. She doesn't have to be alone, either."

Melinda had hugged her before Sherry returned to her friend's bedside.

Now, after a pause of several minutes, Boyd said, "We could go back for your car tomorrow."

"I'd rather get it now."

Out of the corner of her eye, she saw the muscle flex

in his jaw, but he only nodded. Stubble darkened that stubborn jaw. She had a fleeting moment of remembering the texture of his unshaven chin and jaw beneath her palms and fingertips.

She should have asked Daniel for a lift. Or Tom. *Any*-one but Boyd. Spending time with him, *depending* on him, was dangerous in its own way.

They continued in silence for several minutes. Melinda was still oblivious to the landscape outside and to the passing traffic.

"We're no further ahead than we ever were!" she burst out at last.

A big hand covered hers, which was balled into a fist on her thigh. "We are. Did you know that Matson may be moved out of intensive care tomorrow? He's going to make it."

That was good news, but not what she was talking about, and Boyd had to know it.

"Ms. Morgan is now safely out of his hands," he continued.

She made a sound in her throat. "Physically safe. But will she be able to come back from this?"

"Yes, I think she will," Boyd said in his calm way. "He didn't have her for years. I'm impressed with her fortitude. She was determined to walk out under her own power. Maybe she has a stronger sense of self, more confidence, than the two very young women had."

"I'd like to think so," Melinda said wearily. "I didn't even ask whether the crime scene techs came up with anything useful."

"Evidence that will help to convict him. They found an empty magazine for a Glock that has Jonas's fingerprints on it. No convenient phone numbers or addresses on notepads, though."

"A map with certain locations circled?"

His mouth curved in a wry grin. "You're an optimist. Who knew?"

Melinda snorted. That was the last word she could ever apply to herself.

Boyd flicked on the turn signal, and started up a long gravel driveway she recognized. Her Subaru sat alone where she'd parked beside Sherry Williams's garage.

Melinda squared her shoulders. "Thanks for the lift. I'll see you in the morning for the meeting?"

He braked in front of the garage. "You'll see me in your rearview mirror all the way home."

"What?" She swiveled in her seat to stare at the big man beside her. Operating on automatic, she opened her mouth to say, *I'm a cop! I don't need a protective detail!*

Except…she wasn't foolish. Lieutenant Matson would have said the same, wouldn't he?

Boyd was frowning at her. "Dorrance is on the loose, and he's seriously angry. You notice he didn't contact you after he attacked the lieutenant, and not today, either."

"Because both were failures."

"That's right. He blames everything else on you, so why not his current frustration, too?"

"I'd like to think he doesn't know where I live."

"You're not that naive."

No, she wasn't. How had Dorrance known where Miguel lived? Lieutenant Matson? Officer Jonas? Reality was that keeping your name out of a phone book didn't cut it anymore. There was too much information online.

"I want to see you safely in the house," Boyd continued inexorably, his jaw set in a way the men he'd commanded in places like Afghanistan and Iraq would probably recognize.

And truthfully…wouldn't some backup be reassuring?

She'd convinced herself that Dorrance wouldn't come after her yet, but who knew how'd he react to what he'd see as today's debacle following his close call in Lieutenant Matson's backyard?

"Thank you," she forced herself to say, released the seat belt and opened the door. Then she made herself turn back to Boyd. "I'm sorry. I don't know why I even argued. I guess by this time you know I tend to get my back up when—" She hesitated, made momentarily uneasy by her inability to finish that sentence. She didn't like it when someone challenged her—but he hadn't done that.

The line of his mouth softened as he searched her face. "You don't like being scared."

Was that her problem? "No," she admitted, around a lump in her throat. Although, just because today she'd had a weird moment of seeing herself in Kristina didn't mean she was actually afraid. Only that she'd carried her empathy a little too far, given her profession. Cops had to retain some detachment, or they couldn't do their jobs.

Boyd said gruffly, "I wish you'd change your mind about—"

"Going on the run?" She made sure to sound bold. "Not a chance."

Before he could argue, she hopped out, slammed the door and walked to her own car. Her neck prickled with the knowledge that he hadn't taken his eyes off her. Just as she felt his stare drilling into the back of her head during the entire drive to her house.

SHE HADN'T BOUGHT the house until after the two of them quit seeing each other, so Boyd had never been inside, only seen it from the outside the one other time he'd followed her home. It was from Miguel that he'd heard she had decided she would rather live in her own place than with him at the ranch. At the time, he'd been tempted to look up the address and drive by—just curiosity—but wouldn't let himself. The word "stalker" had come to mind, particularly indefensible with him being a cop.

Turning into the driveway right behind her, he studied the single-story ranch-style house from a security standpoint. It reminded him of Guy Jonas's house, except worse, because it lacked a garage. If she'd been able to use a remote and drive right into an attached garage, he might even have honked and gone on his way.

No, he wouldn't. Dorrance had repeatedly demonstrated his skill at breaking into houses. Boyd wasn't going anywhere until they knew Melinda's was clear.

So he parked behind her and got out as she did the same. No eye rolls today. Echoing his movement, her hand went to the butt of her weapon and her head turned as she looked for trouble.

She waited for him to join her before taking the single step up to the small porch. "I was thinking," she said in a low voice. "We should send a unit by Dorrance's house. I'll bet he's gone by and knows it's empty."

"You're right." Boyd frowned. "Jonas's house, too. Hell, Cordova's is another possibility."

He watched their backs as she unlocked the door. Only as he heard the door opening did he start to turn back—just as she sucked in a breath.

She yanked the gun from its holster. He did the same without having to think. Then he saw what she had.

Her living room was trashed. Not ransacked the way a burglar might have done. *Destroyed* was the word that came to him. Mortar fire might have done this much damage.

She'd momentarily frozen just inside, her lips parted,

eyes dilated in shock. He nudged her forward, then signaled toward the opening into a hall.

Melinda swallowed, visibly pulled herself together then nodded. She eased forward to flatten her back to the wall, ready to cover him as he started down the hall. A glance told him no one was in the kitchen, although it hadn't been spared. Food and broken dishes covered the floor. A back door had obviously been kicked open. Weapon held in readiness, she went into the first room on the left, a small bedroom converted to an office. When she backed out, he bumped open a door to see a bathroom, damaged but empty, then entered the last room, her bedroom. His nose had already told him some of what they'd find.

She let out a cry and brushed past him, coming to a stop a few feet from the bed. Her arms slowly sagged until her handgun pointed at the floor.

"This must have taken hours," she whispered.

"He *had* hours."

Bedding and mattress had been slashed. One closet door lay on the floor, where it had been stomped on, what had probably been a full-length mirror shattered into vicious, glittering pieces. The other closet door hung from one wheel on the track. Her clothes had been yanked out, slashed with a knife and then the intruder had urinated on them. Bureau and bedside table drawers all lay smashed on the floor, clothes in torn heaps. He'd slammed a lamp against the wall, opening a big hole in the plasterboard.

"Oh, God," Melinda whispered, her head turning. "He got his hands on *everything*."

Looking at her stricken face, he saw the moment she cried out again. Holstering her gun, she raced to the vicinity of what had been her bureau, dropped to her knees and began frantically digging through the mess on the floor.

"It's the only picture I have! The only one! I have to find it."

Boyd joined her. "Your sister?"

"Yes!"

The sister who'd been murdered by one of their father's best friends. What she'd told Boyd had explained so much about her.

As he searched, too, he remembered the flickers of emotion she hadn't been able to hide, try as hard as she would.

Dad's buddy had been molesting Melinda's younger sister. Dad wouldn't believe it. Melinda had taken to guarding her sister like a pit bull, but Dad went so far as to insist Melinda go with him on what turned out to be a meaningless errand at a time Melinda had believed her sister was at a friend's. They returned to find the ten-year-old girl had been raped and strangled.

Good ole Dad? He reacted by sitting around getting drunk and crying and insisted Pete couldn't have done anything like that.

Since Pete had, he was arrested, tried and convicted. Refusing to stay with her sorry excuse for a father, Melinda had run away from home repeatedly until authorities placed her in foster care. Boyd knew she'd been able to take almost nothing from the house.

The sound that escaped from her throat now held pain he recognized. It was the noise parents always made when they found out a child was gone, or that their husband or wife had been taken from them by violence.

She held a twisted picture frame. Jagged shards of glass clung to the frame, and blood dripped from her hand. She hadn't even noticed. She was fumbling to gather shreds of paper.

Boyd gently took the frame from her and tossed it away, then wrapped her in his arms. "Melinda," he said roughly. "Sweetheart. You remember her. That's what's important."

He'd never seen her really cry, not like this. The sobs shook her slender body. For a minute, she seemed oblivious to his presence, but then she lifted a devastated gaze to his face.

"This was the only thing that mattered to me."

Hearing her despair wrenched something loose in him he doubted could ever be repaired. "It's *not* the only thing," he said insistently. "You know that. It was a photograph. You can still see your sister's face, can't you? Close your eyes and imagine it."

He dug deep to call up the sister's name. Elise. That was it.

She pressed her face to his chest. He was the one to close his eyes and lay his cheek against the top of her head. God, he couldn't stand seeing her so hurt. Maybe *this* was what had scared him as much as the idea of her being injured or killed. A woman so strong shouldn't sound so— No, damn it! Not broken. He had to believe nothing would break Melinda.

Fractured might be a better word. It didn't suggest a permanent state. Fractures could heal.

He was talking to her, with no idea what he'd been saying. Just…trying to give her comfort. He wanted to scoop her up and carry her out of this house, but what if Dorrance was outside watching? He'd love nothing more than seeing her face now.

No, that wasn't happening.

Melinda didn't cry as long as another woman might

have. Any second, he expected her to retreat, physically and emotionally. To be embarrassed and even angry that she'd exposed her grief to him.

He wasn't going to let her get away with that.

Gently, he said, "Let me call Daniel."

"Daniel?" She lifted her face again, her eyes so swollen and red he wondered that she could see him. "What? Why...?"

"This is a crime scene now, and you're not going to be the one who has to process it." He hoped that didn't sound as grim as he felt.

After a moment, she bobbed her head.

He extracted his phone from his pocket and called Daniel, who answered immediately.

"I can tell you where Dorrance went after he found out he'd lost his hideaway," Boyd said. "He must have come straight to Melinda's place. He did his best to demolish it. As she said, he must have spent hours at it."

Daniel spat a couple of choice words. "You're with her?"

"Yes."

"You can stay put until I get there?"

"I won't leave her." Boyd met her eyes. "Just in case Dorrance is hanging around, we're staying inside."

"Then I'm on my way. I'll call the techs again—"

Boyd interrupted. "Let's seal the house and wait until morning to turn them loose in here. It's...worse than you're probably imagining."

Daniel agreed, and cut the connection. Boyd stowed his phone and said, "Let's get your face cleaned up."

Before Daniel or any other of her coworkers saw her. She wouldn't like that.

It took her a minute, but she nodded and let him help her up. Only then, as he steered her toward the doorway, did he see that one of her hands still formed a fist… one that enclosed scraps of the photograph that meant so much to her.

MELINDA SAT STIFFLY in the passenger seat of Boyd's SUV. She was going home with him, even though he'd never exactly asked her if she was okay with that. He just assumed. It was very Boyd-like. Maybe she should be ashamed to have been so compliant, but she couldn't yet work up even any indignation. She hadn't even thrown out an alternative.

She *wanted* to go home with Boyd. And maybe that wasn't smart, but she was doing it anyway.

Even if she'd hated the idea, she wasn't sure she could have summoned the least resistance. The anguish had ebbed, leaving in its place…nothing. *I'm numb*, she thought, except that wasn't quite true. Emotions swirled beneath the surface, a dangerous current. If she let herself think about— But she wouldn't. Tomorrow was soon enough.

What stunned her was discovering how *violated* she felt by the intrusion into her home, the destruction of her possessions. It shouldn't have come as any surprise; she'd seen the reaction over and over when she'd gone out on a report of a burglary. What had happened to her was worse; Dorrance hadn't only gotten into her house, touched things she owned, fingered her lingerie and peered into every private place, he'd then destroyed everything. Slashed and stomped and smashed. Urinated on her clothing in the worst insult of all.

He was making sure she knew he intended to do all those things to *her*.

She must have made a sound of some kind, because Boyd reached over and took her hand in his. He had such big hands, warm, strong and capable of such deftness, even delicacy.

He surely didn't assume she'd go to bed with him. Melinda almost shook her head. Of course he didn't. Whatever else she could say about him, he was too *decent*, too honorable, to take advantage of a woman in shock.

Funny, though, that he'd wanted her all along to stay with him at the ranch.

She focused enough to see that they were now on the ranch road, made of hard-packed dirt.

"Do you have a live-in girlfriend?" she asked, voice scratchy.

His head turned and his fingers tightened on hers. She didn't meet his eyes.

"No girlfriend."

She frowned, having a hard time imagining a man as beautiful as he was, as quintessentially male, ever not having a woman at his beck and call. But at least she wouldn't have to deal with that reality tonight.

"I'm assuming that if you were seeing anyone, you'd have called him instead of coming home with me."

Her couple of attempts to date since she and Boyd parted ways went nowhere. She thought maybe she'd given up. That's what happened when you thought you'd found the one person—

All she did was nod.

They passed the turnoff to his partner's cabin. She'd liked Gabe Decker even though he made her feel a little uncomfortable. It took her awhile to realize that Gabe's impassive face, his seeming stoicism, was his cover, just as Boyd's relaxed charm and confidence were his.

Boyd had been quite different in bed with her. Gabe probably was with his wife, too.

Wow, she was thinking about everything and anything *but* the monster who had to be stopped.

"Don't," Boyd said.

Startled, she looked at him. He couldn't possibly have read her mind.

"Your hand jerked." His voice lacked much inflection. "You started thinking about something that upset you. It can wait until tomorrow. You need a good night's sleep before you become a cop again."

"I'm always—"

"No, you aren't. And I should know."

Heat rose in her cheeks, despite her strange state of mind. He did know. He knew she was a woman, too— and he'd taken advantage of that because he didn't *want* her to be a cop at all. He couldn't possibly think—

"The task force meeting is soon enough." He came to a stop right in front of the massive log house he'd had built six years ago to replace what he'd told her was a shabby, traditional farmhouse with a cracked foundation. She'd never asked why he wanted such a big place, and he'd never volunteered the information. Why *hadn't* they had that discussion?

Because he'd expected her to reveal her sore places but hadn't been willing to do the same, Melinda suspected. She hadn't pushed, because she'd believed they would have time.

Maybe we do.

She didn't move even though he'd gotten out. All she did was watch him circle around to her side.

He hadn't given any indication he still felt the same way about her…but she knew that wasn't true. He was as intensely focused on her as he'd been back then, not trying to hide his tenderness or how protective he felt.

None of which answered the big question: whether

he could accept the woman she'd made of herself after her father's betrayal and the loss of the only person she'd ever loved.

Except, maybe, Boyd.

Chapter Thirteen

"Ah. Lasagna." Boyd removed the labeled dish from his refrigerator. This being Friday, his housekeeper had left him a full casserole dish, intended to feed him for the next three days, needing only to be warmed up. "I hope you like it."

Melinda sat at the old farmhouse-style kitchen table, gazing straight ahead with dazed eyes. It took her a moment to focus on him.

"I love lasagna." She forced a smile. "Especially when it doesn't come out of the freezer case at the grocery store."

A picture flashed into his head of the food trampled on her kitchen floor. That probably included everything from her freezer.

He opened his mouth, about to tell her that his housekeeper was an excellent cook, but he stopped himself in time. She'd eaten Jennifer Langley's food several times. In fact, he'd first met Melinda when she came out to the ranch to interview the terrified little girl that Gabe and Trina had since adopted. They'd sat on the sofa in his living room, him leaning against a doorway trying to be unobtrusive. He'd had trouble taking his eyes off the slender, fine-boned female detective with the soft voice who'd been a natural at encouraging a scared kid to open up.

Frowning at the memory of his powerful reaction to Melinda McIntosh, he popped the dish in the microwave, the garlic bread in the convection oven, and decided not to bother with the broccoli. He didn't much like it anyway.

He poured two glasses of milk and carried them to the table, then set their places with napkins, silverware and plates. He was disturbed to see Melinda sitting so still. Outwardly she managed at the task force meetings, but he could always feel a sort of vibration coming from her. He suspected she was tapping a toe or toying with a rubber band or pen beneath the table. When they'd shared meals, she had been quick to jump to her feet and offer to help. Even sleeping, she was restless.

He gritted his teeth. He couldn't let himself remember how she'd felt curled up against him or squirming in search of a more comfortable position. They wouldn't be sleeping together tonight, no matter how much he wished it were so. *She'd* sleep better in his arms, and he'd prefer having her so close, he didn't have to lie staring at the dark ceiling worrying about her.

Right now, she was dull, her personality in hiding. He hoped that's all it was. She was taking the destruction of her home worse than she would have a physical attack on *her*. Everyone needed a sanctuary, and hers was gone. Plus… Boyd suspected the loss of that single, precious photograph was the worst part. He couldn't forget her thin cry, or the way she'd all but screamed, *This was the only thing that mattered to me!*

In a way, her sister had been killed again today.

After the appliances beeped, he carried their dinner to the table and then, when she still didn't move, dished up for both of them.

Melinda stared down at her serving of lasagna. Once

again, he sensed it took her some effort to say anything. "It smells good, but… I'm not that hungry."

"Did you have lunch?" He knew the answer; their day had been too eventful for either of them to take a meal break.

She lifted her head and blinked a few times. Her forehead crinkled. "I guess not."

"Then eat even if you don't feel like it. Come morning, you need to be strong."

A beat slower than would have been natural, she nodded. Satisfied to see the first bite go in her mouth, Boyd started eating himself. And, damn, he was starved. His big body required a lot more fuel than did her much more slender one.

She paused after a few bites to tear the slice of garlic bread in half, then quarters. Was she going to shred it so that he wouldn't notice she hadn't eaten any of it? But she lifted one piece and took a bite out of it.

She surprised him by asking, "Is Mrs. Langley still with you?"

He liked that she was curious, and glad to talk if that would distract her.

"She is. She claims I'm the perfect employer. I'll eat just about anything she prepares, I'm reasonably tidy and I'm hardly ever underfoot."

Melinda surprised him by chuckling. Maybe good food had been just what she needed. "She's got a point."

"She's a proud mama right now," he added. "The youngest of her two kids just graduated with honors from Pomona University."

"That's in southern California, right?"

"Yep. Top-tier liberal arts school. Her daughter picked it because she was desperate—or so she said—to live someplace that was actually populated with two-legged mammals instead of four. She wanted museums, restaurants, concerts. Since she's been accepted to Columbia University for law school, I don't think she plans any immediate return to ranching country."

Melinda laughed but then said, "That's sad for Mrs. Langley."

"From what I gather, you couldn't pay her enough to live in an apartment in Portland, never mind New York City. I think she'll be happy with visits from her kids. They seem to talk often."

He turned his attention back to eating, as Melinda did the same, albeit slower. She suddenly laid down her fork, though.

"You said you'll eat 'just about' anything. What won't you eat?"

He raised his eyebrows. "Oysters. Cooked spinach. Brussels sprouts. I'm not all that fond of broccoli, either, which is why we're not having a vegetable with dinner."

"But if Mrs. Langley had cooked and served it, you'd have eaten it."

"Yeah."

"I had no idea you'd let anyone persuade you to do a single thing you didn't want to," Melinda said thoughtfully.

Good to know she thought of him as an autocrat.

"I'm capable of bowing to common sense," he countered. "Broccoli is good for me. Taste isn't the point." Was this the right or wrong time to talk about them? He couldn't decide, but did say, "I can change, you know. It…just doesn't come easily to me."

Her startled gaze met his. Neither of them so much as blinked for a good minute. She clearly knew he wasn't talking about his tastes in food.

She nibbled on her lower lip, distracting him from

her haunting eyes. "I've…wondered. If I hadn't just walked out."

"I knew better than to make a demand like that." He had to press the heel of his hand against his breastbone to quell the sharp pain under it. "But…" He gusted out a breath. "You scared me. And I'd made a vow."

"What was that vow?" Melinda barely spoke above a whisper.

"That I'd never again let myself love a woman whose job put her into regular danger."

She shrugged, as if what he'd said didn't matter. "And there I was."

"Yeah." He had to clear his throat. "There you were." She'd come as a shocker to him, no question.

Boyd couldn't just keep eating, downplay how important this conversation was. He could only wait for her to make the next move…if she gave a damn why he'd made a vow that ruled her out.

Melinda tore apart more of her bread, reminding him unpleasantly of the scraps of that photograph.

The only thing that mattered to her. Mattered so much, he'd asked one of the techs to gather those scraps so he could try to have the photo restored.

Now, when he'd almost given up, she said, "You lost someone."

Did her asking mean *he* mattered, too?

"Yeah." Funny, how he had to work to summon a picture of Raquel's face. Passing years did that. But it came. Melinda didn't look anything like Raquel, except for the thick dark hair. Well, similar height, too, and both were athletic women. Fighters, in different ways. "She was a soldier. Part of a unit that guarded supply convoys. I worried, but she spent most of her time on the base. Afghanistan," he added. "She worried about me. It wasn't supposed to be the other way around."

Melinda watched him, expression solemn.

"Her family was traditional. Her grandparents came to the US from Costa Rica. They weren't happy about her joining the army. She was supposed to work in the family business, a growing chain of restaurants in Houston. Get married, have babies. She wanted to see the world, have some adventures." He had a feeling his smile was a failure. "I don't suppose they'd have been any happier about me."

"You wanted to marry her?"

"We'd just started talking about it." He shrugged. "She resisted. I wasn't anywhere near ready to retire from the military, and Raquel had no intention of getting stuck back home, alone in officer housing while I was gone for months at a time."

Man, he thought, who was he kidding? Melinda and Raquel would have understood each other at first sight.

"What happened?"

"IED. She was in the lead vehicle. It went off right beneath her. They couldn't really even come up with a body to bury."

"Oh, Boyd." Melinda stood so suddenly, her chair rocked. She came around the table and put her arms around him.

He buried his face between her breasts and held on. Mostly, Raquel had been a dream, one that had faded in the intervening years, but talking about her brought the memory of pain.

"I'm so sorry," Melinda murmured, her cheek against his head. "Did you have leave? A chance to go home and, I don't know, talk to her family?"

"No. We were in the middle of an operation. It was

almost a week after her death before I even heard about it. I...had to go on."

"Push everything you felt out of sight."

He gave a rough laugh and straightened, letting his arms fall away. Reluctantly, but pity wasn't what he wanted from this woman. "Yeah. I'm here to say that doesn't work so well."

Melinda backed away in recognition of his withdrawal, and after a moment returned to her place at the table, although he doubted she'd eat any more. He'd kind of lost his appetite, too.

"How long ago was this?" she asked.

"Ah..." There was a time, he could have told her to the day. Now, he had to think back. "Seven years ago. You'd have been dealing with Dorrance right around then."

Their eyes met again.

"I should have known there was something like that."

He shoved away his plate. "How about some apple pie?"

"That...actually sounds good. Thank you."

This time, she insisted on clearing the table, rinsing their plates and loading them in the dishwasher while he served the pie, including ice cream for himself. Then they sat back down.

The silence while they ate was peaceful on the surface, but he knew a lot simmered beneath it. He was proved right when she said, "So, if I'd argued back when we split up, would you have backed down?"

Boyd had to be honest. "I don't know. I'd like to think we could have...compromised, but that was never possible, was it?"

"What'd you think, I'd switch to working dispatch? Something like that?"

"Maybe."

"And what were *you* going to give?" she asked, the razor edge not so well hidden in her voice.

"Nothing as meaningful," he had to admit. "I was stunned when you just said, 'Forget about it,' and left."

"You could have called me later. Come after me."

He realized he was glaring at her. "I thought *you'd* be back, calling me a jerk. When I never heard from you—" A chasm had opened at his feet, that's what. All he'd been able to think was, he'd let himself fall for another woman who chose her job over him.

And he'd been too damn scared to accept that, with both Raquel and Melinda, the job had been part of the woman, and therefore a good part of why he'd fallen for each of them.

"So you didn't change your mind," she said now, flatly.

"At the time, no."

She'd heard what he was saying, all right, because skittishness showed. "I can't deal with this right now."

He could do nothing but nod. Had he really been deluding himself that she'd throw herself into his arms and he could carry her up to his bed? After she'd seen a recurrence of one of her worst nightmares today?

Idiot.

"Okay," he said. "What are you thinking for tomorrow?"

The relief on her face at the change of subject shamed him.

"I want to talk to Kristina Morgan. I hope she'll be in good enough shape to tell us what she learned about Dorrance."

"I can't imagine anything she heard will help find him, but I'd sure as hell like to know how he homed in on her."

Melinda nodded. "I would, too. You don't mind driving me to the hospital in the morning?"

An officer at the scene this evening had driven her Subaru to the police station and parked in back. Leaving it in front of her demolished house hadn't seemed like a good idea.

Boyd scowled at her. "Of course not. I'd like to sit in when you talk to Kristina—" Seeing Melinda about ready to fire up, he raised a hand. "I won't even try. She'll be more comfortable talking to a woman, but I'll wait for you. Daniel can hold off the morning meeting until we get to the station."

"Okay." She suddenly looked shy. "Would you mind if I took a shower and went to bed? I'm really beat."

"Of course not." He pushed back his chair and rose. "Come on. I'll find you something you can sleep in, and I can wash what you're wearing, if you want."

"That would be good." Melinda offered him a twisted smile. "I suppose I'd better find time to shop tomorrow, too."

"I'm afraid so," he said gently.

"I need to tackle that mess."

"My advice?" At her nod, he said, "Get a dumpster out there, then hire someone. They can toss everything too damaged for use, set the intact stuff aside for you to go through. A stranger won't take the same emotional hit you would picking up every single item." Seeing the emotions shimmering in her eyes made it hard to go on, but this needed to be said. "You'll need to get repairs done, too, before the house is livable again."

"That's true. I don't know if it will ever feel like home again," she said softly. "Funny, I'd just had that thought about Kristina. I mean, whether she'd be able to live in her house again."

The only, and probably useless thing he could think to say was, "Give it time."

Melinda offered him a shaky smile. "Thank you. For everything. I mean, today."

"You're welcome." Seeing her startled expression, he realized that had sounded curt. He didn't want her thanks. He wanted—

There he went again, wanting to push. Which, he acknowledged ruefully, was his nature.

"Let me show you where you'll sleep," he said, and led the way toward the wide staircase formed of slabs of pine.

He gestured her into a guest bedroom, but she came to a stop in the doorway, looking at him. She dampened her lips with her tongue, betraying some nerves. Boyd couldn't help himself. He lifted his hand and stroked her cheek, ending with his thumb pressing lightly on that tempting mouth. Melinda trembled, he couldn't mistake that, and her eyes darkened. She might have even swayed toward him.

He thought he'd started to bend his head when she jerked and took a big step back, panic awakened.

He clenched his teeth, growled, "Just a second," and fetched a T-shirt and a pair of sweatpants with a drawstring waist from his room. Wordlessly, he handed them over, waited until she passed him her dirty clothes through a three-inch crack between door and frame, and took them downstairs with him. Then he pretty well paced until the washer finished and he could throw everything into the dryer.

She'd been naked, just on the other side of that door.

He wouldn't be sleeping like a baby tonight.

WITH THE COLORS of the bruises on her face turning garish, Kristina almost looked worse the next morning. Her responses came slowly, as if she had to work at grasping the questions. But when Melinda had asked in the first place if she was able to talk, she'd immediately said, "Yes. I... don't know if I can help, but if there's anything..."

True to her word, Sherry Williams had been in the chair by Kristina's bedside when Melinda arrived, a fierce guardian. She'd gone down to the cafeteria to get some breakfast and coffee, having apparently spent the night.

Melinda left the door half open, aware Boyd leaned against the wall in the corridor eavesdropping.

Working their painful way through Dorrance's arrival at the house and the initial brutality took more out of Kristina than Melinda liked, but it had to be done.

Kristina kneaded the bedclothes with arthritic hands. "It was my fault he knew about me," she said in a low voice. "I was...such a fool."

"*Nothing* about this was your fault," Melinda said sternly.

"Oh." The older woman focused on Melinda's face. "You're right. I didn't mean it that way. Only that I got to know him years ago, when I was a nurse here at the hospital. He was severely injured when a lift failed at the garage where he worked. I covered his floor, night shift, and he had to stay for, oh, almost a week, I think." Her mouth twisted into an almost-smile. "Things get slow in the middle of the night. He wasn't sleeping well. We... started talking. It seemed to me that he was lonely, too. There was nothing romantic." The wrinkles on her forehead deepened. "Just...us sharing some of the dark hours. So, you see, he knew I lived alone in a too-big house on acreage. I told him I had no intention of moving, that it was home even if downsizing would have been smarter for me."

As it turned out, Melinda couldn't help thinking, it would have been way smarter.

She shuddered. "I was horrified when he was arrested back then, and I learned what he was really like." She made a sound in her throat. "After he, um, forced himself into my house, he told me he'd looked me up back then. Even driven by the house a few times. Decided I wasn't worth his while. He made a point of saying I still wasn't, saggy old woman I am, but he'd had to *settle*."

Melinda huffed out a breath. "I don't think he has a single redeeming feature. There are men on death row who hold on to their humanity. I'm not sure Gene Dorrance ever had any."

"No," Kristina whispered.

They talked for a while longer. Melinda asked if he'd implied he would let Kristina go.

Her head moved slightly against the pillow in a shake. "He said I'd be glad when he was through with me. 'I like to bury my girlfriends.'" She shuddered. "He actually said that. *Girlfriends*."

Melinda leaned forward. "I've always suspected he'd held other women captive and killed them, but we couldn't prove it. We never had a clue where he might have buried them."

Kristina plucked some more at the bedclothes, her hands shaky. "He didn't say, except… There was something about a grove. He came back one night, enraged—" Her throat worked. "He—" After a moment, she murmured, "You know what he did to me. He said…he said he might just dump me there, instead of burying me, because the cops had ruined it for him."

A grove. One the cops had ruined for him.

It was all Melinda could do to keep from leaping to her feet. No wonder Dorrance knew that clump of quaking aspen trees so well.

Dear Lord, if they could find the graves…

Had Boyd heard? Would he already be making calls? This was the first real clue…but after so many years, the soil would have settled, vegetation regrown.

And Dorrance would still be out there, angrier than ever at her.

Chapter Fourteen

By the time she came out of the hospital room, Boyd had already contacted Daniel, who called for a handler to bring a cadaver dog to the bridge on the south side of the aspen grove.

"Apparently she's in the middle of a training session," he told Melinda. "Her name's Sarah Sutton. She has several dogs she uses for volunteer work. Mostly search and rescue, I guess, but she's trained one to sniff out accelerants in suspicion fires, and has a Lab with a gift for finding bodies."

"I've worked with her," Melinda said, as he drove out of the parking lot, "but I thought she did only search and rescue. Did Daniel tell her how long ago those bodies would have been buried?"

"I'm sure he did. He wouldn't waste her time if she and her dog couldn't help."

"No. God, I hope we can find the graves! At least the women's parents would *know*."

"Yeah," he said in the gruff way that felt like a gentle touch with calloused fingers.

Her cheek tingled with the memory of yesterday evening's touch, and she wished she hadn't been a coward.

He didn't seem to notice her reaction, continuing, "I

just wish we had a hint where Dorrance might have gone to earth."

"Bad pun," she pointed out.

He gave a grunt that was almost a laugh.

Melinda kept sneaking glances at him during the short drive to the police station. She'd shocked herself last night by dropping off to sleep practically the minute she slipped between the sheets, and not waking until Boyd had rapped on her door this morning.

Because I felt safe.

Something she would usually hate to admit. She kept *herself* safe. She'd never been willing to depend on anyone else for something so basic, not since she'd failed to protect Elise.

What surprised her was realizing that she didn't mind knowing that she'd been leaning on Boyd as much as she should. For all their history, he hadn't said anything to make her think he felt that because he was bigger and stronger, it meant he was also superior. He'd even hinted that he knew he was wrong to ask her to give up her job so that he didn't have to worry about her.

At least she understood now. At the time, she hadn't so much as wondered whether he had something in his past that hurt as much as her sister's murder had hurt her. It said something about her that she *hadn't* wondered.

She wrinkled her nose, remembering the way he'd thrown out his demand, completely confident she'd jump to diminish herself because he'd made his pronouncement. And *that* said something about *him*.

Of course, his years as an army officer had given him more practice in throwing out orders and assuming anyone within earshot would jump to meet them than could possibly be healthy for anyone.

"Did I miss anything?" he asked now, after a fleeting, hard to read glance.

"You mean after she talked about the graves? I don't think so." She was quiet for a minute, before exclaiming, "Where *is* he?"

"I wish I knew." That grim tone matched her mood. "I have the helicopter back up in the air, and we have an all points bulletin out on the Camry now that we know the model and color. Switching license plates won't help him."

"No."

"He lost his backup vehicle, too."

That must have made him almost as mad as losing his hostage had.

She focused as Boyd turned just past the police station into the parking lot. It seemed to her that the media presence was diminishing. In one way, she hated the pressure they brought to bear, but what if people were tired of constant tension and had decided to shrug off the worry? After all, there were other stories to follow on the local news.

Actually, she wasn't sure whether that was true or not. *Her* attention had been single-minded for…she had to count. A week now. No, eight days. Nine? She'd lost track.

"Task force meeting," she mumbled.

That earned her another glance from Boyd as he parked. "We have information to share the others probably haven't all heard. Maybe someone else does, too. Or will have an idea worth pursuing."

"Sure." Dispirited, she got out of the SUV and waited for him before heading into the building.

Unfortunately, no one else around the table in the conference room had any meaningful news or even ideas.

Daniel's update on Lieutenant Matson was positive, though; doctors had decided when to release him from the hospital.

Daniel finished his report with a grimace. "Which means putting him and his wife into hiding."

There was a moment of depressed silence.

The FBI agent said thoughtfully, "This guy has a gift for passing under the radar."

"He probably always has," Boyd commented. "And yeah, he's had a way of making people uncomfortable, but not always. Kristina Morgan sounds as if she liked him. Felt as if they had a lot in common. Really, the guy lived in Sadler for a lot of years without drawing much attention at all. None from law enforcement, until Andrea Kudelka somehow briefly overpowered him."

"That's true," Daniel agreed. "Not sure where to go with that, though." When no one else commented, he said, "Detective Yates, have you learned anything about the pickup truck that was in the Morgan woman's garage?"

"It's a 1998 Chevy, black and rusting," the young detective said. "I haven't looked up the VIN number, but finding out where he got it doesn't seem very pressing now. If he purchased it, the seller hasn't turned in the required title change. Given the number of pickup trucks on the road locally, this one would have been good camouflage, but it doesn't want to start and spits out clouds of black exhaust. Joe Bailey—" the mechanic who took care of the department's fleet "—says Dorrance was damn lucky to make it across the state in that derelict. It has a hundred and seventy-three thousand miles on it," he added.

So Dorrance had needed not only a hostage and a

bolt-hole, but also new transportation—all provided for him by Kristina Morgan. All stolen from him yesterday.

"No sightings of the Camry?" he asked, knowing the answer. Someone would have said.

Daniel shook his head, and Aaron Loftis, the CAU rep said, "Calls to the tip line are down. Might be time for another press conference."

Although Melinda suspected that Chief Austin loved nothing more than standing behind the microphone, the center of attention, even he must be losing enthusiasm. The questions weren't nearly as sympathetic as they'd been, for one thing. And he'd be able to do nothing but flash Dorrance's photo—again—and say—again, "We need the public's help to locate our suspect," and declare that this cop killer was likely driving a gray Toyota Camry.

From what Melinda could gather, Kristina's identity hadn't been breached yet, and they wanted to keep it that way. The press wouldn't like being told a victim had been rescued, sending Dorrance on the run again, without the addition of any details.

The group briefly discussed the trashing of Melinda's house, then she detailed the interview with Kristina and the hope that a cadaver dog might be able to locate the grave or graves Melinda had always believed were out there somewhere.

Loftis frowned. "Who is this woman? She's not on my list of resources."

Daniel assured him that she'd assisted several law enforcement agencies in Oregon and northern California, after which Loftis decided to join those at the possible gravesites.

As the meeting broke up, Daniel stopped Boyd and Melinda, letting them know he'd just gotten a text from the dog handler, who planned to meet them forty-five minutes from now. He handed over Melinda's car keys, too.

"You probably saw it parked out back."

She nodded, although she hadn't even looked.

He joined Loftis and the two men departed, talking as they went about the challenges of locating old graves without a fairly precise starting point.

She ought to be worrying about the same thing, but instead had the passing thought that she should stop at her desk, check email and see how high the stack of paperwork on her desk had grown. Somehow, she couldn't work up any interest. Except—oh, God, she was so behind on the reports *she'd* have to write.

Boyd, of course, hadn't gone anywhere without her. Even aside from his physical presence, it was impossible to forget he was there given that those eyes rested on her no matter what else she was doing, or who she was talking to.

Straightening away from the wall in the now empty hallway outside the conference room, Boyd asked, "Any reason we should drive separately out to the aspen grove?"

At least he hadn't questioned her right to be there. Boyd's presence was a given with the site well outside the city limits and therefore in his jurisdiction.

Did she want to drive herself?

When she hesitated, his expression darkened.

That stiffened her spine. "You'd rather I give up even that vestige of my independence?"

His dark eyebrows arched. "That's what you think of me?"

After a moment, she felt her shoulders sag. "No. I'm sorry. I appreciate everything you've done, especially given our past and my, well, attitude. I...hope you won't mind me staying with you for a few more days, until I can figure something else out."

He studied her for a moment, then said calmly, "No hurry. In fact, as far as I'm concerned, you don't need to figure anything out." He smiled slightly. "I have in mind you staying for good."

Melinda's mouth dropped open, but after his bomb-shell he walked away, heading for the exit sign at the end of the hall. She was left gaping at his broad back, torn be-tween astonishment and aggravation that he'd just throw something like that out, and a thrill she couldn't deny. She had absolutely no idea how to respond to what he'd said.

Then her eyes narrowed. She'd trot after him, as he assumed she would—but that didn't mean she couldn't stroll right past him and drive herself after all.

Take that, she thought with satisfaction she knew full well was darn right childish.

FULLY AWARE THAT it was his fault he had to watch her in the rearview mirror instead of having her sitting be-side him within touching distance while they squabbled and maybe even came to some kind of understanding about their future, Boyd gave himself an ass-kicking as he drove. What the hell had he been thinking?

He wasn't, that's what. The truth had just fallen out of his mouth without any thought, and he couldn't remem-ber the last time that happened. It was particularly foolish where Melinda was concerned. He knew how sensitive she was, and why, and then what did he do but confirm her belief he was a dictatorial jackass?

Maybe because he was?

He switched his gaze from the road ahead to scowl at

the sight of her red Subaru, hanging farther back than he liked.

But then one corner of his mouth quirked. No, he hadn't enjoyed her cool, challenging gaze as she sauntered by him, hitting the "unlock" button on her remote, but now that he thought about it, he *had* appreciated the saunter. Her hips had swung that extra little bit to send him a message.

Oh, yeah—she'd still be going home with him tonight. *After* she put him in his place. He grinned.

Nearing Cordova's place, all amusement and anticipation left him. He couldn't help thinking about how close Kristina had come to being murdered, her body tossed out by the side of the road. And then there was their grim purpose this morning.

Boyd slowed down and started watching for the unmarked turn to the left. There it was. His tires crunched on gravel and spit out dust in a plume to envelop first Melinda's Subaru, then Daniel's department-issue SUV.

He slowed even more when he got to the timber-built bridge, but it felt sturdy when he rolled onto it. If there really were ranches out here, the bridge had presumably been designed to support stock trailers.

Not far on the other side of it, a dusty blue pickup was pulled off onto the shoulder. Someone sat inside, and he felt sure that was a dog in the passenger seat. He tucked in behind and parked.

Melinda and Daniel followed suit. Boyd left greetings to Daniel, who'd made the contact with the dog handler, and instead surveyed the dirt verge of the road.

Even as seldom used as this road seemed to be, would Dorrance want to carry a body from his car down a slight incline toward the creek? All it would take was suddenly finding himself speared by the twin beams of headlights.

Instinct said no. Boyd crossed the road to walk along that side. Maybe they'd taken the reference to "the grove" too literally, but the drop-off was more pronounced here, the land too open. He ignored the cluster of two men and two women still conferring when he recrossed the road and kept walking. If there was a way to get down closer to the cluster of aspens, Dorrance hadn't used it the night he'd set up the ambush here, but that made sense. He'd have planned for a quick getaway if events went bad, as they had.

Boyd turned at the soft fall of footsteps behind him. Melinda, of course.

"What are you thinking?" she asked.

He told her.

She nodded. "The only thing is, he probably didn't bury more than a couple of bodies out here. At least, we have only two missing women from that period. Also..." She hesitated.

"It's been nine years plus," he conceded. "If it were only tracks he'd made, they'd be gone. But what I was thinking is that this would be a good place to bring the kids to wade and picnic, or skinny-dip, or throw in a fishing line. If somebody stumbled on an easy route to drive close to the creek, others would find it, too."

"You're right. What if the turnoff is farther up the road? With this scruffy growth, we might not be able to see it."

Back by the cars, the woman, lean and athletic, had clipped a leash on the dog, a big yellow Labrador, and was sliding down toward the creek. Loftis and Daniel followed her.

Boyd nodded toward them. "Why don't you go ahead? I might drive a little farther to check it out."

"I'll come with you," she said firmly. "If there's a

place he could have parked down there, that would narrow down how much ground we have to cover."

They walked back to his vehicle. Daniel glanced over his shoulder, but didn't demand an explanation for why they were climbing in and about to drive away.

Melinda sat tensely beside Boyd as he edged out of the line of parked cars, but kept her mouth shut. Apparently she shared his feeling that this wasn't a time or place for anything that didn't have to do with their purpose here.

The land in this area did some gentle rolling. He saw what might be the crumbling remnants of a basalt formation. The road dropped past it, and damn, there was a track, well-used although clearly not officially maintained, leading back toward the creek. Seeing the same thing he did, Melinda stiffened.

He turned carefully onto it. Not maintained by anybody, it had ruts that made the SUV lurch and his head connect with the roof a couple of times, but led straight through sagebrush and junipers to the creek. The turnaround there would give space for three or four cars to park.

It placed them a good half mile upstream from where the handler was set to start her dog to work.

Boyd pulled out his cell phone and called Daniel.

TWO HOURS LATER, the dog alerted. The handler praised him and Daniel hammered the kind of flag surveyors used into the ground. They were right at the edge of the grove, but far enough outside it that someone digging wouldn't have had to contend with roots, yet the soil might retain some softening moistness from the creek.

Boyd looked around for any natural markers. Would Dorrance have been able to find this exact spot again?

Close enough, apparently, because ten minutes later,

the Labrador alerted again, and they marked yet another spot.

Daniel was on the phone again, calling for help and tools to dig. At this point, the rest of them just watched as the dog searched an increasingly widening grid.

Somehow, it wasn't a shock when the dog found two more places worthy of exploration. After rewarding her dog each time, the handler kept it up for another couple of hours while the CSI team and a couple of off-duty officers joined the rest of them and they started to dig at the first two sites.

The day was hot. Boyd was glad to be wearing flexible tactical boots instead of the polished cowboy boots he wore when he expected to be on camera. During his shifts digging, he had to stop frequently to wipe sweat out of his eyes. He wasn't alone. He'd shed his uniform shirt within minutes but kept on the white T-shirt he'd worn beneath. Between copious sweat and dirt, he could tell it was destined for the ragbag.

Melinda and the two CSI techs present paced between the growing holes. Melinda had wanted to help, but to her obvious annoyance, none of the men gave way.

Boyd's hole was a couple of feet down when his shovel scraped on something. Not for the first time—they'd hit rocks early on, plentiful enough he'd wondered if the gravedigger had piled them on before covering them with dirt.

But, as he had every other time, he stopped and crouched, using his hand to brush away reddish soil to reveal a stained oval object with a couple of cracks. He knew what he'd found.

He stood and called for a tech. "I've got something."

A couple of men kept digging, but everyone else present gathered around the hole and watched as she used a brush to gently expose more of what they all knew was a skull.

Boyd switched his gaze to Melinda, who stood with her arms crossed on the other side of the hole—the grave—and stared unblinking at the evidence of what she'd always insisted she knew: that Gene Dorrance had held and murdered women before the rescue of Andrea Kudelka and Erica Warner.

Her expression was so closed, he hated to think what bubbled beneath the lid she'd jammed tight.

Chapter Fifteen

Melinda had been conscious all day of Boyd's occasional, searching gaze. Because of it—because she didn't dare let him weaken her—she'd kept her distance from him, although she, in turn, couldn't help watching him hard at work, too.

He seemed indefatigable. Sweat plastered the thin fabric of his T-shirt to hard muscle, making him look less civilized than he did in his usual crisp white shirt with pearl snaps, dark trousers and dark suit coat. His hair was wet and disheveled from all the times he ran his fingers through it—and from the once he walked away from a grave to crouch by the creek and splash water over his head and shoulders.

Not until they started toward their cars did he and she have a moment to talk.

"From the minute we got there, you knew Dorrance must have had a way to drive down closer to the creek." The question had nagged at her all day.

Boyd flicked a glance her way. "Made sense."

"I wouldn't have thought of it." She usually kept her awareness of her own shortcomings to herself, but she owed him one. "We'd have wasted hours, maybe even given up."

"Maybe, maybe not. Daniel would have had the same thought once he had a minute to look around."

"Because of your military experience."

"Thinking about routes and tracking is part of it."

She unlocked her door, tired but needing to say this. "I should grovel. I remember what I said back then." Still hurting, she'd lashed out after he was elected sheriff and they'd been forced to work together on the hunt for the serial killer. She couldn't remember the exact words, but she'd been so sure his years in the military didn't give him the qualifications to be sheriff, whatever the voters thought.

A crease in his cheek let her know he was smiling. "But you were right, too. I didn't know anything about criminal investigation."

After a moment, she nodded. Maybe he hadn't, but he had learned. He'd been...more of a partner this past week than she could ever remember having before. Using his head, offering a strong wall at her back.

The knowledge was humbling, and she knew then that she couldn't have been more wrong about him.

It was a shock to realize she trusted him more than anybody but Daniel, and their relationship was primarily a working one. Off the job, they were friends in a casual way because of her friendship with his wife, Lindsay.

Melinda felt a whole lot for Boyd that was light-years past "friend."

As she followed him home to the ranch, she wished she was beside him instead of still maintaining that distance. Her determination to assert her independence this morning felt petty.

He turned off the highway, her right behind, the tires changing sound on the packed dirt and gravel ranch road. She felt weird—almost as if she were having an out-of-body experience—during the half mile drive to his log house. He must have used a remote, because a wide door rolled up on an outbuilding she wouldn't have identified as a garage, revealing two open spaces inside. He parked, and she followed. Having their vehicles out of sight and locked in was smart, she had to admit.

When she got out, Boyd was waiting. The door glided down behind them and he held out a hand, before glancing down at it with distaste and pulling it back.

She didn't care how dirty his hand was. She snatched it up and squeezed hard. For a moment, he only looked down at her, but then his clasp tightened and he led her to the wide front steps to the porch, up and inside.

Boyd stopped, flicking on a light, his intent gaze on her. "You were right about that SOB."

It was the first time they'd talked about it.

"I wish I hadn't been." She'd been haunted by the ghosts of the dead women, but now the graves would take their place.

"I know," he said gruffly. He seemed to be waiting for something more, but finally he released her hand. "I need a shower before we think about dinner."

She hadn't worked hard the way he had, but she'd sweated plenty just standing out in the hot sun for so much of the day. Since she hadn't managed to shop for clothes, though, she'd either be putting the same dirty clothes back on, or Boyd's way-too-big sweats and T-shirt. Or she could wait until bedtime.

"I'll check out your refrigerator," she suggested, backing away. "You go ahead."

"I left a note this morning asking Jennifer to run into town and pick up some basics for you." His smile was so faint, Melinda might have missed it. "Somehow, I suspected you'd be too busy to do anything about it yourself."

"Clothes, you mean? Oh. That was really nice of you. And of her. I'd like a shower, too. I have to admit. I feel like—" She made herself stop.

"You want to wash his contamination off you?"

"Something like that."

"Then come on." He held out that big, filthy hand again. Knuckles were scraped, she saw, and his fingernails were broken and dirty, too, but his strength was just what she needed right now.

They climbed the stairs side by side, as if they'd done so a hundred times instead of the few occasions she'd been with him in this house.

"I had an idea," she heard herself say. Better to concentrate on catching Dorrance than on the fact that the ground had shifted between her and Boyd. That they were alone in his house, possibilities she had given up on open once more.

He looked sharply at her and came to a stop in the hall outside the guest room.

"We've let him take the offensive. You notice he hasn't emailed me in days."

"I've noticed." There was enough grit in the two words to scrape more skin from his body. "I'm surprised he hasn't sent a picture taken at your house."

She was, too, but maybe he didn't consider the destruction to be a victory.

"I snapped a couple of pictures today."

Boyd's eyebrows rose, and for good reason. Cops didn't take their own photos at crime scenes. Otherwise, they were setting themselves up for their phones to become part of the court record.

"Not of the graves or anything. Of you and Daniel opening the back of the hearse. A few like that."

They hadn't really needed a vehicle as big as the

hearse, given that all they found in those graves was bones, lacking substance to fill out body bags, although they'd used those anyway to make sure every tiny bone and piece of dirt—or other evidence—made it back to the lab. Techs, including a contingent from CAU, had used brushes to clear the skeletons and, after endless photographs taken in situ, been careful to remove them and lay them out again just as they'd been in the graves. The body bags were supported by stretchers so that nothing could shift during transportation.

"You're thinking of sending him a photo so he knows we found the graves."

"I'm betting that will shake him up." She wanted to do a lot more than that, but had to take what she could get. "The more we can rattle him, the more likely he is to screw up."

"You need to clear it with Daniel."

"He's heading SPD's investigation, but you're running the county's."

His eyebrows twitched. "As you've pointed out in the past, I don't have the background and experience he does. Or you, for that matter."

Melinda made a face at him.

Boyd smiled, bent forward and kissed her lightly on the lips. "Why don't you shower, then give him a call?"

"Okay." She smiled weakly and let herself into the guest room.

BOYD BENT HIS HEAD forward, savoring the powerful beat of water on his neck and back, but the simple pleasure didn't reduce his tension. Fear for Melinda collided with this powerful resurgence of feelings for her. Did she want him as much as he wanted her? Was she ready to relent and come to bed with him tonight?

The chemistry was still there, he knew it was. Knew she felt it, too. But for the first time in his life, that wasn't enough. Yeah, he'd felt more than physical desire for Raquel, but their relationship had developed naturally, without a lot of agonizing until near the end, when they butted up against where they'd take it. And Melinda—he'd been in love with her the first time around, he just hadn't known how much. Hadn't analyzed why she hit him so hard from the first meeting.

Thus his stupid demand.

With a groan, he tipped his head back so that the hot water ran over his face.

His instinct was to push it with Melinda tonight. Those aggressive instincts were part of him, meaning that patience came hard for him. Even so…he knew he couldn't do that to her. He couldn't forget what Dorrance's assault on Melinda—and that's what it had been, for all that she hadn't been physically present—had taken out of her. Today, he'd seen grief to go along with the satisfaction at finding answers, and he'd heard humility when she apologized for the things she'd said to him, even though he'd known he deserved every word at the time.

The last thing she needed was to have him come on to her like a charging bull.

He mumbled some profanities, got a mouthful of water he had to spit out and turned off the faucet.

The hall bathroom door was closed when he passed it after getting mostly dressed. He had to grit his teeth at the images that filled his head: Melinda's long, slender body, her high, firm breasts, legs that went on forever. Was she toweling off right now? Had she run the water as hot as he had, making her ivory skin pink?

He swore again and made himself keep going, even

when he heard the quiet sound of that door opening behind him.

Some evenings he'd find the makings for a dinner he had to cook himself—say, steaks for the grill, or the already sliced and diced ingredients for a stir-fry. But Jennifer would have observed the long hours he was working, and obviously knew he had a guest, so tonight's meal was one of her casseroles, easy to reheat, along with homemade sourdough rolls and a salad ready to put on the table.

He set the casserole to warming while he listened to Melinda talking on the phone behind him. When he did turn, he saw that she was staring at his bare feet, a blush chasing across her face. His feet weren't particularly sexy—but he thought hers were. She was definitely reacting to something.

Pay attention to what you're doing.

He waited until they'd sat down to eat before he asked what Daniel thought.

She scrunched up her nose. "He decided me making contact with Dorrance couldn't hurt anything. It's not like the guy doesn't already hate my guts."

If she'd meant that to be funny, she'd missed her mark. Knowing a man as vicious as Gene Dorrance fully intended to punish Melinda in the worst of ways stayed with Boyd like an untreated wound, present whether he was waking and sleeping.

He only grunted and focused on splitting and buttering a biscuit.

"I thought I'd wait until morning," she said after a minute.

She'd dished up a lot of greens and only a small helping of casserole, he saw. He didn't expect her to have an appetite like his, but she'd visibly lost weight in barely over a week. She hadn't learned, as most soldiers did, that you had to shovel the food in when you could.

"Try one of these." He lifted his half-eaten biscuit. "They're really good."

She did and ate it with enthusiasm before picking up her fork to start on the rest of her meal.

You can lead a horse to water... he thought and concentrated on filling his own stomach.

"Does Gabe know what's going on?" she asked.

"Everyone in the county knows what's going on unless they don't follow the news at all. But yeah, I've put him and Leon on alert. A couple of other guys, too," he added.

Looking interested, she asked, "Veterans?"

"We hire a lot of them. You know that." Feeling some amusement, he said, "We're going to be hosting another guy shortly. I don't know if he's interested in ranching, but he needs someplace to stay while he gets his head together."

She cocked her head in interest.

Despite the rage of feelings he kept contained, Boyd grinned. "Should be fun. Joseph Marr is Trina's brother. He's a former teammate of mine and Gabe's. Hasn't made it here for a visit yet. Gabe's still feeling a little squeamish about taking Joseph's sister to bed every night knowing her brother is in the guest room."

"They're married!"

"Sure, but I bet they weren't the first time."

"What's he going to do, punch Gabe?"

"You never know. If so, I'm sure Gabe won't fight back."

Shaking her head, Melinda said in obvious disgust, *"Men."*

Boyd laughed.

Melinda kept eating, even helping herself to a second

sourdough biscuit. Getting her thinking about something else had its rewards.

But her distraction lasted only so long. She balled up her napkin and looked at him, the bleakness back in her eyes.

"I wish we had a plan for tomorrow."

Boyd wished they had a plan at all. They'd started with one, but the only part that had paid off was the news barrage and the tip line. Now they were back to ground zero, without the faintest idea where Dorrance was holed up, or who he'd go after next.

And at the forefront of Boyd's thoughts was the wish that he could at least spend tonight wrapped around Melinda while they slept.

Keeping her safe from everyone but him.

MELINDA WAS SURE the meal had been delicious—she knew those sourdough biscuits were—but her mind hadn't been on food. She kept jumping between Dorrance and the horrors he'd perpetuated and might yet loose on someone else, and Boyd. The man who'd somehow persuaded her to come stay at his house, and who'd suggested she stay for good. Somehow, that subject hadn't come up again.

She almost rolled her eyes. She was a coward, that's why she hadn't confronted him right away. Well, and they'd been a little busy, too.

She wasn't used to feeling uncertain or…vulnerable. Emotionally *and* physically. If not for the emotional part, she wouldn't have hesitated to jump into bed with Boyd tonight. *He* wouldn't be likely to object. Her real trouble was that their lovemaking had been so far out of her previous experience, she'd never been able to think of it as just sex.

So if she made that choice, she'd be opening herself to a lot more than sharing her body and enjoying the pleasure of the moment. Did she trust him enough to do that?

She tuned in to find that, as was too often the case, he was watching her. God forbid he read her mind!

Feeling too antsy to just sit under the force of that thoughtful gaze, Melinda leaped up and began gathering dishes to carry to the sink. In a more leisurely way, Boyd did the same, but once he opened the dishwasher and started rinsing his plate, he said, "Why don't you let me finish up here?"

"You cooked." Her cheeks warmed. "Well, pushed buttons on the microwave."

He grinned with the deceptively lazy charm that had sucked her in the first time they met. "I'm good at that."

"I'm sure you are. But you're the one who labored hard today while all I did was stand around."

The humor left his face. "Bet you didn't like to be sidelined."

"No, I didn't, but—" Feeling awkward, she shrugged. "Obviously, I'm a little lacking in brawn."

A nerve in his cheek ticked. "You're not lacking in anything from where I stand."

Hearing the roughness in his voice, she grasped for the nerve to say, *I might have been wrong.*

What came out was, "I missed you."

"God, Melinda." The plate he'd held in his hand clattered into the sink and he turned off the flow of water with a single jab. "It's been killing me."

"You…you mean that?"

"Can you doubt it?"

Seeing the fire in his eyes, she didn't, even though she wasn't the most beautiful woman ever, never worked to make herself sexier for any man's sake, and had tried harder to fit in with the guys than she had to lure anyone like Boyd. And yet the first time he'd set eyes on her, he'd wanted her and she hadn't been able to help being just as drawn to him.

Swallowing, she shook her head and took a step toward him.

The next moment, his arms closed hard around her and his mouth found hers.

This kiss had a quality of desperation she'd never felt from him before or felt herself. There was nothing skilled about it. They kissed deeply, passionately, their bodies straining together. She dug her fingers into his shoulders to hold on, to lift herself to meet him.

He yanked his mouth away to kiss his way down her throat. Along the way, he mumbled, "I was trying so hard not to push you tonight."

"Why?" she whispered.

Boyd lifted his head to stare at her. "You've had a hellish few days, that's why."

"Maybe that's why I need you now," she said simply.

He groaned and said, "Screw the kitchen. Let's go upstairs."

They held hands again. This time, it felt symbolic, although probably she was making too much of what could turn out to be no more than a passionate, satisfying night.

Uh-huh. She couldn't forget what he'd said.

As far as I'm concerned, you don't need to figure anything out. I have in mind you staying for good.

Rational thought ended as soon as Boyd had hustled her into his bedroom. Next to the massive bed, he started stripping her. Even as her shirt and bra dropped to the floor, she wrenched at his shirt until he let her pull it over his head. She was hungry to see him naked, too. Her knees weakened at the sight of a powerful chest with just enough dark hair to almost hide his nipples, and then there was the muscle-rippled belly. She pressed her lips to the hollow at the base of his throat, then slid them downward. Just rubbing her cheek on his pecs sent a rush of pleasure through her.

He growled something under his breath, swung her up in his arms and laid her back on the bed. Before she could sit up, he peeled off the yoga pants and panties she'd found in her room.

She whimpered at the expression on his face as he raked his gaze over her. He made her feel beautiful, whether she was or not.

"You, too," she whispered and did sit up.

His dark eyes flicked to hers, and his hands went to the waist of his worn jeans. She was stunned to see that they shook. Even so, he shed jeans and his boxers so quick, her gaze didn't make it lower than the jutting evidence of his arousal. She reached for him, but he shook his head and backed away before fumbling at the bedside drawer.

"Let me—"

"I'm on birth control." Before, she'd insisted he use a condom, too.

His stare all but blistered her. "You're sure?"

Melinda bobbed her head.

She might as well have sliced the tether holding him back, because he was on her faster than she'd known he could move. Kissing her, then closing his mouth on first one breast, then the other. Licking, suckling, his unshaven cheek adding another sensation. His hands wandered, squeezing her hips, before one traced a path to the junction of her thighs. Once his fingers slid into her slick folds, she was lost. All she wanted was him, and she wanted him *now*.

As big and solid as he was, she wouldn't have been

able to move him until he was damn well good and ready, but apparently he was, because suddenly his knees pushed hers apart and he was there, between her legs. Pressing against her, taunting her, then pushing slowly inside. A huge shudder shook him. And all the while, he watched her.

She moaned. Her back arched in a near spasm, and she used her hands and even fingernails to urge him on. "Now. Please. Now."

He surged into her, sinking himself deep, and for the first time closed his eyes. "So good," he muttered.

Better than she remembered, and that was saying a lot. She'd never needed anyone like this, but he was there, filling her, driving her up. Her back arched, and the excruciating coil of tension broke, flooding her with pleasure and joy.

She cried his name, and felt his body jerk as he came, too, pulsing inside her. She barely heard her name as he whispered it against her neck.

Chapter Sixteen

Sprawled on his back with Melinda wrapped in his arms and her head on his shoulder, Boyd felt amazing. The best in a long time. Ever, maybe. He'd been so afraid they'd never get here again—

She stirred. "That was—"

He lifted his head slightly, but still couldn't see much of her face. "Out of this world?"

Her chuckle vibrated against his side and chest, making him think he might be ready for round two without much of a break.

"Maybe," she murmured. "Only...this doesn't mean—"

Hearing the return to wariness in her tone, Boyd's excellent mood evaporated and his whole body stiffened. "Mean what?"

"You don't have to sound hostile!"

"No?" He reared up, dumping her onto the bed. "We've just made love, and you're already stringing the barbed wire? How am I supposed to take that?"

She sat up, too, eyes wide, silky dark hair tangling around her face and shoulders. "That's not what I was trying to say."

"Then what *did* you intend to say?" He wasn't doing himself any favors, but was too pissed to rein himself in.

Damn it, having her pull back before he'd even caught his breath hurt.

Melinda raised her firm chin. "I'm nervous, that's all. Okay? I'm not quite ready to…to move in yet, even if you seem to think it's that easy!"

He winced at the reminder. She, of all women, had been guaranteed to hate the way he'd tossed out his intentions. Releasing a long breath, Boyd reached to cup her jaw and cheek. To his relief, she tipped her head enough to nestle her face in his palm.

"I know it's not that easy," he said quietly. "When I said that, I was letting you know what I want. I didn't do it very well."

"No kidding." Her forehead puckered. "I don't get it. Every time I see you on TV, you're so…charming. Every woman in your vicinity starts blushing and smiling."

"Would that work with you?"

She stared at him for an uncomfortable moment, not so much as blinking. "Not once I saw through it. I mean, sure, you mowed me right over when we first met. But after you blew it, I realized that I was never sure how deep those smiles went."

"I'm sorry."

She frowned. "It's more than that. Did you ever really pay attention to me? Did you have the slightest idea who I was?"

"Of course I did. Why else would I be so irrational? You scared me—"

"Because of Raquel." She remembered his girlfriend's name. Of course she did.

He cleared his throat. "Yeah. I'm still afraid for you. Back then, I overreacted. Granger County wasn't exactly a war zone."

"But now it is," she said, a little wryly.

"Seems that way, doesn't it?"

In her unnerving way, she studied him for a minute. He dreaded what was to come. He'd never figured out how Gabe, notoriously closemouthed, had engineered a romance with Trina. Maybe being a therapist had taught her how to coax words—and meaningful ones, at that—from a stone.

Unfortunately, it was true that Boyd knew how to charm people on one level, but when it got to anything as raw as emotions, he was as bad as his partner. What she saw on his face right now, he couldn't conceive.

"I love being here with you," she said, surprising him. "Not just in bed." She looked a little shy. "Eating dinner together, talking about our days. You know."

He knew.

"I just…need to be able to trust that you'll understand when I make the decisions I do. And back me up when I need it. Not…assume you know best."

"Have I done that since Dorrance showed up in town? Or earlier when we arrested the bank robbers?"

Her lashes fluttered a few times, as if he'd surprised her. "No," she said finally, "but for most of the time I assumed that was because you didn't have any particular interest in me anymore."

"You assumed wrong," he said gruffly. "I didn't know if you'd give me the time of day, but in the back of my mind, I never quit hoping."

Was that a shimmer in her eyes?

"Then why…?"

"Didn't I charge after you?"

Her head bobbed.

"Partly—" Boyd rubbed a hand over his face. That hand was shaking. He didn't like having no control over whether she decided in his favor or not.

What's more, this much honesty didn't come easily for him. Raquel aside, he'd never had a serious relationship with a woman. Short-term hookups, sure. His most important, lasting friendships were with friends and teammates, but the boys and men he knew, and perhaps especially soldiers, they didn't talk out how they felt the same way. Or at all.

He had to start again. "Partly, it was the way you looked at me with such astonishment and then dismissal. You walked out as if you hadn't been that invested anyway." That had felt like taking a slug to his chest. Maybe he'd been wearing a vest so he wasn't bleeding to death, but that didn't protect him from pain. He forced himself to keep talking, however little he liked doing it. "Then I'd made that vow. I've had some ugly wounds in my years in the army, but nothing that hurt like hearing Raquel was dead. I was looking forward to seeing her, then *wham*. I was convinced I couldn't go through that again. I…didn't see yet that I'd fallen for her, and then you, *because* you were strong women. Warriors. And if I loved you, I had to accept your job instead of treating it like a nine-to-five you could quit in favor of doing something else."

"It took you years to reach that epiphany?"

He grimaced. "I was getting there when we worked that serial killer investigation together. But Daniel and Lindsay came so close to being killed. That could have been you."

"So you chickened out again."

It was more complicated than that, but he chose not to remind her how open she'd been with her dislike of him. If she'd betrayed any suggestion that she'd missed him…

"What about next time?" she challenged him.

"This *is* next time. I haven't gotten in the way of you doing your job, have I?"

"No. That's why I came home with you, you know."

He smiled crookedly. "Although you made sure you had your own car here."

"Seemed smart." She scooted closer to him on the mattress, not quite closing the distance, but getting there. "I'm sorry I started this. I guess I just…"

At her hesitation, Boyd finished her sentence, "Aren't sure you trust me."

Her eyes searched his. "I'm not very good at trust. You know that."

"I know." A ragged sound escaped him. "Come here. I wasn't done with you."

Would never be done with her.

He'd imagined progressing to slow and tender once they'd eased that first frantic need, but their little talk had him feeling as if his horse had just bolted at the same moment he'd realized the girth of the saddle was loose. The need to join with her, and *now*, roared back to life.

Thank God, she met his mouth with just as much intensity and passion.

MELINDA STOOD ON the front porch that stretched the entire width of the huge log house and watched Boyd's black department SUV recede down the ranch road. She kind of wished she'd gone with him; he would have preferred to drop her at the police station and come back for her after he'd finished his business at the sheriff's headquarters. He'd gone back and forth on that, though.

"If you're there at the station, you'd head out with Daniel or any other officer in a minute, wouldn't you?" he'd said. "I think Dorrance has to be planning another ambush. You should be safe here." He'd sighed at that point. "You don't have to tell me that I'm being protective. Not sure how much I can change."

If he could accept her, she had to accept him as well: a former officer and soldier who'd spent years in war zones. He had a way of making her feel safe, too. But as far as today went, she refused to be afraid to be left alone. This was about her, not Boyd. His housekeeper wasn't scheduled to work today, which meant she'd be alone here for however many hours Boyd was gone.

"Do your job," Boyd had said tersely, although his final words were, "I've got Gabe on alert. He and Leon will be somewhere on the ranch and carrying phones."

He'd input both of their numbers into her phone.

Now, heeding his insistence, she went back inside and locked the dead bolt on the front door.

The plan was for her to respond to any calls to the tip line that seemed worthy of follow-up. Maybe from the sheriff's department, too; she didn't know. Boyd's business was apparently administrative, not surprising given how little time he'd spent at his desk this past week or more. She knew he was going to start by firing a deputy. He was mad to have to do it when his small force was already stretched so thin, but negligence couldn't be excused.

Melinda wandered into the kitchen, a room made airy by large expanses of windows looking out on ponderosa or lodgepole pine woods and pastures.

She poured herself a second cup of coffee and sipped it standing right in front of the expanse of windows, smiling despite herself as she watched several older foals bucking and chasing each other along the fence line.

The phone she'd just set down on the counter beeped and gave a little bounce to let her know a text had arrived. She stiffened. There'd been no response to the one she'd sent Dorrance earlier that morning. If it was him—

It was, with an attached photo. A girl with terrified eyes.

Chloe Decker, the adopted daughter of Boyd's partner, Gabe. A child who'd survived seeing her family butchered. Sickened, Melinda scanned the text itself.

I'm watching you. If you try to forward this text or make a call, I'll kill the kid. Drop your phone. NOW. Walk out the back door.

For a fraction of an instance, her fingers tightened. Would he really see if she took the brief moment it would take to send this to Boyd, who might not even have turned out onto the highway yet?

But movement outside drew her eyes, and she saw a man standing not that far away between tall pines. He had a child slung over his shoulder, and a handgun.

Melinda let the phone clatter to the floor.

MAN, HE DIDN'T like leaving her. During their careful discussion, Boyd had hidden the depths of his fear and his paranoid belief he had to stay close to Melinda.

Even as he emerged onto the highway and accelerated southbound, he battled the need to turn back. What if she needed him? But what if she didn't, and was insulted by his lack of faith in her ability to protect herself?

And, damn, what made him think that psycho killer had managed to sneak onto the ranch and was close enough to threaten Melinda, anyway?

Yeah, but he didn't believe Gene Dorrance was holed up in a falling-down barn somewhere brooding and licking his wounds. He knew his time was limited and intended to make the most of it.

He didn't seem to expect to survive unscathed and go

on to live a happy life in some other part of the country. All he wanted was the people he hated to pay for their crimes against him. He must see that his options were increasingly limited, which meant he'd want to be sure to degrade and murder Melinda before he died himself.

Boyd's stomach clenched and his foot hovered above the brake as he fought his instincts.

He'd laid his phone on the console between seats to be sure he didn't miss any important calls or texts. Even as he forced himself to drive on, he kept flicking glances at it, suspicious of the silence. He'd give a lot to be on horseback somewhere on the ranch, Melinda riding beside him. No crime on their minds. He'd begun to hate this stint as sheriff, except what if he hadn't pinned on the badge, giving him the ability to support and protect her?

If he failed—

The damn phone rang. Not dispatch or one of his deputies. The caller was Gabe Decker. It would take more than an everyday problem on the ranch for his partner to need to consult with him right now.

"Gabe?"

"Chloe is missing." His voice was taut, agony thinly suppressed. "This isn't like her. Trina just called. I'm fifteen minutes away from home. Any chance you're closer?"

Fear squeezed Boyd's rib cage. He braked, keeping an eye on his rearview mirror. "Yeah. Hell. I left Melinda alone at the house."

"You don't think—?"

Boyd recognized the sudden sharpness in his partner's voice. He'd heard it when they were under pressure in dire circumstances. Yeah, Boyd did think, and Gabe was seeing the same terrifying possibilities.

"Tell Trina not to go anywhere near my place," Boyd

snapped, and dropped the phone back onto the console even as his speed dropped to a point where he was able to wrench the steering wheel into a U-turn. The tires squealed, and he burned rubber as he stomped on the gas to speed back to the ranch.

The battle-ready part of him calculated despite the fear that could have paralyzed him.

He'd have to park well before he reached the house. Given the lack of rain, he'd raise a plume of dirt once he hit the ranch road. Thank God he had his rifle with him.

He picked up the phone again and dialed Leon. When his foreman answered, Boyd asked, "Where are you?"

"Gabe already called. I'm on my way in, but not close enough to help if anything goes down in the next ten, fifteen minutes."

"Do your best."

Boyd's hand clenched on the phone. *Call Melinda*, he decided.

She didn't answer. She could be on a call made because of the tip line, thinking she could get back to him. He tried again, listened to ring after ring until her voice mail picked up.

Again.

No answer.

Dorrance had figured out how to get to Melinda, Boyd knew with icy certainty. Another child, a young girl again, and this time one Melinda already knew, although Dorrance probably wasn't aware of that. Didn't matter to him; he'd figured out her Achilles' heel.

Back on the packed dirt road, Boyd hardly slowed down. A pothole he hadn't noticed before threw the SUV sideways, but he controlled it with a steady hand. There was the turnoff to Gabe's cabin; time to ditch the vehicle and proceed on foot.

He suddenly wished like hell that Joseph Marr had arrived to provide backup. Gabe would have said if he had.

Boyd gave brief thought to where Dorrance had hidden his car. Then he dismissed the issue. Didn't matter; Dorrance would be on foot now.

He'd have grabbed Chloe, maybe gone so far as to knock her out so she couldn't scream and alert her mother, who handled a handgun or rifle with impressive competence thanks to her army ranger brother's insistence. Trina had proved able to shoot to kill, if that's what it took to protect someone she loved. Boyd had no doubt she had a weapon in hand right now, but she didn't have the skills he could have used to corner Dorrance.

Boyd drove off the road into a stand of pine trees. Some minor undergrowth didn't hide the SUV, but made it less obvious. Dorrance wasn't that close, though. With Melinda not answering her phone—

Even as he took out his rifle and checked to be sure it was ready to fire, Boyd had to fight not to succumb to the tornado of terror and anguish that could have whipped him away. If there'd ever been a battle he had to win, this was it.

For Melinda, and for the cute kid Gabe and Trina loved so much.

Boyd broke into a run.

MELINDA SHUDDERED. Her sidearm in its holster lay on the table where she'd imagined being able to grab it quickly. But he could see her clearly through the windows. If she diverted on her way to the door, Dorrance would see.

And…she felt sure he'd search her when she reached him. If he kept the barrel of his own gun pressed to Chloe's head, she wouldn't dare open fire.

All she could do was walk out that back door, hands

in the air and pray she had a chance to fight back. He despised women. Might he underestimate her, be unable to imagine any female having the ability to overcome him?

Andrea had, she reminded herself—but so momentarily, Dorrance was likely to discount her courage and strength.

If worse came to worst, Melinda could only hope he'd let Chloe go. Gripped by anguish as she accepted the likelihood of her own death, she saw Boyd's face as he'd looked down at her while they made love. The wanting, the tenderness, the commitment. She couldn't have imagined seeing that. If he lost another woman he loved to violence—

Don't think about it. Do what you have to do.

She opened the door and walked out onto the deck, hands in the air.

Chapter Seventeen

Boyd scanned the landscape ahead and to the sides even as he sprinted full out. Reason said Dorrance wouldn't have knocked on the front door. He'd use Chloe to lure Melinda out back, however he accomplished it. He'd obviously waited until Boyd left, so he'd been somewhere he could identify the black SUV as it receded, watch the dust plume all the way out to the highway.

Not hard to do.

What was his intention? To kill Melinda immediately to ensure he got it done, that he could have the chance to watch the light leave her eyes? Or was he set on having time with her? Long enough to reduce her to a broken excuse for the woman she was, to make her beg?

He was deluding himself if he thought Melinda McIntosh would ever beg for her life. But then, nobody could say Dorrance was sane.

If that's what he wanted, he had to have a spot picked out that he believed would give him privacy for a few minutes to a few hours. One of the unoccupied cabins? An outbuilding that was unlocked, or that he'd been able to break into?

Boyd had to believe Dorrance wouldn't go for a quick death for the woman he hated so much. Because if he did, a gunshot would split the quiet day any minute, ending her life.

The house reared ahead.

HANDS SPREAD OPEN so Dorrance could see that she didn't carry either her phone or a weapon, Melinda walked as slowly as she could without being too obvious. She'd opened her every sense, watching for any tiny flicker of movement to one side or the other, the steady clop of a horse's hooves or the engine of a ranch vehicle on the road. A voice. Anything at all that might distract Dorrance…or give her hope that she wasn't alone confronting him.

But the quiet was so absolute, even eerie, she wondered where the birds had gone. Even the yearlings she'd earlier watched running grazed now. As she neared the trees, reddish soil puffed under her every footstep.

Dorrance waited where she'd first seen him. A child lay limp over his shoulder. Not "a child": Chloe. Fine, strawberry blond hair spilled down his chest.

He looked different, she saw, as soon as she was near enough to study him. She'd been right about the weight lifting; despite the added years, he'd become considerably brawnier than he was that day in the courtroom. He'd gone completely gray, though, and his hair was thinning. She doubted he cared. His eyes burned as he watched her approach. Melinda doubted he'd had a thought that didn't have to do with revenge in the intervening years. That hate twisted his face into ugliness.

He was also filthy, which wasn't a surprise after he'd lost his access to a shower and washing machine and dryer. Had he managed to find anything to eat? She hoped not. Hunger would weaken him.

She stopped twenty feet away from him. "I'm here. Let the kid go."

"You're not that stupid. Keep walking. You need to pass me. Go straight ahead. I'll follow behind you."

Melinda wanted to cast a glance over her shoulder. Oh, God, why had she talked Boyd into leaving?

Dorrance would only have waited. Or, if his ploy to use Chloe had failed, he might have killed her and dumped the body.

In sudden horror, Melinda wondered: Was Chloe alive? She hung so limply, Melinda couldn't be sure. *Please, let her only be unconscious.* That might be best. It would...protect her from knowing what was happening. She'd suffered enough horror for a lifetime when she'd seen her family murdered.

Melinda's skin crawled as she passed within a couple of feet of Dorrance. Walking forward with him behind her, unable to see him, was worse. The prickling up and down the back of her neck could have been the path of a scorpion searching for the right place to sting. She couldn't forget the hank of graying brown hair he'd used to taunt her. Would he cut hers off right away?

There was no path, but undergrowth was scanty here on the far edge of forests that covered the eastern side of the Cascade Mountains. The heat and dry climate had a big impact. What clumps she saw of bitterbrush, snowberry, wax currant and Oregon grape were easy to avoid.

Would Dorrance notice if she "accidentally" stepped on a plant and broke a few branches? Would he realize she was trying to lay a trail?

Dorrance ordered her to continue straight ahead. She caught a glimpse from the corner of her eye of the fence line off to her left. They seemed to be paralleling it.

Behind her, she heard a crunching sound and a growl.

He had stepped on something like the low-growing pine-mat manzanita.

"Hands up!" he snapped, and she realized she'd let her arms sag.

Melinda's fingers were tingling, ready to go numb, but she forced her hands higher again.

Where was he taking her?

Boyd was forced to slow his pace before he reached the house. He circled around it, easing from one bit of cover to another. He couldn't disappear here as training and experience allowed him to in a lusher landscape or a sunbaked adobe town with crooked streets, but he studied his surroundings carefully each time before he moved.

He came into sight of the deck—and the back door, standing open as Melinda must have left it. Unless Dorrance had gone *in*, thinking he'd have long enough before anyone came looking?

Boyd's gut said no. He must realize that Chloe's disappearance would be noted quickly. If Gabe had been home and learned that Melinda was here alone, he'd have searched the house after she didn't answer the door.

Boyd sifted through other possibilities, not liking how many there were even with Dorrance and Melinda on foot.

First the garage and then, a quarter of a mile farther, the long string of cabins built for ranch employees lay to the north of the house. There were a couple of empty cabins right now—but Dorrance would take an enormous risk of being seen if he tried to use one. In normal times, as a stranger he might not have occasioned comment, since ranch hands came and went seasonally, but his photo had been spread far and wide. A man carrying a child and either holding a gun on that child or a woman?

He'd need space and privacy. The woods here weren't dense—this land had all been logged at one point—but they extended for several miles. Some minor ranch roads crisscrossed through the second-growth forest, but Boyd and Gabe had made the decision not to log. They had enough pasture. As a result, not much lay this way...but finding Dorrance and Melinda among the trees might be like searching for the needle in a haystack.

And, damn, ideally he'd spot them somewhere he could set up a shot—and get it off before Dorrance could pull the trigger to kill Melinda or Chloe.

If Chloe was still alive.

Boyd gave his head a sharp shake. He couldn't afford to think like that.

Slipping from tree to tree, wishing these trunks were large enough to truly hide a man his size, he watched for footprints or any other sign that someone had passed this way recently. Too bad the earth was dry and hard right now.

Wait. His thoughts snapped to a stop. *Haystack.*

Hay.

There were a couple of decrepit cabins out here, part of the ranch's past. One was close to falling down—maybe had. Boyd hadn't had reason to pass it since winter. But they'd done enough repairs on the other cabin to use it as a hay shed. A narrow track led to it from the main ranch road so that bales of hay could be unloaded and stored there. One of the feeding stations for the horses was just on the other side of the fence.

If Dorrance had explored... Yeah, that was a good possibility. If he knew anything about ranching, he'd be aware that horses and cattle both mainly relied on pasture at this time of year. Late summer or early fall, when the grasses were dry or grazed down, Boyd or Gabe would make the decision to start supplementing the stock's diet, while making sure they had enough hay to last through the winter.

Wary of focusing too quickly on one site, Boyd nevertheless kept moving that way. It made sense.

And then he saw some crushed vegetation.

SHE COULD HARDLY feel her arms and hands. Even if she could get her hands on a weapon, would she be able to use it effectively, or be so blasted stiff and clumsy she'd drop anything she tried to grab?

Uh-huh. And what weapon would that be? She hadn't seen even a fallen branch solid enough to be useful.

Once she turned her head to try to get a look over her shoulder.

A low, menacing voice said, "You think I won't kill her?"

No, Melinda knew better than that. This man lacked any pretense at a conscience or sense of empathy. Although he wouldn't want to shoot—that would draw attention. He wouldn't have to, though; he could break a five-year-old girl's neck with a quick wrench of his hands.

She hoped he didn't see her shudder. He craved her fear, which meant she couldn't betray any.

Where are you, Boyd?

Had anyone noticed Chloe's absence yet? Mid-morning like this, Melinda would expect so. Nap time might have been different.

What would Dorrance have done if Boyd hadn't left? she found herself wondering again. Or if she'd gone with him? Hidden with Chloe, thinking a chance would come? Or killed her, shrugged and dreamed up another strategy while he bided his time?

She heard a whimper.

Chloe. That had to be Chloe.

"Shut up!"

She was alive.

The exhilarating knowledge buzzed under Melinda's skin, energizing her. Whatever else happened, she had to save the little girl.

If only determination was enough.

Just ahead, a tree root had pushed the soil up. She deliberately stepped wrong on it, stumbled and fell into a bush before hitting the trunk of a ponderosa pine and scraping her knuckles over it.

Dorrance stopped. "Get back out here. And don't do that again." Teeth showing, he jiggled Chloe. "Or I might not bother hauling her along any farther."

Cheek on Dorrance's chest, Chloe had opened her blue eyes and was watching, although she looked dazed.

Don't fight, Melinda wanted to beg, even though Chloe could provide the distraction that would allow her to jump him. It was too dangerous, though, and a child her age too fragile.

She pushed her way back through the thin branches of what she thought was a snowberry or maybe a huckleberry bush and pretended to limp once she stepped free.

"Go."

BOYD DEBATED TEXTING Leon and Gabe to let them know where he was, but as much as he'd have liked backup, he made the decision not to. The sudden appearance of one or the other of the men could precipitate a crisis, and potentially a bloodbath. If he thought either had been close enough, he'd have asked them to advance up the dirt track to the hay shed, but by the time they circled around…no. Right now, the best chance was for him to see Dorrance ahead and get a good, clear shot.

He carried his rifle in his left hand and his Glock in his right. Just in case he stumbled on them unexpectedly he had to be prepared, but he would prefer that not happen. He moved as fast as he thought he could without screwing up, setting each foot down with care to be sure not even a twig snapped under his weight.

The unnatural silence made him believe they weren't far ahead, certainly near enough to make the birds and small mammals wary. That didn't mean they hadn't veered to the southwest. Not to the southeast; Dorrance was unlikely to steer them any closer to the fence, where they might become visible to a ranch hand on horseback—or, although he didn't know it, to either Decker or Leon Cabrera, both riding hard to get back.

Not having seen the fence in a while, Boyd began to worry about whether he was still following behind his quarry. Dodging from one bit of cover to another, it would be easy to deviate from a direct line. He wished like hell Melinda could have left a few more breadcrumbs in her path. Or had she, and he'd missed them?

He stood still and carefully examined every bit of undergrowth within a wide radius. Relief hit when he saw the broken whippets on a clump of the ubiquitous common snowberry. Closing in on it, Boyd zeroed in on what he'd swear was a smear of blood higher than he'd expect on the rough trunk of the pine. Would she have reached up to break her fall?

His heart clenched. God—what if the blood was from a previous injury?

It couldn't be severe, he told himself, or she wouldn't still be walking—and still be able to leave him a signpost.

He shouldn't have doubted her.

He continued forward, a ghost slipping through the

dry forest. He didn't think the hay shed was far ahead. If that wasn't Dorrance's goal... Boyd didn't let himself dwell on the might or might not be. At the least, the old log building would provide excellent concealment.

A growl of sound had him freezing in place. Was that a voice? If so, it had to be Dorrance's.

Boyd slid from the cover of one tree to another, his every sense focused on the origin of that sound. He let himself move a little faster than he had been, knowing time had slowed in that way it had during action. He couldn't count on Gabe or Leon.

A faint squeak came to his ears next. Hinges. He increased his pace. Once Dorrance got Melinda and Chloe stashed deep in the shed, it might be impossible to take him out before he could pull his own trigger.

THE CABIN LOOKED like the kind of place Dorrance could have hidden the past few days. A small-paned window in the side couldn't have been washed in years—decades—but let Melinda see what she thought was a heap of hay bales.

"Open the door," he ordered.

No padlock. She turned the hasp and swung open one of the double doors that looked newer than the structure itself. The interior was murky, daylight not reaching far inside the limited opening. Yes, she'd been right about the hay, stacked high and nearly filling the entire space. If there'd once been walls or a loft, they'd been removed.

"Don't suppose anybody will be tossing out hay for the horses today," Dorrance said, sounding almost genial. He waved the gun toward her. "In."

"I know you don't want to kill a child," she said, as

steadily as she could manage. "Why don't you leave her out here?"

"So she can run for help?"

"She wouldn't have any idea where to go. She's only five."

"You know her."

Betraying that much had been a mistake.

She shrugged. "I recognize her. She saw her family murdered a couple of years ago. I have no idea if she's anywhere near recovered from that tragedy yet."

"Isn't that interesting?" Dorrance sounded pleased. "Won't take much effort to bring her to heel then, will it?"

Sickened but hiding it, Melinda said, "You've never gone for children."

He shrugged. "You're right, but she's useful. It's your fault I needed her."

"Oh, bull." She let him see her contempt—but not, she prayed, her terror. "You make your own decisions."

His eyes narrowed and he ground the barrel of the Glock into Chloe's temple again. "Now, do what I tell you!"

She'd irritated him, maybe rocked him slightly off balance. If he'd just turn the gun away from Chloe, Melinda would take any chance to jump him.

"Up," he snarled.

The hay had been stacked in a crude stairsteps. As she clambered atop the first level, two bales high, she heard tiny, scuttling sounds. Mice. Would he freak if one ran across his foot? Shoot at it?

Height gave her an advantage, didn't it? As she climbed atop the next stack, yet another two bales high, she crawled closer to the window. If there were any others, they'd been blocked by the hay. At least this one gave her some light.

The door swung closed behind her, until that small dirty window provided the only illumination, and it was murky.

He tossed Chloe atop the first level and then swung the gun to point at Melinda. "Sit down."

Oh, God, oh, God.

BOTH DOORS WERE CLOSED, although from inside Dorrance wouldn't be able to turn the hasp to secure them. Since they swung outward, he wouldn't have any way to lock them, either. Boyd didn't like the odds of that kind of frontal assault, though.

Fighting to suppress all emotion, needing right now to be a soldier, not a man who loved the kidnap victim, he evaluated the old cabin to determine his best option. He could wait until he had backup, but given that there was only one way in or out of the place, that might not help. And what would Melinda and Chloe suffer during that extra ten or fifteen minutes?

Would Melinda have any chance to make a move?

He couldn't depend on that, but had no doubt she'd fight. That scared him as nothing else could, but he also had faith she'd use her head.

That was the moment he saw movement inside the window. Not clear, but he knew it was Melinda. Standing? Kneeling? Hard to tell. A sinking feeling told him *this* might be his only good chance. But unable to see through the scum and dirt covering the glass increased the risk of him shooting the wrong person.

He closed his eyes for a moment, then holstered the handgun and lifted the rifle to evaluate distance. There wasn't even a breeze he had to account for. The moment he pressed his eye socket to the scope, the small square of the window leaped into focus.

He lowered the rifle and glanced around. If he could find a branch low enough to rest it on, he'd eliminate any possible tremor in his hands or arms.

He saw a jagged Y thrusting out from a pine where a branch had broken off. A little bit more of an angle to the window than from here, but not so much it should make a different.

Now to drag out some facsimile of the clearheaded and dispassionate patience that had once come so naturally to him in combat situations. If only Melinda could know he was here, waiting for that psycho to show his head in the window.

IF HE CONCENTRATED on her, he'd forget Chloe. Would the girl think to shove open the door and run? If she did, would he react fast enough to gun her down?

"Take off your shirt."

Melinda reluctantly peeled her shirt over her head, hating the creepy way Dorrance watched her.

"Now the bra." She wanted him to forget Chloe. If he climbed up here, she had a chance of wrestling his arm to one side or even kicking the gun from his hand. Or...

Boyd, Gabe Decker and Leon Cabrera were all army-trained snipers. Even Daniel was. If there was any chance at all that one of them had tracked her and Dorrance to this cabin, they might conceivably be able to take a shot through the window.

Dream on.

God help her. Moving very, very slowly, she reached behind her. "Not a chance."

He ate her up with lust-filled eyes, apparently assuming she'd obey. "How does it feel, filling in for Andrea and Erica? Sometimes they even enjoyed themselves, you know."

"I doubt that." Her voice shook despite her best effort. But with an abrupt movement, he hoisted himself up the stacked bales and over her, using his weight to press her down onto the scratchy bed of hay. He dropped the gun, but suddenly he had a wicked looking knife in his hand.

He was excited, mumbling something about her jeans—and maybe carving her up some, just to let her know how powerless she was. He hadn't pinned her arms, though, probably discounting her ability to fight back.

Out of the corner of her eye, she saw movement. Chloe. Not going for the gun, but slipping off the hay bales. Yes! Melinda would lose in a battle of strength with Dorrance, but she wouldn't submit without fighting back, and a distraction might give her a momentary advantage.

The door swung open. With a bellow of rage, he turned his head—and Melinda slammed the heels of her hands into his throat. She forced his head up, up, even as he lifted the knife.

And then his head exploded, just as she heard the crack of a rifle.

Sprayed with blood, soaked with it, she shoved him off her, seeing his body bounce down the stairsteps of hay bales.

Only a second later, Boyd appeared in the open doorway.

Epilogue

It was close to an hour before Boyd was free to go home. He'd fired the kill shot and had to account for his choices to Daniel, the first cop to show up. The few questions had been pro forma, though; Daniel wasn't seriously questioning Boyd's recitation of events or his decision to pull the trigger.

He wasn't the only one who was so relieved, his knees shook like a newborn foal's. Gabe held on to Chloe like he'd never let go again.

The paramedic had felt the lump on her head and gazed into her eyes with a scope before deciding to transport her to the hospital.

Gabe rose to his feet with the five-year-old looking tiny in his arms. "I'm going with her."

Nobody argued.

By that time Leon had walked Melinda to the house. She'd yanked her T-shirt over her head to mostly cover her bloody torso.

She sat at the kitchen table when he finally walked in, her fine-boned face marble white. She was clean, thank God, hair wet. He had to wonder how long she'd stayed in the shower. Whether she yet felt clean.

When she heard the back door open and saw him, she shoved back the chair and stood. He groaned, crossed the kitchen floor in three strides and yanked her into his arms. He knew exactly how Gabe felt. If he had his way, Melinda wouldn't leave his sight for weeks to come. He didn't care if she called him possessive.

"I've never been so scared in my life," he mumbled into that wet hair. "I love you. Realizing he had you—" The shudder was so powerful, he might have been ripped open by the San Andreas fault.

"I was afraid I'd never see you again," she whispered, making him realize she'd locked her arms around him and knotted the back of his shirt in her hands. "I told myself if only I could save Chloe—"

"You did. You did that." Around the lump in his throat, he told her the truth. "Unless he'd already killed her, I never had any doubt you'd find a way to set Chloe free."

Melinda lifted her head enough to see him. "Really?"

"Really." God, he sounded as if he'd used coarse sandpaper on his throat. Maybe all those internal screams had done the damage.

"I still feel gross."

"I'm sorry." Gentle didn't come easily right now; despite everything, he was aroused and she must know it. "If I could have gotten there sooner—"

Her eyes shimmered. "I thought you might be out there. I still can't believe you really were." Her breath hitched. This astonishingly strong woman was crying.

"You've never been able to count on anyone."

Damp or not, her eyes held his. "I was wrong about you."

"Not as wrong as I was about you."

"Oh, Boyd." She buried her face against his neck again, but she didn't sob, just maintained her grip on him. Her knuckles dug into his back.

He pressed his cheek to the top of her head, closed

his eyes and prepared to wait as long as he needed to. This was a different kind of patience, and he'd give her as much as she needed.

A long time later she sighed and released his shirt. She freed herself from his powerful embrace and studied him with those mesmerizing green-gold eyes.

"You…you really want me to stay here with you?"

"I want you to marry me. I want us to have kids when you're ready." He didn't so much as blink. "I swear I won't let you down."

Her smile was small and shaky. "I think you've proved yourself. I love you, too, you know. If I hadn't back then, you couldn't have hurt me so much."

"I will never forgive myself."

"I was just as dumb." Oddly, tears brimmed again in her eyes even as she took the step to close the distance between them again. "Do you know what I'd like?"

If it was an ice cream cone, or to be taken to the hospital to see Chloe and Kristina, he'd give her what she wanted even if it killed him.

"What?" he asked roughly.

"I'd like you to make love with me. I need to see *you* looking at me so I can wipe out any memory of *him*."

Incapable of words, Boyd snatched her up in his arms and carried her to the staircase. She wrapped her arms around his neck and held on for the ride.

* * * * *

CAVANAUGH JUSTICE: THE BABY TRAIL

MARIE FERRARELLA

To

Logan Asher Ferrarella Welcome to the world, little man
You are very loved

G-Mama

Cavanaugh Justice: The Baby Trail

Prologue

The heart-wrenching, terrified scream tore through the darkening fall night air. It would have instantly grabbed his attention, even if he wasn't part of the Aurora Police Department. He ran toward the sound even before he could completely identify it or pinpoint the source.

The next second, he knew. It was a child.

As the father of four, Captain Brian Cavanaugh was more than familiar with the sounds made by a screaming child. He was also able to differentiate between the kind of scream uttered in play and the kind that was uttered in pure, unadulterated terror.

This scream was the latter, reverberating with genuine grief-stricken distress.

As a newly promoted police captain, Brian Cavanaugh was keenly aware of sounds that were out of sync with the streets of Aurora. Streets he had sworn to serve and protect from the first moment the badge had been pinned on his chest.

Half a second after his brain registered the terrified scream, he made out the form of the sobbing little girl on the pavement. Eight, maybe nine years old, the distraught child was on her knees, her body rocking to and fro as she clutched the bleeding body of a man Brian presumed had to be her father, or perhaps her uncle.

The image immediately tore at his heart.

Coming off what had wound up being a very long double shift, Brian had just pulled up and gotten out of his vehicle at one of the few convenience stores in the recently incorporated city of Aurora. All he'd wanted to do was buy the half-gallon container of milk that his wife had asked him to get and go home.

They were out of milk again. His four kids went through the white liquid as if it were destined to quickly evaporate.

He had just finished parking his car when he'd heard the three shots ring out in quick succession. The pitiful scream and gut-wrenching cry echoed in the wake of the gunfire.

Brian was running toward the sound, his gun drawn, before he was even aware of doing it. When he saw the little girl, his first thought was that she was wounded. There certainly was enough blood for that.

The small blonde looked up at him. Tears streamed down her thin face.

"Help him," she begged. "Please help my daddy. He's all I've got."

A quick scan of the area told Brian that the person responsible for this dreadful scene was nowhere in the vicinity.

Brian dropped down to his knees, swiftly checking the bleeding man for vitals. After a moment, he located the faintest hint of a pulse.

Relieved, Brian pulled out his phone and called for an ambulance. All the while, he was keenly aware that the little girl on the ground was watching him with huge eyes, eyes that silently said she was praying for him to perform a miracle.

"This is Captain Brian Cavanaugh," he told the responding dispatcher who answered his call. Brian rattled off his shield number, identified the type of crime that had just transpired, gave the address and requested an ambulance be sent out immediately.

By then he saw the convenience store clerk stumbling to the front door. Looking as if he was in his late fifties, the clerk appeared barely able to push the door open. He was bleeding from a head wound and seemed on the verge of passing out.

"You might want to make that two ambulances," Brian quickly amended.

He felt small hands on his arm, holding on to him tightly and clutching him as if contact with this man who had driven up out of the darkness was the only thing that was keeping her father alive.

"ASAP," Brian stressed emphatically in a deep voice that brooked no argument as he slipped a comforting arm around the trembling, sobbing little girl. "It's going to be all right, honey. Your daddy's going to be all right," he assured her.

The future chief of detectives didn't know it then, but that was the night he became Korinna Kennedy's larger-than-life hero.

Chapter One

Looking back at that night, she had no idea where she would be if Brian Cavanaugh hadn't been there to call for an ambulance, one that had arrived just in time to save her father's life. If she were to take a guess, most likely she would have been lost somewhere within the deep recesses of the social services program. Probably bundled off into the foster care system.

Or worse.

To Korinna Kennedy, the larger-than-life Brian Cavanaugh was her guardian angel, hero and patron saint all rolled up into one.

Even at that young age, Kori had known that this police captain who'd come to her and her father's rescue hadn't had to do any of it. His job had ended with calling the crime in. Instead, he had remained with her throughout that whole terrifying night. He had rescued her, but more importantly, she was convinced that he was the reason her father hadn't died that night.

Sometimes, in her dreams, she could still see the whirling, flashing-red ambulance lights, still hear that wonderful, piercing siren sound that told her help was on its way.

For the first year, Korinna had relived the whole traumatic scene in her dreams every night, watching her father being loaded into the back of the ambulance. And rather than being moved aside by paramedics focused on just doing their job and saving a shooting victim's life, she'd been allowed to ride beside her father in the vehicle.

Again because of the man who had showed up out of the blue.

Brian had convinced the paramedics to allow her to go in the ambulance. He'd told them that she'd needed to go with her father. When one of the paramedics began to protest, Brian had told him that it was all right. He was taking full responsibility for the child's presence and planned to also accompany her.

At the time, she'd just thought of him as being the kindest man she had ever met, as well as her hero. She hadn't realized that the tall, extraordinary police officer was also the son of the chief of police, which was what gave him such an air of authority. To her, it was the man's deep, booming voice that made people obey him without question.

In her eyes, because of Brian, her father had gotten the care he'd needed quickly and she'd been there to see it all taking place.

Despite his waiting family and his police duties, the then police captain remained waiting with her in the hospital for what seemed like forever. He'd spent part of the time coaxing her to eat a sandwich he'd gotten from the cafeteria even though she'd politely refused at first, telling him she wasn't hungry. She'd finally eaten the sandwich because he'd said it would make him happy.

To partially distract her, Brian had told her about his daughter and three sons, as well as his many nephews and nieces.

And whenever there was any news about her father's

condition, he'd kept her abreast of that, too. He'd treated her, she felt, like an adult, not like a child. Years later, she'd found out that he'd kept certain facts from her in an effort to keep her from worrying.

And in the end, mercifully, everything with her father had turned out well. He'd survived that terrible night as well as the surgery that followed.

No one could ever tell Kori that it wasn't all due to the efforts of her newly found patron saint.

When she could no longer stay in her father's hospital room, the remarkable police captain had come to her rescue again. Leaving the hospital, there'd been no social worker, kindly or otherwise, to collect her and ferry her over to a group home. Instead, Kori had discovered, Brian had pulled some strings and rather than being taken to a bed in a shelter, she'd found herself going home with the man who had saved her father.

That one simple event wound up shaping her life to the present day.

Brian's diligence and kindness were the main reason she'd become a police officer and eventually a police detective. It was also why she was always so determined to go the extra mile, to go out of her way to help people, especially children.

Even after all these years, she could relate to those distraught children. She could see the haunted looks in their eyes and remember what it had been like to feel that way herself.

In her opinion, being cut off from all hope was just the worse thing possible.

It was also why she tried to be so upbeat even when everything seemed to take on such a hopeless bent. In her heart, Kori knew that, despite everything, hope could always be found. She knew that because, when she had been so beside herself, thinking that all was lost—her mother had died the year before and then her father had been shot before her eyes as he went to buy her something to eat with their last twenty dollars—someone had come from out of the blue to save them both. To make everything right when it seemed to her as if there was no more "right" to be had left in the world.

She remembered how afraid she had felt when Brian had brought her into his home. Afraid of being rejected and sneered at by his wife and children.

But that hadn't happened.

Brian Cavanaugh and his family had showed her nothing but kindness. Showed her that there was "right" in the world. And that it was not an anomaly, but the norm.

Every single member of his family, in their own way, had demonstrated it to her right from the very beginning. That sort of thing, in turn, had gone into building her foundation.

Brian's kindness to her had not been just some fleeting thing. It continued.

She was invited to stay with Brian and his family while her father was in the hospital, recovering from his surgery. And she'd remained there while he was in the convalescent home, undergoing physical therapy and, very slowly, growing stronger. Somehow, Brian had managed to find a program that wound up covering the expenses for that as well.

When her father was finally able to retake the reins of his life and unsteadily get back to his feet, it was Brian who'd found him a job within the police station in a civilian capacity.

She loved her father dearly, but Korinna was convinced that she loved Brian Cavanaugh as well. Not only that, she knew that the undying loyalty he had earned would have her following the man through the gates of hell.

After all, the man had given her back her father and her life. There was no way she could ever return the favor, but that did not stop Kori from continually trying.

"Going out to keep our streets safe, Kori?" William Kennedy asked his daughter just as she walked into the living room.

Both father and daughter had always been early risers. Technically, this was actually late for Kori. It was seven thirty on a Monday morning.

"You might not have noticed, but they pretty much keep themselves safe, Dad," Kori replied.

Aurora was known not just as the safest city of its size in California, but was currently inching its way into that position in the country as well.

"Oh, I've noticed," her father assured her. "Which is the reason I know I don't have to worry about you out there—although I still do," Bill confessed without any embarrassment.

They had had this conversation before. More than once. "Dad, you know I can't live in a bubble," she reminded him, then added with a shrug, "Stuff happens."

Bill Kennedy sighed, nodding his head. "I know, I know," he said, making his way into the kitchen. "But you're my little girl…" he began.

Kori turned as she leveled a look at the still handsome older man.

"Dad, I'm not a little girl," she reminded him patiently. "I'm twenty-five years old."

Bill waved his hand at the statement. "Kori, you

could be eighty-five years old. If I'm still around at that point, you'd still be my little girl," her father told her without any shame.

"Uh-huh." There was no point in arguing. Kori knew she wasn't going to win. Instead, she nodded her head and changed the subject. "You don't look as if you're ready to ride into work. Shouldn't you be dressed by now?" Korinna asked her father.

"And that's why you're such a good detective," Bill quipped. "And to answer your question, I'm not dressed yet because I'm going in later."

That stopped her in her tracks. Her father prided himself on never missing work, even when he wasn't feeling a hundred percent. It was just the way he was. Once close to being homeless at the lowest point in his life, he was grateful to be able to pay his own way. He never took that for granted. It was a point of pride for him.

"Something wrong, Dad?" Kori asked, concerned.

"Nothing is wrong, honey," he assured her in a patient voice. Having her worry about him was nothing new. "Just time for my annual exam, that's all. Nothing to worry about." And then he smiled at her. "Certainly beats the alternative."

"The alternative?" she questioned, not entirely sure what he meant by that.

"Yes. There was a time when it looked as if there wouldn't be any exams, annual or otherwise," he reminded her matter-of-factly.

Smiling at him, Kori bent over and kissed the top of her father's head, a head that still sported a very thick, healthy mane of dark brown hair, although it was now streaked with gray.

"Good point, Dad. Okay, I'll leave you to get to your exam. Give me a call when it's over, okay?" Kori requested.

He arched a brow. "Who's the parent here?" Bill deadpanned.

"We all know the answer to that one, Dad. I am," she told him, sporting a very straight face that told him she was only half kidding. "See you tonight," she said by way of parting.

Getting into the four-door vehicle she had left parked in the driveway, Kori buckled up. But rather than start the car, she sighed and glanced back toward the house.

It had taken hard work on her part to stop constantly worrying about her father, to stand back and allow him to reclaim his independence. It had taken a real effort to stop hovering over him, prepared to instantly jump right in to help whenever she thought he needed her.

That, too, was thanks to Brian's laidback manner and counseling.

Might as well get going, she mused.

Kori turned the key in the ignition and started up her car. With one last glance at the house, she pulled out of the driveway.

Not a day went by when she didn't think of the tall, distinguished, handsome Brian Cavanaugh as her own personal godsend.

The police chief helped her in so many countless ways. Different ways. There was no way she could possibly *ever* find to thank him.

The only way she knew how to even begin to express her gratitude was to do her job to the very best of her ability—and to never complain, no matter what the circumstances were or how frustrated she temporarily might feel.

That wasn't always easy.

Deciding to put her father's annual medical exam out of her mind—it did no good to worry—Kori drove to the police precinct.

First, though, she stopped at the nearby local coffee shop that had recently opened on the adjacent corner.

The precinct coffee wasn't all that bad as far as that went and, in a pinch, it did the trick. But the coffee offered at the coffee shop was so much better.

Kori stopped there to get what had quickly become her customary, exceptionally strong, container of black coffee. Actually, she ordered two containers. One for herself and one for her partner.

It wasn't until Kori was back in her car and buckled up, the newly purchased containers planted securely in the cup holders, and driving toward the police station, that she remembered she no longer *had* a partner to give the coffee container to.

Or at least, not the partner she usually supplied with coffee.

Detective Weldon Wills had decided to go into the private sector to work. Or rather, his wife had decided that he should enter the private sector. Consequently, her now former partner had handed in his gun and shield and given his notice.

Without the slightest warning, Friday had suddenly turned out to be his last day.

Kori was still reeling.

That also meant, she thought sadly, that sometime during this week, she was going to be meeting her new partner.

New partner.

The words echoed hauntingly in Kori's brain, taunting her.

She supposed she was in sincere denial. That was

why the fact that Wills would no longer be sitting at the desk facing hers had just conveniently slipped her mind, sinking to the bottom of the pool like a large lead brick.

If she were being honest, she would have to admit she didn't like change and had always had difficulty adjusting to it. It had been that way ever since her mother had died. Kori freely admitted that was why she had always liked hanging on to the status quo rather than embracing moving on, the way her father—and Brian—had always advised her to do.

Maybe she was being shortsighted, but in her eyes, there was absolutely nothing great about moving on. Nothing.

It was painful.

Before she realized it, Kori found herself pulling into her usual space in the parking lot at the rear of the police station. She had next to no recollection of the trip.

Turning off the ignition, Kori sat there for a moment, looking at the two containers of coffee. Jumbo-sized, one was more than enough to sustain her for the day, but for a number of reasons, she couldn't very well leave the other one in the car.

It had always been beyond her to waste anything, even something as nominal as a container of coffee, she thought as she got out of the car. She supposed the reason for that was rooted in the fact that she could vividly remember, in the days just before her father had been shot outside the convenience store, when he had lost his job and they'd been inches away from living out on the street.

Kori walked into the station. There certainly hadn't been any money to waste or to spend on things that weren't totally and absolutely necessary.

She supposed that she could easily find someone to

give the other container of coffee to. The hard part, she decided, pressing for the elevator, was deciding just who that someone would be.

Since joining the force, she had made it a point to get to know as many of the officers as possible, especially the Cavanaughs. They were Brian's family and so, by proxy, she felt that they were hers.

But there were just so many of them and she didn't want to just single one out arbitrarily. Not that any of them would care—other than to possibly tease her about it—but she would care.

She would definitely care.

Kori really wished that Wills was still there, just for another five minutes or so. Just so that she could hand him the coffee and talk to him one last time.

Maybe he'd stop by, she thought hopefully. Just one last time, to say final goodbyes, or pick up something he'd forgotten to take with him when he'd left the precinct on Friday.

Kori's mouth curved. Now she was really just grasping at straws.

What did it matter who she gave the large coffee to? The Cavanaughs, every single one of them, were not the kind of people to feel slighted by something so minor as being given a container of coffee—or *not* being given a container of coffee.

She was making a big deal out of nothing.

This was just her nerves getting the better of her, Kori thought with a sigh. Well, she had adjusted to Wills when she had partnered up with the man and, she reminded herself, he hadn't been the easiest man to get along with. If she did it once, she could certainly do it again.

And, in the interim, she could find some appreciative soul to give the extra coffee to.

Heading toward her desk, which was located in the middle of the Missing Persons' squad room, she suddenly slowed her fast pace. There was someone sitting at the desk that faced her own.

The broad-shouldered, dark-haired man looked vaguely familiar—

And yet he didn't, she thought.

Closer scrutiny told her she didn't know the man.

It wasn't unusual for people who were escorted into a squad room, looking to speak to a detective, to take a seat in order not to stand awkwardly out.

"Excuse me," Kori said to the man as she set down the two containers of hot coffee in the center of her desk, "May I help you?"

"No, but I think that, if all goes well, we could wind up helping each other," the stranger answered.

And then he flashed her what she could only term to be a wide, magnetic smile; the kind that totally reeled the recipient—in this case, her—in, and created butterflies in her stomach.

Chapter Two

It was the smile that did it.

The moment it appeared on the stranger's lips, curving the corners of his mouth, the warm smile seemed to instantly light up the entire room. It identified the man sitting at what had become, as of this morning, the "unoccupied" desk.

The man seated there was definitely a Cavanaugh, Kori thought.

He had to be.

While every member of that extensive family could easily lay claim to deep integrity as well a number of the same physical traits, the one attribute they all seemed to have in common, at least the ones she had met so far, was that incredible heart-stopping smile.

Granted, she knew that she hadn't met them all. But as mystifyingly improbable as it might seem, all the Cavanaughs she *had* met possessed the same sort of killer smile. One that not only seemed to light up a room, but instantly generate a warmth within the soul of the recipient.

Conversely, the steely look a Cavanaugh leveled at someone could send a chill down the person's spine. It conveyed the message that this was someone *not* to be taken lightly, discounted or messed with.

However, Kori had learned not to jump to conclusions, even if those conclusions seemed to be all but inevitable. So, for now, Brian Cavanaugh's protégé proceeded with caution.

"Let me guess," she said as she slipped into her seat, facing this new person with the incredible magnetic smile. "You're my new partner."

The man at the desk against hers inclined his head as he nodded to himself. "The chief told me you were sharp as well as quick." With that, he half rose in his seat, extending his hand toward her as he introduced himself. "I'm Brodie Cavanaugh," he said. "But I suspect you already knew that."

She felt her pulse jump. There was that smile again. She could swear she could almost feel it burrowing straight into her chest, spreading out and settling in.

Kori did her best to ignore it or, in lieu of that, to sublimate it. If she didn't somehow manage to dampen its effects, she instinctively knew she wouldn't have a prayer of being able to work through any caseload that came along or to even be able to attempt to think clearly.

His smile was *that* potent.

This one was good-looking enough to have his own squadron of groupies following him around wherever he went. He probably did.

"The last name," she admitted, referring to what he'd just said about feeling that she already knew him. "But not the first. Just where are you within the family dynamics?" Kori asked, quickly adding, "Not that it actually matters when it comes to our working relationship."

Brodie nodded, a hint of his killer smile surfacing again. "Good to know," he murmured and then told her, "But if you're curious—and to answer your question— Finn's my brother."

"Finn," she repeated, her mind quickly reviewing all the members she had been introduced to at the various times Andrew Cavanaugh had thrown parties under one pretext or another. These days she didn't have time to attend them any more, but she had initially. "That would make you…" Her voice trailed off and then she happily declared, "Donal's son," as she identified Brodie's place within the family.

She noted that the smile was back—and widening. Was it her imagination, or was it growing warmer in here?

"Damn, you are good," Brodie told her. "There are times that I can't keep who's who straight myself. It was hard *before* Uncle Andrew stumbled across our branch of the family. After he brought everyone together for the most mind-boggling meet-and-greet, I feel that absorbing all that information as to who's who is just about impossible."

There was a spark of admiration in his eyes as he looked at her.

Kori could see that happening. Because she had been so very anxious to assimilate *everything* there was to know about her white knight, she had made it a point to learn about Brian Cavanaugh's family as well—and there was more than the usual amount of information.

The way that had come about was because Brian Cavanaugh's great-grandfather and his great-grandmother had divorced back when that sort of occurrence was far from the norm. When a divorce created a dark stain on the family tree.

Even so, the young couple had split up and never looked back. They'd each taken a son and gone their separate ways.

Consequently, Brian's father, Seamus, because of

his young age, quickly lost track of his little brother, Murdoch. It wasn't until decades later that Brian's older brother, Andrew, Aurora's former chief of police, had learned about the divorce. He, in turn, had gone hunting for his grandmother. She had hidden her trail well and discovering what had happened to her hadn't been easy.

Refusing to accept defeat, Andrew'd kept at it and finally found out what had happened to his father's younger brother.

Sadly, he'd learned that his grandmother had passed away, as had Murdoch. But not before Murdoch had gotten married and fathered three sons and a daughter. Those offspring, Andrew's cousins, all went on to have children of their own.

And that, Andrew liked to say, was when the story turned unique. Oddly enough, Murdoch's children and grandchildren had all either gone into law enforcement within the city where they lived or into some branch *affiliated* with law enforcement.

Once Andrew had found this heretofore "lost" branch of the family, the members had slowly begun to migrate to Aurora. Drawn by what seemed like some sort of a powerful attraction to either be with this new branch of the family or, at the very least, to meet with them and decide whether or not moving to Aurora seemed like the right thing to do.

Eventually, they'd decided that it was and every one of them settled in Aurora.

The new and old members of the family would often joke that they had enough relatives to populate their own entire police force—and very possibly their own town.

"Not impossible," Kori told Brodie, commenting on his assertion that learning everyone's name was difficult. "Just kind of challenging." Without missing a beat, Kori changed the subject. "You transferred from another department." It wasn't a question.

He was new to the Missing Persons department and she'd just assumed he'd had to have transferred from another section within the police department.

"But nobody told me which one," Kori admitted. Then added, "I barely knew that Wills was leaving."

It occurred to her that Brodie might not know who Wills was. She didn't want to start out on the wrong foot and have him think she was taking things for granted— or worse, that she was rubbing his nose in the fact that she knew things and he didn't.

"Wills was—"

"Your last partner," Brodie interjected. "Yeah, I know." Because he didn't want her thinking he had inside information—that wouldn't be the best way to start their working relationship—he said, "At least, I'm assuming that was who you were talking about. Nobody really told me anything. I just applied for a transfer from Homicide on Friday, thinking it would be a long process and that I should at least start by setting it in motion. I was surprised when I was told that one had just opened up that morning in Missing Persons."

Half a dozen questions filled her head, jockeying for position and searching for answers. "Do you mind if I ask why?" Kori asked then realized that her question might have come across as ambiguous, so she elaborated. "Why you applied for a transfer from Homicide, not why one just opened up in Missing Persons. I already know why that happened."

Brodie flashed a smile at her again. This one was just as lethal as the last one—and the one before that.

She would have to learn how to block the effects of that smile. There were just no two ways about it.

"That's easy enough to answer," Brodie told her. "I have to admit that the sight of all those dead people was really beginning to get to me. I want to be able to help people *before* they've gone stone cold." He shrugged philosophically. "Working on a case after the fact might help the victim's family feel as if they're getting some sort of closure, but personally I joined the force to help *save* people, not just bring their killers to justice."

When he saw her smile, he couldn't help wondering if the reason he had just given her came across as being entertaining.

"What?" Brodie asked.

Kori shook her head. "Nothing," she murmured. Then, because she saw he was waiting for some sort of an answer, she told him, "It just sounds like the same reason why I joined the force."

Actually, she had joined the force because she wanted to be like her hero, but the reasons that Brodie cited had been her secondary reasons. That was also why she had opted for the division she was in once she was able to request a division assignment.

Listening to her, Brodie nodded. "Then I'd say that we are going to work well together." Her new partner seemed to take full measure of her, his eyes washing over her. "Mind if I ask you another question?"

Kori braced herself to be on the receiving end of any one of a number of questions from "the new guy," ranging from how strict their lieutenant was to how to most effectively get around protocol. Those were all things that Wills had wanted to know when he had come into the squad.

Instead, Brodie nodded at the two containers she had placed on her desk when she had sat down.

"Are you planning on drinking both of those?" he asked.

That caught her off guard.

"What?"

She looked over to where Brodie had nodded and realized that she had forgotten all about the coffee containers once she had seen Brodie. Kori replayed his question in her mind.

"Oh no." Wrapping her hand around the bottom of the container closest to Brodie, she pushed it in his direction. "This one's for you," she told him, adding, "I hope you like it black. If you don't, there's what passes for sweetener in the break room."

Taking possession of the container, Brodie smiled his thanks. "I take it that the coffee isn't from the break room."

She willed her pulse to settle down as she slowly drew in a deep breath. "Oh lord, no. I wouldn't do that to you on your first day as part of the squad." She nodded at the container between them. "This is from the coffee shop that's across the street," she told him. "It might not be the world's greatest coffee, but it definitely is head and shoulders above anything you'll find in the break room or living in the vending machine."

"'Living in'?" he echoed, arching one eyebrow quizzically.

"Sometimes the vending machine coffee tastes as if it had a life of its own," she warned him.

He decided to leave that alone for now. Instead, he focused on the container in his hand. "And you bought this for me?" he asked, nodding at the coffee.

She was about to say yes, then thought better of it.

The truth was always the best way to go. "Full disclosure, it was my turn to buy coffee for my partner and me. I honestly forgot that Friday was his last day here," she confessed.

Brodie removed the lid on the container and set it aside. "Were you and your partner close?" he asked her as the steam from the coffee seeped into his senses for a moment.

She wouldn't have exactly called Wills and her close, so she diplomatically replied, "Well, we worked well together."

Brodie processed the information. "I'll do my best not to disappoint you. So how much do I owe you for the coffee?" he asked, pausing as he took his first sip.

Brodie drew in his breath sharply as he felt a jolt shoot through him as the all but solid dose of caffeine kicked in.

"You don't owe me anything. Call it a Welcome to Missing Persons gift," Kori told her new partner.

She watched as Brodie's smile formed beneath the container as he took in another, somewhat larger, sip of the inky coffee. His green eyes seemed to penetrate right into her as they shone with humor above the rim of the container.

"On behalf of my now fully awake consciousness," he told Kori, "I would like to offer my sincerest thank-you."

It took Kori less than a second to find her tongue, but, lost in the glow of his smile, it was a second she was acutely aware of.

"No need for thanks. You get to buy the coffee next week." Kori did her best to sound matter-of-fact and removed.

"Sounds fair to me." Brodie took another deep swig,

waiting for the coffee to wind itself through his system. "Where did you say you bought this?"

"The shop is called Morning Wake-up Call," she told Brodie. "The coffee shop is located on the corner across the street from the precinct. You can't miss it. By eight thirty, there's usually a line of police officers feeding into it. There has been ever since the shop opened up. Most of the officers swear by it. These days the only reason anyone drinks what's in the vending machines around here is if they can't get away or are too busy to spare the time to hotfoot it to the coffee shop."

"Seems to me someone should look into whatever it is that they're using to brew the coffee and put that stuff into the coffee machines around here." He finished off the rest of the coffee in his container. "I guarantee you that productivity would go up."

"Well, you're a Cavanaugh. Why don't you suggest it?" she told Brodie.

But her new partner shook his head. "Technically, I'm a new Cavanaugh," he told her. "I'm not into making changes at the moment. Right now, I'm into being part of the team until I get more entrenched in the family."

She looked at him uncertainly. "Hold it," she told him. "You're serious? You're actually 'new'?" That would explain why she hadn't seen him around earlier.

He laughed softly. "Well, not exactly 'new,'" he clarified. "I should have just said new to the Aurora police force. Before that, I worked on the force in Littleton."

"Let me guess, you worked the Homicide Division there?" she asked him.

He grinned. She *was* paying attention. "Very good, you *were* listening. When I applied to join the Aurora police department here, they put me into the exact department I was initially working in the last city I lived in. But, like I said, I really wanted a change."

Kori nodded. "Because you were tired of dealing with dead bodies." Thinking about that now, she had to admit that was rather a sensitive reaction on Brodie's part. In her book, that spoke well of him.

"Nothing like a dead body to make me feel helpless," he told her.

"Certainly can't argue with that," Kori responded.

He nodded, taking in the last remaining swig of his coffee. "I've got a feeling we're going to work well together."

Kori studied him for a long moment over her own container, having only taken a few token sips so far. She could only hope that the good-looking man wasn't just blowing smoke. Just because the other Cavanaughs she had met and interacted with were men and women of integrity didn't necessarily mean that they all were.

In her experience, a lot of good-looking men just depended on their looks to get them through any situation.

Still, she gave him the benefit of the doubt. "Might be a while before we find out. We don't have as much crime here in Aurora as they do in other cities—except, I suppose, when it comes in comparison to small towns, of course."

"That might be a pleasant change. But that's okay. I'm good at kicking back," he told her.

Just then, the door to the lieutenant's office at the rear of the squad room opened and Lieutenant Dan Rafferty peered out. He quickly scanned the area for a moment. Recognition set in when he saw who he was looking for.

"Hey, Kennedy, Cavanaugh," he called, beckoning. "Come into my office."

Kori pushed her chair back from her desk and rose. "Guess he wants to say hello."

"That didn't quite sound as if that was part of meet-and-greet," Brodie observed. Rising to his feet, he gestured ahead of him. "After you," he told Kori.

She smiled to herself as she led the way to their lieutenant's office. At least the man was polite.

Chapter Three

There were rumors that once upon a time, in his early twenties, Lieutenant Daniel Rafferty had been a track-and-field star and had even entertained the idea of competing in the US Summer Olympics. But that was twenty-four years ago.

Looking at the man now, it hardly seemed possible. Rather than move with the ease of a gazelle, Rafferty lumbered back into his office. Reclaiming the seat behind his desk seemed to require a lot of effort on his part.

The body that sank into the upholstery all but spilled out on the sides, seeming to cover every available inch of space. These days Rafferty was always either just going on a diet or just coming off one, the latter motivated by his frustration in not being able to achieve the weight goals he had set for himself.

There was more than a little envy in the lieutenant's dark brown eyes as he scrutinized the young man who had just been sent to join his department.

Kori had the very distinct impression that the words Rafferty uttered to the new man who was just joining his squad weighed rather heavily on his tongue. It seemed difficult for the lieutenant to interact with someone whose physical fitness was an acute reminder of just how much he had let himself go over the years.

After gesturing toward one of the empty chairs in front of his desk, the lieutenant told Brodie, "I've heard good things about you from Captain Jeffers, Cavanaugh. He sounded as if he was really sorry to see you go." Rafferty studied Brodie's face closely for a moment. "Are you sure you want to be here?"

"I'm very sure, sir," Brodie sincerely assured the man.

Rafferty nodded. For several seconds, there was nothing but silence in the room, as if the lieutenant was thinking over his next words. And then, as was his habit, the squad leader sucked in his breath before speaking. "All right then, consider yourself temporarily assigned to this department, Cavanaugh."

That didn't sound quite right to Kori. "Temporarily, sir?" she questioned.

The lieutenant appeared annoyed at having to explain himself. "Well, it should go without saying that if, for some reason, Cavanaugh here doesn't work out, he'll have to go back to his original department." Rafferty narrowed his eyes until they were all but dark slits. "Cavanaugh or not, there is no display of undo favoritism in my department," he told Kori and then he shifted his steely gaze to the newly transferred detective. "Is that understood, Cavanaugh?"

"Yes, sir," Brodie answered, his expression totally unreadable.

Brodie was apparently taking this briefing in stride, Kori thought, but she took offense for him. Rafferty was unduly flexing his muscles. In her opinion, his words could have been more welcoming, especially given Brodie's connection to several of the people in high places of authority, both past and present. If she was the one on the receiving end of this so-called "first meeting," she would have taken offense at the less than hidden meaning in the lieutenant's pep talk. In other words, Rafferty was saying that he intended to watch Cavanaugh like a hawk and if he took one misstep, then Cavanaugh or not, the detective would be out of there.

Once again, Rafferty sucked in his breath and then said, "All right, with that out of the way, looks as if you might just get a chance to prove your mettle, Cavanaugh. Five minutes ago, dispatch got a 9-1-1 call from Aurora General Hospital. According to the caller, a newborn was just reported kidnapped from a mother's room in the maternity ward." Rafferty shrugged, as if not sure just what he believed to be true. "It just might all turn out to be some sort of miscommunication, but just to be on the safe side, why don't you two go and check it out?" the lieutenant suggested. He gestured at the two detectives as if they were joined at the hip.

Kori was instantly on her feet. This sort of thing was the reason why she had joined the police department in the first place. To protect the children who couldn't protect themselves. Who was more defenseless than a newborn?

"Yes, sir," she declared.

Rafferty barely acknowledged her. Instead, he was looking at the newest addition to his department. "Let me know what, if anything, you find, Cavanaugh," he ordered the man.

"I will, Lieutenant," Brodie promised. He waited until they left the lieutenant's office and then looked at Kori. "I'm sorry."

The apology seemed to have come out of nowhere. Kori looked at him. "For what?"

"The lieutenant usurped you." Brodie sounded genuinely sorry that had happened. "I don't think he meant to do that. He was probably just focused on testing what I'm made of. You know, wanting to see if I can really measure up and be part of the team I was 'auditioning' for."

She stopped walking for a moment so that Brodie could hear what she had to say more easily. "I didn't take any offense that Lieutenant Rafferty appeared to hand the lead to this case over you if that's what you're worried about—but thanks for the apology," she told him. "However, you didn't have to worry. I don't have any ego issues here. Especially since there's an infant's welfare concerned."

Brodie took in what she said. "Even so, I know that the case should be handled by you. I'm here to learn and to help," he told her. "Not to try to take over."

Well, that would certainly make him different from her last partner, Kori thought. Until just now, Kori had come to the conclusion that there were some men who couldn't help themselves. For those men, there was just this bone in their body, this mindset that made them inclined to just commandeer the reins of any given investigation.

Her eyes met Brodie's.

"I believe you," she told him. "Now, let's get over there. Maybe there's been some strange, simple mix-up at the hospital that can easily be resolved and that no one actually kidnapped a newborn."

Brodie studied her profile. "Do you really think that's the case?"

She felt as if he were looking straight into her soul. She sighed. "No, not really," she told him. "But I can hope."

When they got to the rear of the precinct, she instinctively headed to where her car was parked. It took her less than five steps to realize that Brodie wasn't walking next to her. He had turned toward his own vehicle.

"Hey, Cavanaugh," she called out and then waited for him to turn to her. When he did, he appeared surprised that she wasn't with him. They had each just assumed that the other was following in their wake. "I think it would make more sense if we drove in one car," she told him.

He picked up on her inflection. She meant in *her* car.

Obligingly, Brodie pivoted and headed for her.

He flashed a rueful smile. "Looks like there are a few things we still have to work out."

Well, that was nice of him. He didn't get his back up over that. She was liking her new partner more and more.

"Looks like," Kori agreed. "Since you just admitted that you're relatively new to Aurora, and heaven knows I've lived in Aurora all my life, I thought in the interest of getting to the hospital quickly, I should drive."

Brodie nodded, his dark hair falling into his eyes. He was amenable to having her behind the wheel. "Makes sense to me," he agreed.

Kori had to admit that she had been prepared for some semblance of an argument. The only reason she was the one to drive when she'd partnered with Wills was that, occasionally, the latter liked to let his mind wander.

Brodie, however, seemed inclined to go with the flow. Maybe this *would* work out after all. This job was hard enough at times without having to worry about jockeying for position and possibly offending a fragile ego.

"So," he said, picking up the conversation where they

had left off as he got into the passenger seat and buckled up, "does this mean that you really think that this *is* a kidnapping?" he asked her as Kori started up her vehicle.

"What makes you think it isn't?" she asked, curious as to his reasoning.

"Well, from what I've heard, hospital procedures have changed drastically from the days that people could just walk into the nursery and walk off with a newborn under some pretext. Security has certainly tightened, mother and newborn ID bracelets are constantly being double-checked and most important of all, nurseries have pretty much gone the way of the dinosaur. Now the baby is in a bassinette in the mother's hospital room. Instant bonding from the first moment," he concluded.

That was pretty astute for a bachelor, she couldn't help thinking.

Kori spared a glance in her partner's direction and saw that Brodie was smiling to himself. "What?" she prodded.

"I was just thinking that arrangement pretty much does away with the new mother's illusion that she's going to get anything resembling a full night's sleep anytime in the foreseeable future," he answered.

She laughed softly. "I think that pretty much is a given when she decides to become a mother," Kori pointed out.

A thought came to him out of left field. "What if she didn't decide?"

She wasn't sure what he was getting at and didn't want to jump to conclusions. "What do you mean?"

"What if becoming a mother was something that

happened totally by accident? An unintended conse-
quence of one moment of wild, unplanned passion?"

He certainly had a point, she thought, but she wasn't
about to get philosophical about this. That path was
too involved.

"We're not here to debate how she became a mother.
We're here to find out if her baby was taken, and if
so, when, how and by who," she specified. Of course,
there were other questions, she thought, but for now
just these would do.

"You're the boss," Brodie told her.

She slanted a look in his direction at the next light.
He seemed way too complacent. "Are you trying to
stroke my ego, Cavanaugh?"

"No, just stating a simple fact," he told her without
displaying any sort of revealing emotion on his part.
"Like I said," he continued, "I'm here to absorb and
learn."

It sounded almost too good to be true. "And you
have no problem whatsoever taking directions from a
woman," she pressed. "A younger woman," she specified since that might have made a difference in this
case.

"I take it you *are* familiar with the Cavanaughs?"
he asked.

She didn't know if he was feeding her lines or if he
was serious, but she answered him as if he were asking
a legitimate question. "Of course I am—and I figure
you already know that."

Brodie didn't answer her one way or another. Instead, he made the point he was trying to get across
to her. "Then you know that my family, especially my
extended family, has a lot of strong-willed, not to mention really stubborn, women in it. Actually, to be com-

pletely honest, I don't think there *is* such a creature as a mild-mannered Cavanaugh female. In our family, every single one of them is stubborn as hell. I'm also proud to say that they all know what they're doing. So no, I have no problem observing how you work and learning from you. Any other questions?"

"I'll be sure to ask them when they come up," Kori replied.

Making a left turn in the middle of a side street that came up, Kori followed the zigzag path that took her into the hospital parking lot. That, in turn, provided parking in front of the emergency room. Following that was a small parking lot directly in front of the hospital entrance. In the distance, a parking structure afforded additional spaces—five levels of them—for people coming to the hospital for the purpose of visiting patients as well as to avail themselves of the various diagnostic tests the hospital offered.

Kori parked directly in front of the hospital's main front entrance. Pulling up her handbrake, she declared out of habit, "We're here."

Brodie wondered if her last partner was a simpleton. "I kind of gathered that from the sign they had right out front that said Aurora General Hospital."

"Well, I see that nothing gets by you," Kori deadpanned.

"I do my best," he answered in an identical tone. And then, simultaneously, the two new partners grinned at one another. If there was any tension, it was laid to rest.

Brodie waited until she got out of her vehicle, then walked with Kori to the entrance.

The moment they entered the hospital, Kori got the distinct feeling that the reported kidnapping had definitely not been made in error. There was chaos everywhere. The tension in the air was so thick, it seemed to make even breathing difficult.

Her eyes on the front desk, Kori approached the distraught-looking woman sitting there. Taking out her ID, Kori held it up for the woman's benefit.

"Detectives Kori Kennedy and Brodie Cavanaugh." She nodded at Brodie. "We're here about the newborn reportedly kidnapped from her mother's room."

The receptionist, a grandmotherly woman who appeared almost beside herself, sighed with what seemed like palatable relief.

"Oh, thank goodness!" she cried.

Rather than telling them where to go to speak to the bereft new mother, the receptionist was immediately on her feet and making her way around her desk. Flustered, she walked *into* the desk once before managing to clear the area and finally get out into the aisle.

"Nothing like this has *ever* happened here before. At least, not since I've come to work at Aurora General." She considered her words, then added for clarification sake, "But probably never."

"Miss, you need to take a deep breath," Brodie advised calmly.

The fact that he had addressed her as "Miss" instead of "Ma'am" put the woman in a more receptive, calmer frame of mind. The hospital receptionist did as he said, taking in a deep breath and then slowly releasing it.

Kori noted that the older woman actually seemed grateful, but that obviously didn't diminish the horror she felt regarding what had happened.

"The maternity ward is on the fifth floor," she told the two people she felt were here to rectify a terrible wrong. "I'll take you up there."

"That really isn't necessary. We can certainly get there on our own," Kori said.

However, the look on the woman's pale face told her that she was wrong. "Oh, but it *is* necessary," she declared in a quaking voice.

Brodie's eyes met Kori's and she could see that he was telling her they shouldn't contradict the woman. It was obvious that the receptionist would feel better if, in her mind, she'd somehow contributed to the solution of this heinous problem.

"Then please," Kori encouraged the older woman, "lead the way."

She saw Brodie smile his approval. She had no idea why that would make her feel good.

But it did.

Chapter Four

The hospital receptionist, who introduced herself midway as Amelia Saunders, was still talking nonstop as she walked into the elevator with Kori and Brodie. Rather than abate, her babbling grew more pronounced as they rode up in the elevator.

"Security put the entire hospital on lockdown," she told the detectives. "Belatedly, I know, but better late than never, right?" The question was followed by a high-pitched, nervous laugh.

"Do you know any of the details about how the baby was taken from her mother's room?" Kori asked Amelia. Since she had to listen to the woman go on and on, she felt that she might as well channel her toward hopefully useful information.

Confronted with an actual question, Amelia abruptly stopped talking. Instead, she raised her hands, palms up, toward the elevator ceiling as she shrugged. Her eyes appeared huge as she answered. "All I know was what I heard. One minute the baby was in her bassinette, the next, she wasn't." Amelia shook her head helplessly. If there was a theory as to how the abduction had been pulled off, no one had let her in on it.

"Were all the surveillance cameras checked?" Brodie asked.

"No one tells me anything," the woman lamented as the elevator came to a stop and the doors opened up. They had reached the fifth floor.

It was on the tip of Kori's tongue to ask the receptionist if she had made any inquiries about the cameras and actually *asked* if anything had been caught on video, but she had a feeling that both questions would lead nowhere. The woman was completely caught up in wringing her hands and proclaiming how in the dark she was about the whole situation.

So instead, Kori merely nodded her head, as if sympathizing with the receptionist and how locked out of everything she felt she was. She just sensed that it was simpler that way.

The sooner they got to question the mother, Kori felt, the better. Maybe they would get somewhere there. At least, she could hope so.

As if reading her their minds, Amelia proclaimed, "That poor mother's room is this way."

It was an unnecessary declaration. Anyone would have suspected that something out of the ordinary was happening and it was all centered around room 509.

There were a lot of concerned-looking people coming and going, not to mention the sound of high-pitched, anguished crying that emanated from that room.

Kori glanced at Brodie. "Well, it looks like this is the right room," she said just before she braced herself and entered.

Brodie made no comment in response, but Kori could all but feel her new partner's smile, resigned but still very much in play, slipping its way under her skin.

The next second, Kori's heart went out to the woman in the hospital bed.

Rose Williams's flushed face was in direct contrast

to her white hospital gown. Her eyes were red-rimmed. She had obviously been crying and there were tear tracks on her cheeks. The petite, gaunt young woman definitely looked worn out and right now appeared older than her age, which, according to the information that they had been given, was twenty.

When they entered the single-care unit, the bereft young mother had her arms wrapped around herself and she was rocking to and fro in her bed. The action was obviously intended to somehow comfort herself, but it wasn't working.

Just then, the young woman began talking. At first Kori thought the words were meant for them, but then she realized that the infant's mother was saying the words to no one in particular. Her agitation increased with every single syllable she uttered.

"It's my fault. All my fault. My fault that my baby girl's gone," she cried.

"Ms. Williams…" Kori began in a soft, kind voice, trying to get the young woman's attention. It took her two more attempts before she managed to finally succeed. The bereft mother looked up at her with wide, frightened eyes. "Ms. Williams, I'm Detective Kennedy and this is Detective Cavanaugh," Kori said, introducing herself as she drew closer to the young woman's bed. "We're here to investigate your daughter's abduction." She held up her badge and her identification for the mother's benefit.

The expression on the tear-stained face was blank, as if the distraught new mother was being addressed in a foreign language and none of it was registering.

And then, slowly, the words Kori had said seemed to penetrate. Rose took in a deep, shaky breath, as if that could somehow help her cope with the ramifications of this terrible situation.

"She's gone because of me," the young woman cried again. The look in her eyes was wild, as if she didn't know where to go, what to think. "My baby's gone because of me."

"Why would you say that?" Brodie asked. He had been prepared to let Kori do all the talking, but in the face of all this anguish, he'd been unable to maintain his silence any longer.

"Because I said I didn't want her," Rose answered, her voice breaking at the end of her sentence. "But I do. I do want her," the woman cried. She looked wildly from one detective to the other. "I was just scared," she explained, sobbing.

Any second, the woman was going to start pulling out her hair and ripping her clothes, Kori thought. She tried to redirect the young mother's attention by getting Rose to talk to them. "Scared? Scared of what?"

Rose's breathing was labored. "Scared of dropping her. Of doing everything wrong. Of not being good enough to raise a baby." She searched their faces for some sign that they understood. "But now I'm even more scared that I'll never seen her again," she wailed, her voice cracking again as she tried to suppress the overpowering fear that threatened to literally swallow her whole. She was trembling now, unable to keep her body still.

"Every new mother—and new father—is afraid of messing up. It's only natural, and it goes with the territory," Brodie assured the young woman who seemed to be completely unraveling right before their eyes.

"But I was going to give her up, give her away, as if she was a sweater I didn't want. I thought she would be better off without me." Her voice dropped as she added, "And I'd be better off without her." There was self-loathing in her voice. "Except once I saw her, I realized that I couldn't go through with it. I mean, I knew I wasn't going to be the best mother or even what she needed," Rose protested, "but heaven help me, I fell in love with that tiny face. And now she's gone."

She raised her tear-filled eyes to look at the two detectives, silently pleading for their help to rectify this awful turn of events. "Please find her. Please find my baby."

"We'll do our best." Kori's vague words were immediately swept away by her partner's far more forceful promise.

"We'll find your baby," Brodie told her, drawing closer to the tearful, distraught young woman. He was rewarded with a look from the mother that all but canonized him where he stood.

"I'm counting on you," Rose told him, emotion quaking in her voice.

"When was the last time you saw your daughter?" he asked the young woman, hoping he could get an answer without having her break down on them again.

The question seemed to throw Rose for a moment as she attempted to think. It was obvious that she was having trouble keeping events straight in her mind. Everything appeared to be a jumble right now.

Finally, she was able to formulate an answer.

"At breakfast. I saw her at breakfast," Rose declared, nodding her head as if agreeing with herself. Her eyes met Kori's then swept back to Brodie. "I was finally able to eat something—I've been too upset to eat these last couple of days," she added. "And then I guess I must have fallen asleep. I shouldn't have."

"And do you remember where your daughter was when you fell asleep?" Kori asked. She was fairly certain she knew the answer to that, but she wanted to hear Rose say it.

As Rose pointed toward the bassinette, her hand was trembling. Looking at the empty, tiny, enclosure was a painful reminder that the baby had been stolen from her by any one of a number of people, all of whom she had felt she could trust.

Until now.

"She was right there." Rose looked at the detectives, stricken. "I can still hear the sound of her breathing. It was such a peaceful sound, I guess it lulled me to sleep," she told them ruefully. "I should have realized that something was wrong when it stopped. The silence should have woken me up," she cried, her voice growing frantic again. "Why didn't I wake up? She was my baby, I should have been in tune to her, to her sounds," she declared as if she felt it was some sort of a given. Rose's eyes moved back and forth between the two detectives, searching for confirmation of her omission. "Right?"

"Not necessarily," Kori answered, doing her best to be tactful. "This was all new to you." Kori tried to move on before Rose had another outburst. Having the baby's mother blame herself wasn't going to help them with the investigation. She looked at the tray with empty dishes. "Was the tray here when you fell asleep?"

Rose stared at Kori, a bewildered expression on her face, as if the simple question was too much for her to comprehend.

"Think, Rose," Kori coaxed. "Whatever you can piece together will help us find your daughter. Now, was the tray still in the room when you fell asleep?"

Rose's eyes moved from side to side, as if that would

somehow help her think and remember. When she finally spoke, the young woman didn't sound very confident. "I guess so."

Brodie turned to the receptionist. Amelia was still hanging around, like someone observing an accident unfolding and just couldn't get herself to turn away. Amelia dropped her eyes, as if suddenly embarrassed at being caught this way.

Brodie made it a point to keep any accusation out of his voice. "Who would have collected the breakfast tray, Amelia?" he asked.

This time there was no hesitation when she answered. "One of the orderlies would have come in. It's their job to collect the tray," she declared.

Brodie nodded, taking in the information. "Is there just one orderly who does that for every floor?" he asked the woman.

Amelia looked pleased at the question, as if relieved that there was another one she could answer. Her smile entered her eyes. "Yes, as far as I know."

Kori assimilated the information. Could be something, could be nothing, she thought. "All right. Where can we find him?"

"Her," Amelia corrected. "The orderly who works this floor is a woman. Edith Woods," the receptionist recalled belatedly. "She specifically requested this floor." Amelia remembered. "She said she likes to work on the maternity floor."

Kori exchanged glances with Brodie. She could see they were both thinking the same thing. Maybe there was a reason why this Edith Woods had initially requested to work the maternity floor.

"And where is this Edith now?" Brodie asked the receptionist.

Amelia looked over her shoulder, as if visualizing the space she was going to tell them about. "Security has everyone in the break room, questioning them until the police got here," the receptionist told them, happy to be able to share that information.

"Well, the police are here," Kori told her, spreading her hands as if to underscore the fact. "Where is the break room?"

Amelia jolted, as if she was suddenly waking up. There was almost a rueful expression on her face. "Oh, it's this way. I can take you to it."

"Please," he requested.

"And you're going to find my baby," Rose said. It wasn't quite a question but a hopeful statement. "I'm counting on you. I didn't mean the part about giving her up for adoption. I really didn't."

This time is was Kori who paused at the woman's bedside. She squeezed Rose's hand. It felt icy to the touch.

"We know you didn't," she told her because she felt that the young mother needed to hear the reassurance.

Rather than look consoled, the distraught new mother surprised them by beginning to sob again.

Kori felt at a total loss.

Brodie saw the helpless look on his partner's face. He leaned in to her and whispered, "C'mon, let's find the orderly. Maybe she saw something."

"Maybe," Kori murmured. Right now, it was all they had to go on—maybe.

EDITH WOODS LOOKED like everyone's idea of a grandmother. Heavyset, with kindly eyes, she appeared more than willing to tell the two detectives everything she knew, which unfortunately didn't really amount to very much.

They could see that there was nothing out of the ordinary happening on the floor. A variety of people were coming and going from the various rooms, visiting the new mothers, and oohing and aahing over the brand-new little people who had come into the world. While it vaguely appeared that there was something unusual going on, no one seemed to realize the hospital was on lockdown because, unless someone attempted to physically leave the building, life went on as usual.

"In other words, nothing unusual?" Kori guessed.

The woman shook her gray head. "Nothing at all out of the ordinary."

"Did you see anyone in Ms. Williams's room, either entering it or leaving it?"

"No." Pity came over the orderly's face. "As far as I saw, the poor dear didn't have any visitors. Oh, some of the nurses lingered in the room to talk to her, you know, try to make her feel good about her decision..." Her voice trailed off.

"You mean her decision to give up her baby?" Brodie asked.

"Yes, that. You could see that she was agonizing over the decision, but some women just aren't cut out to be mothers," Edith said.

"And in your opinion, Ms. Williams looked as if she belonged to that group?" Kori asked, studying the orderly, who nodded her head with authority.

Right before their eyes, Edith seemed to retract her words. "Well, that's just it."

"What's just it?" Brodie asked, not quite following what the woman was telling them.

Edith cleared her throat, then told them, "You could

see she was wavering about that, that she couldn't quite make up her mind. If you ask me," the orderly continued, lowering her voice as if this was all a guarded secret, "she thought what she'd decided was for the best, but then she just changed her mind. I've seen enough of this sort of thing to know."

Kori reverted to hard and fast facts. "And you're sure you didn't see anyone in her room?"

"Not when I came in to bring her the tray—and not when I came by later to collect it—except that she wasn't finished yet, so I left it," she added. "I only saw her nurse go in as I was distributing trays to the other mothers."

The two detectives were suddenly alert.

"Which nurse?" Brodie asked.

"Nurse McGuire," Edith recalled. "I think she's been here as long as the hospital has," she added.

"And where can we find her?" Kori asked.

"Security just told her she was free to go," the orderly answered.

Kori and Brodie went back to the room where the remaining personnel on the floor were being questioned to ask about the nurse who had been told she was free to leave.

The hospital security guard appeared to have been sent directly from central casting, representing a studio's idea of what a run-of-the-mill hospital security guard should have looked like. The rumpled, stocky man reminded Kori of someone who was doing this sort of work only after having tried and failed at several other types of occupations along the way.

"Well, it's about time," the man cried with relief the moment he saw Brodie and Kori enter the room and come toward him. Rayburn Smith instantly seemed pleased to be able to pass the buck.

What was up with that? Kori wondered. "I guess we must have 'police' stamped on our foreheads," she murmured to the man walking next to her.

"Maybe it's our official demeanor," Brodie commented, humor curving his mouth. "Mr. Smith," he said after half a beat during which time he read the man's name on the badge pinned to his chest, "we're Detectives Kennedy and Cavanaugh." He indicated Kori and then himself. "If you have the time, we'd like to ask you a few questions."

"Of course, of course," he said agreeably enough. "But unfortunately, I didn't see anything," he told them right off the bat.

That seemed to be everyone's story, Brodie thought. He still held out the hope that *someone* had seen something useful.

"Maybe you don't even realize that you saw something. Sometimes even the smallest detail can help break a case," he told the security guard.

Smith's dark eyes grew wide as he looked from one detective to the other. "You really think so?"

"You never know," was all that Brodie would commit to. The next second, he suggested, "Why don't we go over there where we can talk without anyone interrupting us?" Brodie nodded to a far corner of the room.

The security guard brightened. He appeared to be more than happy to comply. And then his eyes darted toward the rest of the people still waiting to be told they could go home.

"You want me to tell everyone else they can leave?" he asked.

"Not quite yet," Brodie told him.

Smith nodded, more than happy to comply. "You got it, Chief."

Brodie didn't bother to correct him.

Chapter Five

In the end, after speaking to the security guard, as well as all the hospital employees who had been gathered and held in the maternity floor break room, everyone was finally released.

Kori and Brodie found the interviews entirely unsatisfying, not to mention draining.

Brodie blew out a breath as he shook his head. "I never saw so many people who saw nothing even remotely suspicious," he said wearily. "Either whoever took that baby was exceptionally good at making themselves inconspicuous or invisible, or the baby wasn't taken from here."

"She had to be," Kori insisted.

"Then how would you explain 'Now you see her, now you don't'?"

Kori thought for a moment then ventured one explanation. "My guess is that everyone on the floor was too busy doing their job—one of the nurses said that there've been cutbacks recently, so the employees here are trying to do more than their share," she confided.

"What about the people visiting patients?" he asked. They had interviewed a number of visitors as well.

"That's easy," she said. "They were too absorbed in their own little world, oohing and aahing over the newest addition to the population. That could have easily prevented them from noticing anything unusual that might have been going on."

Tunnel vision. That was a simple enough explanation, he thought. "You're probably right. We should hit the surveillance cameras next just in case *they* picked up anything useful," he suggested.

"You mean like someone making off with a baby?" she asked grimly.

"I was thinking more in the way of a wiggling backpack or duffel bag," Brodie said, scanning the immediate area as they walked away from the break room.

Kori shook her head. "If only," she said with a wistful sigh. "That would make things so much easier. Okay, let's see if whoever is manning the monitors turns out to be more helpful than the security guard was and gives us copies of the fifth-floor videos from the last twenty-four hours." She figured that should cover it on the outside chance that the kidnapper had made the mistake of surveying the immediate area *before* finally going through with the abduction.

"You might want to review videos taken from all the ground-floor exits in that time frame as well," Brodie told her. "After all, the kidnapper had to have left the hospital with their 'prize' somehow."

Kori's quizzical look melted into a smile as she nodded at him with approval. "You just might work out after all, Cavanaugh."

"Is that your idea of an 'atta boy'?" he asked Kori.

"It might be," she allowed, rolling the term over in her head. "I don't like being predictable."

Brodie laughed, amused. "Something tells me that's not one of your shortcomings."

She raised her chin, pretending to dismiss his comment. "I don't have shortcomings."

"Of course you don't. What was I thinking?" Brodie quipped.

"Hey," Kori suddenly called out to Brodie as he bypassed the elevators. "You just walked right by the elevators," she said, pointing to the closed silvery doors.

"I know," Brodie answered as he continued walking down the hallway.

A thought suddenly occurred to her. "You're not one of those people who likes to take the stairs every time he gets a chance, are you?" She was all for exercise, but there was a time and a place for it and that time was not now.

He looked at her as if she were spouting nonsense. "Hell no!"

Her brow furrowed. "If you're not taking the stairs down and you're bypassing the elevator, where are you going?" she asked.

"I just wanted to go see the baby's mother before we left," he told her.

She still didn't understand why he was going back. "Did you think of something else that you want to ask her?" she asked as she quickened her step to catch up to Brodie.

"Actually, I did," he answered. "I want to ask her if she has anyone to call who could be here for her. That orderly mentioned that she didn't recall seeing anyone coming by to visit Rose, and I just want to make sure she has someone she could stay with or talk to." He turned down the hall toward the woman's room. "She shouldn't be going through this by herself."

Kori stopped walking and looked at her new partner in surprise.

When Brodie realized that she wasn't keeping up, he turned around to look at her. He couldn't read the expression on her face.

"What?" he asked.

"Nothing," she answered, waving away his question. And then she replied, "You're just being very thoughtful, that's all." Her mouth curved ever so slightly. "I had no idea that my new partner came with feelings."

Brodie laughed at the comment. "I'm a Cavanaugh," he reminded her, then deadpanned, "I'm told that we all come with feelings."

"Well, there's always an exception," Kori pointed out diplomatically.

He pretended to take her comment seriously. "Not to my knowledge," he answered after a moment.

They reached Rose's single-care unit and pushed open the door. The second they walked in, the young mother sat ramrod-straight, instantly alert.

"Did you find her?" she cried eagerly. "Did you find my baby?"

Brodie hated to have to tell her the truth, but he wasn't about to lie. "No, not yet…" Brodie began to answer.

Rose refused to surrender all hope. "But you do have some leads, right?" she asked breathlessly. "Things you can follow up on, right?"

He didn't look in Kori's direction and he certainly didn't have the heart to tell Rose that so far they had come up empty. He saw no reason to crush her.

So he worded his answer as positively as he could. "We're examining every single possibility. In the meantime, we—" he glanced toward Kori, including her in on this "—wanted to ask you if you have anyone you could call to come down to the hospital. Like a friend or a relative," he supplied when she didn't say anything in response to his question.

Rose seemed lost for a moment. Her eyes moved back and forth, seemingly staring at nothing as she tried to think.

"I suppose there's my cousin, Rachel," she finally said. A small, disparaging laugh escaped her lips as she considered her cousin. "I haven't seen her in a few years, though. Not since she went away to college." She raised her eyes to Brodie's face, suddenly dismissing that choice. "But I can't call her. I'm not part of her life anymore. She doesn't even know I had a baby. And her mother—my aunt Gloria—would be horrified if she found out that I had a baby and wasn't married. They wouldn't want to have anything to do with me," she said sadly. The very thought was pure anguish to her.

"Your aunt might surprise you," Brodie told her. "You'll never know if you don't try to get in contact with them," he predicted. "Why don't you give me her number, or at least her name, and I'll see if I can reach her for you?"

Rose looked very doubtful about the suggestion. But in the end, she relented and gave him her aunt's last name and her last known address.

Writing it down, he pocketed the piece of paper. Patting it, he told her to think "good thoughts."

Rose offered him a weak smile. "That didn't help with my grandmother."

Brodie and Kori exchanged looks. "You have a grandmother?"

"Yes. We were pretty close, too. But something changed when I told her that I was giving the baby up for adoption. She seemed really disappointed and distant. We still talk, but not as much," she lamented.

"Have you tried calling her?" Kori asked.

Rose pressed her lips together and nodded. "But she's not answering."

"Keep trying," Brodie advised. "Tell her what happened. I'm sure she'll come," he told her. He couldn't imagine a relative staying away after hearing that.

Rose nodded, though she seemed unconvinced. "Maybe."

Brodie said a few more encouraging words to Rose, and then he and Kori left the hospital room.

He was well aware of the fact that Kori had kept her silence throughout the entire exchange between the kidnapped baby's mother and him as he was trying to build up her hope.

"Go ahead," he told Kori as he pressed the down button for the elevator.

"Go ahead?" Koru repeated, raising her eyebrow as she looked at him.

"Yes. Tell me what you're thinking. I know you've been dying to give me your opinion about what I just said to Rose," Brodie said. Partnered with her for a few hours, Kori had impressed him as the type who didn't hold things back when they occurred to her.

Her answer surprised him. "I think you're a lot more thoughtful than I'd expected you to be—and a hell of a lot more thoughtful than any of the other detectives I was partnered with."

"'Partnered with,'" Brodie repeated. "As in plural?" he asked. "Just how many partners have you had?"

In response, Kori laughed to herself. It was a dry, almost humorless laugh as she thought about the men who had filled that position.

"Off the top of my head, I'd say too many," she answered.

"Why so many?" Brodie asked, genuinely curious. Was there something about her that he should be aware of? At first meeting, the attractive young woman seemed nice enough, but he could be wrong. If so, he needed to know in order to be prepared.

"Looking for people who have disappeared out of their lives can take a lot out of a person." She half shrugged as they rode down to the first floor. "I suppose that some people can't handle it."

"But you can?" Brodie asked, studying her face.

Her answer was straightforward. "I live for it." Her eyes almost glowed as she said, "There's nothing like being able to reunite people who never thought they would see one another again."

Brodie caught the note in her voice. "You sound like you speak from experience," he noted.

"I do," she said proudly, thinking of the cases that had gone well. And then she asked Brodie, "Did your uncle tell you about the night I met him?" If he already knew, then there was no sense in repeating the story, she thought.

"Which uncle?" he asked as the elevator came to a stop. The doors yawned open and he put his hand out, holding the doors back as she got off. Brodie followed her out. "You forget, I have an entire stable full of uncles."

She smiled at the way he'd put that. She would have loved to have had more of a family than she did. But she was grateful to have her father alive.

"Brian," Kori answered.

"Oh." He nodded. "You mean the chief of detectives. No, he didn't. Probably didn't think it was important to our working together," Brodie guessed.

He was probably right about that, Kori thought as she began to go over the particulars of that night. "I was going with my father to the convenience store. We were having hot dogs for dinner," she recalled, then added, "He couldn't afford anything else." There was no shame in her voice. It was just a simple fact. "It turns out that the convenience store was being robbed at the time and we walked right in on the robbery. My father grabbed my arm and bolted out of there."

She paused for a moment, a lump forming in her throat. "He used his body to shield me so I wouldn't be hurt." She shivered as she said, "I just remember this awful sound—the robber fired his gun and he shot my father. Twice. My father fell to the ground right before my eyes." She stopped again, trying to catch her breath and keep her tears back. She always cried when she remembered that night.

"I just remember trying to keep my father's blood from spilling out of his body with my hands over the wound. I was nine," she told Brodie, as if that explained her futile, foolish attempts to stop the bleeding with her hands.

Her mouth curved slightly from the memory. She had been so desperate, so hopelessly naive.

"That was the night I met your uncle. He was just coming off a double shift and his wife told him to stop at the convenience store on the way home so he could get some milk. I will forever be grateful that he did.

"He called for an ambulance and then stayed with me until they came. He even insisted that the EMTs let me ride in the ambulance with my father. They weren't happy about it, but they did," she recalled. "That's when your uncle Brian became my hero," she confessed.

"He stayed with me in the hospital waiting room while my father was in surgery. And when it was finally over and it looked as if my father was going to survive,

instead of handing me over to a social worker—I had
nobody else—" she explained ruefully. "Your uncle
took me home with him," she recalled fondly. "His wife
didn't look too happy to see me instead of the milk," she
recalled. "That was his first wife," she added. "When
she died, he married Lila," she explained. Given Brodie had said he was relatively new to the family, she'd
thought he might need to have the dynamics reinforced.

Since they had reached the first floor and had gotten off the elevator, they began walking in the general
direction of the room where the hospital surveillance
cameras were kept.

"Wow," Brodie said to his new partner, impressed.
"I'd say you definitely know a great deal more about
my family than I do."

"Only certain members." She didn't want him giving undue credit where it didn't belong. "Your uncle
Brian was my guardian angel. All I ever wanted to do
was be like him and find a way to repay him for what
he did for my father," she told him. "Trying to reunite
missing people is my small way of paying a little back."

"If I know my uncle—any of my uncles—he would
probably just say that he was only doing his job," Brodie
told her. His mouth curved. "That's how they all think."

"Well, it might have just been his job, but it was my
life," Kori stressed. She stopped walking because they
had managed to reach the hospital's security office with
its multiple bank of monitors. "Okay, let's hope that the
hospital's surveillance cameras didn't suddenly all go
down for some reason or wound up malfunctioning in
the last few hours."

"Well, if you ask me, that would be one hell of a coincidence if it happened," Brodie told her.

Knocking on the closed door, he didn't wait for an

invitation to come in. Instead, he opened the door and then held it for Kori so she could walk in first.

The lone security guard sitting there, watching the various monitors, looked surprised and was on his feet instantly.

"You can't be in here," he informed the duo indignantly.

"On the contrary," Kori said, holding up her badge and ID for the guard to see, "we can." Giving the man both their names and the police department they were with, she told the man exactly what they needed from him. "We would like copies of the surveillance tapes from this morning. Specifically the ones from the maternity floor and the ones monitoring all the hospital ground-floor exits from the last twelve hours."

The guard, a nondescript man in his fifties, didn't appear to be the type who enjoyed deviating from the norm. "You want copies of *all* of them?"

"Unless you want to give us the originals," Brodie specified.

The guard looked horrified by the suggestion. "Oh no, no I don't. The originals tapes have to stay here."

"Good policy," Brodie said cryptically. "But we need to review them and unless you want us sitting here, crowding you for however long it takes to look those videos over, you're going to have to make copies of them for us." Brodie's eyes met the guard's. "Do you have a problem with that?"

The man's eyes darted back and forth between the two detectives as he took in a deep breath. He seemed ready to protest the decision then, looking at Brodie, he seemed to think better of that.

"No, no I don't," he replied. "I don't have a problem at all. I just have to find where Herman kept the empty tapes."

"Herman?" Kori questioned. Was that the man's supervisor?

"Yeah, the security guard who usually runs this area. He called in sick today."

Brodie could feel his partner looking at him and he didn't have to guess what she was probably thinking. Was this Herman's absence merely a coincidence, or was it all just a well-orchestrated plan set in motion to facilitate the newborn's abduction?

Everything was suspect. He would have to work at finding a way to shed these suspicions once he walked out the door. But for now, he made a mental note to go to this Herman's house and talk to the man—on the outside chance that the guard had had something to do with the abduction.

As for shedding these suspicions, this wasn't like other jobs that could be left behind once he walked out the door. It remained on a person's mind, preying on it in order for him to be able to make something of all the puzzle pieces that he wound up picking up. He needed to try to make sense out of all of these pieces and form them into some sort of a coherent whole that would lead to an answer.

"You have this Herman's address and phone number?" Kori asked the security guard before Brodie could.

"Of course I have it. What kind of a security guard do you think I am?" the man asked her indignantly.

"A conscientious one," Kori answered without any hesitation.

The guard seemed to relax a little right in front of her eyes, placated by her response.

"Okay then," he said. "I'll go get what you asked for."

With that, the security guard went to fetch the information for them.

Chapter Six

Valri Cavanaugh belonged to the family members heretofore thought of as the lost branch and, once discovered, had transferred to Aurora. In short order, Fergus Cavanaugh's daughter had become an indispensable member of the computer lab that was a vital part of Crime Scene Investigations.

Brenda, Brian's daughter-in-law and head of that computer division, had been quick to see the young woman's potential and had taken Valri under her wing, where the latter had flourished.

These days, Valri was the one everyone approached when they needed something done "yesterday." Consequently, Valri could usually be found swamped beneath a pile of do-mine-first requests.

It had taken her time, but Valri had finally developed a tough skin and had learned to turn a deaf ear to all those needy pleas.

Or most of them.

Hence, when Kori finally came to the computer lab and approached the "wizard of the lab" with the stack of Aurora General surveillance tapes, Valri said, "I'm afraid you're going to have to wait your turn," as she gestured toward all the other requests currently covering her desk.

"Normally, I would," Kori told the attractive woman, adding, "Really. But this is an emergency."

"Honey," Valri replied wearily, "they're *all* emergencies." She didn't even bother looking up from the project she was immersed in to make her point.

Brodie knew exactly what button to press when it came to his cousin. "A baby was stolen out of her mother's room in the maternity ward at Aurora General Hospital sometime this morning."

Valri was somewhat partial to the Cavanaugh whose first name was the same as her husband's last name: Brody. But more than that, it was the nature of the crime that had snared her attention.

"Why didn't you say so in the first place?" she asked. Valri stopped what she was doing for now and, for the first time since they had entered, really looked at the two detectives standing beside her desk. "Okay, hand them over," she instructed as she put out her hand.

Brodie did as she asked, putting the stack on her desk. The number of different tapes was not lost on Valri but, in the long run, it wasn't anything she couldn't handle. "What is it that you're looking for?"

"Anything that looks suspicious to you." When Valri raised an eyebrow, Kori got a little more specific. "Someone making off with an infant and making their way out of the hospital rather than back to the mother's room. We had security give us copies of everything they had from the fifth floor as well as from all the ground-floor exits, but we haven't had a chance to review anything yet," she confessed.

Valri was quick to cut off what she suspected was going to be a rambling apology. That wasn't going to do anyone any good and would only eat away at the time.

"Leave that to me," she told Kori. She directed her question at both of them. "How long has the baby been missing?"

"Sometime between seven and ten this morning," Brodie answered. Ten was when they had been called in.

"That's rather a large window," Valri commented.

Kori agreed with her. "The mother fell asleep right after she ate breakfast. She had apparently been under a huge emotional strain."

Interest flashed in Valri's eyes. "What sort of a strain?" she asked as she made notes to herself.

Brodie recalled what the mother had tearfully told them in the hospital room. "Apparently, she had decided to give the baby up for adoption and then had second thoughts about it," he told his cousin. "Consequently, because she had wavered, she felt that the baby's abduction was all her fault."

Valri nodded. "It looks like someone decided to take that decision out of her hands."

"You have to admit that, from one angle, it does look that way," Kori agreed.

Valri frowned to herself as she wrote down more notes. "I guess keeping the baby in the mother's room doesn't completely eliminate the problem of hospital abductions," she said under her breath. Nodding, she looked at the stack of tapes she was going to have to review. "Okay, I'll let you know if I see anything 'suspicious,'" the computer expert promised them.

And then she offered Kori what she hoped passed as an apologetic smile. "I didn't mean to snap at you like that when you came in. It's just if I didn't try to prioritize what's really important and what someone only *thinks* is important because they've been asked to look into it, I would never get out from behind this desk."

She quietly laughed to herself, adding, "Not even for a bathroom break."

Kori could easily see that happening. How many times has she stayed at her desk, working into the wee hours of the night? There were even times when she all but slept in the squad room. She could fully sympathize with the other woman.

"Apology more than accepted." Kori flashed a smile at Brodie's cousin. "Thanks."

But the other woman shook her head. "Don't thank me yet," she told Kori. "Wait until after I've come up with something."

In the face of that, Kori amended her initial statement just slightly. "Thanks for trying."

But Valri barely seemed to hear her. The computer tech was back in work mode.

Brodie led the way out of the computer lab.

"Why don't we grab some lunch and then see if Herman Garcia is as sick as he claimed to be when he called in this morning," Brodie said as he made his way to the elevator.

Brodie's suggestion surprised her. Kori hadn't thought about food since they had caught this case. The very idea of the baby being stolen the way it had, under everyone's nose, had completely destroyed her appetite.

"You can eat?" she intoned as the elevator doors opened and they got on.

"I can always eat," Brodie told her, adding, "I work a lot better if my stomach isn't rumbling and distracting me.

"Besides," he pointed out, "you need fuel to work an investigation." He pressed the button for the first floor. "So, drive-thru or takeout?"

Kori had to think for a moment before answering

his question. Her mind was definitely not focused on food. She made her decision based on expediency. "The drive-thru," she finally said. "That way you'll waste a minimum of time."

He wasn't sure how she meant that, but he sensed this wasn't the time to get into any sort of a debate not based on the case.

"Works for me," Brodie replied. Then he couldn't resist adding, "I chew fast."

That meant he'd wind up taking in a lot of air, she couldn't help thinking. "Isn't that bad for your rumbling stomach?"

Brodie smiled, amused. "Do you enjoy arguing?"

She had to pause and think for a moment to word her answer properly. "I enjoy solving crimes," Kori told him. "Anything that gets in the way of that is consequently a problem for me."

His grin grew wider. "So then that's a yes," he assumed.

Kori shot him a look, wondering if this was some sort of game for him. Was he trying to test her or just annoy her?

Maybe she'd been too hasty, thinking they'd work well together. There was still a lot about this overly good-looking man that she didn't know.

"We can skip the drive-thru, you know," she told Brodie. Since she was the one driving, that meant she could call the shots.

Brodie raised his hands innocently, surrendering. "I never said a word."

Since she viewed that as more or less of an apology on his part—he didn't press the matter or attempt to flex his muscles to put her in what he thought was her place—Kori felt she could afford to relent.

"I had a feeling that you'd see things my way," she said. "Okay, what's your preference?" she asked, referring to the drive-thru.

He really didn't care as long as he got to eat. His tastes had always been eclectic, which made him easy to satisfy. "You pick."

She wasn't about to make a selection. For one thing, she didn't know if one place was better than another because she didn't frequent any.

"I don't go to fast-food places," she informed him.

Her disclaimer surprised him. Because of the nature of the life cops led at times, he thought that all law enforcement agents frequented fast-food establishments to a lesser or greater degree.

"You're kidding," Brodie said, thinking she was pulling his leg for some reason.

"I kid on occasion, but never about food," Kori replied. She could see that her answer confused him. She was going to leave it that way, then decided to open up to him just a little. "I like to cook, not grab things on the run." He still looked as if he was having trouble processing that, so she added, "Cooking relaxes me."

When she slanted a glance in his direction, she saw that her new partner looked amused by her answer. "I'll keep that in mind," he told her. "But for now, I don't think we have the time for you to demonstrate your culinary abilities for me—although I'd like to revisit that offer later."

"What offer?" Kori asked, baffled. She hadn't made any sort of an offer, she thought. What was he talking about?

"Sampling your cooking," Brodie answered. "You've piqued my curiosity."

Kori shot him a look. Maybe she had really made a

mistake. Maybe the man was an egotist after all. "And you've piqued mine," she replied. "Just when did you hear me make an offer to cook for you?"

"I thought it was implied," he told her.

"No," she replied definitively. "In your case, it wasn't implied, it was imagined."

His eyes smiled at her. "Po-tay-toe, po-tat-toe," he countered. "Let's hit the drive-thru and then get to Herman Garcia's apartment."

Kori sighed as she pressed her lips together. "Tell me, did you willingly transfer out of Homicide or did someone strongly suggest you make the change?" Right now she had the uneasy feeling that Brodie Cavanaugh was a problem waiting to explode. She could easily see a superior wanting this to be someone else's problem.

Brodie laughed. "As a matter of fact, they tried to talk me out of it."

"Out of making the transfer or out of remaining with the police department entirely?" she asked pointedly since his statement sounded so ambiguous.

"Since you seem to have your doubts about me, maybe you should investigate that matter for yourself," he suggested.

Cavanaugh was bluffing, she thought. She decided to call it. "Maybe I will," she replied, looking over briefly to see if Brodie's expression gave him away.

It didn't. The man probably made a hell of a poker player. Okay, Cavanaugh wanted to eat, she thought, so they were going to get that out of the way first.

"Any particular fast-food place you want to go to?" she asked.

"Whatever is closest. I'm easy," he replied, his eyes teasing her.

The hell he was, she thought. Cavanaugh was challenging her and that was far from easy in her book. "So you say."

"Are you saying I'm not?" he asked. There was no missing the amusement in his voice. He was enjoying this. Well, she was not about to encourage that.

"I don't know you well enough to say anything one way or another." Scanning the block as they drove by, she saw a sign proclaiming they were about to pass a taco place. She slowed her vehicle. "How's *Arriba* sound?" she asked him.

"Edible," he answered with a smile.

"Is that a yes?" she asked, wanting to be absolutely sure. She didn't want to go through the drive-thru only to have him change his mind at the last minute and say he wanted to go somewhere else.

"That's a yes," he answered, then added with a laugh, "If this was some other time, I'd be thought of as a cheap date."

Oh no, they weren't going to go that route, Kori thought. "Except that this isn't a date. However, what it does mean is that you have no taste buds," she informed him. "You know what you want?" she asked as they approached the order window.

He looked at her for what felt to Kori like a very long moment. "I do," he answered.

A wave of warmth shot through her. Something in Brodie's voice gave Kori the very distinct feeling that he wasn't referring to the menu. But if she said that, she knew he would make some sort of a crack that would totally get them off track, so she bit her tongue and refrained.

Brodie placed his order, telling the disembodied

voice coming from the sign that he wanted a quesadilla. And then he looked at her.

"Do you want anything?" he asked. "It's on me,"
he added.

She was tempted to say something about his being
the last of the big spenders, but then thought better of
it. That would have been mean-spirited. It also wasn't
like her.

Maybe she *was* hungry, Kori considered. That sort
of response was something a cranky, hungry person
would have said, not her.

She really did need to get more sleep, she silently
upbraided herself.

Kori looked at the sign and decided to go with the
item pictured on it.

"Maybe I'll have a taco," she told Brodie.

"What kind?" he asked. When she didn't answer
him, he tried to make the choice easier for her. "You
want bean? Chicken? Beef? Or a combo that includes
all three?"

"Chicken," she said, choosing the lightest thing she
could that was on the menu.

Brodie nodded, adding the item to his tab. "And a
chicken taco."

The sleepy voice told them to drive up to the next
window to pay and collect the items.

When they reached the next window, their order was
already there waiting for them. Brodie paid for it then
collected the large paper sack with all the items stuffed
inside.

Kori drove away from the last window. She had to
admit, if just to herself, that the smell filling the air
was really tempting.

"You want me to pull over somewhere?" she asked,

nodding toward the parking lot located behind the fast-food restaurant.

Brodie read between the lines. "No need. I can eat while the car's in motion," he told her and then realized she might take that as a criticism. "But if you want to pull over somewhere—"

She shook her head, vetoing that idea. "I'll feel better once we get to question Garcia and find out if he's really sick or if this was somehow part of an elaborate plan to steal a baby."

"If Garcia is really sick, I doubt ten minutes is going to make any difference. If he isn't, then my guess is that he's not home anyway." But one look at his new partner's face told him which way he needed to go with this. "Why don't we find out if he is really sick and just didn't come in?"

Since he was being selfless, she could relent, Kori thought. "Aren't you afraid your quesadilla will get cold?"

"That's the good thing about fast food. It tastes the same whether it's cold or warm. Like I said," he repeated, smiling at her. "I'm easy."

This time, she offered no argument. Instead, she just nodded. "Right."

Parking in front of the Wakefield Arms, an apartment complex that had been one of the first built in Aurora, and while none of the apartment complexes in the city look old, it was apparent that the Wakefield Arms had seen better days.

Garcia's apartment was located on the second floor. Because someone was exiting the building at just the right moment, there was no need to ring a bell to enter.

Moving swiftly, Brodie slipped in and then held the door open for Kori.

Once inside the building, they went up to the second floor, taking the stairs.

Apartment 204 was to the right of the stairwell.

Kori pressed the doorbell. When there was no response, she tried again.

Still nothing.

Before she could try a third time, Brodie gently moved her out of the way and banged on the door. He announced their presence by declaring, "Aurora P.D., Mr. Garcia. We need to have a word with you!"

When there was no answer from inside, Kori realized that Brodie was going to break down the door. Putting her hand on what was a surprisingly rock-hard chest, she stopped him.

"Why don't we go get the manager and see if he or she can—?"

At that moment, the door to the apartment opened just a crack. They could see a watery set of eyes looking at them. A hoarse voice that sounded as if it had gotten that way thanks to a night of next-to-nonstop coughing asked, "Why is the police department looking to talk to me?"

The question was punctuated by several sneezes in a row.

Kori stumbled backward to get out of the range of the sneeze and wound up against Brodie's chest.

"Sorry," Brodie murmured only loud enough for her to hear.

Doing her best to ignore the almost rock-solid chest she'd backed up against, Kori directed her attention toward the man they had come to talk to.

"Mr. Garcia, you called in sick today..." Kori began.

The sick man looked surprised. "Boy," he cried, his

voice totally nasal, "when they said that the hospital was
going to be cracking down, I guess they really meant it."

The security guard punctuated his statement with
another sneeze.

Chapter Seven

Kori decided to tackle the situation head-on and not waste any time mincing words. "The hospital didn't send us, Mr. Garcia," she told the rather pale-looking, sweaty security guard.

She realized that the somewhat overweight man appeared to be holding on to his front door more for support than to keep them out. He was looking at them blankly, as if trying to unscramble the words they had just said.

"Then why are you here?" Garcia finally asked in a thick, nasal voice.

"Mind if we come in?" Kori asked him.

Garcia stared at the two detectives, apparently weighing whether or not he should invite them inside. And then, taking a labored breath, the man, swaddled in his bathrobe, stepped back. He cleared the threshold for the detectives, although, even now, he was still partially holding on to the door.

Kori came into the tiny apartment first, followed by Brodie.

"We're here because there was a baby stolen from Aurora General Hospital this morning," Kori told Garcia as she turned to face him again.

"Your absence from the surveillance camera monitoring room seemed to strike us as a rather a convenient coincidence," Brodie added. "We wanted to verify that you were really ill."

Watery dark eyes widened as the security guard stared at the two detectives standing in the small hallway in his apartment. He sneezed then, covering his mouth with a bunched-up handkerchief that had apparently seen much better times.

"A baby?" the man repeated, clearly horrified. Belatedly, his brain seemed to kick in as he blinked. "But you got it on the surveillance tapes, right?" he asked anxiously. "The baby-napping."

"The tapes are being reviewed right now," Brodie told the security guard, answering the man's question honestly. "But so far, we haven't come up with anything we're able to use."

Stunned, Garcia shook his head, as if to clear it. And then he sneezed again before he was able to say anything. When he did speak, what came out was a hoarse protest. "That's not possible," he cried.

"That's what we thought," Kori told the guard, watching his face. He sounded sincere enough, but she wasn't a hundred percent convinced. It could have just been an act.

"Unless there are some dead zones in the hospital," Brodie said, referring to areas that either had no cameras set up or where the cameras that were installed couldn't capture any actual images. "Are there any known dead zones on the maternity floor, Mr. Garcia?"

The man clutched his threadbare robe as he grimaced, attempting to think. Apparently, the effort hurt his head. Kori guessed that he might have been dealing with a killer migraine, but this matter superseded something as mundane as a headache. He sat down on his sofa.

"There are a couple on every floor but that's because the hospital doesn't have the most high-power cameras installed. There're plans to put them in, but..." His voice trailed off and then he sneezed again, his eyes watering before he was finally able to conclude, "Yeah, there are dead zones."

Brodie and Kori exchanged glances. "Looks like we're going to have to talk to everyone on those tapes to find out if they saw anything even remotely suspicious going on," Kori said.

"Or question them to find out if they *did* anything suspicious," Brodie deliberately added.

A loud sneeze prefaced the guard's declaration. "I'll go with you."

It was a halfhearted offer as Garcia pushed himself off the sofa and unsteadily back up to his feet.

At this point, Kori believed that the man was actually as sick as he seemed.

"That's okay, Mr. Garcia," Kori said. "The hospital doesn't need you risking getting all those mothers and babies sick. You just need to take care of yourself. We'll see ourselves out."

Garcia offered no argument. Brodie thought the man even looked relieved to an extent.

"I take it you believed him about being too sick to come in today?" Brodie asked her as soon as they closed the door behind them after leaving the second-floor apartment.

"Garcia looked downright miserable and his eyes were genuinely red-rimmed. The man didn't strike me as being that good of an actor." Because she and Brodie had only been partners for a matter of a few hours and she didn't want him getting the impression that she was steamrolling him, Kori made a point of saying, "Unless I'm missing something here."

Brodie took her question for what it was: a gesture. But he did appreciate it. He'd encountered people, male and female, who came across as if they had chips on their shoulders, or thought of themselves as having the final word in everything. Kori didn't appear to have that problem.

"Not that I can see," he told her. "The guy looked pretty miserable to me. Not only that, but I got the impression he was really upset that this baby kidnapping took place in his hospital when he wasn't there to catch whoever did it in the act."

Well, at least they were in agreement on that, Kori thought.

Leaving the building, they proceeded to Kori's car. Kori's brain was whirling. "All right, next order of business," she told Brodie, "is to get someone from the hospital to identify all the hospital personnel who were captured on the surveillance tapes."

Brodie nodded, but he just wanted to make sure that his partner hadn't lost sight of one very salient point. "You realize that the baby is long gone by now," he told Kori.

"I know," she answered, "but if we can find out with who, we'll be halfway toward getting that baby back," she emphasized. She refused to entertain any other sort of outcome for this situation.

There was no arguing with that, Brodie thought, although, quite honestly, he didn't hold out all that much hope that they'd be able to locate just who had taken this baby—which meant that, in all likelihood, they weren't going to get her back, at least not any time soon.

Brodie roused. He couldn't allow himself to entertain negative thoughts.

"How can someone do that?" Brodie asked after maintaining several minutes of silence once they had gotten into the car and were traveling on the road again.

Lost in her own thoughts, Kori looked at Cavanaugh, startled. "Did you say something?"

Brodie rephrased his question. "How can someone just take a defenseless infant and make off with her like that?"

He had seen all sorts of bad behavior while on the job, but this sort of thing was beyond him.

Kori glanced in her partner's direction. "Oh, there are lots of reasons," she told him.

"Like what?" he asked.

Because he was probably dealing with this for the first time, she could see how this could be a gut-wrenching mystery to him. Sadly, she had more experience with this sort of thing. At this point, very little surprised her, but it could still sicken her.

"Maybe whoever took her wanted a baby of their own and, for one reason or another, they couldn't have one. Or maybe this person knew that Rose would give the baby up for adoption and they thought, 'Hey, no harm, no foul,' they'd just eliminate the middle man and find a couple who wanted this baby and were willing to pay any sum to have her.

"Or maybe," she said grimly, "whoever took the baby intended to sell it on the black market." She squared her shoulders as if that could somehow protect her from letting this thought eat into her soul. "It's barbaric, but you would be surprised how many babies are actually abducted and sold."

Brodie shook his head as he felt a cold chill work its way down his spine.

"It's an ugly, ugly business," he murmured more to himself than to her.

"That it is," she wholeheartedly agreed.

"How can you be part of it?" he asked, wondering how she could immerse herself in this sort of thing.

"I'm not 'part' of it," she informed him tersely. "What I am part of is reuniting the stolen babies and children with the people who love them and are totally out of their minds with frantic worry. Doing my job right is what makes everything else worthwhile."

Brodie nodded, taking her words in. "I guess I have to apologize."

Kori wasn't sure what Cavanaugh was telling her. "For what?"

"For underestimating you," Brodie said. "You've got a tougher skin than I gave you credit for."

Kori's laugh rang hollow. Then just before she pulled into the precinct, she told him, "I don't have tough skin, Cavanaugh. Under this exterior is just one big bowl of mush."

Brodie caught himself thinking that the woman sitting in the driver's seat had to be just about the most tempting-looking "bowl of mush" he had ever encountered—but he felt he couldn't say as much. That might get him into trouble at this point in their association.

And besides, they were working a case that was far more important than the way he felt himself reacting to this new person in his life.

THEY WENT BACK to see Valri.

They could tell the moment they entered the computer lab that they wouldn't be hearing the news they were hoping for.

Valri raised her eyes. "Just how fast do you think I am?" she asked the duo. There was an edge to her voice, partially brought on by the fact that, so far, she hadn't succeeded in her efforts to locate whoever had made off with the baby and she was taking this abduction personally. "I mean I'm good, but you people are expecting superhuman good."

Kori felt bad about putting this sort of pressure on a woman who was already overworked. But before she could begin to make any apologies, Brodie rescued the moment.

"We were just looking to spare you the trouble of having to make a phone call, one way or another. We're all aware of the fact that time is of the essence in this case and we were hoping against hope that something would pop out at you from the surveillance tapes," he told his cousin. "Whatever tapes you've gone through, we're going to take those back to the hospital and see if someone there can give us the names of any of the hospital personnel who do appear on the tapes so we can question them.

"Maybe, between all that effort, we can find some information to help us find this baby," Brodie said.

Kori mentally applauded her new partner, impressed by his creativity.

Valri stopped and pulled three of the tapes over toward herself. Those were all she had managed to go through during the time that Kori and Brodie had been gone.

"Have at it," she said, gesturing to the tapes. "You think you can get someone to confess to taking the baby?" Valri asked her cousin skeptically.

"No, but we can question them regarding whatever they might have seen. Sometimes people don't even know that they've seen what they've seen," he told the petite young woman sitting behind the computer.

Valri pressed her lips together, nodding. "I suppose that makes sense," she agreed. Having turned over the reviewed tapes, she sat back in her chair. "Now, if you don't mind, I've got a ton of work waiting for me. Some of it's not even yours."

Valri actually could get back to what she had been doing.

"Thanks for all your help," Kori told the other woman with sincerity, squeezing Valri's arm.

Valri merely murmured something unintelligible in response, then looked up for a moment to smile at them before retreating into her work.

Half a second later, Valri was totally lost in thought.

"You know, she seemed so preoccupied, I don't think she even heard me," Kori told Brodie, talking about his cousin as they made their way to the elevator.

"Oh, make no mistake about it, Valri heard," he assured his partner. "She's exceptionally good at multitasking."

However, Kori wasn't all that sure about what he had just said. She was fairly certain that in Valri's place, she wouldn't have that ability. She usually needed to focus on one thing at a time. "How do you know?"

Brodie laughed as the elevator doors opened and they both stepped in.

"Trust me, the woman has hearing like a bat," he told her. "I don't know how she does it, but somehow, my cousin manages to hear everything, even when there's noise that would normally interfere with her being able to hear clearly."

"'Hearing like a bat,'" Kori repeated. "Lovely description."

"Accurate description," Brodie countered. "And that's all that counts right now."

ARMED WITH THE copies of the surveillance video tapes, Brodie and Kori returned to the hospital. This time their destination was the personnel department. They went straight to the head of that department.

When Kori and Brodie walked into Wade Murray's office, the man looked as if he was getting ready to go home for the night.

He didn't seem pleased to see them. "I'm sorry but you're going to have to come back in the morning. I'm afraid that I'm on my way out for the day."

"And I'm afraid you're not," Brodie countered.

The head of personnel looked as if he might drop a few choice words on these strangers invading his office when Brodie took out his badge and ID. The man swallowed whatever words he was about to utter.

His sloping shoulders seemed to slope even more. "This is about the baby that was taken, isn't it?" Murray asked.

"Smart man." Kori flashed the man a humorless smile, showing the head of personnel her own identification and badge.

In response, Murray dropped into his chair like a man who suddenly was unable to stand under his own power. He sighed helplessly.

"I'm not sure what more I can tell you. The police were already here, and I gave them my statement." He gripped the armrests as he looked from one detective to the other. "I'm afraid I didn't see anything."

The regular department would have sent out officers to take down statements, Kori thought, but she and Brodie, as well as other members of their team, were more organized and focused when it came to abductions.

"This isn't about what you might have seen, it's about what someone else might have seen," Kori told the head of personnel.

Murray's eyebrows drew together in a deep frown. "I'm afraid I don't understand."

"We have copies of all the surveillance tapes that were taken of every conceivable hallway and escape route the kidnapper might have taken with the baby he or she abducted," Kori told the director. "As you can imagine, there are a lot of hospital personnel visible in these tapes. Unnamed people," she emphasized.

"That's as should be expected," Murray said, then added, "This is, after all, a working hospital. A very popular working hospital."

"Yes, Mr. Murray, we understand that," Brodie said. "We'd like to have all the people in these tapes identified. Or at least as many who work in the hospital as possible."

Murray nodded his head almost absently. "Of course," the man agreed as he began to push himself up from his chair.

Just as he reached his feet, Brodie delivered the knockout punch.

"Today," Kori's partner stressed.

Murray eyed him, as if he were having trouble processing what was being asked of him. His gaze moved from Kori's face to Brodie's.

"Today?" he repeated, surprised.

"Yes," Brodie confirmed. "This is time sensitive. So yes. Today."

A huge, heartfelt sigh escaped Murray's lips and his eyes stared in helpless resignation at the tapes that Kori was holding.

"Today," he murmured.

Chapter Eight

As it turned out, most of the employees the personnel director saw and could actually identify on the various surveillance tapes had ended their shifts and gone home for the day.

Other than a couple of orderlies who had opted for overtime by taking on a second shift, the employees Murray had named were no longer on the premises.

Drained, Murray leaned back in his chair. He mopped his forehead with his handkerchief and rubbed his eyes. "I'm afraid that you're still going to have to wait until tomorrow to question these people. As a matter of fact, in a few cases, you're going to have to wait until the day after tomorrow," Murray said, correcting himself.

Kori didn't understand why the man was being so thick-headed. Didn't he understand what they were up against? "We don't have time to wait," she told the head of personnel.

"I understand your position. I really do," Murray told the two detectives. "But you have to understand mine. I can't release these people's home addresses without a court order. I'm sorry, but my hands are tied."

Brodie nodded, stepping forward. "I understand," he told Murray in a soft, quiet voice. Out of the corner of his eye, he could see the furious look entering his partner's vivid blue eyes, but he pretended not to notice. "Did I happen to mention that my sister is a journalist writing for the *Aurora Gazette*? As a personal favor to me, she's sitting on the story—for now—about the abduction. How fast do you think the story about the uncooperative head of hospital personnel obstructing our search for the kidnapper—or kidnappers—can circulate after it hits the paper as well as its online companion?" Brodie asked innocently as he pinned the man down with a sharp look.

Murray's shallow complexion turned almost a bright scarlet. "But I'm not being uncooperative," he protested. "I sat here, *after hours*, and looked over all the tapes you brought me. I'm not releasing the employees' addresses and phone numbers because I'm just obeying the law."

"I don't think people are going to see it that way when there's a baby's life involved. Can the hospital withstand that sort of bad publicity? Can you?" he pressed. "How long do you think people will continue bringing their children to this hospital?"

Murray raised his hands in blatant surrender, giving up. He'd half agreed with the detective all along. Now it was totally out of his hands if he didn't want this blowing up in his face.

"You've made your point."

Brodie didn't take the opportunity to gloat. It wasn't about that. He merely said, "I hope so." And then he got back to business. "We're going to need a printout of names, home addresses and phone numbers—ASAP," he informed the man.

Murray nodded, beginning to type again. "Way ahead of you." Kori stepped back, away from the director's desk and out of his earshot.

"I didn't know your sister worked for the *Aurora*

Gazette," she whispered to Brodie in a barely audible voice. She had been under the impression that practically all of the Cavanaughs were involved in some form of law enforcement.

Watching Murray as he compiled the information he had requested, Brodie hardly spared her a look. He didn't want to distract the head of hospital employment from what he was doing.

"She doesn't." Brodie's voice was so low, it barely registered.

Kori stared at him. Turning her back to the intimidated head of personnel, she had to ask her partner, "You mean you lied?"

"Not exactly." When she looked at him for an explanation, he gave her the best one he could. "Skylar took a couple of journalism courses when she was in college. At the time, she was toying with the idea of becoming a journalist. That lasted for about six months before she torpedoed the idea."

"But you asked him how he'd feel about the *Aurora Gazette* running a story about him not being cooperative," she reminded Brodie. "You made that up?"

"A fair question," Brodie agreed. "I never said that Skylar could get the *Gazette* to run it."

He looked at her to see if she disapproved of his method or had something to say about his deception. Or worse, if Kori's sense of self-righteousness might egg her on to tell Murray the truth and consequently cause him to stop what he was doing right now.

But none of that happened. Instead, Kori appeared to be waiting for the man to finish printing the list of names and addresses he had come up with.

When the computer stopped printing, she took the

list from Murray and quickly scanned it, doing a mental tally.

All in all, it looked like there were twenty-seven people they needed to talk to.

"Thank you, Mr. Murray. If we wind up finding Rose Williams's daughter, we'll make sure that you get the credit," Brodie said, taking the list from Kori, folding it and tucking it into his shirt pocket.

Murray shook his head. The bottom line was that he just wanted this to be behind him so that the hospital could move on.

"Just make sure you find her," the personnel director told them.

"We fully intend to, Mr. Murray," Kori replied, shaking the man's hand. "And thank you for all your help."

Murray merely nodded as they left his office. The man still looked very shaken.

As THEY LEFT the building, Brodie focused on the list in his pocket. There were a lot of names on it. "We're going to have to get a task force together," he told Kori. "There are too many people on that list for the two of us to be able to talk to in any sort of a timely manner. Not if we want to do a thorough job. Any time we spend talking to one person is that much more time the actual kidnapper might utilize to escape with the baby."

Kori decided that there was no point in her taking offense, but this was *not* her first rodeo and he should have realized that. "I've already got people on standby," she told him.

Brodie nodded. "I kind of figured you would," he replied as they walked down the hospital's driveway.

"By the way, what you did back there with Murray…" she began.

Still not quite sure how to read this woman, Brodie braced himself for anything, including a possible lecture. "Well, you know, desperate times…" he said, allowing his voice to trail off.

She smiled at her partner. "I was going to say that I was pretty impressed by how quickly you picked up on being so innovative," she said, referring to his story about his sister.

Brodie slanted a look at her, feeling relieved. "So then you're not mad about my taking a liberty?"

"Why would I be?" she asked. The truth was that she'd been prepared to be a great deal more creative to get the director's cooperation. "There's a baby's life at stake here," she told him. "The only thing that would make me angry is if we were forced to drag our heels. And thanks to you and your 'sister the journalist'—" the corners of Kori's mouth curved in an amused smile "—we weren't."

Her smile widened as they reached her vehicle and got in. "You know, I really think that this partnership definitely has possibilities, Cavanaugh."

Brodie didn't say anything. He merely flashed a smile at her.

Maybe it was because she had had so little to eat today and was basically operating on fumes, but she could feel his smile burrow into her chest and then spread out warm fingers that seemed to touch every single part of her.

Damn, she was definitely tired, Kori thought.

Kori did her best to block out the effects that Brodie's sizzling, sexy smile managed to generate, but it took concentrated effort on her part.

WALKING INTO THE squad room, before she contacted the people she used to make up a task force, Kori decided to take a little time out so that she could call her father. Given the nature of her job, she knew he worried.

Hell, she thought, the man would have worried if she worked in a library. The specter from the night so long ago hovered over both them, casting a dark shadow. She didn't want her father's imagination running away with him, especially since she normally had a habit of contacting him if she was planning on being late.

It took her five rings to get her father to answer the phone.

"Hi, Dad. Sorry I didn't check in with you earlier," Kori said. It wasn't until just now, when she heard her father's voice, that she remembered he had gone to see his doctor for a checkup. "So what did the doctor say? Is everything all right?" she asked him, mentally crossing her fingers. Since that night when she had almost lost him, she took nothing for granted.

"Yes," Bill's booming voice reassured her. "The doctor gave me a clean bill of health. According to him, I'm going to be around for a really long time." Deftly, her father changed the subject. "So, are you going to be late?" he asked. She was ordinarily home by now unless something was going on at the station.

"I'm afraid I am." She glanced toward the squad room doorway. One member of her team had walked in. "It looks like I might be pulling an all-nighter, Dad."

She and her father had always been on the same wavelength. Now was no different. "Is it bad?"

She wasn't about to insult her father's intelligence by attempting to pretend the situation was better than it was.

"I'm afraid it is, Dad," Kori confessed. "Someone kidnapped a baby girl from her mother's hospital room today."

"And no one saw anything?" her father questioned. His tone told her that he already knew the answer to that, but was hoping to be told differently.

"No one saw anything," Kori confirmed, frustrated.

Her father was quiet for a moment before he said in a confident voice, "You'll find her."

Kori sighed. "I wish I had as much faith in me as you do."

"That's okay, honey. I have enough faith in you for both of us," he assured her with a soft laugh. "After all, you're the reason I'm still alive," he added in all sincerity.

Kori smiled to herself as she turned away from the others to ensure her conversation remained private. "Dad, Brian Cavanaugh is the reason you're still alive," she tactfully reminded him.

"That's not how I remember it, honey. It wasn't Brian Cavanaugh's arms that were around me in those crucial moments, anchoring me to this life and refusing to let me die and slip away," her father said.

This was familiar territory and while Kori appreciated what her father was saying, right now, she didn't have time for it. The rest of her task force had just showed up. She didn't expect them to do much at this hour, but at least they could get started.

"Dad, I've got to go. I've got a task force to put together," she told him.

Kori heard him chuckle. "That's my little girl. You go do what you have to. I'll leave the porch light on for you."

"Oh good," she quipped. "I hate to come stumbling home in the dark."

She heard her father laugh again. "You know, honey, someday that smart mouth of yours is going to get you in a whole lot of trouble."

"It hasn't so far," she returned.

"It's just a matter of time," her father assured her. "Your luck can't last forever."

"Huh. Who says?" were Kori's parting words to her father. "I've really gotta go, Dad. I'll see you later." She terminated the call.

As she tucked away her cell phone, Kori turned around and saw that Brodie had been standing close enough to be able to listen to most of her end of the conversation without any trouble.

"You always eavesdrop?" she asked Brodie in surprise as she crossed the last few steps to him.

He wasn't about to deny that he had overheard. "In my defense, I wasn't intentionally eavesdropping."

Her eyes swept over him. "I don't see any handcuffs holding you in place."

"Not any real ones, anyway," he told her. When she lifted an eyebrow, he clarified. "After all, you said you were going to brief your task force, so I didn't want to go wandering off so that you wouldn't be able to find me when you got started."

She gave him a very cryptic look, not believing a word of his excuse. "How very thoughtful of you."

Brodie pretended to take her words at face value. "I always try to be," he answered. Then he asked her, "Everything okay?"

Rather than automatically say yes, Kori felt her back going up. "Why?"

Brodie shrugged. "It's your tone. You sounded worried when you were talking to your father. I thought maybe something was wrong."

She felt her irritation growing, then managed to talk herself out of it. The man was a Cavanaugh. Cavanaughs took an interest in everything and everyone around them. He was just being nice, she silently insisted. He wasn't trying to be invasive, or nosy.

"Everything's fine," she told him. "Or it will be once we find this baby and hang whoever took her by their thumbs from the nearest yardarm."

Brodie looked at her, cocking his head. "The nearest what?"

"Yardarm," she repeated. Then, because Kori realized that Brodie probably hadn't read the same books as a child as she had, she elaborated on the term. "It's a mast on a ship."

He looked a little dubious. "Okay, I'll take your word for it."

"You didn't read much as a kid, did you?" Kori asked with a laugh.

"Obviously not the same books that you did," he replied.

"Actually, there wasn't much money when I was growing up. To entertain myself I would read everything I could get my hands on," she confessed.

The smile that curved his mouth was self-depreciating. "I spent most of my time playing video games," he replied.

"That must have made your father very proud," she quipped.

"I don't know about that," he told her. "But it did help build up my reflexes."

She nodded her head. "Which will come in handy if we ever have to battle it out with the undead."

As she said that, she eyed some of the officers in her task force, They didn't look overly happy about having to be here at this hour.

The oldest member, as well as the shortest member of the team, Roy Valente, was immediately alert as he picked up on the last thing that was said.

"We're going to be up against the undead?" He looked both uneasy and intrigued. "Since when did the undead invade Aurora?" he asked, looking at Kori as if he were seriously asking the question.

"No forces of the undead," she said. "What we've got is a baby stolen from her mother's room in the hospital. If you ask me, that's definitely enough of a 'bad guy' in any book," Kori told the four other members of her task force, looking at Alex and Roy.

"You're right." Mark Baxter agreed with Kori. He looked at the other men gathered around Kori's desk. He zeroed in on Brodie. Raising a shaggy eyebrow, he asked, "And you are?"

Kori realized that she had definitely dropped the ball. She really was tired, she thought. "Everyone," she announced, "this is Brodie Cavanaugh, the newest member of our team. He'll be replacing Wills, who left us on Friday."

Fresh-faced and eternally eager, Richard Spenser was the first to extend his hand to Brodie. This was obviously Cavanaugh's first case with Missing Persons as well as his first day. "I guess you get to hit the ground running," Spenser speculated.

"Best way to learn," Brodie replied.

Spenser grinned at Kori, his recently straightened teeth spilling into a whiter-than-white smile.

"He's a Cavanaugh, all right," the detective declared,

then grew serious as he asked the leader of their group, "So what are we doing here in the middle of the night?"

Mark Baxter, another member of the team, rolled his eyes. "This is *not* the middle of the night. You're more of an old man than I am," he pronounced. "This is what we normal people think of as the shank of the evening. But his question is valid…" Baxter continued, looking expectantly at Kori. "What *are* we doing here? I had to break a date with this gorgeous creature that took me *forever* to finally arrange."

"What we're doing here is that we have twenty-seven people to talk to about what they might have seen in the hospital," Kori told her task force. "They showed up on the surveillance tapes in the same time frame that the baby was taken. They were on the maternity floor at the time. We're hoping that at least *one* of them gives us some kind of a lead."

"We're talking to them at this hour?" Valente questioned.

"Yes," Kori answered. She wasn't happy about the hour either, but she had to work with what she had. "You have a problem with that?"

"Not me." Valente spread his hands. "I was just thinking how popular this is going to make us, knocking on doors at this hour," he pointed out.

"I don't care about being popular," she told her team. "All I care about is finding that baby as soon as possible," she told the others.

As she spoke, she divided the list of the twenty-seven people who had been on the maternity floor at the time of the abduction into three separate piles, then handed the pages out. "Spenser, you're with Baxter. Simon, you're with Valente. And Cavanaugh," she said, turning toward her new partner, "you're coming with me."

He bowed his head in compliance. "I hear and obey," Brodie said.

She shot him a look that had been known to melt lesser men, then just continued walking.

"This should be interesting," Baxter murmured, only saying what the other members of the task force were thinking.

Chapter Nine

"Well, that was an immensely frustrating couple of hours that led nowhere," Kori said to her partner as they walked away from the last of their share of people to question.

In the interest of fairness, she had given each set of detectives nine hospital employees to interview. However, of the nine that they had drawn, only six were actually at home and none of those six had had anything productive to offer when they'd been questioned. Nobody had seen anything out of the ordinary.

"I sure hope that the others had better luck than we did," Brodie told her as they walked down the street to where Kori had parked her vehicle.

Kori frowned, frustrated. Things could have gone a lot better. She was beyond tired. "The only way they could have had worse luck would be if none of the people were at home," she said.

Brodie didn't quite see it that way. "Actually, not finding these people at home leaves the possibility open that when they *are* questioned, they might have something viable to offer by way of an observation." He glanced at Kori, who wasn't saying anything. "In other words, they might have actually seen something."

Kori sank back in the driver's seat. Her car key was in her hand but she hadn't put it into the ignition yet.

Brodie leaned forward, looking at her profile. "You know, I think I can actually *see* the wheels turning in your head," he told her. "What are you thinking?" In his opinion, Kori was being almost unnaturally quiet.

She shifted in her seat, then glanced at Brodie. He was right. Something *had* occurred to her. "That the people we did get to talk to, for one reason or another, might not have been all that forthcoming."

"Okay," Brodie said gamely. "So how do you propose we find out if they were or not?"

The fastest way she knew of was to look into bank statements. Most criminals weren't nearly as smart as they thought they were and were very prone to making amateur mistakes.

"The best way I know of is to take a look at their bank records or examining their lifestyles. If someone is suddenly spending money like water, there's usually a reason for that and it's not because a long-lost relative died and left them money," she told Brodie. Kori warmed to her subject. "Think about it. This might not be our kidnapper's first time stealing a baby. There might have been other infants taken from other local hospitals."

"Maybe," Brodie agreed thoughtfully. "Or maybe this is just a one-time deal and the kidnapper was prompted by something else—like they want to have a baby but can't—and then they saw Rose's infant daughter and decided to take their shot."

It sounded way too plausible. He could very well be right, she thought darkly.

She frowned at him. "Do you always rain on people's parades?" she asked.

"No," he answered. "I just wanted to point out what we're up against."

"Trust me, I am *very* aware of what we're up against," she returned. Stretching, she rotated her head. She ached in places she didn't know she even had. Kori sighed. "Lord, I feel like someone mopped the floor with my whole body," she complained.

He grinned at her. "Well, for a mop, you look really great."

Kori laughed. "If that's supposed to be a compliment, I think you need to work on it," she told him. Taking a deep breath, she finally put her key into the ignition and started up her car. "Okay, let's see if the others had a more productive evening than we did."

"I'M GUESSING THAT they didn't," Brodie said to Kori in a low voice as they walked into the squad room less than half an hour later.

He looked around the all-but-barren room. None of the four other task force members was giving off any sort of a breakthrough vibe and he was guessing they would be if they'd had any sort of success tonight.

The next moment he heard Kori making it certain. "Did anybody find out anything tonight after questioning their list of hospital employees?" she asked, looking from one task force member to another.

"Yeah," Valente said, speaking up. "That I can't pull an all-nighter the way I used to." The recently divorced detective looked far from happy about the revelation.

"Well, I don't know about anyone else, but in our case, not everyone answered the door," Baxter told the others.

"Yeah, I don't know if they weren't home," Simon

chimed in, "or if they just weren't willing to answer their doors at that hour."

"Well, either way, you're right. It's late," Kori said, clearly not happy about today's outcome. If it were up to her, she would go on knocking on doors and asking questions, but she knew she had to pull back. There had to be a happy balance between doing her job and pushing her people beyond endurance. "We're going to have to stop and get a fresh start questioning the hospital employees in the morning."

"Tomorrow," Baxter repeated as he scrubbed his hand over his face, then looked at his partner. "That's the day after today, right?"

Spenser didn't answer immediately. He had to stop to think for a moment before he could actually answer with any sort of conviction, "Yeah," he finally said, "last time I checked."

Simon stared at the detective and laughed. "Just how tired are you?" he asked.

"Apparently very," Spenser answered. He looked at Kori, not sure if she had actually said they were free to go home or if that had been wishful thinking on his part. "If it's okay with you, Kennedy, I'm going to call it a day and go home."

"You wait any longer, and it'll be tomorrow," Brodie quipped.

Because of the nature of the crime, she had been pushing them hard, Kori thought. Too hard. She wasn't asking anything of them that she hadn't asked of herself, but that wasn't really a good excuse. The others had lives to get back to. They weren't like her. This *was* her life.

So she nodded toward Brodie. "Yeah, what he said. Right now, looking at all your bright, shiny faces, I'd say that we're all too tired to be productive. Like I already said, we'll pick this up in the morning," Kori told the rest of the task force.

"You'll get no argument from me," Valente said as he gathered up his things.

He was immediately joined by three other, barely audible voices, all expressing their agreement.

The task force quickly filed out, leaving the squad room and heading for their separate vehicles in the precinct parking lot.

Because he was technically "the new guy," at least in this department, Brodie took his time getting ready to leave. He was well aware that it was never a good idea, as "the new guy," to gain a reputation of being the first one out the door.

About to leave, Brodie noticed that Kori was still at her desk. Taking a closer look, he saw that she was reviewing something as she made notations on her computer. He didn't have the impression that she was just finishing something up so she could leave as well.

He debated just walking away, then decided to say something to her. "You're not going home?" he questioned.

"I will," Kori answered absently. Her attention was on something that she was rereading and she really wasn't paying attention to what he was saying.

"But not now," Brodie surmised.

His voice finally penetrating, Kori raised her eyes to his. Was he actually pushing for her to go home? "I don't need a keeper, Cavanaugh," she told him.

He made up his mind and crossed back to her desk. "Oh. I don't know. Maybe you do."

Kori felt her temper flaring but managed to bank it.

No, he couldn't have said what she thought he'd said. The man would have known better.

"Excuse me?" she challenged.

He shrugged, then told her simply why he had said what he had. "I've got a lot of people in my family who push themselves too hard and they don't even realize it."

Kori realized she was clenching her hands into fists and forced herself to relax—she was only marginally successful.

"I'm sure they all appreciate you taking an interest in their lives—" her eyes narrowed as she concluded more sharply "—but I don't need that."

He knew she expected him to back off—but in good conscience, he couldn't. "Oh. I don't know. I think everyone needs that once in a while," he said.

Maybe he didn't realize how dangerously close he was getting to having her explode, Kori thought.

"No offense, Cavanaugh, but I don't really care what you think." Her eyes pinned his. "Is that understood?"

She expected him to back off, but he didn't. Instead, Brodie told her, "I thought that was the whole reason I'm part of the team."

"Are you *trying* to get on my nerves?" Kori asked, doing her best to get back to the notes she was making to herself.

"Not particularly," Brodie answered with an innocent expression. "But then, Pinocchio didn't appreciate having Jiminy Cricket right away, either."

Okay, enough was enough. She was through trying to be nice about this. Kori stopped making notes and put down her pen. "If you were Jiminy Cricket, I could at least squash you like a bug," she informed him, hoping that would get her message across and get him to back off so she could finish what she was attempting to do.

But Brodie ignored what she was saying. Instead, he decided to level with her. "Look, I know the chief of D's is going to ask me how you're doing—I don't really need to tell you that he takes an interest in all his people and that you, because of the nature of the way your relationship began, have a special place in his heart. If I tell him that I stood by and watched you work yourself into a total frenzy, he's not going to be very happy with me—or you, for that matter. I don't want to have to give him a negative report—so help me out here," Brodie requested.

Was he actually missing the point? she wondered. "The negative report, Cavanaugh, is that we haven't gotten anywhere."

"And we're not going to," Brodie stressed, "if you wear yourself completely out. C'mon, Kennedy, do me a favor. Call it a day and go home. Even a superhero like you needs to sleep once in a while." He saw her open her mouth and put up his hand like a traffic cop in an effort to stop her. "Tell you what, since my car is still in the lot, let me drive you home. That way," he told her with emphasis, "neither one of us has to worry about you falling asleep at the wheel."

"I have *never* fallen asleep at the wheel," she informed him indignantly.

Brodie was unmoved. "Doesn't mean that this won't be the first time."

The laugh that escaped her lips was a very dry one. "You really like to argue, don't you?" she charged,

He didn't even try to deny her accusation. "I've got two sisters and a whole bunch of girl cousins. Kennedy, I was *born* arguing," he replied. "So you might as well just retreat," he told her. "Because you're not going to win this."

"You realize that I could just order you to go home," she said.

The look he gave her in response told Kori that she was free to try, but it might not quite go the way she anticipated that it would. "You could waste time like that, sure."

Leaning back in her chair, Kori stared at him, then she sighed and pushed herself away from her desk. "I'm too tired for this."

"Finally," he declared, taking that as a sign of victory. But he made no effort to leave the squad room until she gathered her things together and began to make her way out.

"You know, maybe I should have you meet my father," Kori said as she walked through the door that Brodie was holding open for her. This time, when she smiled, she wasn't forcing it. "I've got a feeling he'd really like you."

He took her assessment in stride. "Why shouldn't he?" Brodie asked. "I'm a really likable kind of guy."

Kori gave him a look as they went toward the elevator. "I'd say that is up for debate."

He was unfazed by her tone. "That's okay. We'll let your father cast the deciding vote."

Did he actually think she was about to bring him home to meet her father? That was not about to happen. She'd only said that in a moment of weakness.

Wow, she really *was* tired.

"In your dreams," she responded to his suggestion that her father cast the deciding vote.

Brodie glanced at her as Kori pressed for the elevator. He noted that her expression had turned rather sad. Something else was up, he thought. Something that didn't fit in with the banter.

"What's the matter?" he asked.

She shrugged, looking away. "I'm just thinking about how Rose must feel."

"Rose?" he questioned. For a moment, he didn't make the connection.

"Rose Williams," Kori elaborated. Then because there was no recognition in his eyes, she said, "The baby's mother."

For a moment, because of the bantering between them, the baby's mother's name had eluded him. But not anymore.

"Don't dwell on that," he told Kori. "Focus on how Rose is going to feel when we bring her little girl back to her."

He was taking things for granted. "*If* we bring her little girl back to her."

"We will," Brodie told her with unmistakable confidence.

"You can't know that," Kori insisted.

"The first step in making something happen is believing that it can—and will," he told her. "The next step is good police work. And your team," he reminded her, "is the best."

She frowned at him as she stepped into the elevator. The doors closed with a resounding whoosh.

"Don't patronize me."

"I'm not," he replied. "What I'm doing is just repeating what my uncle told me when he brought up my being your partner."

"Your uncle really said that my team is the best?" she questioned.

The corners of his mouth curved slightly as they got off the elevator. "He did."

Was he deliberately setting her up? she wondered.

After all, she didn't really know this man yet, outside of the fact that he was a Cavanaugh.

"In those words?" she questioned uncertainly.

Brodie didn't hesitate for a second. "In those words."

Kori still wasn't a hundred percent sure if she believed him, but she made a decision. "I think I should quit while I'm ahead."

Brodie's smile began in his eyes and radiated outward. "Good idea. So..." he said as they went outside "...should I drive you home or should I just follow you?"

She didn't understand. "Why would you follow me home?" Kori asked. Was he talking about stalking her?

He looked at her as if the answer to that was self-evident. "To make sure you got there."

Okay, now he was really pushing it. "I don't need you watching over me, Cavanaugh."

"Probably not," he agreed, "but humor me. Just in case the chief of D's is going to ask me, I need to be able to honestly tell him that, one way or another, I saw you home."

"Cavanaugh." Kori's voice went up, a warning note practically vibrating within it. She was very close to telling him what he could do with his insulting effort to keep tabs on her.

But Brodie talked over her. "The chief of D's cares about you, Kennedy. The way he cares about all of us."

"All of us, huh? So does that mean he's going to ask me if *you* got home safely?" she challenged.

"Probably somewhere down the line," Brodie answered without so much as blinking an eye. "The sooner you stop fighting me on this, the sooner you can get home and go to bed." He saw suspicion flare in her eyes, so he felt obligated to add, "Alone," just in case she thought he meant something by that.

Kori lifted her chin defiantly. "There was never any question about that," she informed him icily.

Brodie smiled at her. *Really* smiled. Even though she was exceedingly exhausted, she could still feel the effects of his smile as it seemed to burrow into her stomach, throwing it into complete chaos.

Brodie was right. She *was* too tired to work, at least productively, Kori told herself.

She needed a good night's sleep so that she wasn't subject to these sorts of thoughts tomorrow and could turn her attention to her work full-time.

"Okay, you can drive me home," she told him almost grudgingly as she got into his police-issued vehicle.

SHE STRUGGLED TO keep her eyes open so that she could direct him to the small house she shared with her father. Damn, she was more tired than she had originally thought.

Brodie pulled up at her curb, then turned toward her. "Do you need me to walk you to your door?" he asked her gamely. "No charge," he added.

She didn't know if he was being serious, but she was taking no chances. "I think I can find my way home," Kori informed him.

Rather than make a comment one way or another, Brodie decided to tactfully retreat. He felt it was better that way for both of them.

"All right, Kennedy. I'll swing by in the morning to pick you up," he told her as she opened the door on her side to get out.

She looked at him blankly. "You don't have to do that."

"Yes, I do. Your car is still in the rear of the police station," he reminded her.

Kori rolled her eyes. She'd forgotten about that. "I guess I really am tired," she admitted.

He shrugged as if that were no big deal. "We all get that way sometimes," he told her. "Well, good night, Kennedy. I'll see you in the morning."

"Yes," she said with resignation, "I know." Kori mumbled something else in response as she let herself out and walked up her driveway.

She felt his eyes on her as she closed the door behind her. The man obviously took his promises seriously, she thought.

Chapter Ten

Kori was halfway up the stairs, making her way to her bedroom, when she realized that her father was sitting in the living room, sound asleep on the recliner she had bought him for Father's Day several years ago.

Turning around on the stairs, she felt a pang of guilt.

It was obvious that her father had fallen asleep waiting for her to come home. Kori shook her head. He hadn't done that in years. But then, she thought as she made her way back downstairs, she was usually home at a decent hour. This was way beyond a decent hour.

Crossing over to the living room sofa, she picked up the blanket that had been thrown over the back of that piece of furniture for as long as she could remember. Bringing it with her, Kori very carefully covered her father with it. Lately, the nights had been unusually chilly, and she didn't want him getting cold.

"Oh, Dad," she whispered as she spread the blanket over him, "you should know by now that I can take care of myself. You didn't have to wait up."

Finished, Kori pressed her lips together as she stepped back to make sure that she had covered all of him. For the umpteenth time, she thought how grateful she was that Brian Cavanaugh had been there that night to save her father—and, consequently, her. If he hadn't been there, there was no doubt in her mind that she would have missed all this.

Satisfied that she had done what she could, she moved away very quietly. Retracing her steps, she went to the stairs.

"You haven't found the baby yet, have you?"

Kori stiffened. Her father's sleepy voice, suddenly coming out of the blue like that, caught her off guard.

For a second, she thought she had imagined it. But one look at the man's face told her that she hadn't.

She might have known. He must have heard her come in no matter how quiet she tried to be. The man had hearing like a bat.

Turning on the stairs to face him, she confirmed his suspicions. "No, we didn't."

"You will, Kori," he told her with a certainty that sadly eluded her. "You will."

"Go to bed, Dad," she replied. She wasn't feeling very optimistic right now and she was much too tired to debate over whether or not she and her team would be successful in recovering the kidnapped infant.

Her father drew back the blanket she had thrown over him and left it on the side of the recliner. Holding on to the chair's arms, he pushed himself into a standing position and got up.

"I can now that I know you're back safe and sound," he told Kori as he made his way to his first-floor bedroom.

"Uh-huh. G'night, Dad," she said as she continued on her way up the stairs.

Exhausted though she was, it took Kori a while to unwind and finally fall asleep. Miscellaneous details of the case kept popping up in her head. Not only that but, in the middle of it all, she would suddenly and completely unexpectedly, experience this warming, all-encompassing feeling slipping throughout her entire body. The same one that she felt when she reacted to Brodie's smile.

She did what she could to block it.

Kori finally fell asleep, almost in self-defense.

IN THE MORNING, she felt as if she was fighting her way to the surface through an unusually thick serving of oatmeal. Struggling to open her eyes, she was about as rested as someone who had slept on a bed of hot, lumpy coals.

If anything, Kori felt more tired than when she had fallen asleep. She made her way into the kitchen from memory.

Hearing her coming in, Bill, busy preparing breakfast, turned around to greet her. The greeting died on his lips, unspoken as his eyes grew huge. "Wow, honey, maybe you shouldn't go in today," her father commented as his eyes slid over her. "You look as if you're coming down with something."

"I'm fine, Dad," she insisted, taking her usual seat. "Or at least I will be once I find the miserable lowlife who stole that defenseless baby girl and bring her back to her mother."

"Very noble plan," her father replied as he brought over the black coffee he'd just made and filled the empty cup he'd placed in front of Kori. "But right now, I'm thinking of my own little girl."

"Dad," Kori said patiently after she took a long sip of the coffee and let it wind throughout her body, warming it and bringing it back online, "we've talked about this. I'm not a little girl anymore. I haven't been one in a very long time."

They had a difference of opinion on that score, Bill thought, saying, "You will *always* be my little girl. Case closed," with finality. "So, how's the new partner working out?" he asked as he buttered two slices of very lightly toasted white bread for her.

Kori shrugged. "Not great," she replied noncommittally.

"Why? What's wrong?" he asked. In his experience, the Cavanaughs were all good, decent people dedicated to their professions as well as their commitment to keep the citizens of Aurora safe.

She blew out an irritated breath. "Brodie Cavanaugh was the one who strong-armed me into calling it a night and coming home. I was all for staying at work, but he insisted I go home. He even drove me here so I wouldn't fall asleep behind the wheel." Kori frowned.

She didn't like being told what to do and her father knew it. Even if he didn't, the touch of disgust in her voice would have given it away.

Still, Bill couldn't help grinning. "I like him already." Just then there was a knock on their door. Her father looked at her. "Are you expecting someone?"

"Well, my guess is that it's either a very polite home invader, or my new partner." She scowled at her plate. Now she wasn't going to be able to finish her breakfast. She should have come down earlier, she thought. "Since he drove me home, he's here to pick me up so I can get to my vehicle. It's parked at the police station."

Bill went toward the front door to open it. "Well, at least you know it'll be safe there," he said. "Nobody's going to steal a vehicle from the police station." With that, he opened the door. "Hello," he said to the tall young man in his doorway. "I'm Bill Kennedy. You must be Korinna's new partner."

"I must be," Brodie agreed. "And you're her dad."

Bill nodded as he drew open the door further for Brodie. "Guilty as charged," he said with a smile.

"You know, I think we met once at one of Uncle Andrew's parties." Brodie walked into the house. "As I recall, you came alone," he told Kori's father, glancing in her direction.

Bill nodded. "I think you're right. C'mon into the kitchen," he urged his daughter's new partner as he closed the front door. And then, as they walked into the kitchen, Bill nodded at the stove. "Have you had breakfast yet, Brodie?"

"I grabbed some coffee on the way over here," Brodie admitted.

"That's not answering my question," Bill said and then rethought his statement. "Or maybe it does. Grab a seat." He gestured to one of the remaining empty chairs. "How does scrambled eggs sound to you?"

Brodie saw the plate of eggs her father pointed out. "Great, but I don't want to eat your breakfast."

Bill waved away the other man's protest. "Go ahead, eat. There's more where that came from," he assured Brodie.

"Dad," Kori pretended to complain, "if you feed him, we'll never be able to get rid of him."

Brodie smiled at Kori, as if this was the first time he'd noticed her sitting there. They both knew that wasn't the case. "Maybe if you feed me, you'll bring out my better qualities."

"That's assuming that you *have* better qualities to bring out," Kori countered.

Bill looked from his daughter to the detective who had already gone out of his way for Kori. The older man thought he detected things in her voice that he wasn't aware of ever hearing before.

Bill smiled to himself as he pushed his plate over in front of Brodie. "Anything else I can get you?" he asked.

"Oh no, this is more than enough," Brodie assured him with feeling. "Really. I just came to pick up your daughter." Belatedly, the young detective realized that he hadn't told her father his name. Half rising in his seat, Brodie extended his hand to Kori's father. "I'm Brodie Cavanaugh, sir."

"Cavanaugh," Bill repeated. "I take it that you're also related to Brian Cavanaugh."

It was a given that all the Cavanaughs were related to one another in some fashion, but since Kori rarely talked about her work other than in general terms, Bill was rather curious as to exactly how the man who had saved his life was related to this young man who had been partnered with his daughter.

"Dad, we have to get going," Kori told her father. She was already on her feet and taking her empty plate to the sink.

She wanted to stop her father from asking more questions. He meant well, but that didn't mean he wouldn't ask embarrassing questions.

Bill raised his hands, symbolically indicating that he was backing off.

"Sorry, despite attending some of your uncle's parties, I don't usually get a chance to meet any of the people that Kori works with. I just wanted to make sure that she had someone to have her back."

Heaven only knew what her father was going to ask Cavanaugh next, but she wasn't about to hang around to find out.

"Time to go," Kori announced loudly.

On his feet, Brodie picked up the remaining piece of toast, nodding toward it.

"Thanks for the breakfast, Mr. Kennedy. It was great," he said with genuine enthusiasm.

Her father was preparing a fresh serving for himself. "It was my pleasure, Brodie," Bill said.

"See you tonight, Dad," Kori declared. She paused to brush a quick kiss across his cheek. She was impatient to get going and was out the door in seconds.

Brodie was right behind her, the last piece of toast disappearing behind his lips.

"My car's parked at the curb," he told her.

"I see it," she told him, adding impatiently, "I've got eyes."

He pretended to glance at them. "Pretty ones, too," Brodie acknowledged, then, in case she had some choice words about the compliment he had just paid her, he added, "I like your dad," just as they reached his car.

She slanted a look at her partner. "He seems to like you, too."

Brodie caught the less than thrilled note in her voice. Rather than just ignore it, he asked, "Is that a problem?" When she didn't answer, he pushed it a little further. "Did I miss something here?"

She had the nagging suspicion that her father was attempting to play matchmaker.

Kori sighed, getting into Brodie's car. She was probably just being edgy, but once the thought had entered her head, she couldn't get rid of it. Now that she thought about it, lately her father had been talking about how maybe she should start thinking about starting her own family, and while that seemed like a good idea somewhere down the line, she really wasn't ready to entertain that thought now—or maybe not even for a long while.

"No," she denied. "That's not a problem."

Brodie laughed, shaking his head. "Wow, that wasn't convincing at all."

She was not about to justify herself to him. He might be a Cavanaugh, but as far as she was concerned, he was the "new guy."

"Can we get back on point, please?" she said, buckling up.

"Actually, if you want to know the truth," he told her, starting his vehicle. "I was trying to distract you."

"Distract me?" she echoed, her eyebrows drawing together as she stared at him, perplexed. Why?" she asked, confused. And then her expression transformed to one of concern. "Why?" she repeated. "Did anything happen with the case that you're not telling me? And why would you be the one who was notified anyway? I should be the one in charge of this investigation."

"No one is disputing that," he told her. "I just thought if you were able to be a little more clear-headed, it might be a lot easier for you to think and investigate this awful kidnapping."

"Clear-headed?" she questioned.

"Yes." Looking to his left, he pulled away from the curb and headed straight for the precinct. "From what everyone told me about you when I asked them, they all agreed that you have this laser-like focus. And if anything else got in your way, you could just eliminate it and zero in on what you felt were the important details of the case."

"You *asked* about me?"

He hit her with another lethal smile. "Hey, I'm a Cavanaugh. Cavanaughs like to know what they're getting into."

She didn't care for being dissected this way—or the

way he had put it—but there was no sense in reading him the riot act. That wouldn't help any of them find the baby any faster—or get along any better. He was right about one thing, though. She needed to focus.

"Well, the first thing we're 'getting into' is getting the rest of the team together for a strategy session. We're going to rattle some cages until someone says something that we can use to find out just who took this baby and what happened to her. Babies do *not* just disappear into thin air."

"This one apparently did," Baxter muttered, frustrated when Kori said the same thing to the four other members of her task force in the conference room half an hour later.

"Well, I am not about to accept that," Kori informed Baxter passionately. She turned toward another member of the team. "Spenser, find out just how much this baby weighed when she was born and how many inches she measured."

"On it," Spenser replied. The detective started to leave the conference room to head for his own desk in the squad room.

"She was six pounds, two ounces and a total of nineteen inches long." Brodie spoke up before Spenser was able to leave and log onto his computer in order to get that information.

Pleased, as well as surprised, Kori nodded at Brodie. "Good work," she told her partner.

"How is knowing how much she weighed at birth supposed to help us?" Simon asked.

"Simple," Kori answered. "Since according to all the surveillance tapes we reviewed, the baby didn't appear to be carried out in plain sight, I have to assume that she was smuggled out in something." She glanced around the room at the men working the case with her. "This gives us a starting point. We're going to go over all the tapes again—" her words were met with groans, but she continued talking "—to see if we can see something that the kidnapper might have used to smuggle the baby out of the hospital.

"For instance, a laundry hamper, or those food delivery wagons the orderlies use to bring trays to the patients. A drugged baby could just as easily be smuggled out in one of those."

"You want us to check the whole hospital?" Baxter asked.

"Only as a last resort," Kori answered. "For now we concentrate on just that morning and just on the maternity floor—as well as the exits during that time period." Getting warmed up, the volume of Kori's voice increased. "We'll be looking for large handbags, backpacks, or the aforementioned laundry hampers, wagons and anything that could have been used to transport an infant without arousing any suspicions."

"Valri already reviewed the tapes," Brodie reminded her.

Kori nodded. "Yes, but she was looking for someone who was transporting a baby outright, not attempting to smuggle her out inside something. C'mon people, we've got six sets of trained eyes," she said to her task force. "One of us should be able to see something that looks out of place."

"Don't forget you wanted us to look into bank records and credit card statements," Simon reminded her.

"I'll get the list of names and get started on that," Brodie volunteered, adding, "I know some people who can get us those records pretty quickly."

Ordinarily, she might have challenged him. But she wasn't about to ask questions, not when there was possibly a baby's life at stake.

"Then do it," she told him. "The clock's ticking, people, and we're running out of time."

The declaration was greeted by the sound of chair legs scraping along the floor as everyone went to do their part.

Chapter Eleven

Because she thought there was something they might have overlooked or missed when their second day of investigations turned up nothing useful, on the third day, Kori decided to try another approach. In order to implement it, she didn't go to her lieutenant. Instead, she went straight to the chief of detectives.

Ultimately, he was the one who would have to approve this anyway.

Since Detective Jennings, the woman in charge of the chief of D's schedule, wasn't at her desk, Kori knocked on Brian Cavanaugh's door. When she heard his resonant voice respond, "Yes?" she peered into his office.

"Got a minute, sir?" she asked him, remaining just outside his door.

Brian was just finishing a report he wanted to issue. Looking up, he nodded at Kori. She didn't usually take it upon herself to just pop up in his office this way. This had to be important.

"For you? Always. Come on in, take a seat," he invited, half rising in his chair. "So, what can I do for you?"

Although they shared a special relationship whose roots went all the way back to that night in front of the convenience store, Kori had never just presumed that she could barge in on the man at will. But this situation was different.

"Well, you know about that case we caught, the one involving the baby who just seemed to disappear from the hospital." Replaying what she had just said in her head, Kori laughed at herself. "Of course you know. You're the chief of D's, you know everything."

"Well, not everything," Brian replied. "But I am aware of most things," he allowed, then urged, "All right, go ahead."

"We keep coming up against dead ends," she told him, distressed at the way the investigation was going. "I think we need someone to go to the public and make an appeal. See if someone saw anything that we could use."

Kori was well aware of the downside of making such an appeal. "I know we'll wind up getting a lot of blind leads that go absolutely nowhere." She slid to the edge of her seat, enthusiasm getting the better of her. "But all we need is that one lead that turns out to be real—and it'll all be worth it."

She was all set to try to talk him into it, but it didn't turn out to be necessary.

"That's a good idea," Brian told her. "I'll have Jennings set it up. She'll let you know the specifics as soon as she has them."

To Kori that just represented an extra step that wasn't really necessary. "I don't need to be informed, sir," she told the chief. "I just wanted to get the situation going."

"Of course you need to be informed," Brian contradicted. "After all, you'll be the one who's going to be making the appeal to the public."

The chief's words caught her completely off guard. She replayed them in her head. It didn't help.

"Wait. What?" The import of what Brian was saying finally hit her. "Oh no, sir, I didn't mean to imply that I was the one who was going to make the appeal," she protested.

"Why not?" he asked, then challenged, "Who better than you? You're familiar with all the details of the case, which means that you can answer any questions the reporters might ask," Brian pointed out.

What he was proposing terrified her. "I don't do well in front of an audience outside my own task force. The public…" Her voice trailed off as she shook her head, negating the very thought of having to stand up behind a podium and brief the general public.

Brian didn't accept her excuse. "Don't sell yourself short, Kori. You care," he emphasized. "That's the important thing here. The public can sense that you're being genuine." His tone indicated that, as far as he was concerned, this was a done deal. "I'll tell Jennings to set it up."

Suddenly feeling desperate, Kori said, "Your nephew would be better."

Intrigued, Brian felt compelled to ask. "Why would you say that?"

She shrugged haplessly. "I get the impression that your nephew's used to getting people to listen to him. I guess what I'm trying to say it that he can charm people into seeing things his way."

"I see," Brian replied, rolling the situation over in his mind. "Here's a thought. Why don't you bring Brodie to the press conference for moral support?"

Kori looked at the man she would have willingly followed through the gates of hell if he had asked her to. She had a bad feeling about this. "I'm not going to get out of this, sir, am I?" she asked him.

Brian's smile unfurled very slowly, working its way up to his eyes. In that, she suddenly realized, the chief of detectives reminded her a great deal of his young nephew.

Kori sighed and nodded, resigned to what she was going to have to do, even though the idea really did unsettle her.

"All right, sir. Have Jennings call me when the news conference has been set up."

The chief beamed at her. "Atta girl," Brian readily pronounced.

There was no mistaking the pride in his voice. He had made no secret of the fact that he felt as if he had a personal stake in Kori and in everything that she did and accomplished.

Not leaving anything to chance, Brian was on his landline, calling Brodie the moment that Kori walked out of his office.

He told his nephew exactly what had gone down and what he needed from the younger man. "Your new partner doesn't like the spotlight. All things considered, she would prefer to avoid it."

Brodie tried to read between the lines. "So you want me to be the one to make the appeal to the public?"

"No," Brian said. "I think she needs to learn how to do that. This job requires a lot out of its people." And he envisioned a great future for this young woman he had taken under his wing. "I just want you to back her up, offer her moral support," Brian told his nephew. "I'm counting on her earnestness getting the public on board."

Brodie neither craved nor shunned the spotlight. It was just another tool to be used if the occasion called for it. "You got it, Uncle Brian."

Brian had expected nothing less from him. "I knew I could count on you to help properly represent the department. Jennings is putting the press conference together right now. My guess is that it'll take place within the hour."

"Don't worry. I'll hold her hand," Brodie assured the chief. As a thought hit him, he suddenly added, "But only if she wants me to."

Brian laughed softly in approval. "Good man, Brodie," he told his nephew.

Kori was positive that the swarm of butterflies was going to overwhelm and get the better of her. Standing there, clutching the sides of the podium and staring into the cameras that were all pointed at her, recording every nuance, every word she was uttering, Kori thought her throat was going to close off, making her strangle on the words she was attempting to utter, all before a live audience.

Doing her best to pull herself together, she didn't even realize that Brodie had left her side as well as the podium. Belatedly, she saw that he had made his way down to the front row of newscasters, all of whom had gathered before her, ready to listen to whatever it was that she had to tell them before firing their questions at her.

Catching a glimpse of him now, Kori saw that Brodie had the most encouraging look on his face, aimed at her. It was as if he was mesmerized by every word she had to utter.

That was some bit of playacting on his part, she thought, considering that the man was already briefed on everything she had to tell this gathering of reporters and newscasters.

And then an incredible thing happened.

Kori found herself talking to only Brodie—just the way one of her teachers had once counseled her to do when she had to give a speech and it all but paralyzed her.

She didn't attempt to dissect it, she just went with it because, for whatever reason, delivering this briefing to Brodie seemed to help her not just manage to get through this ordeal, it also helped her get her message across to the reporters.

By the time Kori finished her briefing, she could feel her head spinning wildly. But at the same time she felt fairly certain that she had managed to drum up the necessary response from her audience to motivate them to get out there and search for some viable trace of this baby, who had somehow managed to disappear from her mother's room and vanish into thin air.

The inside of her mouth was as dry as a desert when she finished and turned away from the reporters. Only then did she blow out a shaky breath. Behind her, she heard the sound of people—reporters—gathering up their things and moving away. She surmised that they were preparing to carry the message she had imparted to them and take it to their various audiences.

The first person at her side was Brodie.

"How did I do?" Kori heard herself asking her partner. The next moment she was bracing herself for an answer she felt would most likely be critical.

"You were every bit as good as the chief of D's thought you'd be," Brodie told her. "Now let's get back to the precinct because the second this hits the airwaves we're going to be inundated with calls." As soon as he said that, another thought hit him. "We're going to need more people manning the phones."

Coming out of a self-imposed trance, Kori nodded as his words penetrated. While giving her briefing to the cameras, she hadn't been able to think past the moment. But now that this uncomfortable ordeal was behind her, her mind began whirling a mile a minute.

The very next moment she was striding toward her car, barely aware that she was leaving Brodie behind her until he called out to her.

"Hey, slow down, Speedy," he cautioned. "Unless, of course, you're planning on running all the way back to the station."

There was an unbelievable amount of energy surging through her veins. So much so that the idea of getting back to the police precinct on foot actually had some merit—for a moment.

"All right—for your sake, I'll slow down," Kori told him.

An amused expression playing on his face, Brodie told her, "I appreciate that, Kennedy."

MANY HOURS LATER, Kori felt as if, any minute, her head was going to just come right off.

It seemed as if she, Brodie and the rest of her six-person task force, not to mention the score of people commandeered to answer the phones, had been at this forever.

And not really having that much to show for it, she thought ruefully.

Leaning back, she ran her hand across her throbbing forehead, acutely aware of the pounding headache that had moved in and taken up residency there.

In a daze, it took her a moment to realize that someone was saying something to her.

Hanging up, Simon looked around the room. "You

know how people are always saying that all babies look alike?" he asked wearily, aiming his question at no one in particular.

"Yeah, people who have never had a child of their own say that," Valente responded. "As the father of two, I can definitely tell you that all babies do *not* look alike," he said. "Even when they're tiny little people, there's a personality there. Ask my wife," he added, picking up a receiver as yet another call had been put through.

Simon refused to surrender the point he had just made. "Well, I've just taken at least ten phone calls from ten different people who all swear they've seen our missing baby being taken from the premises by one person or another. What do you want to bet they didn't see anything?"

It was tempting to believe that, but that wasn't why they were here. "We can't assume that until we've sent someone to check out these different so-called sightings," Brodie told the man sitting to his left. And then, realizing he might have treaded on Kori's toes, he glanced in her direction. "I'm sorry. Did you want to say that to Simon?"

She didn't know if he was being serious or sarcastic, but because he had been there for her earlier at the press conference, silently supporting her, she decided to take his statement in a positive light.

"No, I think you took care of that nicely," she told him. And then she turned to look around at the rest of her team. "Cavanaugh is right," she told them. "We're going to need to check out every so-called sighting just in case it turns out to be the one we're looking for."

"All right," Valente said with a resigned sigh. "Who's going to go?"

There was only one fair way to do this. "We'll take

turns," Kori answered, then scanned the room. "Is that okay with everybody?"

Baxter was the first one to answer her. "Sure."

Valente nodded. "Yeah. Because of you, I get to skip a PTA meeting my wife was dragging me to."

Simon gave Kori a three-finger salute. "You got it, boss."

"I'm not your boss," Kori insisted. "All I am is the temporary leader."

Spenser merely laughed under his breath and said, "Yeah, right."

"Admit it, Kennedy," Brodie said, joining Kori as they left the room to check out a possible lead ten minutes later.

"Admit what?" she asked. She was relieved to take a break from the phones as she led the way to the elevator.

"That you like being the leader, temporary or not," he clarified.

"And if I do?" she challenged, pushing the down button a little too hard.

"That makes you human," he told her with an enigmatic smile.

"I am human," she readily admitted. "No arguing with that."

His eyes were warm as he looked at her. "Good to know."

The call they were responding to had come from a Cyndy Kellerman who had said she had been in the vicinity of the Aurora hospital approximately at the time of the abduction. Working, she couldn't come to them, so they came to her.

Cyndy worked in a fast-food restaurant that prided

itself on the number of different kinds of tacos offered on its menu.

"You hungry?" Brodie asked his partner.

Agitated, she wasn't even mildly tempted. "I'll eat later," she told him.

They walked into the small sitting area, which appeared as if it could seat about twelve. At the present time, there were only three people in the restaurant, all seated at different tables.

Brodie led the way to the counter, but he let Kori do the talking.

Showing the tall, gangly teenager behind the counter her identification, Kori asked him, "Is there a Cyndy Kellerman here?"

The teenager looked at the badge in front of him as if he were examining it for authenticity, and then raised his eyes to the woman's face.

"Did she do something bad?" he asked, his voice cracking. Kori decided the teen had to be a late bloomer.

Brodie had a feeling he was shooting the teen down when he said, "No, we just need to talk to her."

"You got one of those, too?" he asked, nodding at the identification Kori was just putting away.

"Yes, I do," Brodie answered, although he didn't bother taking it out. "Now, is she here?"

The teen nodded. "But she's taking a break, man."

Of course she was, Kori thought. "And where does she go when she's taking her break?" Kori asked.

The teen nodded in the general direction of the front door. "Outside."

Kori felt her patience ebbing away. "*Where* outside?" she asked, allowing the edge back into her voice. It had been another exceptionally long day and she was coming dangerously close to the end of her patience for today.

Nervous now, the teenager pointed to the back of the lot behind the building. "She likes to smoke. The boss wants her as far away from here as possible. I guess he hopes the walk back will be enough to get the smoke off her clothes. It's not," he confided, lowering his voice. "I can still smell it on her when she comes back."

"Sounds positively delightful," Kori murmured under her breath as she made her way out the door to talk to the young woman.

Kori and Brodie quickly scanned the area.

Cyndy wasn't hard to spot. The woman, who looked as if she was out of place working at the fast-food restaurant, was standing at the extreme left of the building, an absent expression on her face as she stared off into space.

"Lord, I sure hope she's sharper than she looks," Kori murmured.

"My guess is that she'd have to be," Brodie responded. "But don't judge a book by its cover. She might surprise us."

Kori laughed as she held up her crossed fingers in the air. "Well, here's hoping that you're right about that."

Chapter Twelve

Brodie and Kori had their wallets open to display their IDs and badges as they approached the woman they assumed had called the precinct, saying she was certain she had spotted the baby that had been talked about on the news.

"Cyndy Kellerman?" Brodie asked as he and Kori crossed to where the young woman was standing, smoking her cigarette. She stared sleepily at the approaching duo.

"Who's asking?" Cyndy asked.

"I'm Detective Cavanaugh and this is Detective Kennedy," Brodie said, indicating his identification and then Kori's.

The woman looked at them blankly, as if unable to fathom why the two detectives were there.

"You called the station, saying that you were certain you had seen the baby everyone was looking for on the day she was abducted," Kori prodded.

The light seemed to dawn on the young server's face. And then her eyes shifted from one detective's face to the other's.

"I did," the server told them defensively. She raised her chin.

"Tell us exactly what you saw," Kori urged, doing her best not to sound as impatient as she felt.

"To the best of your recollection," Brodie added. He deliberately ignored the look that Kori shot him.

"I saw this old lady with this baby in her arms, on the side of Aurora General." She looked from Kori to Brodie then appeared to consciously decide to give the details to Brodie. "She was in a hurry," Cyndy added. "The old lady, not the baby."

"How big was the baby you saw?" Brodie asked. Anything larger than a newborn meant she hadn't actually seen the baby in question.

Cyndy paused to think, then told him, "Not big. Like the one they keep showing on the news bulletins that they keep broadcasting." She became defensive again. "I wouldn't have wasted my time calling in to you guys if what I saw was a big baby."

"Okay, fair enough," Brodie said when he saw that Kori was about to say something he thought might wind up being off-putting. "Can you describe the woman who was holding this infant?"

"I said she was an old lady," Cyndy insisted and then emphasized the key word again. "*Old.*"

"How old?" Kori asked.

"Well, she was older than you," the server said flippantly. Then looking at Kori more closely, Cyndy added, "Yeah, I guess a lot older."

"Nice to know there are people older than me," Kori murmured under her breath as she turned away from Cyndy.

But Brodie heard her and he struggled to mask his amusement.

"Can you give us an estimate? How old do you think this woman was?" he asked Cyndy. "Was she forty?

Fifty? Sixty?" Each time he gave her a number, he looked at their potential eyewitness's face to see if he had guessed a number that came close enough.

But there was nothing to indicate that there had been a breakthrough.

The girl shrugged. "Look, I don't know," Cyndy stressed. "She was just old. Like grandmother old," she told Brodie.

That wasn't good enough in Kori's book. "All right, let's try this," she proposed. "What was this old woman wearing?"

"I dunno. Frumpy stuff," Cyndy said.

"Like a nurse's uniform?" Kori asked.

There was no recognition on the server's face. "I don't know. Maybe. I wasn't looking at her clothes. All I know is I wouldn't have been caught dead in those shoes she was wearing."

"Her shoes," Brodie repeated. He doubted this would lead them anywhere, but maybe it was better than nothing. At least it was worth a shot. "What kind of shoes was she wearing?"

"They were all crepey, rubbery-soled." The fast-food server shivered as she described the shoes. "I'd say they were probably good for a burglar. Nobody could hear you coming if you wore those," Cyndy surmised. There was a bit of vague admiration in her voice.

"Which way was she going?" Kori asked.

The server looked annoyed that the female detective kept breaking into her conversation with the tall, good-looking detective.

"Away from the hospital…" she said, her voice trailing off. "Or maybe she was going to it. Anyway, she was in a big hurry. At least for an old lady."

This wasn't getting them anywhere, Kori thought.

From the looks of it, this Cyndy person was just trying to flirt with Cavanaugh. It was time to wrap things up.

"Well, thank you very much," she said with finality. "If you think of anything else—" Kori took her business card out of her pocket and presented it to the girl "—give me a call."

Cyndy glanced down at the card in Kori's hand but made no effort to take it. "Can I give him a call instead?" she asked, nodding toward Brodie, a wide, inviting smile on her face.

"Sure," Brodie told her, taking out his card and giving it to the girl. "Whatever makes you more comfortable."

A very interested light came into the fast-food server's pale brown eyes. "You know, I wasn't looking to get comfortable."

At this point, Kori decided that maybe she needed to come to her partner's rescue before Cyndy made an even more aggressive move on Brodie. Hooking her arm through his, she pretended to draw him over toward their vehicle. "Well, we've got other leads to follow."

"Oh wait!" the server called just before they were able to get away. "There's one more thing."

Kori sighed and turned around. Doing her best to look patient, she asked, "Yes?"

"I found this on the ground. The old lady might have dropped it in her hurry to get away from there," the server said, holding up something she had dug out of her pocket. "But I'm not sure. It might have already been there when she went by."

"This" turned out to be an ankle bracelet, the kind that hospitals put on infants to start buzzing if they were being taken out of the hospital illegally.

Kori stared at her. "Why didn't you go to the police with this?"

"I didn't think it was anything important. I just picked it up off the ground and I forgot about it, I guess," the girl said with a shrug. "Like I said, it might have already been there before she went by."

"We're going to hang on to this," Brodie told her.

The young woman shrugged. "Sure. Whatever."

That was one clueless young woman, Kori thought. She waited until they were out of hearing range before she cryptically said to Brodie, "Maybe she needs a date for the prom."

Brodie laughed at her assessment, relieved to leave the young server behind. "Not my type," he told Kori as they got into the car.

"So, out of curiosity, what is your type?" she asked Brodie, buckling up.

He spared her a look before answering. "Older and wiser," he said significantly.

Kori started up the car, barely aware of doing it. She looked down at the ankle device one last time. "Speaking of wiser, this definitely belonged to our missing infant. At least we now know that whoever stole that baby had to work at the hospital." As she talked, Kori worked the situation out to her satisfaction. "How else would they know how to remove that ankle device?"

"Good point," Brodie said.

She barely heard him. "We need to re-canvass the maternity floor, see if we missed something else."

"We didn't miss that ankle device. That girl just happened to find it," he pointed out. He brought up another point. "There are five more names left to question on our part of this list." Taking out a folded paper from his pocket, he held it up. "That means there are five more potential witnesses."

"Five more people who *thought* they saw something," she said, pulling away from the taco restaurant.

"All it takes is one person," Brodie reminded her. "One potential witness felt they'd seen something and took it upon themselves to call in. You need to hold on to that," he told her.

He was right. She needed to hold on to that, to the fact that if everyone on the team kept at this long enough, they *would* find that one lead that would bring them to the right conclusion.

She nodded. "You're right," she told him. "Let's get going."

Out of the corner of her eye, she caught the look he sent her as she stepped on the gas. The smile caused every single nerve ending in her body to suddenly stand up and salute. It took her more than a second to focus on the road.

"My thoughts exactly," he told her.

NONE OF THE so-called witnesses panned out, although Kori was fairly certain that the people who had taken the trouble to come forward actually did believe they *had* seen something, be it the kidnapper or some sort of plan going down to either smuggle or steal the baby from of the hospital.

Then she thought of Cyndy Kellerman. Without realizing it, the young woman had provided them with their only single clue, such as it was.

Maybe they would get luckier, she thought, attempting to remain optimistic. Even so, a sigh managed to escape her. "I really hope we're not just spinning our wheels," she lamented as they drove back to the precinct.

"Those wheels just need to make contact once and we'll have our answers," Brodie told her.

"When you graduated the academy, did someone give you a box of quaint sayings you could just whip out and use to spread joy around?" she asked, her voice growing sharp. "Or do these 'uplifting' words just naturally roll off your tongue?"

Rather than get annoyed, Brodie just grinned at her again. "I guess these things just come to me because there is no box full of sayings for me to reach into," he told her.

"Too bad," she quipped, turning down the street toward the back of the police station. "If there was, I would have requisitioned it so that we'd have something to burn for the next bonfire."

"Okay," he said gamely, "now I have a question for you."

She supposed that she had this coming to her, whatever it was. She needed so stop saying what popped into her mind. "All right. Ask."

"Your mood," he said, watching her expression for any telltale signs of her next eruption. "It does get better, right?"

Yup, she thought. She'd had that coming. But she stopped short of an apology. This was her. If he didn't like it, then Cavanaugh could request another department transfer.

"When there's something there to improve it," she answered.

His eyes met hers—and then he nodded. "I'll hold you to that."

Hold you.

For a moment, completely out of the blue, the image of Brodie holding her just flashed through her mind, wrapping her with an all-encompassing warmth she couldn't immediately shake off.

And then, just as quickly, it was gone.

How the hell could she be thinking of something like that at a time like this? Kori silently upbraided herself. They had a kidnapped infant to find. She had absolutely no business letting her mind go elsewhere.

"Hey, where are you?"

Brodie's voice broke into her thoughts, pulling her out of her mental reverie and back into the front seat of her vehicle.

Blinking, she spared a glance at him. "What?"

"That expression on your face...you weren't here," he told her. "But you were definitely thinking of something. What was it?"

Floored and at a loss for an answer, she grabbed the first thing that occurred to her.

"Dinner," Kori answered. "I was thinking about dinner," she said, recalling one of the things he had said that first day. She built on that. "And how I haven't had it. Or lunch. I guess not eating is finally catching up to me."

"I knew it would," he told her. "Why don't I take you to get something to eat after we sign out at the precinct?"

"That wasn't a hint," she told him almost indignantly.

"No," he replied mildly, "that was a suggestion on my part. You've got to eat. I've got to eat. So why don't we just do it together?" Brodie could see that his partner was about to turn him down. He cut her off before she could. "Partners do grab something to eat together—and they even talk while they're doing it. It's called getting to know each other." He looked at her, his mouth curving in amusement. "Unless you're afraid to spend time with me."

Her eyebrows drew together. Was he that full of himself? He was handsome, but not *that* handsome. "That's ridiculous. Of course I'm not afraid."

"Great. Because I know this really great place where we can grab a meal and talk for as long as you'd like."

As long as *she'd* like? He was lobbing the ball into *her* court? Just what did he think he was doing? She'd set him straight. "So it's a dine-and-dash place."

Brodie just shrugged. "It's anything you want it to be."

"I'm not sure I follow you," Kori said, her voice getting an edge to it again.

As if to tease her, Brodie went literally with the words and not the gist behind them. "Why, Kennedy, you're not a follower. You're a leader. We both know that."

"Right now, I'm just a tired detective. I just want to pick up the next list of people to interview so I can be ready to go tomorrow—and call it a night," she concluded.

When they got back to the conference area that had been set aside in the squad room, Kori found that the list of possible witnesses had shrunk—by a great deal.

"Where are all the other names?" she asked Baxter, holding up the short sheet of names that was left.

Baxter nodded at Brodie. "Why don't you ask him," he suggested.

"Cavanaugh?" Kori questioned incredulously. "He was going around in circles, same as I was. Why would I ask him?"

"Because the chief of D's—otherwise known as Cavanaugh's uncle—thought we could use some more people to conduct those interviews. Enough detectives were requisitioned for us to do the work properly," he told Kori.

There was only one thing she wanted to know. "Have we made any progress?"

"Well, we've had a few more leads," Simon told her, "but it's going to be a while before we know if any of those leads pan out."

"So no," Kori concluded from what the other detective said.

"For now," Valente allowed, catching the tail end of the conversation. "But that doesn't mean that one of these leads won't be able to finally bring us to the actual kidnapper."

"You know, there's even talk that this might be the beginning of a new baby abduction ring forming," Spenser told her. Joining the group, he seemed even more exhausted than she felt.

Tired as she was, Kori exchanged looks with Brodie. They had the same thought and both shook their heads.

"I don't know," Kori replied. "I don't really think so. It just doesn't feel like that's the case here. Think about it," she said to the men in the room who comprised her initial task force and were now preparing to leave. "Unless this baby was the first, why haven't we heard about any other recent abductions taking place?"

Spenser shrugged. "Because maybe this baby *is* the first."

"You know that old saying?" Brodie said to the others.

It was Kori who sighed. "Another old saying, Cavanaugh? Okay, what sage piece of advice are you imparting this time?"

"When you hear hoofbeats, think horses not zebras," Brodie said with a straight face.

Simon looked at his partner and shrugged in confusion, then asked, "And that means?"

Brodie explained patiently. "That maybe this is just a single abduction. Maybe whoever made off with the baby just wanted *that* baby, or *a* baby. They didn't want to begin their own nursery." He didn't wait for anyone to agree with him—or argue, either. Instead, he went another route. "Anyway, I think we're all pretty much too wiped out to hash this out now. Let's all just go and get something to eat, then go home and get a good night's sleep. We'll take another look at this in the morning when we can think more clearly."

Baxter glanced at Kori. It was clear that he agreed, but wanted to see if she was on board. "That okay with you, Kori?"

"Right now, that's just great with me," she said without a trace of sarcasm. "But then, I'm so tired that I'd probably agree to anything—within reason," she specified when she saw the light entering Brodie's eyes.

Brodie grinned broadly at her. "Define *reason*."

"Off the top of my head, I'd say anything that doesn't cross your mind," she answered.

"Well, that's fair—I think," Simon pronounced.

"Nobody asked you," Brodie pointed out.

"Also true," Simon said, inclining his head. "Well, I'm going home. Good night, cellmates. See you in the morning," Simon told no one in particular as he walked out.

Chapter Thirteen

Leaving the building, Kori paused on the top step before descending the rest of the stairs and out into the parking lot.

Brodie looked at her. "Something wrong?"

"You know, about going together to grab some dinner…" she began, searching for a way to word what was probably going to come off as a rejection in his eyes. "I think I'll take a rain check."

"Oh?"

Kori continued walking to where her vehicle was parked. "Yes. I'm just way too tired to chew," she told her partner. "Besides, if I know my father, he probably has something warming on the stove for me. No sense in letting that go to waste—again."

"You know," Brodie told her, "I'm getting the impression that you don't want to be seen out in public with me."

She couldn't read his expression. She didn't think that he looked annoyed, but his comment made her wonder if maybe he felt insulted. She couldn't really tell.

"What are you talking about? I've been seen out in public with you everywhere for the last few days," she pointed out. "Every time we leave the precinct, we've practically been joined at the hip."

"Work doesn't count," Brodie answered. When he saw her begin to protest, he added, "It's not voluntary."

"I beg to differ," she told him. "If you recall, I split the task force into three groups. I could have picked anyone else, but I told you that you were with me." The moment the words were out, she realized she'd set herself up.

Amusement curved Brodie's mouth. A mouth she noticed seemed to be getting progressively more sensuous. "Why did you do that?"

"Because I needed my head examined," she answered tersely, then sighed. "And because you're my partner." She closed her eyes for a moment, regretting this path she'd just taken. But now that she had, she might as well get the rest of this out. "And as far as partners go, you're all right," she told him grudgingly.

Brodie clutched his chest. "Wow, that's a really heady compliment."

Kori frowned. Okay, time to wrap this up and go home. "Speaking of heads, don't let that go to yours."

Brodie laughed. He looked as if he knew the sound of that laugh was burrowing into her consciousness, unsettling her.

"Don't worry, I won't," he promised. Kori had already started to walk to her car. Brodie called out to her. "Hey Kennedy, you sure you don't want to stop somewhere and get a beer and some pretzels?"

She was a sucker for pretzels, although the thought of beer didn't move her. "I'm sure—and when we do go out, Cavanaugh, I'm not going be that cheap a date. Count on that."

He grinned at her. "Then I guess I'd better start saving up so I can do this right."

"I guess so," she agreed.

As she turned to her car, she felt her mouth curving in an amused smile. *Okay, so maybe he isn't so bad after all*, she thought.

BILL KENNEDY LOOKED at his daughter in genuine surprise when she opened the front door and walked in. "I wasn't expecting you home before midnight," he told her.

"Yeah, Cinderella called. She said she wanted her slippers back," Kori quipped.

It was an inside joke between them. When she had been a little girl, Cinderella had been her very favorite fairy tale. She had made her father read it to her so many times, she could actually recite the story by heart. She had even gone so far as to sew herself a makeshift ball gown. She'd worn it three years in a row for Halloween until she'd finally outgrown it.

Remembering, her father smiled. "Did you tell her she couldn't have them?"

"No," Kori answered, keeping a serious expression on her face. "I felt sorry for her. Besides, keeping those slippers would be stealing and you taught me to always be honest."

"I didn't need to teach you to be honest," Bill told his daughter with pride. "You were born that way." Then, changing the subject, he asked, "You haven't eaten, have you?"

There was no point in denying it or making up excuses. Her father would see right through that. He always had.

"You know me too well, Dad. As a matter of fact, for the last half hour, I've been fantasizing about your fantastic roast beef sandwiches. Any chance you can whip me up one of those?"

"Every chance in the world, honey. You want it in the kitchen, or should I bring it to you out here?" he asked, thinking that every step she took at this point was an effort. If he knew his daughter—and he did—she had pushed herself too hard again.

"I'll have it in the kitchen, Dad—as long as you agree to join me and have one as well," Kori told him.

When Bill smiled, people told him that he looked just like his daughter. He smiled now. "I thought you'd never ask."

Bill Kennedy led the way into their kitchen, attempting to gauge his daughter's mood by what she was saying. Over the years, he had found that the direct route was always the simplest—and the most satisfying.

"So, how's the investigation going?" he asked as he opened up the refrigerator and rummaged around on the shelves. Because Kori was such a fan of roast beef, Bill always made sure that he had at least half a pound of the meat, thinly sliced and rare, on hand, as well as tomatoes and lettuce.

"Still stuck in first gear," Kori lamented. For now, she decided not to mention the tracking device that had been tossed away and found on the ground. It might not lead them anywhere, either.

"After that great appeal you made to the public this morning?" Bill asked his daughter in amazement. "I would have thought that you would have gotten a great many calls in response."

"Oh, we did. Trust me, we did," she told her father, a sense of weariness slipping into her voice. Kori paused for a moment to sink her teeth into her first bite of the thick roast beef sandwich, savoring the familiar, wonderful taste.

"But?" her father asked, waiting to hear the downside of the story. The way she had phrased it, he knew there had to be a downside.

"*But*," she echoed, "none of those so-called tips that were called in led us to anything remotely productive. That's not to say that they won't," she quickly corrected, "but to get to that point involves having the team wade through all those calls that had come in and *keep* coming in."

"You need help?" Bill asked, about to volunteer his services.

"Thanks, Dad, but luckily, Chief Cavanaugh gave us a boatload of officers to help man the phones." She paused again to take another bite. "He also recruited a bunch of detectives to conduct the face-to-face interviews with all the callers whose stories seemed to be at least partially credible."

"Brian Cavanaugh's a good man," her father said as he sat down opposite her at the table. "But then, you and I already knew that," he concluded with a smile.

"Yes, we did," Kori agreed absently.

"But?" Bill prodded. He could see that something else was bothering his daughter.

Kori put down her sandwich in order to share what was eating away at her. "The longer this takes, the harder it's going to be to find that little girl, Dad. I'm afraid that we might wind up missing our window of opportunity and being too late."

Bill closed his hand over hers and squeezed it for a moment, trying to will his strength to her. "You'll do it, Kori. I've got faith in you, remember?"

She laughed dryly. It was going to take more than just her father's faith in her to get the job done. "You forget one little thing. I'm not a miracle worker."

"Don't sell yourself short, honey," he told her. And

then his tone changed to a more uplifting one. "By the way, how's your new partner doing now that he's gotten used to what the job requires?"

Kori thought back to earlier that day. "Well, we went to interview the first eyewitness who called into the precinct and she wound up flirting with him. Does that give you any idea how things went?"

Her father nodded, taking the information in stride. "You never know. That sort of thing might turn out to be useful, Kori."

"How?" she asked. "How is that going to turn out to be useful?"

He thought for a second. "Well, someone calling in with a 'tip' might see Brodie and want to impress him with what she's seen."

That was what happened today and, as far as she was concerned, that sank like a lead balloon. "Dad, if what the 'witness' tells us turns out to be a lie, then what good is it?"

"Might not be a lie," her father pointed out. "It might actually be the truth, just drawn out to keep you enticed and on a string."

Kori read between the lines. "And by 'you,' you mean Cavanaugh."

"Yes," he told her, adding, "Whatever brings that little girl home."

Well, she certainly couldn't argue with that, Kori thought. She'd be willing to use whatever method she could. What was important here was to bring that infant home to the girl's mother.

Kori looked down at her empty plate. "Great sandwich, Dad—and great talk," she added. "As always." She smiled at the man she considered to be her anchor. "You always make me see things more clearly."

"Glad to help, honey. That's what I'm here for." He picked up her plate and put it on top of his. "And glad to hear that you and Brodie are working well together."

"Well, I wouldn't go so far as to say that," she cautioned.

"But you will," Bill assured her with confidence. When he saw the skeptical look on her face, he told Kori, "Don't forget, I met your partner at a few of Andrew's family gatherings." He liked the fact that he and his daughter had been assimilated into the family. It did bother him that in the last couple of years, Kori always seemed to find excuses not to attend. "You should attend those things, you know."

She shrugged a little too carelessly to be convincing, Bill thought. "Maybe someday."

"And maybe the next time you're invited," Bill stressed.

Kori shrugged again. She didn't want to be pinned down and wind up having to lie. "We'll see."

But for once, her father wouldn't let this go. "As a favor to your old dad, Kori."

"Maybe," Kori allowed. And then she smiled. "As soon as I find this 'old dad' you speak of."

Bill laughed, pushing himself to his feet. Bending over his daughter, who was still seated, he kissed the top of her head.

"Get some sleep, Kori. Morning will be here before you know it."

She nodded, rising to her own feet. "I'm much too tired to argue with you, Dad."

"Thank heaven for the little things," he acknowledged. Picking up the plates to take them to the sink, Bill watched his daughter as she walked to the stairs.

Kori didn't bother to turn around. She could *feel*

her father's eyes on her, watching her make her way to her room.

"I can get to my room on my own, Dad. You don't need to watch me walk up the stairs," she deadpanned.

"It's one of my few pleasures, baby—and so is calling you that," he told her, anticipating the next words out of her mouth would be to protest his referring to her in that way.

Kori merely laughed and shook her head. "Good night, Dad. See you in the morning."

It occurred to her as she went the rest of the way to the stairs that she never grew tired of saying that and never took saying it to her father for granted. She still occasionally dreamed about that awful night in front of the convenience store when she'd tried to stop her father from bleeding to death with her hands. The memory was never far from her thoughts.

She was really lucky, she thought. *Really* lucky. And the only way to show her gratitude was to pay it forward.

"So, is everyone all well rested?" Kori asked the next morning. Walking into the squad room, she had called her task force into the conference area.

Simon snorted, dismissing her question. "You ask me, Rip Van Winkle had the right idea with that twenty-year nap he took."

"Well, if you take that kind of a nap, when you woke up, you wouldn't be the stud you fancy yourself to be now," Kori told him.

The men sitting around the table exchanged surprised looks. "Hey, looks like our fearless leader is back among us," Baxter said to the others.

"I was never gone," Kori informed Baxter. "But this

case involves a really grim situation and, I don't know about you guys, but I'm not about to 'whistle a happy tune' until we locate that baby and I'm holding her in my arms—or at least one of us is."

More of Brian Cavanaugh's handpicked recruits kept walking in. She recognized several of them from the day before. They all appeared to be ready and willing to help field all the phone calls that were coming in again, hot and heavy.

Kori looked around the room. "Okay, so where are we?"

Officer Alexandra Harper spoke for the volunteers. "We're still talking to the 'good Samaritans' who are calling in, claiming they saw someone taking the baby off the premises. At this point, there seems to be no end to them."

"I'll say," Drew Montgomery agreed, adding his voice to Alexandra's. "We've got reports describing everyone but Santa Claus abducting the baby from the hospital."

Another officer, Kirk Conway, nodded and spoke up. "One woman swears she saw the baby being carried off in a laundry basket."

"A laundry basket?" Brodie repeated. "Why didn't she call someone immediately?"

"Well, according to our so-called eyewitness, she *thought* she saw something wiggling like a baby in the laundry basket, but when she went to try to investigate, the woman making the rounds and gathering the laundry together shooed her away."

"'Shooed her away'?" Kori questioned as she paused to take a long sip of her extremely bracing, eye-opening black coffee.

"The witness's words, not mine," Conway explained to Kori.

"And what did this woman say when she was 'shooed'?" Kori asked.

"According to our so-called eyewitness, the older woman collecting laundry was territorial. She claimed that she would get into trouble and maybe even lose her job if she let everyone touch the hospital laundry. I dunno, I guess there's a lot of call to touch hospital laundry. Anyway," Conway continued, "she asked our 'eyewitness' to move away from her and the basket."

"Doesn't that strike you as rather odd? This woman being so protective of the hospital's laundry," Brodie commented.

"Yeah, but hey, it takes all kinds," Baxter said with a shrug.

Kori thought of the taco server's story about an older nurse holding a baby. "What did this protective hospital worker look like?"

Conway thought for a moment. "All the eyewitness said was that it was some older woman who looked as if she should have been retired long ago instead of doing laundry like some kind of old-fashioned washer woman."

"'Washer woman,'" Brodie repeated. "Now there's a term I haven't heard used in decades. Maybe longer," he commented.

Simon looked at this newest member of their team. "Just how old are you?"

"We can discuss Cavanaugh's youthful appearance later," Kori told the others, then turned toward the policeman. "Tell me more about the woman who called in and this laundry basket that attracted her attention. Was she sure she saw the laundry moving?"

"That's just it, she wasn't sure. She just *thought* it might have been moving, but she didn't get a chance to check that out one way or another. For all we know, it was just wishful thinking—in hindsight."

"Hindsight?" Kori questioned.

Conway nodded. "You know, when someone is trying to be a part of the solution that led to finding the little girl."

"In other words, this so-called eyewitness might have had some sort of a desire to play hero by association," Brodie suggested.

"Or maybe just good intentions that were being pushed too hard in order to register. We'll find out today," Kori told the others. "Okay, people, we've got our list of supposed witnesses to talk to. Same partners as before. Let's hit the streets."

"You got it, boss," Simon said, speaking for all of them just before the task force filed out of the office.

Chapter Fourteen

Kori wearily closed her phone and put it away. She had just had to tell Rose Williams that there was no new news. They still hadn't been able to locate her baby or discover who had taken her. With all the working surveillance cameras on the various floors, they had not been able to record so much as a glimpse of the crime being perpetrated. The only thing that they had managed to do was rule out a simple kidnapping because there had been no calls asking for a ransom.

Kori felt that telling the new mother, who was now home, that they hadn't been able to find the baby had just about crushed Rose.

Kori was keenly aware that she, her partner, and the rest of the task force had been working the investigation almost nonstop for close to a week now. They still had nothing of substance to show for it. Every time Kori thought they were finally getting closer, whatever they were working on just seemed to fall through and the team wound up back at square one.

Faced with yet another dead end, Brodie looked at her as they walked to their vehicle. He found himself thinking that his partner was taking this last setback particularly hard, especially after hearing her end of the phone call. In his opinion, she seemed to be wilting.

When she got into the vehicle and began driving again, Brodie debated saying something, then decided that he really needed to.

"You do know that there are some kidnapping cases that are never solved," he warned Kori. He just wanted her to keep things in perspective.

Working the case, she had done a complete about-face and was now determined to cling to hope. "I don't care about other kidnapping cases. I care about *this* kidnapping case," she snapped. Then murmured, "Sorry. I didn't mean to bite your head off."

Brodie saw that she was clutching the steering wheel to the point that her knuckles were white. *Not good*, he thought. Since Kori had initially said that she liked to be the one driving, he hadn't contested the arrangement. But now he began to think that this might have been a bad idea—at least for now.

He could detect the tension gripping her body. He could especially see it in her arms and shoulders, not to mention that it showed in her face. He felt he had to do something to help Kori deal with it before she wound up driving into something and causing an accident.

"Pull over," Brodie told her.

Kori gave him a look as she continued driving, certain that she had misheard. "What?"

"Pull over," Brodie repeated, enunciating each word slowly.

"Why?" she asked sharply.

He wasn't going to get into a discussion while they were driving. Or, more to the point, while *she* was driving. "Just do it," he told her.

Kori pressed her lips together, keeping back a host of choice words that, voiced, might have made her feel temporarily better but eventually she knew she would regret saying. Annoying though he was, she knew that Cavanaugh undoubtedly meant well.

So, taking a deep breath, she did as Brodie instructed and pulled over to the side of the road. "All right, I've pulled over," she declared, spreading her hands. "Now what?"

"Now get out of the car," Brodie told her with finality.

She stared at him, stunned. Just what was he trying to accomplish?

"What?" she cried.

"You heard me, Kennedy," he said, then repeated, "Get out of the car."

"Yes, I heard you," she agreed. "And I want to know why."

"Because I want to switch places with you," he told her patiently.

She rolled her eyes. This was getting annoying, not to mention repetitive. "Again. Why?"

All right, he would spell it out for her. "Because you're tired, you're preoccupied—" he ticked off his fingers "—and you're in no condition to drive."

Okay, she was now officially angry. "In your opinion."

"In *anyone's* opinion. C'mon, Kennedy," he urged, trying to appeal to her common sense. "You're an accident waiting to happen and I, for one, still have a lot of living left to do—and I figure you do, too."

For the second time, a number of words rose to her lips. This time it was harder keeping them back than before, but she managed.

"Maybe you're right," she allowed, "but there is a little girl out there who might not have a lot of living left to do and I want to find her before some crazy person decides that she's used her allotment up."

"We all want to find her, Kennedy, but pushing yourself way beyond human endurance isn't going to help find that little girl. And neither is getting into an accident," he stressed.

"What are you talking about?" Kori demanded heatedly.

"If you hadn't just swerved in time back there," Brodie pointed out, "we would have undoubtedly wound up being tree ornaments a couple of minutes ago."

Kori glared at him, angry because Brodie had said that. Angrier because part of her knew he was right. "But we *didn't* wind up being tree ornaments, did we?"

"No," he agreed, "but I'd rather not take another chance on that. Now switch places with me," Brodie said a little more insistently. "I don't want to have to tell your father that you won't be coming home tonight— or any night—because you were too stubborn to listen to reason. Now, are you going to get out of the car or am I going to have to get physical and carry you out?"

The next moment he saw Kori raise her chin like a boxer about to go into the ring and face an avowed enemy. Just when he thought he was going to have to make good on his threat and carry her out of the driver's seat, Brodie saw his partner drop her chin again, obviously surrendering.

"All right, have it your way," she snapped sharply, throwing open her door.

Swinging her legs out, she stood and then deliberately rounded the vehicle's back end. She made her way to the passenger side. Getting in and buckling up, she slammed her door defiantly. The action made the car vibrate on her side.

"Happy?" she asked between gritted teeth as she glared at Brodie.

"Let's just say I'm mildly content," he told her. "The word *happy* is reserved for when we find that baby," he told her, then stressed, "*When,* not *if.*"

Kori sighed. Cavanaugh was trying, she acknowledged, and she wasn't being fair to him. But that was because she felt so drained and really disillusioned.

"I'm sorry," she told him, apologizing in a moment of weakness "I'm usually not this down."

"You're taking this too personally," Brodie pointed out, beginning to drive. It was way past the time when they should have clocked out.

Kori's eyes flashed as she turned to look at him. "I take *every* case personally," she informed him indignantly. "It's the only way I know how to work."

"Funny you should mention that," Brodie responded.

"'Funny'?" she repeated incredulously. "I can think of a lot of words to use here, but *funny* isn't one of them."

"Which was why I was going to suggest something to help you broaden your base."

She stared at him, suddenly grateful they were calling it a day and heading back to the precinct even if they hadn't made any discernable headway.

"I don't know what you're talking about, Cavanaugh, and right now, I have to admit that my brain is way too tired to make any sense of it or to attempt to untangle the words."

"All right, I will speak in short sentences that you can understand without even trying," he told her, doing just that by speaking very slowly and carefully.

Her eyes flashed again. "Don't patronize me, Cavanaugh. If you do, I won't be responsible for my reaction."

"No patronization intended," Brodie told her in an easy, calm tone. "Anyway, there's going to be a gathering this Saturday..." he began, staring straight ahead at the road in front of him.

He wasn't able to get any further because she declared, "No."

"You're not being very fair, you know," he told her. "You're turning this down without even knowing what it's all about."

She made an annoyed noise under her breath. "You just said it was a gathering."

"Yes, but you don't know what kind of gathering it's going to be—" Brodie noted.

"Doesn't matter," she said, cutting him short. "I don't do gatherings when I'm working a case."

"That's ridiculous." Didn't she realize how absurd her statement sounded? "Only hermits don't 'do' gatherings," he informed her, telling her decisively, "And you're not a hermit."

"No," she agreed. "I'm a frustrated detective."

He refused to back off. "And this will help take the frustration away."

"Okay," she said gamely, "you have my attention. At the risk of sounding like I'm totally lost, just how is this going to take the frustration away from me? Or are you just talking?"

"I can't speak to that lost reference you just made," he conceded, "but I am *not* just talking. This gathering on Saturday is going to include, among others, a number of seasoned veteran detectives discussing some of their old cases. Their old missing-persons cases," he stressed, "some of which involved kidnapped children. Who knows, you might pick up something useful. We all might," he added so she didn't feel singled out.

"You'll also have a chance to blow off some steam—
and make your father happy."

"My father?" she asked incredulously. "What does
my father have to do with it?"

"Well, for one thing, he'll be one of the people attending." Brodie eased into a stop at the red light.

All right, she thought, now she knew he was just
pulling her leg. "In case this little fact escaped you, my
father's not a seasoned detective."

"No, you're right," Brodie agreed, taking his foot off
the brake and going again. "But Uncle Andrew likes
your father—a lot. He'd never exclude him from a gathering he was throwing. He hasn't done it in all the years
he's been having these get-togethers."

She sighed as she shook her head. Did Cavanaugh
really think she didn't see through this? "You're just trying to get me to go to one of these things and I really—"

Brodie laughed, interrupting her. "Getting you to
come is just a side benefit. But it really is a gathering
to discuss old cases." She was still looking at him as
if she didn't believe him, so he added, "I should know.
I'm the one who suggested it to Uncle Andrew when
I saw how much not finding this little girl was really
getting to you, Kennedy."

Kori raised an eyebrow. "And I suppose it doesn't
bother you?" she challenged.

"I didn't say that," he pointed out. "Yes, it bothers
me, but I'm not pushing myself so hard that I'm going
to get sick over it, because if I did that, then I wouldn't
be any good to the investigation." He paused for a moment before saying, "And there's nothing good to be
gotten out of that scenario."

Kori glared at him. He had her cornered and they

were going around in circles. "Got an answer for everything, don't you?"

"Not everything," Brodie told her. "But I do try my best." He glanced in her direction as he took a corner. "So, how about it, Kennedy? Can I tell my uncle that you'll be coming to this thing he's pulling together in order to help you out?"

Guilt, she thought. Now he was using guilt to get her to go. "To help me out?" she repeated, stalling for time to come up with a way out.

"That's what I said," he answered.

Kori sighed and then became silent for a good ten minutes. When her silence threatened to draw out even longer, Brodie decided to press the matter. "Well? Are you going to come?"

She blew out a long, annoyed breath. "You're not going to give up until I say yes, are you?"

His smile all but lit up the interior of the vehicle. She had her answer. "Now you get the idea."

"Why is my coming to this gathering so important to you?" she demanded.

There was no point in beating around the bush. Brodie was honest with her. "Because it's important to Uncle Andrew and to your father. And I'm thinking, in a way, to you."

"Why would you even say that? That it's important to me?" she stipulated. "Don't you think that if it actually was, I would have gone a long time ago?"

"No, you wouldn't have. You wouldn't go because you're afraid."

She stared at him, stunned and annoyed. "And what makes you think that?" Kori asked. She was just about coming to the end of her patience—and she was getting there really fast.

"You're afraid to go because you might be reminded of everything you don't have—meaning a full family life," he explained. "Even when we, meaning my family, feel that we're alone, we're not. There are cousins, uncles, aunts—hell, there're so many relatives, it's a challenge just keeping track of them. In comparison, taken at face value, your life might feel stark to you—but it doesn't have to be."

"It's not," she insisted heatedly. Who did he think he was, analyzing her life like this? "I have my father. That's enough for me."

"All right, then come tomorrow because it's important to him. Having you there is important to him," he said with emphasis.

Kori closed her eyes, searching for strength. This man wasn't going to give up, she thought, annoyed. "And you're not going to stop badgering me until I go, are you?"

Brodie smiled at her. "Nothing slow about you. Except maybe when you drag your feet," he allowed.

She'd had enough. "All right, all right, all right!" Kori cried. "I'll go. Just stop badgering me, okay?"

"Absolutely," he said with an obliging smile.

"Yeah, right," she responded with a mirthless laugh.

"No, really."

She decided to push. "And if I ultimately don't come?"

"Well, then that's called reneging and, if you do, I'll be free to do the same," he warned with a mischievous smile.

"You're saying that all bets will be off then?"

"No, what I'm saying is that if you don't show up, I'll be free to come get you and bring you to the gathering. So you see, there really is no way out and you might as well just go with it, because one way or another, you *will* be there." He glanced at her again. "It's a lot easier that way."

"Why is this so important to you?" she demanded again, still not really understanding why it mattered to him.

"Because," he told her, "ultimately, it'll be important to you."

She sighed. "You do realize that you talk in riddles."

"All right, if it helps, think of this as a riddle. A riddle that'll be unscrambled somewhere in the middle of tomorrow—right about the time you wind up attending the gathering."

"And just so I'm clear on this, if I don't go, you'll come and get me."

"Yes."

"How? Are you going to tie me to the roof of your car?" Because, Kori decided, making up her mind, there was no way Cavanaugh was going to get her to attend on her own power. She absolutely refused to be manipulated into going.

Brodie looked completely unfazed by her sarcasm. "If I have to."

She looked at him uncertainly. "You wouldn't."

But her partner didn't back off. Instead, he gave her this look she couldn't really read no matter how hard she tried.

"I wouldn't push it if I were you," he warned. "You don't know me that well and some of us Cavanaughs can be very unpredictable. You going along with this is a lot easier than digging in your heels. Trust me on this."

"Trust you?" she echoed incredulously. "And why would I do that?"

"Because I've never lied to you."

"Yet," she pointed out.

His smile was indulgent. "For now, all we have is the present," he told her. "So, how about it? Do we have a deal?"

"Sure," she answered, thinking it was the only way to get him to back off. She didn't have to mean it.

"Good. I'll be there tomorrow to pick you and your father up," he told her just as he pulled the car into the police parking lot.

She could feel herself literally being backed into a corner.

Chapter Fifteen

Over the course of the next twelve hours, in the privacy of her own mind, Kori came up with one excuse after another. All the excuses were centered around why she wouldn't be able to attend this latest gathering at the former police chief's house.

But, in the end, she decided that her partner was ultimately right. It was simpler just to go along with this whole thing than to fight it and have Brodie keep bringing it up infinitum, asking her about it and teasing her about being too afraid to attend.

Even though she dawdled, Kori still wound up dressed and ready way too early. Being early was a lifelong habit she couldn't shake.

Taking in a deep breath, she came down the stairs.

Her father had just slipped on a blue-and-white pullover sweater with his gray slacks. He looked over as she came to the bottom step and smiled.

"You look very nice, Kori," he said with approval. "I'm glad you finally decided to socialize with the Cavanaughs. Don't know why you stopped. I never bought that excuse of yours about not wanting to mix business with pleasure. You're not going to regret this."

"I'm already regretting it," Kori murmured. When

her father looked at her, an expression of dubious surprise on his face, she was quick to set him straight about *why* she had just said what she'd said. "This is time I could be using to work on the case, maybe even get somewhere."

"Baby, I know better than anyone what a dedicated workaholic you are," her father told her, "but maybe listening to the voices of experience might just help you actually think of something to help you solve this investigation."

Kori laughed dryly. "That's the same thing that Cav—Brodie said," she responded, deciding at the last moment to use her partner's first name rather than the surname she'd been using when referring to him. This situation, she was sure her father would point out, called for friendliness, which called for first names. "According to him, that was actually the chief's idea."

Bill nodded, agreeing with what his daughter had just said. "Just because someone retires doesn't mean his brain automatically goes into sleep mode and stops working. As a matter of fact," he continued with a genial smile, "the opposite is usually true."

Just then, the doorbell rang. Bill's smile widened. "And, unless I miss my guess, there's our ride now," her father said brightly, striding toward the door.

Out of the corner of his eye, he caught his daughter's frown. He was starting to wonder if perhaps there was another reason why Kori was fighting attending this gathering as hard as she was. Was there something going on between her and Brodie?

Or was she afraid that there would be something going on if she came to this party?

Bill smiled to himself as he opened the door, feeling a surge of hope suddenly dancing through him.

"Hello, Brodie," Bill said, greeting the young man standing in his doorway. "We were just talking about you."

Brodie laughed. "Let me guess. My new partner was enumerating all the reasons she has just decided she can't possibly attend my uncle Andrew's gathering with us."

"No," Bill replied, pleased as he took a step back to physically invite the younger man in. "As a matter of fact, she just said she could see the merit in finally doing this—or words to that effect," the older man wound up saying. For the moment, Bill avoided eye contact with either one of the younger people.

Even so, Brodie gave Kori's father a very skeptical look as he crossed the threshold into the Kennedy living room.

Still, having learned, long ago, the benefit of quitting while he was ahead, Brodie chose not to pursue the matter any further. He felt that if he did, Kori might use that to change her mind and withdraw from the gathering.

So instead, Kori's partner gestured behind him toward the opened door.

"Your chariot awaits," Brodie announced to the two people he had come to bring to his uncle's party.

Kori's attendance meant different things to different people, but the bottom line was that it was important—to his uncle, to her father and, if he were being honest, to him.

"By the way," he told Kori, his green eyes washing over her and lingering at the way her dress's soft, blue material seemed to cling to her body, "in case I didn't mention it, you clean up really nicely."

Kori told herself that she was just imagining her

stomach suddenly tightening. And her mouth growing dry was just a coincidence, too.

"I could say the same to you," she finally responded. A beat later, she realized what she had just said, but it was too late to take it back.

Brodie was surprised by her comment. He didn't know if she was being serious or not, but again, he chose not to prod her for any sort of a deeper meaning. Instead, he merely smiled at her and said, "Glad you approve."

"Isn't anyone going to say anything about me?" Bill asked, extending his arms and pretending to be hurt that he had been left out.

"You are *always* lovely, Dad," Kori replied.

Bill pretended to fluff his still full, albeit gray-streaked hair.

"I know," her father answered, tongue-in-cheek. "It's just nice to hear once in a while, that's all." And then he said in a far more normal voice, "Well, shall we go?"

"Right this way," Brodie said, leading the way to the front curb and his car.

Seeing the vehicle for the first time, Kori stopped dead in her tracks. Her mouth nearly dropped open.

"That's a Cadillac," Kori said in surprise as she looked at the very large vintage vehicle. She had to admit that she had *never* envisioned him driving anything like that.

"So *that's* what it is," Brodie cried, pretending to be enlightened by her reaction.

Kori had to steel herself not to glare at him in front of her father.

"Very funny," she responded. "I just didn't see you driving something so elegant."

"What did you see me driving?" he asked, curious. "A truck?"

She shrugged, slowly walking up to the Cadillac. "I guess I thought you'd be driving something fast," she admitted.

Brodie smiled at the image. "There's a lot about me that you don't know," he told her. And then he mysteriously added, "Maybe tonight will turn into a night of more than one discovery."

Unlocking the car, Brodie held the passenger door open.

"I'll take the back seat," Bill volunteered. He sat in the rear of the vehicle before Kori had a chance to contest the matter, closing the door behind him. "More room for my legs," he explained when Kori gave him a look that told him she thought he was being way too obvious.

"Right, because you're so very large." Kori pointedly looked at his five-foot-eight frame.

"I like to stretch," her father told her, nonplussed.

"Today is about you relaxing and unwinding," Brodie reminded her as he rounded the vehicle and got in on the driver's side. "So you might as well go with the flow. You won't regret it."

"For that to happen," Kori informed her partner, making eye contact and looking at him pointedly, "I would need a time machine."

"So in other words, you're regretting this already?" Brodie asked.

Kori made no answer, but she did smile at his assumption.

Bill wasn't the type to butt into his daughter's business, but this one time, he decided to speak up.

"I guess it's up to us to prove her wrong, boy," Bill said.

Brodie glanced over his shoulder at the older man—and grinned. "Apparently."

Kori pressed her lips together. For the moment, she decided that it was better not to say anything at all. She knew when she was outnumbered.

WHEN THEY ENTERED Andrew Cavanaugh's development twenty minutes later and drove toward his house, Kori couldn't help staring at all the cars parked up and down the residential streets.

"Wow," she finally said, "there are an awful lot of vehicles parked here." More than the usual amount, in her opinion. She looked at Brodie. "Is today some kind of holiday?" she asked as she began to unconsciously search for a space where Brodie could park his overly large vehicle.

"Yeah," Brodie answered, his mouth curving in amusement. "One of Uncle Andrew's parties."

"You're kidding," she cried. "There are *this* many people attending one of your uncle's gatherings?" she asked in disbelief. The number had certainly increased from the last time she had attended.

"I told you they were big gatherings," her father reminded her. He had been invited—and attended—more than his share over the years. Once the so-called "lost branch" had been found, the numbers had really increased.

"I know," she replied, "but there's 'big' and then there's *big*," she emphasized. "I thought you were exaggerating."

"Exaggeration was never my thing, honey," her father told her. About to say something else, he suddenly called out, "Wait!" As Brodie came to a sudden stop, Bill pointed ahead of them. "I think there's a space right up there. Right at the end of the street," he specified. "If you angle your Caddie, you might be able to get into it," he told the younger man.

"Might be worth a shot," Brodie said, studying the space.

Two attempts and some fancy angling later, he finally managed to park his vehicle.

Getting out, Brodie surprised her by helping her father out first. She didn't say anything, but she gave her partner points because he hadn't immediately jumped out on his side to help her out.

"It's a bit of a walk," Brodie said to Bill apologetically.

"Walking is good exercise for me." Kori's father smiled. "I never take that for granted," he told the younger man.

Kori still made no comment as she fell into step next to her father. Brodie was on her father's other side. That, too, surprised her and, once again, she mentally gave him points for being so thoughtful.

Brodie just glanced in Kori's direction to make sure she was there a moment before he rang his uncle Andrew's doorbell.

The door opened almost immediately and a distinguished, genial-looking man measuring at least six feet tall in Kori's estimation stood in the doorway. Deep green eyes swept over the two men on his doorstep, but they came to rest on the young woman with them.

"You've finally decided to come back," Andrew declared with a satisfied smile. He put out his hand, strong fingers taking hold of Kori's and shaking it.

Kori found that his handshake was still very strong, yet surprisingly gentle as well.

"Welcome back, Kori," he told her, still holding her hand.

His hair had gotten grayer, but it was just as thick as ever. She would have recognized him immediately. What did one say to a legend? she wondered, struggling to say something intelligent that didn't sound as if she was about to become tongue-tied.

At a loss, Kori fell back on a standard response. "Thank you for having me, sir."

Andrew laughed at that, glancing back at both her father and Brodie.

"And we only had to resort to bribery to get you to come back," Andrew told her with an amused chuckle. "But whatever it took," he concluded philosophically, "I—we—" he corrected "—are glad you're finally here. Come in, come in." He opened the door further. Once they were inside, he closed his door, leaving it unlocked. "I'll let Brodie show you around. Some things have changed. He can answer any questions you might have."

She didn't want to lose sight of what had actually brought her here. "Um, Brodie said something about veteran detectives…" Her voice trailed off, but there was no missing the hopeful note within it.

"Oh, there's no shortage of those here," Andrew assured her. "And, as promised, they'll be discussing some of their more interesting kidnapping cases. As a matter of fact, we probably won't be able to get them to stop. We are hoping that those stories might trigger something for you and Brodie to use in your investigation," Andrew told her. And then his expression sobered visibly. "Nothing more reprehensible than someone kidnapping a defenseless child, be it an infant or an older one."

Andrew turned to look at Brodie. "Brodie, do the honors, please." And then he turned toward Kori's father.

To her surprise, the chief put an arm around her father's shoulder, drawing him into the kitchen. "Glad you could make it, Bill. I've got something new for you to try," the chief told him. "Based on what you told me the last time, I think you're really going to like this."

Satisfied that her father was in good hands, Kori turned to her partner. "Your uncle's really nice," she told him, watching the two men.

"He doesn't breathe fire on the weekends," Brodie wisecracked. "That's just during the week."

She frowned. "Maybe you had the wrong idea," she suggested. "I didn't *not* come to these gatherings because I thought the chief had become some kind of fire-breathing monster."

Brodie waved away her words. "Hey, what matters is that you're here," he insisted. "C'mon, let me introduce you around to some of the people you *don't* know and then maybe they can get down to swapping a few interesting old war stories before dinner is served."

"Dinner?" she echoed, looking at her watch. It was just past ten in the morning. "Isn't it just a little early for that?"

"Officially," he told her as he began to guide her toward the living room and the spacious patio just beyond that, "Uncle Andrew likes to serve Sunday dinner at around two. But you might recall that, unofficially, he begins feeding people the moment they cross his threshold." Brodie gestured to the serving tables that were scattered around the area. "Be ready to weigh approximately five pounds more when you leave than when you first walked in."

Her father had said something about the food served

at these parties, but she had thought that he was just exaggerating. "You are kidding, right?"

The amusement in his eyes threw her off. She didn't know whether to believe him or not.

"Ask around. You probably know most of these people. By sight if not by name," he added, then amended, "At least the ones who work at the precinct. This is a chance to meet their 'other halves,'" he pointed out. "It'll round out who they are as people, not just as officers and detectives." Brodie watched her expression to see if he had gotten through to her.

Kori was about to protest that she didn't need to have the people she worked with "rounded out" in order to do her job, but something inside her protested her taking that stand, just as it made clear to her why she was resisting this closer association.

The idea of loss—of her losing people she'd gotten close to—had always been there, on the perimeter of her mind. If she didn't get to really know these people, then it wouldn't really be a loss if they were no longer part of her world.

That was the moment Kori realized that the night she had almost lost her father had left her indelibly marked. It made her fearful of making any other attachments because she really was subconsciously afraid of losing people. After all, her mother had died a couple of years before the incident with her father.

So she didn't make any attachments, reasoning that if there were none, then there was no danger of losing anyone. She supposed that was why her cases meant so much to her. The cases were substitutes for any real, lasting attachments.

She had grown silent, Brodie noted. He turned to

look at her and saw the odd expression on her face as if she were experiencing some sort of an epiphany.

"Kori? Kori?" He repeated her name three times before he got her attention. When she looked at him quizzically, he asked, "What's going on?"

Denial was her immediate go-to place. "Nothing."

"That wasn't a 'nothing' expression on your face," he insisted. "Now," he asked again, "what's going on with you?"

Kori sighed. She had a feeling they were going to continue working together so she might as well be honest with him. "You were right," she said grudgingly.

"I'm going to need more," he told her. "I'm right about a lot of things."

"You're right about my resisting coming here—about *why* I resisted," she clarified.

Kori fully expected her partner to gloat.

Instead, Brodie said, "Well, now that you've admitted that to yourself, we can build on it and move on." He took hold of her elbow, gently guiding her to an area toward the left. "Come with me. There are some veteran detectives you might find interesting to talk to."

She certainly hoped so, Kori thought as she went with her partner.

Chapter Sixteen

Kori didn't realize it at the start, but as the day wore on, it became clear that it was destined to be one of those days that she would always remember. For two reasons.

The major reason was, as Brodie had predicted when he'd talked her into coming to the gathering, the stories she listened to over the course of the day as well as the evening triggered something in her own mind. Something that she and Brodie might be able to use when attempting to resolve the kidnapping investigation— maybe even to actually find the infant. For the first time since the investigation began, Kori found herself able to really nurse some real hope.

The second thing that made this a day for her to remember was that she could view Brodie in an even better light. She was able to see him for the person he actually was. Rather that just a cocky, confident, glib-tongued detective who was a member of a revered law enforcement family, Brodie had transformed into a kindly, thoughtful person right before her eyes. A person who had put her father's needs ahead of his own, certainly ahead of any need he might have to attempt to impress her by displaying his vast array of knowledge when it came to law enforcement.

What she found that she liked about Brodie most

was that he didn't just pretend to be a man who cared about his family—Brodie actually *did* care about his family. Not just some of the members, but apparently *all* of them.

It wasn't something he'd said to her. Kori could see it in his actions, in the way he treated the various members they came in contact with during the course of the evening.

She caught herself thinking that that was an awful lot of members for him to be concerned about. Watching Brodie in action definitely contributed to her growing regard for the man.

"So," Brodie said, turning to her as the evening was winding down and approximately a third of the guests, those with young children they needed to put to bed, had gone home or were in the process of going home. "Am I forgiven for making you come?" The glint in his eye said he already knew the answer to that. His asking the question was just a mere formality.

"Yes," Kori answered in a monotone voice, "you're forgiven for making me come."

"And can I take that to mean that you're having a good time?" Brodie asked, giving her his undivided attention and studying every nuance that passed over her face, a face he fancied himself studying for a very long time and still finding something there to fascinate him.

"Yes, I'm having a good time," she replied through gritted teeth because she felt as if she was giving him a card to play against her sometime down the line. "Do you want me to write it for you in blood?"

"No, I'll accept a verbal confirmation—for now," Brodie qualified, and then his mouth curved in a smile that showed his amusement.

Kori shook her head. "Has anyone ever told you that despite your attributes, you can have a very annoying way about you?"

Rather than take the bait, he picked up on something else. "My attributes, huh? Tell me more about what you see as my 'attributes,'" he coaxed.

"And make your head even larger than it is?" she asked with a laugh. "No, thank you. If I mislead you by using the word *attributes*, I apologize. I was wrong to say that."

Brodie pretended to be dumbstruck as he stared at her, wide-eyed. "Stop the presses," he declared, one hand flying to his chest as if to keep his heart from popping out. "Kori Kennedy claims to have been wrong about something. Unbelievable."

She shook her head. "You're an idiot, you do know that, right?" she asked, but she couldn't quite make her voice sound as if she were actually annoyed.

"Sometimes," Brodie admitted. "But then, I've never been perfect like you." There was no animosity in his tone, which was why Kori found that she couldn't take any offense at what her new partner was saying.

Still she couldn't just keep silent, which was why she told him, "I never claimed to be perfect."

"No," Brodie agreed. "Not in so many words anyway. But you have to admit that you did give off that kind of vibe."

"Fine," she conceded. "I'll be sure to work on my 'vibe.'"

"Oh please, don't change a single hair, Korinna Kennedy," Brodie told her, punctuating his words with a warm smile that insisted on dancing up and down her spine no matter how hard she struggled to block that reaction to him. "You're unique just the way you are."

He actually sounded as if he meant it. Kori had never been comfortable talking about herself, even if Brodie was just saying what he had just to pull her leg. But right now something more important had caught her attention. She deliberately shifted his attention to it.

Nodding over to a section on the extreme left, Kori indicated a pretty, animated, older woman. Every time that Kori would look in that direction, for the last hour or so—maybe even longer—the older woman seemed to have been talking to her father. In essence, the woman had been monopolizing him.

Observing the two people, Kori had noticed that the pair seemed to exclude everyone else from their small circle of two.

Unable to contain herself any longer, she asked Brodie, "Would you happen to know who that is?"

He looked toward where Kori was indicating. Recognition instantly set in as he nodded. "Oh sure. That's Maeve."

"Maeve," Kori repeated, as if saying the woman's name would answer the host of questions that had suddenly just popped up in her head. It didn't.

"Uh-huh. She's initially from Murdoch's side of the family chart. She's one of his children," he explained, referring to Seamus's late younger brother. "In a nutshell, Aunt Maeve is one hell of a dynamo. She owns an ambulance company. I hear that the lady still drives a rig on occasion."

He could see that she wanted more, so he elaborated. "Aunt Maeve also raised five kids on her own after her husband died in an accident." Brodie saved what he felt was the best for last, knowing it would set Kori's mind at ease about his aunt. "She wouldn't accept a dime from her three brothers. She had—and still has—too much pride. Sound familiar?"

She didn't rise to the bait. Instead, Kori focused on what she felt was the important thing. "So your aunt is a widow?"

Brodie nodded. "She said she never found anyone who came close to taking her husband's place. Of course, working as many hours as she did, I can't see how anyone would have been able to have a shot at measuring up to the man. Aunt Maeve was always just much too busy to even attempt to have a social life. Why do you ask?"

Kori shrugged, avoiding his eyes as she continued to watch her father and Maeve. He was laughing, like he was really enjoying himself, she thought. He almost seemed boyish.

"No reason."

Brodie laughed, drawing her attention back to him. "You know, you're going to have to brush up on your technique when it comes to lying because, as it stands right now, you really do stink at it."

Kori shrugged again, doing her best to seem indifferent. "In my defense, I never aspired to be 'good' at lying."

"Sometimes," Brodie told her, "in this line of work, you have to be."

When it came to her father, she had always been very protective, even before she had almost lost him so long ago. "It's just that my mother died when I was really young and my father never got over it," she told him. "To my recollections, the man never had so much as a single date in all those years. He swore that loving my mother had spoiled him for anyone else."

"Maybe it's time that he got back in the game," Brodie suggested.

She knew that, technically, her partner was right, but that still didn't evoke any agreement from her. "I just don't want to see my father get hurt."

"Number one, it's not up to you," Brodie pointed out kindly. "Your dad's a big boy. Number two, Aunt Maeve is not a femme fatale who gets her kicks stringing men along. She's a decent, really hardworking woman. When you think about it, this might actually be the start of something for both of them," he told her. "My advice to you is just be happy for them."

Her eyes flashed. Where did he get off, telling her what to think and feel? "I didn't ask for your advice."

"That's okay. There's no charge. The advice is free," he told her with a grin.

He was surprised to see her face cloud over and even more surprised to see her suddenly turn on her heel and walk away. When she kept on walking toward the door, he decided it was time to stop her and find out just what was going on in her head.

Mindful that she wouldn't tolerate being embarrassed in front of his family, Brodie didn't call out to stop her but he did pick up his pace. He managed to catch up with her just beyond the front door.

Grabbing her arm, Brodie turned Kori around to face him.

"You know, you *can* walk home from here, but it'll take you a very long time," he warned. "I wouldn't suggest you try it."

She attempted to pull her arm away, but she couldn't get him to loosen his grip. That just incensed her. "Let go of me," she ordered.

But Brodie just went on holding her arm. "Not until you calm down."

That just earned him an intense glare. "You can't tell me what to do," she warned.

"I'm not telling you what to do," Brodie informed her. "I'm just making suggestions until you come to your senses and act on them."

"So now I'm being irrational?" Kori snapped angrily.

Brodie continued being maddeningly calm and answered her mildly. "Your word, not mine. Now what are you *really* so angry about?"

About to protest that she wasn't angry, she realized she couldn't say that because she was.

"I don't know," she cried. She saw that he was actually waiting for an answer, so she tossed out the first thing that came into her head. "Not being able to protect my father if this blows up in his face." She remembered Brodie's comment about her father being able to make his own choices. He was right, she thought darkly. It was just hard for her to keep out of it. "Not being able to hate you."

Brodie felt somewhat confused by her response. "Not sure I can make any sense of that, but I do know I like where this is going." He smiled at her. "Especially the 'not hating me' part."

Frustrated, Kori doubled up her fists and tried to beat on him. But he caught her hands in his, keeping them still.

And then, in a move completely dictated solely by gut reaction rather than any sort of rational thought process, Brodie found himself responding to the hell-cat who was his partner as if he had no free will. He brought down his mouth to hers.

The moment that his lips touched hers, rather than

defuse the situation, that simple action ignited it—and very effectively managed to set both of them on fire.

The kiss took on length and breadth as well as a tremendous power that he found he wasn't able to safely measure.

That explosion morphed into something else, something gentler and, consequently, a great deal more powerful than anything in its origin had been.

An eternity later, as he drew his head away, Brodie could see that she was as dazed and confused by what had just transpired as he was.

The next moment, unable to resist, Brodie framed her face with his hands and brought his mouth down to hers again, this time in a far gentler action that still managed to burrow its way down into his soul.

As the kiss went on to build in depth and scope, it left Brodie completely shaken for the very first time in his life. Drawing his head away, he looked at Kori, totally stunned, wondering what in heaven's name was going on here.

"Are you all right?" he finally managed to ask her.

"I'm not sure," she admitted breathless with the soul-deep effects of his passionate embrace. The next second, feeling extremely vulnerable, she said, "Let's go back inside."

"Sure." It was safer that way, he thought.

Quickening his pace, he opened the front door and held it for her, then followed her back into the house.

"There you are," Bill said the moment they came in. "I thought we got our signals crossed and you had left."

Wow, this woman has really managed to rattle his brain, Kori thought.

"No, Dad, we wouldn't have left you behind. That would have been irresponsible. We were just outside—

getting some fresh air," she said, avoiding Brodie's eyes, although she had to admit that she felt her face growing warmer because of the lie anyway. "Are you ready to go?"

"As a matter of fact," Bill told his daughter, "I am."

"Okay. Then we'll all say our goodbyes and we can get going," she told her father and Brodie.

"Well, that's just it..." Bill began. "I'm not going to be leaving. That is, I won't be leaving with you."

"You're planning on staying here?" Kori asked uncertainly.

People were slowly trickling out of the house, but if her father wanted to stay longer, she was certain Brodie could be talked into hanging around for a while longer. After all, it had been his idea to come to this gathering in the first place.

Kori turned toward him to suggest just that when her father's answer stopped her.

"Not exactly," Bill said. He turned to the petite woman standing next to him. "Maeve has offered to show me around her place."

Kori thought of the station where the ambulances were undoubtedly being housed. It was getting late and taking a tour through there didn't make any sense to her.

"Now?" she questioned in surprise, looking at her father uncertainly.

"What's wrong with now?" Bill asked.

"Well," Kori pointed out, "it's getting late, not to mention dark. Wouldn't you be able to see more if you did this in the light of day?"

"Every part of the day has its good points," her father answered.

He just wasn't making any sense, Kori thought. "But the ambulances..." she began to protest.

It was his turn not to understand what she was driving at. "Who said anything about the ambulances?" he asked his daughter.

"You just did," Kori pointed out.

"No, I didn't." And then it dawned on him as Brodie laughed at the error. "Maeve isn't going to show me around where the ambulances are kept. She's going to show me around *her* place. Where she lives, not where she works."

"Oh. That's great," Kori said, knowing she didn't exactly sound convincing. All this time, she had been hoping her father would get out there and find someone. He was a good man and he deserved to be happy. Now that it was happening, she told herself that she should feel happy. So why did she feel like an eight-year-old who had just been abandoned by her only parent?

"Take good care of him," she instructed the older woman.

"Oh, I intend to," Maeve said, exchanging glances with Bill.

"And don't drive too fast," Kori cautioned.

Maeve smiled knowingly. "I never do."

"Okay, I think it's time for us to hit the road," Brodie announced, putting an end to the awkward conversation. "Let's say our goodbyes," he told Kori. "Have a good time you two," he said to his aunt and Kori's father as he ushered Kori toward where the former police chief was standing.

Chapter Seventeen

Brodie could sense his partner's uneasiness as he pulled his car up in her driveway. He was aware of the fact that Kori's mind had been elsewhere throughout the entire drive to her house.

Turning off his engine, he remained where he was as he looked at her, "Are you going to be all right?" he asked, concerned.

Her answer was automatic. "Yeah, sure. I'm fine," she replied almost too cheerfully. And then, as she began to open the passenger door, she stopped. She could sense that Brodie could see right through her. Maybe she could stand to talk to someone for a while.

"Would you like to come in for a drink or some coffee or anything?" she asked.

Kori was aware of how awkward that had to sound, but the words were already out of her mouth and she couldn't exactly take them back.

It wasn't hard for Brodie to read between the lines. Kori didn't want to be alone right now, at least not yet.

"Sure," he replied. "The 'or something' sounds interesting." With that, he opened the door on his side and got out of the car.

Kori waited until she had unlocked her front door and then walked in before suddenly turning toward her partner and asking, "What you said before…about your aunt," she clarified.

"Yes?" he prodded, closing the door behind him and flipping the lock for her.

Kori took a breath. Because he was related to the woman, this was *not* as easy as she would have thought. But this was about her father, so she pushed ahead. "She is a nice person, right?"

Brodie smiled. Temporarily, he made himself comfortable on the sofa.

Appearing to think her question over seriously, he told Kori, "Well, there's been talk about nominating her for sainthood."

Annoyance flashed in Kori's eyes. "I'm serious, Cavanaugh," she insisted.

"I'm doing my best to set your mind at ease. And to make you understand that, much as I'd like to, I can't give you a hundred percent guarantee that no one will be hurt here—this does go two ways," he reminded her. "But if your question is whether or not Aunt Maeve is a fair-minded, decent person, then my answer is an unequivocal 'yes, she is.'" He could see by the expression on Kori's face that what he had just said still didn't put her mind at ease. "Don't worry, Kori. It'll be all right."

Brodie's reassurances notwithstanding, Kori was still worried, and she couldn't help it. She didn't want her father being hurt. She should have spent more time with him, she thought, feeling guilty. Then maybe he wouldn't have gone looking for companionship.

Kori absently poured pitch-black coffee into a cup and brought it over to her partner, handing the cup to him. "Can I have that in writing?" she asked as she sat down next to him on the sofa.

"I can cross my heart," he told her loftily, then saw

the error in saying that to her. "But then, if anything goes wrong, you'll probably want to cut it out."

He could create quite an image, Kori thought with a laugh. "So, in other words, you're saying I don't get to have any fun?"

Brodie placed the cup she had handed him on the coffee table, his eyes never leaving her face; a face that seemed to fascinate him more each time he looked at it.

"Maybe we can find some other kind of fun for you to have," he suggested in a light tone.

There it was again, Kori thought. That electricity, those sparks that insisted on shooting all through her, making her vividly aware of the attraction that had been steadily growing between them. Growing significantly larger and more intense every time they shared a kiss.

Her breath had caught in her throat, trapped there by the look in his eyes. "What did you have in mind?" she heard herself asking.

Every fiber in her being was screaming for her to "run for the hills" and yet, for some unknown reason, she stayed exactly where she was.

She didn't move.

It was as if she was just frozen in place, suspended in time and waiting for something—although part of her didn't have a clue what that "something" was.

Kori was only vaguely aware that she was holding on to her own half-filled cup of coffee as if it were some sort of a life preserver. But when he gently removed it from her hand, she just let it go without so much as a single protest or any effort to continue holding the cup. Brodie seemed to want it gone, so it was gone.

He set her coffee aside, placing it next to his own cup on the coffee table. He never took his eyes away from her face.

With the coffee cups safely out of the way, Brodie was free to focus his attention entirely on her.

"This," he whispered, answering her question from a thousand years ago.

And before she could ask what "this" referred to, Kori knew. Knew in her soul because Brodie had brought his lips down to hers and, just like that, had effectively managed to erase her questions even while causing an entire slew of brand-new ones to spring up in their wake.

Kori knew this was dangerous, kissing Brodie here like this in her home without a single thing she could possibly use to distract him from taking things to another higher, much hotter, level.

A level where she would wind up doing the exact same thing she worried that her father was doing.

And even so, as Brodie's delicious mouth found hers, creating havoc, Kori could just *feel* that this was something her soul had been waiting for.

For *more* than an eternity.

As Brodie continued kissing her, the kiss built in intensity, drawing her further and further into a heated area from which there was no retreat.

She felt herself surrendering before she was even remotely conscious of the process.

His hands were everywhere, worshipfully caressing her, stoking her inner fire. But even so, his fingers didn't delve beneath her clothing. Instead, his hands only made her desire for him utterly insatiable.

She wanted him.

Desperately.

It made Kori want to rip her clothes off just to feel his touch on her bare skin.

Ever mindful of the fact that her father could just

come in at any moment and effectively extinguish this growing blaze with his very presence, Kori suddenly rose to her feet.

Never drawing her mouth from his, with small, measured steps, she began to guide Brodie toward the stairs.

Bracketing her shoulders with his hands, Brodie dragged his lips from hers and looked at her quizzically. "Not that this shadow dancing isn't really turning me on, but am I missing the bigger picture here?"

She hadn't a clue what he was talking about. "Bigger picture?"

"Yes." The smile on his lips encompassed his eyes as well. "Are you trying not to hurt my feelings, but are really attempting to get away?" he questioned. "Because I have to admit, this technique? This is all new to me."

Kori caught herself laughing at the bemused expression on his face.

"You know," she whispered, "for a detective, you can be awfully dense. I'm trying to get you to come to my room before my father gets home and we have to stop before he turns the hose on us."

"Can't have that," he agreed. "Where is your room?"

She didn't answer. Instead, she pointed upward just before she returned to her first method of getting her point across. She laced her arms enticingly around his neck.

Brodie paused at the base of the stairs to kiss her again, putting his entire heart and soul into it before pulling his head back and saying, "In the interest of safety, as romantic as the notion might be, kissing while making our way up the stairs is really taking unnecessary chances. Besides, we can get there much faster if our lips aren't sealed together."

With that, he grabbed her hand and raced up the stairs.

Delighted, Kori could only laugh as she raced the rest of the way just ahead of him, pulling on his hand as if that would urge him on even faster. They reached the top of the stairs in a blink of an eye, and then she was drawing him into her bedroom.

She pushed her door closed and Brodie took his cue. There was no more hesitation, no more waiting, no more delays. Clothes were tugged free, meeting the floor one after the other until there was no longer anything in the way, no longer anything to form any sort of a barrier between them.

His hands felt hot on her body, all but leaving a sizzling imprint as he glided them over every inch of her, caressing, possessing and slowly setting the groundwork of what was to come.

Somewhere along the line, although she wasn't quite clear exactly when, they wound up tumbling onto her bed. Body parts wound up around one another in a very warm, palpitating tangle of yearning flesh that forged an eagerness for fulfillment.

His body created a hot imprint against hers, which in turn excited her even more. The feel of it sent her to heights she hadn't even dreamed were possible.

Growing anticipation continued to throb demandingly through every part of her, making her suddenly want him with an intensity that shook her down to her very core. More than that, it frightened her because, outside of the night she had fervently prayed for her father to live, she had never experienced something of this magnitude and intensity before.

Kori felt as if she were literally on fire.

Brodie could feel the change in her immediately. Could feel her reaction to him, her desire to take this to a level that previously hadn't been there.

A level he could honestly say he had never experienced before.

"Oh baby," he breathed, his words blending into her hair. "Slow down before we both burn up."

But Kori didn't slow down.

If anything, she sped up and all he could do was try his very best to keep up with her, thinking that, any second now, they would both wind up being burned to a crisp.

But that was all right, he couldn't help thinking, because if that happened, it would be one hell of a way to go. Men went their whole lives without coming close to experiencing anything even remotely as soul-jarring as what he was feeling with Kori right at this moment.

Each intense kiss, every worshipful caress, had just brought him closer to the final moment of exquisite passion just before the all-encompassing explosion and release undulated through his body.

Brodie held back as long as he could, then, after having feasted on her exquisite body and at the same time, having experienced as much ecstasy as a human being possibly could without imploding, Brodie laced his fingers through hers. He held her hands above her head and then, his eyes on hers, making her feel like the center of his universe, Brodie united their bodies and slipped himself into hers.

He heard Kori's sharp intake of breath. The very sound just excited him even more. He saw her eyes widen and then fill with an emotion he wasn't altogether sure he recognized, but even so, it spoke to him.

Responding to a melody he felt rather certain only he heard, Brodie began to move, at first slowly then faster and faster still. When she began to respond in kind, he realized the same melody must have taken possession of her as well.

From then on, they moved as one being with one purpose: to climb the summit before them together until they could finally get to the very top of it.

Hearts pounding in unison, they kept moving higher and higher until they could achieve that final exhilarating thrill.

And then it happened.

The explosion came, ricocheting and vibrating through them at the exact same moment, raining an exquisite shower of mind-blowing ecstasy over them as they clung to one another, lips and souls sealed for what felt like all eternity.

Or, at the very least, for that moment.

Kori held on to him tightly, not wanting to let go because, if she did, she was certain the feeling would end.

But even now it was receding, swirling off into the mist.

She tightened her arms even more, refusing to surrender to the theft that was threatening this incredible new place she had just found.

She loathed giving it up.

"Who *are* you?" she heard Brodie whisper against her ear.

Kori shifted her head just a little, just enough to look at him.

"I was just going to ask you the same thing," she told Brodie, her voice coming out so softly, it was practically nonexistent. And then she smiled at him. "Maybe we're hallucinating," she said. "Because I've never felt anything quite like this before," she confessed. "So it must be a hallucination."

"Must be," he echoed, nodding his head. "Unless it's real."

The smile that encompassed his face drew her in, making her want him all over again.

"Well," Brodie murmured, slipping his fingers through her hair, "there's one way to find out."

She could feel the smile building within her. "And what's that?"

"We could test it out," he proposed, kissing her with each word he uttered.

She turned into Brodie, the close proximity of her nude body teasing his. "It does sound like a plan," she agreed. Her smile grew. "Well, I'm game."

"Oh, you definitely are that," he agreed, his body beginning to heat again, making demands on him. Slipping his arm beneath her shoulders, his lips marked a brand-new trail along her face, her lips and her throat.

Kori could feel that wild, whirlwind ride starting all over again.

But this time, even though the demands on their bodies were pronounced, they took it slower, savoring every step, enjoying one another now that they both knew what to expect.

And because there was more patience involved, the rewards were even more gratifying than they had been the first time around.

The explosion more intense.

When they finished, falling back against the pillows and taking refuge in each other's arms, they listened to their hearts beating in harmony.

Who would have even thought that that sound could turn out to be so very reassuring? Kori thought. For the next few moments or so, she allowed herself to revel in this and to allow herself to be vulnerable without trying to put up any barriers to protect herself.

Chapter Eighteen

The warm glow created with last night's lovemaking, and that had wound up enveloping her, all but receded in the light of day. It left Kori suddenly bracing herself for what she felt might come in its wake—something a great deal less than the heart-stopping happiness she had experienced in Brodie's arms.

Reality might very well be a cold splash of water.

Would he think, now that they had made love, that he could tell her what to do? Or worse, would he suddenly behave like someone who had made a mistake and was worried he would have to face the consequences of that behavior, consequences he had no intentions of dealing with?

Would he think that their night together entitled him to be the one who was in charge now?

She had no answers, only questions.

Concerns whirled through her head.

Nowhere in *any* of those scenarios was there room for a live-and-let-live attitude. So when Brodie continued to act as if they were on the same footing as before, and that they were becoming friends, respectful of each other's experience and opinions, not only was she stunned, she thought it was a trick on his part.

But all that would come later. First, she had to deal with the "morning after."

Kori hadn't meant to fall asleep. The plan—all along—was for her to hustle Brodie out of the house before her father came home. Unfortunately, the rosy contentment that had taken hold after they'd made love for a second time brought with it a peacefulness that had her contentedly falling asleep in Brodie's arms—and remaining that way until after dawn.

Kori's eyes flew open nearly six hours after they had both fallen asleep. This time when her heart began pounding madly in her chest, it was because of all the consequences and resulting problems that having Brodie here in her bedroom like this created should her father walk in on them. Never mind that she was a grown woman who could do as she chose. What she didn't choose was to flaunt that in her father's face.

The only way out, as far as Kori could see, was for *both* of them to get dressed and slip out of the house as soon as possible, leaving under the guise of getting back to working the case. If they could dress quickly and make their way downstairs, they might be able to leave without waking up her father.

Kori couldn't shake the feeling that they were on borrowed time.

"Wake up," she hissed at Brodie, bending over so that her mouth was close to his ear. At the same time, she covered *his* mouth with her hand in case Brodie yelped at being summarily woken this way.

Instantly awake, Brodie stared at her in utter confusion when he opened his eyes.

Forcibly removing her hand from his face, he asked her, "What's going on?"

Unless there was a burglar in the house, there was no

reason for her to attempt to keep him silent this way. On the slim, outside chance that he had actually guessed the reason for this dramatic enactment, Brodie obligingly kept his voice very low.

"I want to leave without waking my father," Kori told Brodie in what amounted to a whisper that was barely audible.

"Okay," Brodie replied gamely in the same sort of whisper.

"Now," she stated emphatically.

Throwing off the covers, she hurried into jeans and a sweatshirt. When she glanced over her shoulder, she saw that Brodie hadn't moved a muscle. Instead, he was watching her dress and was obviously enjoying what he saw.

"*Now*, Cavanaugh," she ordered in a low growl.

So they were back to Cavanaugh again, were they? He was going to have to make her see that they were way past that at this point, he thought with a smile as he complied with her order and started to get dressed.

"Ready," he announced, spreading his hands to facilitate her view.

Kori stopped getting her things together, looked in his direction and frowned slightly, although it wasn't because of anything she saw. Her thoughts were at odds with one another. She would love to crawl back into bed with Brodie, but that wasn't possible. For all the reasons that had just gone through her brain. In lieu, Kori wanted to put this scenario behind her and slip out of the house, even though she felt cheated because she would have much rather stayed in bed and relived some of last night's highlights with the man who had helped her create them.

Slowly.

"Okay, let's go," she said once he was dressed. "When we pass my father's room downstairs, please be extra quiet."

"I guess bursting into song is out of the question," he quipped.

The fact that he didn't know which was her father's room was a point Brodie decided not to raise. He figured that would occur to her soon enough.

They quietly made their way down the stairs, then cautiously moved in the direction of the front door.

Kori's sharp intake of breath as she came to a stop before an open door alerted Brodie that something was most definitely wrong. Kori was staring into a bedroom. A masculine bedroom, from the looks of the decor.

Kori's next words, mumbled under her breath and strictly to herself, confirmed his suspicions. She appeared genuinely worried, not to mention upset.

"He never came home."

The *he*, Brodie assumed, referred to her father. "What makes you think your father didn't come home?" he asked.

"Because his bed's made," she answered sharply, walking into the room.

"Maybe he made his bed after he got up," Brodie suggested.

Kori glared at her partner, uttering a dismissive noise. "My father's a wonderful man, but he has *never* made a bed in his whole life," she told Brodie. Distressed, she could only come to one conclusion. "He didn't come home last night."

Brodie gave her a look that had "calm down" written all over it, although he did refrain from using the phrase.

"Kori, your father's a big boy. He deserves a night

out once in a while and, from the way you're reacting, I take it that the man never goes out. Ever."

Her face clouded over. "That's not the point," Kori insisted.

"Then what is the point?" he asked her patiently, waiting to see what she would come up with.

"I didn't want him thinking less of me for casually sleeping with someone and it obviously doesn't bother him if I think that about him." She quietly closed and locked the front door behind her.

He didn't see why anyone had to think less of anyone for going with their feelings, but he knew that raising that point was just asking for trouble. It would undoubtedly sink him further into this pool of quicksand that was forming, so he decided the best thing was to gloss over it.

"Chalk it up to a life lesson and just move on," he advised. "We've got bigger things to focus on. Or have you decided to give up on our current case?"

Kori glared at him. "I hate it when you're right."

"I'll try to be wrong once in a while," Brodie told her, then couldn't resist adding with a grin, "But it won't be easy."

Kori made a guttural sound and just continued walking toward his car.

They wound up driving to the precinct in Kori's car because as Brodie went to open up his vehicle, Kori put her foot down.

"I am not going to the precinct in a tank. If you want to drive over there together, it's going to have to be in my car," she informed him.

Brodie spread his hands genially. "Fine by me."

They drove in silence for exactly two minutes before,

unable to keep her concern to herself, she glanced in Brodie's direction and asked, "Do you think he's okay?"

Brodie congratulated himself on not laughing at her question. He sensed that, to her, her concern about her father was very real.

"I'm sure he is, Kori. Unlike a black widow spider, Aunt Maeve does not eat whoever she, um…spends the night with," Brodie said tactfully. Keeping a straight face as he said this was definitely *not* easy since he was biting the inside of his cheek to keep from laughing out loud.

"I'm not worried about that," she informed her partner, annoyed. "I'm worried about my father being hurt."

Brodie looked at her profile for a long moment. He decided to answer her seriously and stop teasing. "Well, we all risk that if we let our guard down and get close to someone."

Was he warning her about himself? Kori wondered. No, she couldn't let herself go there, she insisted. She already had enough going on without worrying about Brodie's feelings about her—or lack thereof.

"Why don't we stop for breakfast before we go in?" Brodie suddenly suggested out of the blue.

Food was just about the last thing on her mind. "You could eat?" she queried, her voice filled with marvel.

Brodie laughed in response. She had to be kidding. "I could always eat, Kori."

She had already gotten too personal last night. It was time to retreat, to rebuild barriers before something went very wrong and she wound up paying for dropping her guard.

"I liked it better when you called me Kennedy," she told him tersely.

"And I liked it better when you called me Brodie," he

countered. His eyes washed over her. "Guess we can't always get what we like."

Suddenly, Kori found herself wanting to put him in his place, to raise her voice and yell at Brodie, or maybe just punch him. But as she tried to summon the proper amount of indignant anger, all she could manage was to relive last night as images flashed through her mind, warming her all over again.

Annoyed with herself, Kori deliberately shut her mind to any extraneous thoughts and instead just focused on Brodie's last request. Breakfast. At least that was safe.

"Do you want to go anywhere in particular?" she asked him.

The moment the words were out of her mouth, Kori realized her mistake. She had wanted to look like the one in charge.

"Never mind, I'll pick," she announced, negating any selection Brodie might have been about to suggest.

"Fine with me," he told her with a broad smile.

She got the feeling that he could see right through her.

Kori sighed. She had to stop looking at him, stop letting that smile of his get to her. She was a decorated detective for heaven's sake and she had a case that needed her entire attention, not just a piece of it.

If nothing else, she was being totally unprofessional.

"Mind if we get that breakfast to go?" she asked.

She was extending a courtesy to him by asking. The fact was she had already made up her mind that whatever order they got would be "to go." She had no intentions of sitting across from him at any fast-food restaurant, giving him another chance to totally wear her down with those liquid green eyes of his that were already wreaking havoc on her entire being.

"I was just going to suggest that," Brodie told her cheerfully, managing to catch her off guard again.

So Kori could only nod her agreement. "I guess great minds do think alike," she told him with a touch of sarcasm.

But Brodie seemed to be entirely serious as he answered, "I guess they do at that."

IT WASN'T UNTIL breakfast had been ordered and secured and they were driving to the precinct that Kori finally dug deep and apologized. It was, she told herself, the right thing to do.

"I'm sorry, Cavanaugh, I didn't mean to bite your head off back there."

"No harm done. My head's still where it's supposed to be, firmly attached," he told her, amused as he let her off the hook.

Stubbornly, Kori ignored his absolution. Instead she forged on with her apology. If she didn't do it now, she never would—and then she would feel guilty about it.

"It's just that I've never been in this situation before, going to work with the man I slept with the day after I slept with him." She avoided his eyes and stared straight at the road.

"No explanations necessary," Brodie told her, doing his best to make her see that he didn't need her to make any apologies. His skin was tougher than that. Much tougher.

She lost her patience. "Damn it, Cavanaugh, it *is* necessary. I don't know what I'm doing here. It's all new for me," she said, referring to the situation she found herself in.

He nodded, but it was a noncommittal nod and she didn't know what to make of it. And then he said, "Even God had to have a first day. It's okay, Kori, really," he stressed. "If it helps, I've never been in this kind of situation before, either. And for the record," he added softly, "I'd really like to see where this goes."

Kori smiled at the man in her passenger seat, oddly comforted by what he had just said even though there was a part of her that upbraided her for being a fool and baring her soul this way to him.

"And," Brodie continued, "I'm going to call my aunt sometime later today to see if she had a nice time at Uncle Andrew's gathering—and afterward," he added significantly after a pause.

She saw the smile in his eyes and tried not to be drawn in by it. "Won't she get angry at you? You know, for prying?"

"Maybe," Brodie allowed. There was no defensiveness in his voice. "But we're Cavanaughs. It's what we do. We pry into each other's lives because we care about one another," he explained. "It might not be spoken, but it is still understood."

She stared at him in disbelief. "And your aunt really won't get angry with you for prying?" Kori asked in surprise.

"Perhaps," Brodie replied, not certain about Maeve's initial reaction, "but ultimately, one way or the other, I'll get to the bottom of this and find out what happened—and then you'll have your answer."

From where she stood, that sounded like a pretty big favor. The man was going out on a limb. "You'd do that for me?"

"Yes, but having you affected is a by-product of this whole exchange. I'm doing it for Aunt Maeve because I do care about her and want her to be happy. I also want to know if she's not happy for some reason. I owe the woman a lot."

"You're a good man, Brodie Cavanaugh," Kori told him with feeling.

"That's what I've been trying to tell you," he deadpanned. And then he said, "Drive faster, partner."

She didn't understand. "Why?"

"Because the smell of breakfast is really tempting me and I can feel my stomach growling—big-time."

"Are you sure that's your stomach?" she asked, slanting a glance in his direction.

"We could pull over somewhere, act like a couple of teenagers in one of their parents' cars and find out," Brodie suggested.

Kori shook her head as she kept driving. "You are totally incorrigible."

"That all depends on what the situation is," he answered. "But right now, if you don't drive any faster, I can't be responsible for what I do."

"To—?"

"That breakfast you're packing back there," he said, indicating the back seat.

"Driving faster," she announced, stepping on the gas in order to arrive at their destination a little quicker than she intended.

His laughter was ringing in her ears.

Chapter Nineteen

Brodie was on his way with Kori to talk to one of the hospital employees they hadn't interviewed yet when his phone rang. He stepped to the side and turned away to answer his phone.

Kori watched Brodie's body language and sensed that this call wasn't about the case, but she couldn't begin to guess what it actually was about. She knew she was going to have to wait until he got off his cell phone.

Waiting patiently had never been her strong suit.

She held her breath as he ended the call and tucked his phone back into his pocket. "Well, you'll be happy to know Aunt Maeve just called back," he told her. He'd placed at call to her earlier and had been forced to leave a message on her voice mail.

"And?" Kori prodded, wanting to jump in and squeeze the words right out of his throat. He was drawing this out and taking much too long.

"And," Brodie told her with a smile, "she thinks that your father is an extremely nice man."

Kori wanted to scream. This wasn't telling her what she asked.

"I could have told her that," Kori said, and then looked at him as questions insisted on popping up in her head. "'Extremely nice man' as in 'I wouldn't mind having Bill Kennedy sit next to me in a movie theater' or as in 'where has he been all my life' nice?" Kori questioned.

"I got the impression it was the latter," Brodie answered.

Kori's smile worked its way up to her eyes with lightning speed. "Really?" she asked, making no effort to hide how pleased that made her.

"Really," Brodie confirmed. "Which brings me to my own question. Just how nice is your father?" he asked, doing a theme and variation of the question she had asked him yesterday at the gathering.

"The kind of nice they rarely make anymore," Kori told her partner.

"Good, because Aunt Maeve could use a little personal happiness in her life. It's always been about her kids, or her job, or the family. It's never about her."

Kori heard what he wasn't saying, "And you think it's about time that it was."

"Absolutely," Brodie said with enthusiasm. "Isn't that how you feel about your father?" he asked.

"Yes," she answered. Then a thought hit her. "Well, what do you know. We seem to be in agreement here."

"Twice in two days," he joked with a laugh as they got to the car. "Who would have thought?"

"And by twice, you mean…" She let her voice trail off because she wasn't about to take *anything* for granted.

There was a sparkle in his eyes when they met hers. "I do," he confirmed. The way he said it left no doubt in her mind as to his meaning. He wanted to make sure that both her father and his aunt enjoyed one another.

A lightness filled Kori, making her feel happy, much the way she had last night when Brodie had made her feel like she was walking on air and collecting rainbows for the very first time in her life.

It was way past time to get back to the case and focus her attention on it. Maybe, given her fresh frame of mind, something new would jump out at her, something that they had missed earlier.

"Did Valri make any headway with the tapes we had her look at?" she asked Brodie after they had gone to see yet another hospital employee. Valri had called him right after that.

Brodie shook his head. The news wasn't good. "She didn't and the tech she had looking over her shoulder didn't find anything new, either," he told her.

"Think it might be worth another go-round?" she asked him. "Maybe if we took another look at the tapes…"

"Honestly, no," he answered flatly. "If Valri couldn't find anything, and her assistant couldn't find anything, then there's just nothing to be found in those tapes."

Kori reexamined his reply and her face brightened slightly. "Which in turn does tell us something."

He looked at her, trying to understand where she was going with this. "How do you figure?"

"Don't you see? Whoever took that baby had to know where all the surveillance cameras' blind spots were located. Which, in turn, just confirms what we already suspected because of the removed tracking device—that this had to be an inside job." Her voice grew in excitement. "That means that the baby was taken not by some random visitor coming to see someone in the hospital. That little girl was taken by someone who works at the hospital," she concluded, barely containing herself.

Brodie rolled over what she had just said in his mind,

nodding. "You're right. And it just reinforces what we already thought when that so-called eyewitness we talked to told us she had found that ankle bracelet the hospital uses as a tracking device. I mean, it was cut off. Someone had to know how to do that without setting it off."

Kori leaned back in her chair for a moment, closing her eyes and centering herself. She knew what they needed to do.

Brodie saw the expression on her face. "You all right?" he asked, concerned.

She opened her eyes again and nodded. "I'm fine," she answered wearily. "But I think, focusing on this idea that it was an inside job, we're going to have to re-interrogate all the hospital employees who were on the maternity floor any time before the baby went missing that day." It was a daunting idea, but there was no way around it. "It's the only way we can effectively follow up on all this."

Brodie nodded, looking none too happy about the matter. "I know."

They went back to the beginning.

SINCE THIS WAS the second time around for a lot of the people—in some cases, this actually made three times—those whom Kori, Brodie and the rest of the task force spoke to were not exactly ecstatic to retrace old ground that was now painfully familiar. Not to mention, for the most part, fruitless.

One of the nurses, Jenny Wong, one of the first people they had originally questioned, seemed almost hostile to be going over all this with the police again.

"Look, it's not that I don't sympathize with that mother—although I hear she was going to give that baby up for adoption anyway," the less-than-patient nurse told Brodie. Rather than sit for the interview, she'd insisted on continuing to work while he asked her questions. "But I've already told you everything that I know," she pointed out. It was obvious that the woman was barely containing her irritation. This was a stain on the hospital's reputation and she just wanted to move past it and have it buried.

"If you wouldn't mind, could you tell me again?" Brodie prodded the sharp-featured woman with an encouraging smile.

The nurse rolled her eyes and made an impatient noise, then began to answer in an almost robot-like tone of voice.

"I came in that morning, checked Rose Williams's vitals, then did the same with the baby after first reading the baby's name on her small wrist bracelet to make sure that the right baby was with the right mother." When Brodie looked at her with an unspoken question in his eyes, the nurse said, "Yes, I know it *does* happen. But I did my part. End of story, end of contact," she concluded. "I didn't see either one of them until the alarm went out that a baby—that baby—had been stolen. Nothing has changed since the last time I went over this with one of your other people. Now, if you don't mind, I have a lot of work to get back to," she said. With that, she turned away from Brodie.

"One more question." Brodie spoke up. The nurse reluctantly turned back to face him, waiting. "Would you know how to remove the tracking device from the baby's ankle?" Brodie asked.

"I would—but I wouldn't," she insisted. "Removing those tracking devices is not part of my job description. Why are you asking me that?" she challenged.

"Because whoever took the baby had to know how to remove the ankle bracelet without setting it off," he told the woman.

"Well, all I can tell you was that it wasn't me," the nurse replied flatly. "Now, can I go?"

Kori, who had listened to the entire exchange—feeling that she needed to back Brodie up with this hostile nurse—nodded and gestured toward the doorway, silently indicating that she was free to leave… for now.

"Thank you," the woman said icily, her words directed at both of them just before she left the area.

Kori sighed. "You know, this is starting to feel like we're stuck in a rerun of *Groundhog Day*," Kori complained. "We're just going around and around the same territory, leaving tread marks and getting absolutely nowhere."

"Until it winds up all falling into place for us and makes sense," Brodie insisted.

"You're right. We're missing something. Something that's staring us in the face," Kori said. "I just don't know what it is." Frustration all but vibrated in her voice.

"It's a process," Brodie told her, then promised, "Don't worry about it, Kori. We're going to get there—as long as we don't give up."

"Will we?" She found herself battling a hopelessness that threatened to swallow her whole. "In time?" she questioned. "I'm not as sure as you are."

"One foot in front of the other, Kori," Brodie counseled. "We still have a lot of people left to re-interview."

Kori looked at the list she had complied earlier. There were still a great many names on it. "Back to *Groundhog Day*," she said with a sigh.

THE RE-INTERVIEWS CONTINUED through the day. Most of the people they wanted to talk to weren't at the hospital and weren't very happy about having to talk to police detectives on their day off and on their home territory. But, to a person, because there was an infant's life at stake, they did all cooperate.

Some, however, were a bit less willing than others.

By the end of the day, Kori, Brodie and their teams were still no wiser about the abducted child's whereabouts than they had been to begin with.

"Second verse, same as the first." Kori mocked herself, feeling like they were just spinning their wheels, going nowhere. "What are we missing, people? What am I not seeing?" she asked of no one in particular.

"Maybe it'll be clearer in the morning," Spenser suggested hopefully.

"And maybe it'll be that much further away," Kori said, crushed. "Sorry," she apologized. "You're right. We should go home. Shower. Change our clothes. Maybe that'll help."

"Hug our kids," Valente, the only team member with children, said, adding his two cents to Kori's plan for the evening. "We get this guy—or woman—" he added "—and I get dibs on stringing him up from the nearest flagpole."

The man was only putting into words what they were all secretly thinking, Brodie thought. "I'll help, but first let's find this baby," he said to the rest of the force, getting his things together in order to leave the squad room for the night.

Concurring murmurs greeted his statement as the other members of the task force filed out of the room.

Brodie found an excuse to hang back until only Kori

and he were left in the room. "Want to get something to eat?"

She laughed, shaking her head. "I keep forgetting that you're a growing boy," she told him. "No. But I'll watch you eat."

"What fun is that?" he asked.

"I wasn't thinking about fun." She sighed, deciding to level with Brodie. "I was thinking that I don't want to be alone just yet. My dad took your aunt out dancing." Even as she said it, she laughed, shaking her head. "Dancing. The man I was so terrified would never walk again is out dancing tonight." A smile took over her features. "You were right, Brodie. Your aunt *is* very good for my father."

Brodie was very pleased at the conclusion she had reached. "I told you. She's got a big heart even if, at times, she comes on a little gruff."

Kori slipped a couple of files into her purse. She thought she heard something in his voice. "You sound as if you have a special connection with her."

Brodie smiled and nodded. "I do."

When he didn't say anything to follow that up, she asked, "Are you going to tell me about it, or am I going to have to use my detective skills?"

"Save your skills," he told her. "It's no big secret. I'll tell you." The truth of it was, he didn't like revisiting that period of his life even though it was years ago. "My mother died when I was still pretty young. Despite everything she was involved with and that put so many demands on her time, Aunt Maeve stepped in to help my father cope with his loss. Moreover, she made sure she was there for every one of us—my brothers and sisters and me," he specified.

"She did what she could so that none of us would feel

as if we'd been abandoned by the woman we all loved and needed. But that's just the way that Aunt Maeve is," he told Kori simply. "I'd go to hell and back on my knees for that woman."

"Wow," she said, impressed. "That is some endorsement."

"I don't know about an endorsement, but I wouldn't say it if I didn't mean it. Now, about that dinner..." Brodie's voice trailed off as he looked at her for any input.

Kori shrugged. She had no preferences. "It can be whatever you want. My only request is that we get it to go."

Brodie smiled. "You read my mind. And since we're on the subject, can it 'go' to my place?"

Her eyes met his. For a moment, she thought it was just wishful thinking on her part, that she was just reading into what he was saying, but a second later, she realized that he *was* inviting her over to his place.

Much as she wanted to go, she didn't want to push it. "Are you sure about this?" she asked Brodie.

"Very sure," he replied. "But if you'd rather not, I understand completely."

"You might," she laughed dryly, "but I wouldn't."

His eyebrows drew together. "I'm not sure that I follow," he admitted.

"That's okay. I promise I'll walk slow so that you don't lose me." And then she smiled. It was a weak smile, but it was definitely there.

They wound up getting Chinese food—several entrées when she had trouble making up her mind which one she wanted.

"Makes for a good breakfast the following day," he told her, paying the tab and then carrying the oversize large bag out of the restaurant and to her car.

"I've never had leftover Chinese food for breakfast," Kori admitted.

"Then you are definitely in for a treat," Brodie promised, getting into the car on the passenger side. The bag filled with their order was put on the floor.

"There's just one problem," she told him as she turned her key in the ignition.

Brodie braced himself. "And that is?" he asked.

She looked at him. "If we're going to your place, I have no idea where you live."

He laughed then, as relief slid through his body. He'd been prepared for almost anything, including her changing her mind, or even doing a complete about-face. Having her confess to this minuscule lack of knowledge was exceedingly gratifying.

"Fortunately, that's a very easy problem to solve," he told her, and then proceeded to give Kori directions to his home.

Chapter Twenty

As she followed the directions Brodie gave her, Kori wasn't really sure just what to expect. She had to admit that she'd thought Brodie probably lived in some sort of an apartment complex. Since no building in Aurora was over fifty years old, she'd just assumed that Brodie lived in one of the newer residential complexes.

She hadn't thought that he actually owned his own home.

So when the address he gave her turned out to belong to a single-story, newly painted structure, it was a surprise. There was even more of a surprise, she discovered, when Brodie unlocked the door.

Leading the way, he walked into the kitchen and put the bag of Chinese food on the counter. Since Kori hadn't said a word from the time he had opened the door, Brodie turned around to look at her.

"You're not saying anything. Is there something wrong?" he asked.

"No, nothing's wrong," she replied, the words coming out slowly as she continued taking everything in. "I was just admiring the place." She looked back at her partner. Everything looked absolutely immaculate. "I guess your maid must have just been here today."

"My 'maid'?" he echoed, bewildered as he unpacked

the bag he had brought in. Where had she ever gotten the idea that he had a maid? "I don't mean to correct you, but I don't have a maid."

"Sure you do," she argued, looking around again. The place looked so clean, Kori thought, she could have eaten right off the floor. "Everything looks so incredibly neat and clean. You *have* to have a maid."

So that was it, he thought with a smile.

Brodie finished emptying the bag, then absently folded it before lining up the containers next to one another. "Well, contrary to popular belief, not all men are slobs," he told her. "My mother, bless her, always insisted that we clean up after ourselves. After she got sick, we kids just kept on doing it. We were trying to please her." Brodie smiled more to himself than at Kori. "Skylar and I thought that if we were very, very good, then our mother would eventually get well and stay with us.

"When she didn't," he continued, "we were pretty devastated, certain that we had somehow failed in some way."

Kori ached for him then, ached for the wounded boy he had been all those years ago.

"Oh, Brodie, I'm so sorry," she whispered.

"Don't be. At least I got into the habit of being neat. See, there's something positive to be gleaned out of every bad situation." He prudently changed the subject. "Now, I know you said you weren't hungry…" he told her as he opened the last of the containers. The alluring aromas all melded together, wafting up so that they could both smell them. "But you have to admit that this does smell tempting."

She smiled. He was right. And now that she thought

about it, maybe she *was* hungry. "All right, you win. I'll have a little bit," she relented.

"Atta girl." He took two plates out of the overhead cabinet and brought them over to the containers. "I knew I could get you to change your mind and eat something."

"Well, don't get your hopes up. Hitting dead end after dead end has just about killed any appetite that I might have had budding up inside me. I keep thinking about what I'm going to say to that poor young mother if it turns out that we can't find her baby. It's tying my stomach up in knots," she admitted, helping herself to a serving of Beef Lo Mein.

"The chief of D's gave me some really good advice when I originally started working in the homicide department."

He held up a fork as well as the chopsticks that had been packed with the containers, giving her a choice.

Since she wasn't all that handy using chopsticks, Kori reached for the fork.

"I was afraid of falling flat on my face," he continued, "you know, not living up to the Cavanaugh name and all that. Let's face it, there's a lot to live up to—not that anyone would rub my nose in it but, well, I didn't want to be remembered as the guy who failed. Anyway, the chief saw that I was struggling with some issues," Brodie said, taking a serving of Moo Goo Gai Pan. "He took me aside and said, 'Don't think about failing. Just focus on succeeding. The rest will take care of itself.'"

"Nice sentiment," she said as she took an egg roll out and put it on her plate. "But—"

"No. No 'buts,'" Brodie told her, then underscored the one word that he wanted her to take away from all this. "Succeeding."

"Succeeding," she echoed, indulging him.

Brodie flashed her a smile. Somehow it managed to hearten her even though she felt as if she were initially just going through the motions and playing along with what he said.

KORI DIDN'T GO home that night, but then she knew that she wouldn't.

Things between them progressed naturally and although she had promised herself that there wouldn't be a repeat performance of the night before, she neither needed it nor wanted it. But deep down inside, she knew that was a lie, created just to protect herself from being hurt if Brodie pulled away from her.

But he didn't pull away.

The complete opposite was true.

Brodie acted as if this was a very natural part of the evening. That after a full day of working together and then spending the evening together, they would wind up retreating to their own personal haven, have a little dinner and then find solace in each other's arms—not out of habit but out of a strong, mutual need to enjoy one another.

And, to Kori's delight, this time was even better than the night before.

When the lovemaking was over and Brodie fell back, stunned, pleased and completely spent, he drew Kori to him and cradled her against him in his arms.

"You know," he said once his breathing began to level off and return to normal, "we're going to have to come up with a safe word."

"'A safe word'?" she repeated, unaware that her breath was tickling his bare skin as she spoke. "Why would we need a safe word?"

He smiled at her. "Because you get my blood rushing so much and so hard, I just might wind up expiring while I'm making love with you."

She slanted a dubious look at Brodie. "Okay, now you're just making fun of me by exaggerating."

Brodie tightened his arms around her. "I would never make fun of you," he told her. He took one of her hands and placed it on his chest, putting his own hand over it to emphasize his point. "And does that feel as if I'm exaggerating?"

She could feel his heart all but pounding against her palm. He might be teasing her, but oh lord, she wanted him again. Those walls that she had kept around herself had been up for so long, she had just assumed that they were a fixture.

A permanent one. Which was why she was so stunned by the feelings madly racing through her like a herd of wild horses that had been set free.

Kori took a deep breath and then said, "Elephant."

Brodie blinked. He raised his head slightly and looked at her, somewhat bewildered.

"What's that now?" he asked, thinking he had to have heard wrong.

"I've decided that's my safe word," Kori explained and then said it again. "Elephant."

"Elephant," he repeated and then he laughed, delighted. "You know, you really are a very unique woman, Kori Kennedy," he told her as he leaned in and pressed his lips against hers.

A quick, fleeting kiss bloomed into something more, something longer and far more stirring, within a matter of seconds.

Before either one of them knew what was happening, they were making love with one another again and soaring above the clouds, creating an indescribable rapture that wrapped itself tightly around them. Within moments, they had managed to seal themselves away from the rest of the world as they slipped into paradise.

THE INSISTENT BUZZING of the cell phone she had placed on his nightstand muscled its way into the dream she was having. The very nice dream that had brought indescribable contentment with it and managed to evaporate without leaving any sort of form or even a hint as to its content once it receded from her brain.

Brodie had trained himself to be a light sleeper years ago and was already awake.

"Your phone's ringing," he told her, rubbing his face and erasing the last trace of sleep from his system.

Kori sat up. "It must be the precinct," she noted, reaching for her phone.

"I don't think so," he told her. "My phone's not ringing." And he was fairly certain that if it was something that had to do with their current case, both of their phones would be ringing.

Kori pulled the phone to her as she leaned against the headboard. Blinking, she focused on the screen. If it wasn't the station, she was fairly certain that it was probably her father, wondering if she was at the station, pulling an all-nighter again.

But it wasn't her father, either. The number on her screen was one she didn't recognize.

Well, she was up now. She might as well answer.

"This is Detective Kennedy," she said. "Who am I speaking to?"

There was a small sob on the other end in response and then she heard a very shaky, timid voice begin to speak. "Detective Kennedy? This is Rose."

Kori braced herself. The young woman was going to ask her if there had been any progress made in locating her baby. She didn't know how to give Rose a negative response and still find a way to keep her hopes up. This was the part of her job she really hated.

Unconsciously, she leaned into Brodie, as if that would somehow help her through this.

Her voice sounded almost hollow to her own ears as she said, "Hello, Rose."

She could feel Brodie become instantly alert.

He took her hand, wrapping his fingers around it and silently giving her his support as he listened to her end of the conversation.

"I wish I had something positive to tell you, Rose, but right now—"

Rose cut in, breaking into what Kori was about to say. She sounded almost breathless as she told the detective, "I got a letter."

Kori quickly assimilated the information, straightening. "From the kidnapper?"

"I think so," she answered uncertainly, then followed that with a slightly more positive, "Yes."

Kori was kicking off the covers and looking for her clothes. "You still have the letter?" she questioned. She wasn't about to take anything for granted.

"Yes, it's right here. Someone slipped an envelope under my door. I found it this morning and put it on the table. I called you as soon as I read it." Rose was talking faster and faster.

"Good," Kori told her. "Don't do anything with it. Leave it exactly where you put it."

"Okay," she answered. "Are you going to want to see it?"

"Oh yes," she said with emphasis. This could be

the break they'd been waiting for. "Are you calling from home?"

"Yes." For good measure, Rose rattled off her address, stumbling at first, as if she was having trouble remembering the exact order the numbers came in.

Kori nodded out of habit, committing the address to memory. "Don't go anywhere," she told Rose. "We'll be right there."

Getting all the way out of bed, Kori terminated the call.

Brodie had put two and two together, but now that Kori was off the phone, he wanted to be sure, so he asked, "Was that what it sounded like?" as he began to throw on his clothes.

Kori was gathering up her own clothing. All the items were scattered all over the floor. In the middle of all this, Kori found it ironic that she had been so amazed at how neat Brodie kept everything while she was the one whose clothes were tossed all over the place as if they had weathered a really severe blizzard of disarray.

"Rose just called that someone had pushed an envelope under her door. She didn't go into any detail, but I'm assuming that there was a message inside about the baby," Kori said as she pulled on her sweater.

"Asking for a ransom?" Brodie prompted as he put on his shoes.

The call had been scarce on details. Kori hadn't pressed because she'd wanted to read the note herself.

"Rose didn't say anything one way or another," she admitted. "Although probably. Why else would the kidnapper drop off a note? "She just sounded very confused when I talked to her. But she seemed pretty certain that whatever that note said, it was written by the kidnapper."

Brodie nodded, taking everything in. "We'll need to notify Crime Scene Investigation. They're going to have to bag the letter and put it into evidence so they can dust it for prints."

They were both thinking the same thing, Kori thought as she heard Brodie say, "With any luck, our kidnapper just made his or her first mistake and we'll find some telltale fingerprints on the envelope or note to trace. Maybe we can finally put a face to this monster who made off with Rose's baby."

Kori slowed down and swung by the kitchen. She knew that Brodie had set the timer on his coffee maker to go off first thing in the morning—which was now.

The scent of brewing coffee greeted her even before she walked in. Breathing it in, Kori turned to look at Brodie, who was right behind her. "You know, you are definitely going to make someone a very thoughtful, wonderful wife," she teased as she poured coffee into two vacuum mugs, then put on the lids, tightening them so that there wouldn't be any mishaps when they took the mugs with them.

Brodie, meanwhile, was packing two containers of the leftover Chinese food to serve as their breakfast on the run.

"Don't go getting ahead of yourself," Kori warned him.

"I'm going to need more before I can take you up on that," Brodie told her, not sure just what she was referring to. He'd learned very quickly that he needed to reserve any sort of judgment until Kori clarified things for him.

"About this note that the kidnapper probably left. It might not have any fingerprints on it, or anything else we can use. This person has been clever so far, avoiding the surveillance cameras, getting rid of the baby's tracking device. Most likely the note was handled when the kidnapper was wearing gloves."

"You know, your optimism can really be overwhelming at times," Brodie quipped.

She gave him a long-suffering look. "It's called being a realist."

"Whatever you say." The expression on his face told her that he wasn't buying the excuse she was giving him. "You know," he suggested, "why don't we reserve judgment like you said and deal with things as we come up against them?"

Kori nodded. There was no point in arguing about it. Besides, part of her was really hoping that Brodie was right.

"Works for me," she told him. "Did you happen to bring the rest of the egg rolls?" she asked him as they left his house.

"As a matter of fact, I did. I figured they would be easy enough to eat without needing to use a fork."

"You've thought of everything," she said, smiling and nodding her approval.

"I usually do," he answered. "Now let's go and find out if that so-called clever kidnapper slipped up and made his or her first mistake."

The fact that he was holding up crossed fingers didn't escape Kori. She figured that Brodie wasn't quite as certain about things as he pretended to be.

Chapter Twenty-One

"According to this address," Kori said as she drove herself and Brodie to Rose Williams's apartment, "if I'm reading this right, I think Rose lives on the ground floor of one of the oldest apartment complexes in Aurora. These days real-estate agents like to refer to them as 'apartment homes.' I guess that's to make them sound more appealing to the renter."

"Apartment homes, huh?" Brodie scoffed. "Whatever happened to truth in advertising?"

She pulled up in what she mused served as a guest parking area. "There is no such thing," Kori said, turning off her engine.

Stepping out, she looked around the grounds. "Not homey, but definitely better than some of the places I've seen." Getting her bearings, she pointed to her immediate left. "I think her 'apartment home' is right over there."

Taking a breath, Kori knocked on the ground-floor apartment door. Less than a second later, they heard a timid voice ask, "Who is it?"

Kori looked at the man at her elbow. "That has to be Rose," she said just before she announced, "Detectives Cavanaugh and Kennedy, Rose. You called me to say you received a note under your door."

She was barely finished saying that before the door flew open. "Please, come in," Rose cried, beckoning them into what was a very small studio apartment.

Kori was surprised at how crammed it appeared.

Given the limited space, the first thing that struck Kori as she walked in was that there was a crib set up next to what had to be a fold-out sofa. For the moment, it took her attention away from how very pale Rose looked.

Kori stared at the crib. A crib meant that the new mother had been expecting to come home with an infant, not give it up for adoption. Had she somehow gotten her facts mixed up?

She looked quizzically toward Brodie. The discrepancy had apparently struck him as well, because Brodie was the one who brought the crib up to Rose.

He turned to face her as he closed the front door. "Maybe I got things mixed up, but I thought you said that when you went into the hospital, you were going to put the baby up for adoption."

The reminder brought a wave of fresh tears to a person who had obviously been crying off and on since the baby had vanished.

Rose struggled to collect herself. "I was," she answered Brodie, a labored sigh escaping her lips as she wiped her eyes.

Wadding her handkerchief up, she looked from one detective to the other, searching for words that she could use to make these two people understand what she was going through. And then she blurted out what had been haunting her since the moment she'd realized that the baby had been taken.

As she spoke, a fresh wave of tears began to choke

her. "I didn't deserve this little being and now I'm being punished for it."

"Explain something to me," Kori requested, trying to get the distraught mother back on track.

"Anything," Rose breathed, looking at the two detectives as if they performed miracles on a regular basis.

"If you were going to give the baby up for adoption, then why did you buy a crib?" Kori asked. She could see by Brodie's expression that the same question had crossed his mind.

"I didn't," Rose protested.

"Then how did this crib get here?" Brodie asked.

She stared at the piece of furniture as if she hadn't noticed it until just now. "Oh, that. My grandmother bought it." Guilt colored her cheeks. "She didn't know I was going to give the baby up," Rose confessed. "She's a very religious person and I couldn't bring myself to tell her until just before I was being wheeled into the delivery room. She was really upset when I told her. I guess none of that matters now."

Brodie could see that Rose was slipping away from them. They needed her to be as clear-headed as they could get her so that she was able to answer their questions.

"When you called earlier, Detective Kennedy said you mentioned that you thought the kidnapper had slipped an envelope under your door," he prodded, trying to get her talking about the incident.

Rose seemed to come to then, as if she had one last purpose to see to before she totally withdrew from reality. Nodding, the young woman pointed toward the small table where she took her meals.

"The letter is over there. I opened it," she said, as if

they couldn't already guess as much. "But I put it back in the envelope and away as soon as you told me to."

"We're going to need your fingerprints," Kori told her as she pulled on a pair of rubber gloves before picking up the letter.

"Why?" Rose asked, confusion and fear in her voice.

"So we can rule you out when we look for other fingerprints on the envelope or letter," Brodie explained to the quivering young woman.

It struck Kori that her partner sounded as if he was speaking to a frightened child rather than to a grown woman. The man had patience, she'd give him that.

The next moment, she turned her attention to the envelope and, more importantly, to what was inside it. Gingerly opening the flap, she very carefully withdrew the folded paper. Even before she unfolded the paper, she could see that they weren't going to need someone to analyze the writing.

Because there *was* no writing to analyze.

"Brodie, come look at this," she called to him.

Brodie excused himself from the frail young woman who, despite the words of encouragement he was giving her, seemed to be slowly falling to pieces.

"What's up?"

The words were no sooner out of his mouth than he saw why Kori had called him over. He emitted a low whistle, careful to keep the sound under his breath.

"Looks like our kidnapper is a fan of grade B murder mysteries," he commented.

Kori frowned. "Maybe, but the person is being clever, not to mention extremely patient," she commented, staring at the note. The sheet of paper contained a missive completely comprised of letters of all sizes, shapes and colors that had been cut out of at least half a dozen different publications so that none could be used for even the slightest identification purposes.

The resulting note read:

Do not worry about your baby. She is safe and being well cared for.

"This must have taken *hours* to cut out and paste," Brodie commented, reading the message over Kori's shoulder.

Kori glanced back at her partner. "You sound as if you almost admire the kidnapper's patience."

Instead of answering, Brodie raised his eyes and looked in the baby's mother's direction. Speaking up, he asked her, "Do you have any idea why the kidnapper would send this to you?"

Rose appeared just as bewildered by the note. "I don't know. I think I might have told someone that I just wanted to be sure that my daughter wasn't being harmed. That I wouldn't worry so much about her if I just knew that she was okay."

"Who, Rose?" Kori pressed. "Who did you say this to? Think, honey."

"I don't know," Rose cried, covering her face with her hands as she began to sob. "I don't know. Maybe it was the orderly who was there. Maybe it was someone else. Everything is all jumbled up." Totally distraught, she looked from one detective to the other. "I don't remember."

Letting out a long breath that sounded suspiciously like a shudder, Rose made another halfhearted attempt to try to collect herself. "Maybe this is a sign," she said to the two people in the room.

"A sign?" Kori questioned.

Rose nodded again, her head bobbing up and down like a cork being tossed around in a flood. "Maybe I shouldn't be trying to find her to get her back. She's probably better off without me. Whoever has her says that they're taking care of her. They could probably do a better job of it than I can," she told them, her lower lip quivering again.

Kori stared at the young woman. This was something she hadn't expected. She decided that the only way to snap Rose out of her mental quagmire was to get tough with her. "And maybe the kidnapper is going to lose his or her patience with your baby the first big crying jag she has and sell her to the first couple who comes along—after knocking her around a little.

"No, Rose, he or she had absolutely no right to steal your baby. This person needs to be brought in and made accountable for what they've done, and your baby needs to be in the care of a law-abiding person or persons. If you feel you can't give her the kind of care that she needs, then you're free to make that sort of decision. But you don't just give those rights away to someone who stole the baby in the first place."

Kori was struggling to hold on to her anger and keep it from erupting. This case was hard enough to deal with without having to try to make the baby's mother not just mentally abandon the baby in a fit of so-called selflessness.

She saw Brodie looking at her. Taking a deep breath, Kori regained control over herself.

BRODIE CALLED THE CSI team so they could dust for any and all prints that might have been on the envelope as well as the paper with all the cut-out letters.

The team arrived in what felt like record time. When

they came, the head of the investigative unit, Sean Cavanaugh, was with them.

Nodding at his nephew and Kori, the tall, rugged man who looked like a younger version of Brian Cavanaugh, his older brother, modestly explained his presence to Kori. "When I heard it was that kidnapping case you two caught, I thought that maybe I could help."

Kori was grateful for the man's interest as well as his offer. "We'll take anything that you might be able to give," she told him in all sincerity.

Sean looked over to the area where his two assistants were dusting for prints. "Caleb, why don't you dust around the bottom half of the outside door?" he suggested. When Kori gave him a quizzical look, he explained his thinking. "You said that someone slipped that envelope under the door."

"They did," Brodie confirmed.

"Maybe they braced themselves against the door when they knelt down. You never know. The knees are the first to go," he commented. "At least it's worth a shot," Sean said.

"I would have never thought of that," Kori admitted. She had been completely focused on the actual note to the exclusion of every other possibility. "I guess that's why you're the head of the crime scene investigations," she told Sean with a grateful smile.

Sean laughed. "I'm already on your side, Kori. There's no need to try to flatter me," he assured her. He glanced in his nephew's direction. "Tell her, Brodie."

"I think she's already picked up on that, Uncle Sean," Brodie said. He winked at Kori. "She's quick that way."

"I just wanted you to know that I'm really grateful for any and all help," Kori explained. "And I know you're busy," she added.

Sean inclined his head. "Message received," he told Kori. "I'll get back to doing my job. The sooner we dust everything for prints, the sooner we can get out of that poor girl's hair," he concluded, nodding toward the baby's mother.

Since the apartment was so small, there was hardly any place for Rose to go in order to be out of everyone's way, but she still tried. Sitting down by the window, she seemed to almost completely draw into herself as the CSI team did their work, dusting for prints and being as thorough about it as they could.

Kori's attention was drawn over to Rose. She seemed so sad and forlorn, Kori could almost feel her heart breaking for what she knew Rose had to be going through. Not only had the child she had just given birth to been taken from her in less than two days after the momentous event, now her very belief that she had a right to keep that child had somehow been stolen from her as well.

She and Brodie needed to get going, but there was no way she was going to leave Rose when the young mother was all but drowning in self-doubt and who knew what else.

Kori made up her mind and crossed to the young mother. Squatting down in front of Rose, she took the young mother's hands in hers.

The look in Rose's eyes was almost excruciatingly sad. "It's going to be all right, Rose. We're going to find your baby."

Rose's lower lip trembled. "You haven't yet."

There was no blame, no recrimination, in her voice. It was just a sad, simple statement of fact, one totally devoid of any hope.

"No, we haven't," Brodie agreed, coming up behind

Kori and adding his voice to hers. "But that note from the kidnapper just might have given us the ammunition that we need."

Rose turned her body toward Brodie. "How?" she asked.

"Well, first of all, the kidnapper just assured you that your baby is not just still alive, but is also being cared for. And second, this kidnapper went out of his way to put your fears to rest. He took a chance on being caught just to get that note to you. That has to mean something to you."

Following Brodie's example, Kori picked up where her partner had left off.

"It means that he doesn't want to cause you any undue anguish about your baby's welfare. The kidnapper undoubtedly took the baby because he or she must have found out that you were going to give the baby up for adoption—"

"But I changed my mind," Rose pointed out.

"Yes, you did," Brodie continued patiently, "but maybe the kidnapper didn't know that and hadn't heard that you'd changed your mind at the time when he took your daughter."

"But you said he put together that note for me to put my mind at ease," she cried.

"We don't have all the answers yet," Brodie told her, feeling it safer to back off for now. "This is still a work in progress. There might very well be an explanation for all of this that'll come out in the end," he said, doing what he could to keep her hopes up about the matter without getting too involved in any sort of further explanation.

Still sitting beneath the window, Rose wrapped her arms around her knees and hugging them to her, she began rocking in her seat. It was obvious that she was trying to generate some sort of self-comfort from the action.

Kori rose to her feet. She lightly placed one hand on Rose's shoulder, briefly making contact. "We're going to go now," she told Rose. "If you think of anything else—or if you just want someone to talk to—you do have my card."

Rose nodded. "Thank you." She sniffed. "I usually just talk to my grandmother, but she hasn't been around for the last few days."

"Oh?" Brodie said, pausing before they left the apartment. "Is that unusual for your grandmother?"

"Yeah, even though things have been strange between us, she's come to see me when she had time off. But these days, work does keep her pretty busy. I guess she just got busier this last week. It doesn't seem fair because I could really use her now."

She couldn't quite put her finger on it, but alarms went off in Kori's head. She exchanged looks with Brodie. "What does your grandmother do?" Brodie asked Rose. She had a gut feeling they were on the brink of something.

"She's a nurse," the young mother replied. As an afterthought, Rose told the two detectives in her apartment, "My grandmother works at Aurora General Hospital."

Chapter Twenty-Two

Kori could feel her breath suddenly standing still in her chest and her eyes darted toward Brodie's. This was just *way* too much of a coincidence. She could see that the same thing was obviously going through his mind as well.

Still, she knew that neither one of them wanted to get ahead of themselves. "Would you happen to have a picture of your grandmother anywhere?" Kori asked in as calm a voice as she could manage.

"Yes," Rose answered. Standing, the young woman crossed to the tiny, pseudo fireplace that was up against the opposite wall. The fireplace with its small mantel was decorative rather than functional. "The picture's right…" Her words disappeared, much the way the photograph she wanted to show them had. Rose looked bewildered. "Well, I thought it was right here," she told Kori and her partner. She looked at the empty mantel, then sheepishly back to the detectives. "I guess I must have put that picture someplace else."

The only problem was, Brodie thought, there was hardly any place else where she could have misplaced the photograph.

"Will this do?" Rose asked, taking her wallet out of her purse. Searching through several credit cards, she found a faded photograph of herself when she was around ten or eleven years old. She was standing next to a stern older woman. "That's my grandmother," she told them.

Kori looked at the photograph. It wasn't all that clear, but at least it was something.

"How about a name?" Brodie asked their victim. "Can you tell us your grandmother's name?" Armed with that information, he felt it would be simple enough to obtain everything else they needed. That would include a better, updated, picture that they could circulate and finally get somewhere, provided Rose's grandmother had been the one who'd kidnapped her own granddaughter's baby.

It sounded unbelievable, but he was also aware that stranger things had happened.

"Sure," Rose answered him. "But why would you want that? I mean, she's my grandmother."

Kori quickly came to the rescue. "She might be able to shed some light on all of this, see it from a different perspective," she explained. "Right now, we're still pretty much groping around in the dark. Your grandmother might have seen something we missed."

"It's usually the smallest clue that winds up breaking a case," Brodie told her, adding his voice to the explanation.

Rose appeared almost solemn as she nodded her head. "Her name is Peggy McGuire, although she might be going by Peggy Larabee. Grandma was married a couple of times," Rose explained, "and I don't know which name she likes to use better."

That sounded like a very strange explanation, Kori thought, but then this was turning into a very strange case. The woman they were looking to interrogate might have a number of aliases. This whole thing wasn't as simple as it had initially seemed.

"What's your grandmother's maiden name, Rose?" Kori asked, thinking that might be as good a place as any to start.

"Her maiden name?" Rose repeated, looking somewhat confused.

Brodie rephrased the question. It occurred to Kori that he was showing a great deal more patience with their victim than she was feeling. "What was her name before she was married to her first husband?"

"That happened before I was born," Rose replied in all innocence.

"We understand that," Brodie continued. "But a bright young woman like yourself could still know that piece of information," he told her, his voice still sounding very calm and soothing.

Kori could only marvel at how controlled he was. Either Rose was so stressed by what had happened that she was incapable of thinking clearly, or she had never been able to do so in the first place.

Meanwhile, Rose had paused, thinking. And then her face lit up as the answer to Brodie's question came to her. "It was Williams," she announced proudly. "Same as mine."

Brodie nodded, appearing pleased. "Good. Very good, Rose. We're going to go now, but we'll let you know the minute we find anything out."

Rose nodded her head, taking what he said to heart and appearing to clutch it to her chest with both hands. "Okay," she replied. And then, looking over her shoulder at the CSI team still in her studio apartment, she asked Brodie, "What about them? Are they going to go with you, too?"

"They'll be going as soon as they finish up. It shouldn't be much longer," he told her.

Rather than look happy to be gaining back her tiny apartment, Rose just grew sadder. "Oh," she cried. "Then I'll be alone."

Kori glanced at the young mother. Rose's words felt like a sharp arrow going right into her heart. Though they needed to get back to doing their job, she couldn't bear just to leave her like this.

"Rose, is there anyone we can call for you?" Kori asked and then came up with several possibilities. "A friend, a relative, someone you worked with?"

But the young woman shook her head in response to every suggestion.

"I don't have any friends," Rose told her. "And except for my grandmother, there is nobody else. My mother doesn't want to have anything to do with me after I got pregnant. And that goes for my cousin, too."

"How about the baby's father?" Brodie asked, knowing that was probably a very long shot.

His last question was met with a negative response as well. Rose shook her head and said, "He took off the minute I told him about the baby and said I wasn't getting rid of it—not in the way he wanted, anyway," Rose clarified. She flushed. "I guess part of me always knew I was going to keep it. Except now I can't because I don't know where she is."

"Hang in there," Kori urged.

She turned toward Brodie to have him back her up, but her partner was talking to someone on his phone. Anticipation surged through Kori. She hadn't heard the cell ring, but there was noise in the tiny studio apartment. Maybe they had finally gotten a lead.

"Skylar," she heard Brodie say into his phone, "you mentioned you were taking a few days off."

He was talking to his sister. Why? What did his sister have to do with anything? It didn't make sense in the middle of all this. And then, as Kori listened, it all began to fall into place.

"Listen," Brodie was saying, "I need a big favor. Yes, I know I already owe you big-time, but this is important," he stressed, apparently cutting into what his sister was saying. "I need you to come and spend a couple of hours with that young mother I was telling you about. Right, the one whose baby was stolen from the hospital," he confirmed. "You will?" As Kori watched, that smile she had become so partial to took over his features. "Knew I could count on you, Sky. Let me give you the address. It's a ground-floor apartment. Oh, and Uncle Sean's here with his team, collecting evidence."

As she listened, Kori could tell from Brodie's body language that his sister was asking him more questions.

"Right, I'll let him tell you all about that when you get here," he said, winding the discussion up. "You're one in a million, Sky. Okay, one in two million," he amended with a laugh. "See you in a few minutes."

With that, he ended the call. Crossing back toward Rose, Brodie told the young woman, "You won't have to be alone when we leave, Rose. My sister said that she can come by and keep you company. She's a police officer, too," he added.

Rose watched him, wide-eyed. "There certainly are a lot of cops in your family." She sighed, somewhat awed. There was a trace of wistfulness in the young woman's voice that was impossible to miss. "It must be nice to have a big family."

Kori caught herself thinking the exact same thing.

"Yes, it is," Brodie readily agreed with a wide smile as he made eye contact with his uncle who had come in a couple of minutes ago. The latter had apparently overheard at least part of what was going on and he nodded his approval.

Making his way over to Sean, Brodie told the man, "Skylar is coming over to keep Rose company. She's already on her way and should be here pretty soon. Would you mind staying until then?" he asked. He nodded toward the distraught victim in the center of all this, his meaning clear.

Attuned to the situation, Sean didn't need convincing. He readily agreed. "Sure. It should take us a while to pack up all this evidence anyway. We'll just pack slower," he told Brodie with a wink.

Brodie's smile deepened. "Knew I could count on you," he told his uncle.

Sean spread his hands wide. "Hey, as your father would have said, 'what's family for?'"

"'Would have' said?" Kori repeated. It was obviously a question, aimed at her partner.

But it was Sean who answered her, looking to spare his nephew. "His father, Donal, passed eighteen months ago."

Open mouth, insert foot. She hadn't known, she thought, distressed that she'd asked so clumsily.

She looked at Brodie. It was the first time she had seen a totally impassive expression on his face.

"I'm so sorry," she said. Since she had broached it so awkwardly, she might as well know the rest of it. "In the line of duty?" she asked, assuming that, given the nature of the Cavanaughs, it probably had to be.

"In bed," Brodie corrected.

Kori's face turned crimson as she thought she had made another awkward blunder.

Seeing her color change, Brodie was quick to set her straight. "From the flu that turned into pneumonia. My father's biggest failing was that he took care of everyone but himself," he told Kori.

Kori debated how to rescue this situation when she heard the doorbell. *Saved by the bell*, she couldn't help thinking.

Brodie was instantly alert. "That should be Skylar," he said, anticipating his sister's arrival.

Going to the door and opening it, he smiled. "You're a life saver," he told his sister.

The tall, slender, pretty blonde dressed in jeans and a comfortable work shirt walked in, instantly owning the space she crossed.

"Remember that when I need your kidney," Skylar told her older brother. Bright green eyes swept over the small room. She nodded a greeting at her uncle's assistants and smiled at Sean. "Hi. Brodie told me that you were working the crime scene."

"That I am. Hopefully," he told Brodie and Kori, "I'll have something you can use soon." He closed the case he had been packing up with a decisive movement of his hands. "All right, see you at the old homestead," he said, addressing his niece and nephew. And then he nodded at Kori. "Detective Kennedy, nice to be working with you."

Sean glanced toward the large-eyed young woman whose home they had just dusted for prints. With all the evidence that had been collected ready to go, he crossed over to Rose. He couldn't help thinking that she looked like a lost waif.

"Don't worry, Ms. Williams. If anyone can find your

baby, it's these two," he promised her, nodding at Kori and Brodie.

Rose raised her eyes toward him, gratitude shining there. To her, Sean Cavanaugh was a father figure—something she hadn't had in her life—and he was kind enough to take the time to reassure her. Rose was more than happy to believe what he'd said to her. She hung on to it like a lifeline.

Brodie was quick to take care of the introductions. "Rose, this is the sister I told you about, Officer Skylar Cavanaugh."

Skylar smiled at the petite woman. "You can just call me Skylar," she told Rose, putting out her hand to shake it. She readily dispensed with formalities since she could see how very vulnerable the young woman obviously was.

It didn't take much to envision her being afraid of her own shadow.

"Rose," the stolen baby's mother said, grasping Skylar's hand like a lifeline and shaking it.

Brodie made eye contact with his sister and mouthed, *Thank you*, before taking the lead and telling Rose that they were leaving now.

"But if you need anything at all, just tell Skylar," he advised. "She knows how to reach me."

The relieved smile he saw on Rose's face told him he had made the right call, asking his sister to come and keep Rose company for the next few hours.

Saying goodbye to his uncle and the rest of the CSI team, Brodie left with Kori.

"YOU REALIZE THAT this doesn't solve the problem," Kori told him as they walked to where she had parked their vehicle. "It just puts a temporary Band-Aid on it."

"Maybe by the time the Band-Aid has to be ripped off, between all of us, we will have located that stolen infant," Brodie replied.

Kori looked at him. Just when she thought she knew what he was capable of, he surprised her by rising to an even higher level. "That was really nice of your sister to agree to stay with Rose—and really nice of you to think of calling her."

"What can I say?" Brodie quipped. "We're terrific people."

Kori got into the car. She wasn't about to let him shrug it off this time.

"Yes, you are," she agreed. "I'm really beginning to see that."

"Just beginning?" he asked with a laugh.

Opening up like this wasn't a joke to her. "Hey, this is hard for me."

Brodie turned his head in her direction and his eyes were smiling at her. He could tell she was being sincere. "And you're doing very well. Although I have to say that there is room for improvement," he deadpanned. "But don't worry, I'll go slow."

She thought of their night together as well as the night before. The very memory made her skin tingle even though they were in the middle of a very serious case. "Oh lord, I hope not," she murmured under her breath.

The very wide smile on his face told Kori that he had overheard her.

Kori forced herself to focus her attention on what was important at the moment, not in the way Brodie made her feel.

"C'mon, let's find out if we can put a face to Nurse Peggy-McGuire-Larabee-Williams-or-Something-or-Other," she urged.

KORI HADN'T THOUGHT it was going to be easy and she was right. When they went to the head of the hospital's HR department, they found the director had taken some time off. But his assistant was there. They asked the woman to help them with their search. The older woman listened to them, then shook her head.

"We don't have a nurse named Peggy here," she informed them.

For a moment, that seemed to take the wind out of their sails. Had this supposed grandmother lied to Rose about what she did for a living? Had Rose gotten confused about where the woman worked for some reason? The young woman was definitely not the brightest bulb in the array, but they both doubted that Rose would knowingly mislead them.

"Wait a minute," Kori said suddenly. "Isn't Peggy short for something?" she asked. She looked at Brodie for his input.

"Don't look at me," he told her. "Nicknames aren't exactly my field of expertise."

His response had Kori turning toward the assistant personnel director. Her own mind had temporarily gone blank. "Help us out here, Mrs. Fielding. Isn't 'Peggy' short for something?"

The woman thought for a moment, then brightened. "Yes, it's short for Margaret."

"Okay, do you currently have a nurse named Margaret or Maggie working here?" she asked. "This nurse would be at least sixty—probably older," Kori amended. "And she could have any one of three last names. Williams, McGuire, Larabee or maybe even something else." Kori looked at the assistant director hopefully.

The woman laughed, shaking her head. "You don't make this easy, do you?"

"Trust us, this is a lot easier than it was an hour ago," Brodie assured the older woman.

The woman merely rolled her eyes. Moving her chair in, she began surveying current personnel files on the computer records.

Chapter Twenty-Three

"Ah, here we are," Angela Fielding declared, seeming very pleased with herself. She had finally managed to locate the person whose file she had been trying to find for the last half hour. "Margaret McGuire," she proudly announced. Scanning a few of the lines in the file, she looked up at Brodie. "We don't have this woman working on the maternity floor. Margaret McGuire is one of our pediatric nurses." The assistant personnel director kept reading. "But she's been with the hospital for over ten years. Before that, she worked over at Madison General. She did work on the maternity floor there. Anything else?" she asked brightly, looking from one detective to the other.

"Yes," Kori interrupted. "Do you have her picture on file?"

"Of course we have her picture on file," the woman replied shortly. And then she apparently heard her own tone of voice and attempted to temper it, sounding more amicable. "These days, everyone's got a picture everywhere," she added with a weary sigh. "This is probably the most photo-obsessed generation in history."

"May we see it?" Brodie gently prodded.

The small, dowdy woman seemed to come around. "Sure. Help yourself," Mrs. Fielding said, turning her monitor around so they could both get a better view of the photo of Margaret McGuire that was on file.

It wasn't a very flattering photograph and if Kori were to make a guess, she would have said that it had probably been taken on the day the nurse had been hired, which meant that the photograph was dated. But there definitely enough of a resemblance to a nurse they had seen on one of the surveillance cameras on the day the infant had been kidnapped.

Kori studied the photograph. Maybe it was her imagination, but the woman in the photograph definitely looked a lot like an older version of Rose. That *couldn't* have been a coincidence, Kori thought.

"And that's Margaret McGuire?" Brodie asked the assistant personnel director just to be completely sure.

"That's what her employee record shows," Mrs. Fielding answered.

"Could we speak to her?" Kori requested. She couldn't help feeling that they were on to something. Or maybe it was just wishful thinking on her part. But either way, they needed to speak to the woman.

"Let me see," the assistant personnel director said, holding up her index finger as she pulled up the latest information that had been entered into the file and scanned it slowly. Coming to the bottom of the page, she looked up and shook her freshly colored ginger head. "I'm afraid that's not possible right now," Mrs. Fielding told them.

"Why not? She's not in today?" Brodie prompted, thinking they would just seek the nurse out in her home.

"According to her file, she's not going to be in any day, at least not for the next month." Her eyes met Brodie's. "Nurse McGuire put in for a leave of absence from the hospital."

Kori had a bad feeling about this. "When?" she asked.

"As a matter of fact—" the assistant director went back to scanning the file for the answer "—she took it three days ago." The look on the woman's face was clearly sympathetic. "The poor thing, I think the turmoil at the hospital because of the kidnapping was just too much for her. According to her file…" Mrs. Fielding paused to read further in the file. "She's always been a very dependable, slow and steady worker. She didn't like her routine deviating from its normal path." She looked at the two people sitting before her. "I guess you could say she's a perfectionist. But her patients' parents loved her."

"Good to know," Kori mumbled. She really wasn't interested in how much her patients' parents loved her, she was only interested in her interaction with one patent in particular. "Do you have her current address and phone number on file?"

The woman looked as if she took that question as a personal insult. "Of course we have her current address and phone number on file. What sort of a hospital would we be if we didn't keep up on things like that?" she asked.

One that apparently could be easily fooled, Kori thought, but she kept that to herself. She also avoided Brodie's eyes, sensing that he might disapprove of the way she was handling this woman.

"Thank you for your help," she told the assistant personnel director as the woman handed them a printout of what she had just asked for. Kori was anxious to leave to see if they could find the woman in her home. "We'll get back to you if we need to," Kori promised.

She and Brodie left within a couple of moments.

Kori was all but pulsating with eagerness to see this

nurse. "So, what do you think?" she asked Brodie the second they were out of Mrs. Fielding's office and had closed the door behind them.

"I think that we need to pay Nurse McGuire a visit," he told her. "Because unless Rose's grandmother has a twin or a doppelganger somewhere, that is most definitely Rose's grandmother in that file. The one she doesn't seem to be able to reach," he added significantly.

"This doesn't make any sense to me," Kori admitted as they got back to the car. "Why would the woman steal her own grandchild?"

"I'll be sure to ask her that once we find her," Brodie said. "But the important thing right now is that we do find her—*and* the baby."

THEY DROVE TO the address that was listed in the nurse's personnel file. Though Aurora had the very unique distinction that none of its neighborhoods, no matter how old, were run-down, this was definitely one of the oldest residential areas in the city. It had been built before Aurora had even been incorporated.

Margaret McGuire's house was an older, single-story home. It appeared somewhat dated, but it still seemed far from falling apart. It looked as if it had been painted in the last decade and, while fading, had not yet begun to peel or flake.

"What do you think the odds are of finding Rose's grandmother here?" Kori asked.

Rather than parking right in front of Margaret McGuire's house and possibly alerting the woman that anyone was coming, Kori parked her vehicle in front of a house several doors down.

"Honestly?" Brodie asked as he got out of the car on his side. "Slim to none, but you never know. My guess is that for whatever reason, the woman is obviously not thinking clearly."

"I'm not so sure about that," Kori said, slowly scanning the immediate area around the grandmother's house. There was no sign of the woman's car, but it could very well be parked inside the garage. "To her way of thinking, this woman is probably sacrificing everything in order to save an innocent child."

"From what?" Brodie challenged. "From being adopted?"

Kori shrugged, trying to put herself in the older woman's place. "From being passed to someone else like an unwanted stray cat or dog."

That sounded rather extreme to him. "Well, here's hoping that she's not too far gone and we can still reason with her," Brodie said as they walked up to the house in question.

Approaching the door, Kori knocked on it. "Mrs. McGuire? This is the Aurora Police Department. Please open the door. We need to speak to you about your granddaughter."

Only silence met her request. After a couple of beats had passed, Brodie knocked on the door. His deep voice asked that she come to the door and open it.

Still nothing.

"Mrs. McGuire, please open up. We don't want to have to break down your door," Kori said, raising her voice as she tried again. "But we will if we have to."

"She's not home," a reedy, high-pitched voice behind them said.

Surprised, Kori and Brodie both turned around to see a woman in her late sixties, possibly early seventies, with wispy, blond-colored hair framing her round face like a fluffy halo. She was standing on the sidewalk several feet away from the house in question.

Brodie addressed the neighbor first. "Do you know where Mrs. McGuire is?"

The woman, who obviously enjoyed knowing everything that was going on in the neighborhood, shook her head. "No. I saw her drive away on Thursday and, as far as I know, she hasn't been back since. I just thought she went on vacation, which is odd," the woman confided, "because Peggy *never* goes on vacation. I've lived here for fifteen years and in all that time, I've never seen Peggy do anything except go to work and come back. She's very dedicated that way," the woman told them as if she was imparting a major confidence. "I'm Edna Barrett, by the way," she said, introducing herself to them. Her sharp eyes shifted from Kori to Brodie. "Why are you looking for Peggy?"

So, the woman apparently did go by Peggy, Kori thought.

"We have some questions for her," Brodie answered the neighbor.

"Is it about the kidnapping?" the woman asked, clearly thinking that it most likely had to be.

"How do you know about the kidnapping?" Kori asked.

Had Rose's grandmother let something slip while she was talking to this woman? Or maybe she had even confided something to her. Kori felt her hope rising.

But that hope quickly evaporated when Edna looked at her as if her intelligence had been insulted. "Huh. Everybody with a TV knows there was a kidnapping. That poor little girl who was stolen from Aurora General," the woman said, shaking her head like a lamenting member of a Greek chorus. And then she sniffed. "Well, if you ask me, Peggy doesn't know anything about it. If she did, she would have definitely told me."

"So I take it that you two are close?" Brodie asked, leaving the end of his statement up in the air.

Edna sniffed again. "I live next door to her," the woman replied, as if her proximity was the answer to the question he had asked.

"So, WHAT DO you think?" Brodie asked after they had left the curious neighbor holding one of their cards in her hand and promising that she would call them the moment that she saw "Peggy" return home.

Kori laughed softly under her breath. "I think that if Nurse Peggy was close to this woman, that would have been the very first thing out of Neighbor Edna's mouth," she told her partner.

Brodie tended to agree as he nodded in response. "Yeah, I think you're right. She's not the type to keep that—or anything—to herself."

Kori got in behind the wheel, but she didn't start the car right away. Instead, she took out her phone and tapped in the phone number the personnel director had given them for the nurse.

She let the phone ring, counting each ring. When she had reached ten rings, she was about to terminate the call, but she abruptly stopped when she heard what she took to be the nurse's voice.

"Hi," a rather bright, cheerful voice said. "You've reached Peggy McGuire. I can't pick up right now, but leave your name and number and I promise I'll call the minute I'm free."

Kori saw her partner looking at her as she terminated the call, an obvious question in his eyes. "That was the nurse's voice mail. At least we know her phone is on," she said philosophically.

Brodie knew exactly what she had to be thinking. "That means that Valri can trace it for us and tell us where she is." They were all the way on the other side of Aurora, far from the police station. "How fast can you drive?"

He didn't really ask her that, Kori thought. "Just fasten your seat belt, Cavanaugh, and do your best to hold on."

Brodie grinned as he saluted her. "Yes, ma'am," he said.

Taking a breath, Kori put the siren on and stepped on the gas.

THE TWENTY-FIVE-MINUTE TRIP took less than ten minutes.

"You weren't kidding when you said to hold on," Brodie told her as Kori brought their vehicle to a stop in the precinct parking lot. Pretending to look over his shoulder, he commented, "I think my breath is still trying to catch up." He unbuckled his seat belt. Part of him still felt as if they were driving. "Who taught you how to drive like that?"

"Sorry, I promised never to tell anyone his name," Kori deadpanned, pretending that someone had actually taught her how to make hairpin turns like that and drive like a racecar driver.

"Yeah, I can understand why," Brodie replied, opening the passenger door and getting out of the vehicle. Damn, his legs felt wobbly, he thought, taking a cautious step. "If I'd taught you how to drive like that, I wouldn't want it getting around, either." He looked down at his sides. "I think it's going to take a few minutes for my hands to unclench."

"I didn't know you had such a penchant for over-statement," she said as they made their way to the back stairs that led to the police station entrance.

"There's a lot of things about one another we still need to get to know," he replied.

Kori looked at him just as they entered the building. If she didn't know better, that sounded like a plan for their future.

The next second she told herself she was letting her imagination run away with her. There was no time for this. All that mattered was solving this case and, if the anticipation coursing through her veins was any indication, they were right on the brink of that. This feeling she was experiencing was coloring everything else right now, distributing hope where it had no absolute business being.

She could feel her heart pounding with every step she took as her hope kept multiplied. "Do you think that Valri can ping this phone for us and actually locate where Rose's grandmother took her baby?"

"Are you kidding?" Brodie asked her. "Hell, this is the kind of thing that Valri lives for. She can do it in her sleep while juggling building blocks with her free hand."

"While I admire and envy family loyalty, I really hope that your faith in your cousin isn't misplaced," she said to Brodie.

Brodie looked at her. It occurred to him that Kori had obviously not availed herself of his cousin's services on any sort of actual level, otherwise she would have already had her answer.

A smile played along his lips as they went to the elevator. "I won't tell Val you said that. As a rule, she's too sweet to carry grudges, but there is always a first time and I wouldn't want your kidnapping case be the first place it starts," he told her. "That doesn't mean that she won't do what she needs to do to help, but after the dust settles, you will have been relegated to the bottom on her list."

Kori hardly heard him as they rode down to the basement. She was trying her best not to get excited, but it was really hard not to. If all this went right, then they were just hours, possibly even less than that, away from recovering a baby that everyone believed had been stolen and whose fate could have wound up being a great deal worse than it now promised to be.

As she stood there next to Brodie in the elevator, she was hardly able to breathe.

"Hey, are you all right, Kori?" her partner asked, concerned, as he suddenly realized that the woman standing next to him wasn't breathing, or at least she wasn't breathing in any sort of normally accepted way.

"Just praying," she murmured as the doors closed and the elevator began to descend.

Brodie thought over her answer. "It couldn't hurt," he replied. And then Brodie took her hand and wrapped his fingers around it, giving it a squeeze. "But don't worry, it's going to be all right," he promised Kori. "I can just *feel* it," he added as the elevator doors opened and they got out.

They quickly made their way to the computer lab and Valri.

"I really hope you're right," she whispered. And then she thought of Rose. "It's time for this awful nightmare to finally be over for that poor girl." Kori raised her

eyes to Brodie's. "Over in a *good* way," she emphasized with feeling.

She wasn't about to get an argument out of him,
Brodie thought.

Chapter Twenty-Four

Valri looked far from happy to see her cousin and his partner approaching her again. Anyone could see that they obviously were going to make yet another request. Drowning in work, she felt her patience slipping away at an incredible rate.

She frowned at the duo before either one of them could say a single word.

"You do realize that there's a system here, right?" she asked her cousin. "I'm sure you're familiar with it, Brodie. Every fast-food place in the state uses it. It's called 'waiting in line.' And all these people—some of whom, amazingly, you are related to," she said, waving her hand at the piles of paper on her desk, "are in line ahead of you."

"Valri, please..." Kori began.

But Brodie cut in, saying what he felt needed to be said to win Valri over. "This is the same case we were working earlier, Val. We think that the baby's great-grandmother stole her from the hospital," he told her, getting down to the crux of the matter. "The woman's a nurse and could have easily moved in and out of the rooms without raising any suspicions. Moreover, when we went to her house, she appears to have taken off. Nobody's seen her since she took a leave of absence from the hospital right *after* the baby was taken," he said, his voice growing progressively more intense.

Talking, Brodie drew closer and closer to his cousin. "We've got Margaret McGuire's cell phone number. We've tried calling, but all we get is her voice mail," he said, answering the question he sensed his cousin was about to ask. "That means that, for now, her cell is on, but that can change at any second. She could just shut it off at any time and then we won't be able to locate her. We've got a limited time frame here," he emphasized.

His eyes pinned Valri down, silently appealing to her humanity.

Valri sighed and put her hand out for the cell phone number. "You're lucky your partner's got puppy dog eyes," she told Brodie, nodding at Kori.

Amused by the description, Brodie laughed and glanced over toward Kori. "You're right," he agreed, his smile deepening. "Maybe I should start calling you Sparky."

"You do and I'll rip your tongue out," Kori told him with a complacent smile that was nowhere as easygoing as it appeared at first.

"Okay," he nodded. "Looks like 'Sparky' is out for the time being."

"Try forever," Kori replied.

Meanwhile, Valri's fingers were flying across the keyboard, typing the cell phone number Brodie had given her into the website that she had pulled up.

"All right," the lab tech declared as her fingers continued typing at an almost breathtaking speed. "I've managed to triangulate the phone's signal." She drew her words out as more screens came up. Valri hit a few more keys, which brought out a triumphant, "There!" from her lips.

"There?" Brodie questioned, waiting for more of an explanation from his cousin than just that single word.

"I've managed to narrow it down," she told them. "The signal's coming from the Airport Inn across the street from the Aurora County Airport on—"

"That's all right, Valri," Kori said, cutting Brodie's cousin off. "There's no need for us to take up any more of your time. I've lived in Aurora for a good part of my life," she told the lab tech. "I know where the airport is located, and so, I'm sure, does Brodie. MacArthur and Main," she said to prove her point, referring to the major cross streets right at that area. "Okay, let's go, Cavanaugh," Kori said, not bothering to hide her eagerness as she looked at Brodie.

Her partner grinned as he pretended to salute her. "Yes, ma'am."

Swamped though she was, Valri paused to grin at the departing detective next to her cousin. "I *knew* I liked you the first time I met you," she said just before she reimmersed herself in the files that were spread out all over her desk, still waiting for her attention. "Good luck," Valri called out, never raising her eyes from the file she pulled over and had initially been working on when her cousin and Kori walked in.

THE AIRPORT AND the motel that catered to the passengers who availed themselves of its facilities were located only a few miles from the police station.

Without impeding traffic to get in their way, they managed to reach their destination rather quickly. For once, the numerous traffic lights along the way cooperated, allowing them to experience practically an unencumbered trip to the motel.

"Not bad," Kori commented as she parked the car in a lot that was only partially filled.

He caught the surprised note in his partner's voice. "Did we catch you in a lie, Detective Kennedy? I thought you said you were familiar with the place," he reminded her.

"I'm familiar with the airport, not the motel," she told Brodie.

He smiled, his eyes all but shining. "I guess that makes us the perfect pair because I'm familiar with the motel."

Kori picked up on what he *wasn't* saying. "Have you been here before?"

Brodie's shrug was noncommittal. "A time or two."

"Oh?" The single word was probing, asking for more information.

Though he could have continued with this for a while longer, he decided to just tell her the truth. "I was undercover—and alone," he emphasized. "Nothing 'oh' about it."

She believed him. Heaven help her, but she believed him, Kori thought. He wasn't the player that she had initially thought he was. That was a role other, less secure people had assigned to him, most likely out of jealousy.

Kori gestured toward the front of the motel entrance. "I bow to your superior knowledge. Lead the way, Cavanaugh."

He grinned and winked at her as he proceeded in front of her. "I could get used to this."

Kori only had one word for him. "Don't."

Brodie opened the door to the motel registration office and held it for her.

When they walked in, the man behind the desk didn't notice them at first. He appeared to be completely engrossed in the game show he was watching on the small set tucked to the side of the reception desk.

Clearing his throat, Brodie rapped on the desk and spoke up to get the man's attention. "Hey, fella, we're going to need your help here."

Embarrassed at being caught, the man pulled back his shoulders and straightened his shirt. The latter was having some trouble fitting adequately over his expanded girth.

"Sorry. I guess I didn't hear you. Welcome to the Airport Inn," he said, greeting people who he took to be potential customers. "And how long will be you staying with us?" he asked as he flipped the motel's registration book around to face them.

Kori ignored the book. "That all depends on your answer, Mr....Clovis," she said, reading his name on the nameplate on the desk. "Have you seen this woman?" she asked him, holding up the photograph she had taken of Margaret—or Peggy—off the employment file with her phone.

"Why, yes. She checked into the motel three days ago. She had only one request—that I give her the room that was located the farthest from the motel entrance. She paid cash, which was a first for me," the reception clerk confided.

"What room is she in?" Brodie asked.

The clerk didn't have to look to know. "She checked into room twelve, but if you want to catch her, I'd hurry if I were you. She just paid her bill and is checking out of the room right now."

The man ended up saying the words to their backs as Brodie and Kori turned on their heels and hurried out of the small office.

"Come again," he called after them, retreating to the game show he had been watching.

The words *so near and yet so far* echoed in Kori's head as she all but sprinted toward the room number the desk clerk had given them.

What if they had just missed the baby-snatching grandmother? If the woman wound up boarding a plane and flying to another location, they might never be able to find Rose's baby.

She *really* needed to catch up to the woman, Kori thought, moving fast.

Brodie found he had to really pour it on to keep pace with his partner. That caused him to be both surprised and really impressed. There had been nothing about Kori Kennedy to alert him to the fact that she was a runner.

The woman, he thought, was just full of surprises.

At the very far end of the parking lot, Kori saw an older-looking woman carrying what looked like a small, wrapped-up loaf of bread, at first. But as she came closer to the woman, Kori could have sworn that she heard a mewling noise coming from the bundle in her arm.

It was most definitely *not* a loaf of bread.

"That's her!" Kori cried to Brodie. "That's Rose's grandmother. With Rose's baby!" Raising her voice, she shouted, "Stop!" To the woman. Kori was holding her credentials up in the air for the woman to see. There was no way their escaping fugitive would be able to read those credentials from where she was, but Kori knew the woman would be able to surmise what they were.

"Mrs. McGuire," Brodie called out to the woman, "This is the Aurora Police Department. Stop where you are immediately!" he ordered.

A haunted look descended over her features as the woman they were trying to detain looked around, desperately searching for an escape route. She looked like a hunted animal that had been trapped—and knew it.

"Mrs. McGuire, it's over. You can only help yourself if you cooperate," Brodie gently advised. "The baby belongs with her mother," he told her, talking in a slow cadence so as not to fire the woman up. He was fairly certain she wouldn't hurt the baby, but he wasn't about to risk everything on that.

Rose's grandmother looked incensed. "She belongs with someone who doesn't want to give her away like she's some sort of inconvenience."

Kori cut in, thinking that if she and Brodie chipped away at the nurse on two fronts, they could get her to give up.

"Mrs. McGuire, Rose has been crying ever since you abducted her daughter from her room. Your granddaughter doesn't want to give her daughter away. She wants to keep her. To raise her," Kori emphasized.

"She wants to keep her now," the nurse stressed, her arm unconsciously tightening around the bundle she was holding. "But what about tomorrow?" she challenged. "What if she decides to give the baby away tomorrow?"

"You'll be there for her," Kori told the nurse. "You can help her over the rough spots, just like you can help her savor the good moments as well. Raising a baby is hard work," Kori said, her voice low and gentle, as if she were trying to approach a skittish pet. "You know that." All the while, she took small steps toward the nurse, her body language coaxing the woman to eventually give her great-granddaughter to her. "But if she has someone who can be there for her, someone she knows can help her, then she'll be able to get through anything."

Peggy made a small, helpless noise as she looked down at the infant she was holding. "I won't be able to help Rose," she said, raising her chin as if to keep her tears from falling. "I'll be in jail," she told them, looking first at Kori then at Brodie. "I know the consequences of what I did."

"Then why did you do it?" Kori asked her gently.

"Because I wanted this baby to be raised with love," Rose's grandmother insisted. "Strangers can't love her the way family can."

"I beg to differ with that," Kori said, thinking of the couples she knew who had adopted children. "But that's not the point right now. And I can understand your motivation," she said with all sincerity. She turned her attention toward Brodie. The way she saw it, if there was any way around this, then he would be the one who would know. "You've got connections, right, Cavanaugh?"

He understood where she was going with this. Kori was talking about finding a way to keep this grandmother from being arrested and made to pay for taking the baby from her mother.

Brodie wasn't sure if anyone within his family's network was capable of pulling that off.

"I've got connections," he admitted and then added guardedly, "Within reason."

She pretended not to hear the last part. "Well, see if you can reason with your group and find someone in their number who can pull a few strings and have this family reunion become a reality," she said, nodding at Rose's grandmother and then at the baby she was holding in her arms.

Brodie shook his head. "You don't ask for much do you?"

Her eyes met his. "I have faith in you, Brodie," she told him quietly.

He took a deep breath, as if to fortify himself for what he was about to do. And then he took out his phone. "Well, that makes one of us," he murmured.

She put her hand on his. Brodie looked into her eyes, an unspoken question in his own. "Don't make a liar out of me, Brodie."

"I'll give it my best shot not to, Kori," was all he could promise.

She smiled at him. "That'll do just fine." And then she turned toward the nurse who had come so close to making off with the infant she had taken from her granddaughter's room. "It's time, Peggy. You need to hand the baby over to me," she told the nurse in an extremely calm, coaxing voice.

She and Brodie watched as the tears filled the woman's eyes. Holding the small bundle to her, Peggy raised the infant up to her face and brushed her lips against the very soft skin.

"Goodbye little one. I only wanted the very best for you. Great-grandma loves you," she whispered, her voice breaking. And then she looked up at Kori. "Take her," the nurse cried, "before I change my mind."

They both knew that was an empty threat, uttered just to underscore the inner turmoil that Peggy McGuire was going through as she contemplated surrendering the tiny infant.

Very carefully, Kori took the baby into her arms. "You obviously care about your granddaughter's state of well-being, Mrs. McGuire. Otherwise you wouldn't have gone through all the trouble of getting that letter to her, letting her know that her baby was all right. You meant well, and you have a good heart. That's all going to count in your favor," Kori told the older woman.

"The only thing the law cares about is that a crime was committed and I was the one who committed it. Reasons don't matter," Peggy said as if she was already resigned to her fate and to living out the rest of her days behind bars.

"Let's go, Mrs. McGuire," Brodie said, taking the nurse by the arm. He began to steer her toward the vehicle that Kori had driven.

The nurse looked at him in surprise. "Don't you want to handcuff me?" she asked, confused.

"Not really," Brodie answered. He looked toward Kori for confirmation and the latter nodded her head, indicating that she was willing to forego that as well.

"You're not planning on running away, are you?" Kori asked the nurse.

The nurse looked down at her legs. "My running days are long over," she confided.

"Then, no," Kori said. "No handcuffs—as long as you stay on your best behavior."

Brodie escorted the nurse into the back seat of their vehicle, then turned to Kori, prepared to take the baby from her.

But his partner didn't seem ready to relinquish the infant.

"Why don't you drive us back to Rose's apartment?" Kori suggested.

Peggy McGuire looked surprised. "You're not taking me to the precinct?"

"Not to the precinct," Kori confirmed. "I think that this little girl's been away from her mother long enough and it's time for a reunion. That takes precedence over everything else." Holding the infant to her with one hand, she dug into her pocket with the other. Producing the car keys, she held them out to Brodie. "Let's get this little girl home, Cavanaugh."

"Absolutely," he agreed as he carefully helped Kori and her precious bundle into the back seat.

Chapter Twenty-Five

When he looked back at it later, it would have been hard for Brodie to say who cried more when they were reunited with the infant who was the center of the drama, Rose or her grandmother. In his opinion, it was a tie.

Wanting to afford them space, Brodie backed away from the two women, allowing them to fully unleash all the pent-up emotions that had been building inside them during this last chaotic week.

As he glanced in Kori's direction, he saw that she wasn't above shedding a few tears herself, although he could see that she was doing her best to attempt to hide them from him.

Maybe she felt that tears were unseemly, Brodie thought.

"Here," he murmured, handing his partner the handkerchief he always kept on him. The handkerchief was something his late mother had insisted on. He kept up the habit as a way of keeping her memory with him all these years later.

A week ago, Kori would have pushed his hand away, pretending she didn't need the handkerchief, saying it was just dust that had gotten into her eyes. But because of the intense way they had worked together, there weren't any more walls or pretenses left between them.

There was only the honesty of what each of them was going through at the moment.

"We're going to have to take you in, Peggy."

"You're taking me to jail," the woman concluded. "I deserve it," she said, tears gathering in her eyes.

"We're going to take you before my cousin Callie's husband, Judge Benton Montgomery. Benton's fair and he'll be willing to listen to the extenuating circumstances. With any luck, you'll wind up paying a fine and have to do a lot of public service, but there won't be any time served in jail."

Hope instantly entered the older woman's eyes. She looked from Brodie to Kori. "Do you really think so?" she cried.

Brodie nodded. "Yes, I do. For now, stay here with your granddaughter and great-granddaughter. I'll have a police officer stay with you until this can be resolved. Meanwhile, we're going to make an appeal on your behalf with the judge."

The sobbing woman threw her arms around Brodie, thanking him profusely.

WHEN THE POLICE officer arrived, Brodie and Kori left to see the judge. Because of the circumstances, Benton Montgomery had agreed to meet with them tonight.

"So we're not bringing her in?" Kori asked, wanting to be perfectly clear as to exactly what he was thinking.

"Not until after we talk to Judge Montgomery. It's not like Peggy McGuire was part of an active baby kidnapping ring that was stealing babies in order to sell them. This was a very specific occurrence that was slated to only happen the one time. I'm pretty sure that the judge will see it that way."

"What about all the money that this cost the city?"

she asked. "People are going to want answers, not to mention a resolution."

Getting back to their vehicle, Kori paused by the car, then got in behind the steering wheel. She put her key into the ignition, but for the time being, she left it where it was.

"That's why we're going to go see Callie's husband. In this particular case, all Judge Montgomery will care about is that there was a happy resolution to what could have wound up being a really terrible situation," Brodie informed her.

That explanation sounded far too simplistic for her. "Are you sure?" she asked doubtfully.

Brodie didn't even have to spend any time reviewing the facts. "I know the man," he told Kori. "I'm sure. All we have to do is tell him that there was a family misunderstanding, that somehow things got out of hand. Lord knows the man is familiar with those. And if we can assure him that this is the end of it, I'm sure that the judge will be more than happy to accept that as the final result to an uncomfortable episode. Trust me, he would only place that grandmother in jail if there was no hope of this being resolved. Everyone just wants life to get back to normal."

"So we just tell him that mother and child have been reunited and it's all over but the shouting?" she questioned.

"It'll be a little more complicated than that, but essentially, yes," he told her.

Still leaving her key inserted in the ignition, Kori leaned to her right, framed Brodie's face between her hands and then kissed him.

Hard.

When she drew her lips away from his, he said, "Not

that I minded what just happened in the slightest, but what was that for?"

She was suddenly relieved and happy, not just that the baby had been recovered, but that Rose and her grandmother had a good shot at rebuilding their lives—for the better this time.

"For absolutely nothing at all," she told Brodie. "I'm just happy."

"Okay, I can work with that," he told her, nodding his head. "Why don't we go in to the station, give the team the good news that the baby's been recovered alive and well, and after we sign out for the day, we conduct our own private celebration?" he proposed, looking at Kori to see if she was on board.

He could read her answer in her smile. "I think I'd like that."

Brodie nodded. "I don't plan on making you regret saying those words."

"You know," Kori said nearly four hours later after meeting with the judge, presenting the case and getting the man to see things their way, "I am really glad all that is behind us."

It had gone more or less the way Brodie had predicted. The judge had ruled for a great many hours of public service, plus a small fine, but no jail time. Everyone involved was infinitely grateful.

"Considering what a disaster it could have been—at any moment," Kori said. "I'm really amazed that everything went as well as it ultimately did. And not just with the kidnapping," Kori added, turning her body into Brodie's.

Despite the fact that they had just finished making love a few minutes ago, Brodie was finding it very hard to concentrate. The closeness of Kori's nude body was creating havoc within him, making him want her all over again.

Desperately.

There was just something about this woman that made him completely insatiable and sapped his ability to even think straight. He'd never felt like this before and it did scare him a little.

"'Not just with the kidnapping.'" Brodie repeated the words she had just said, confused. "Well, what else is there?"

"Well, for one thing, there's my father and your aunt," she said, reminding Brodie that the issue of their relatives was still very much in the offing. "That whole thing could have ended in a disaster seven ways from sundown," Kori stressed. "Instead, I don't think that I've *ever* seen my dad any happier. And I gather, from the few things he's told me, the same sort of thing can be said about your aunt."

Brodie grinned at that. "Oh yeah, that. I think we're seeing the making of quite the couple," he agreed, running the tips of his fingers lightly and seductively along the outline of her face. He knew that aroused her—as it did him.

Kori could feel herself heating up all over again as her breaths grew shorter.

She wasn't all that experienced when it came to intimate relationships and she willingly admitted it. But the way her heart was hammering, she *knew* she was standing on the brink of something that was really special. Something that was incredibly wondrous.

"Wouldn't it be wonderful if they wound up getting married?" she heard herself saying. The next moment she was reeling back the question. "I know, I know, I'm getting ahead of myself," Kori granted, talking quickly before he could interrupt her, "but I think my dad is way overdue for some happiness in his life and I really believe that your aunt is the one who is more than capable of delivering it."

"No…" Brodie began, but got no further.

"No?" Kori cried. She propped herself up on her elbow, ready to launch into a lengthy explanation of why he was wrong.

Brodie put his finger against her lips, stopping the flow of words he knew were about to burst forth. "No," he repeated, "I don't think you're getting carried away. I happen to think that you're absolutely right. I've never seen two people who were more right for each other than your dad and my aunt—except maybe for you and me," he added.

Kori stared at him, her eyes wider than he'd ever seen. "You and me?" she repeated in disbelief. Was he teasing her?

"Maybe it's 'you and I,'" Brodie amended.

"I'm not correcting your grammar here, idiot!" Kori cried in frustration. "I'm trying to get to the bottom of what you're saying. What *are* you saying?" she asked him in the next breath. "Because it sounded to me as if you were saying that we belong together."

Kori waited for Brodie to correct her, her breath once again threatening to back up in her lungs.

"I was," he told her quietly. "Because I do. Maybe I'm the one getting ahead of myself," he said, repeating her initial statement, "but I've never met anyone who made me as crazy as you do."

"Thank you?" she said uncertainly, not sure if that was a compliment or a criticism.

"And I never met anyone who made me so happy to

be crazy at the same time," he continued. Warming up to his subject, Brodie talked faster. "And I don't want to just be related to you by marriage because my aunt winds up marrying your father. I want to be related to you by marriage because we're the ones who are married to each other."

Her mouth fell open as she sat up so that she could stare down at Brodie. "Wait, did you just propose to me?" she cried, stunned.

He looked almost embarrassed as he nodded. "Badly, but yeah, I did. You don't have to answer right away. As a matter of fact, I'd prefer that you didn't—if the answer's no. It would be better if you think about it—for a long time, because I know that this is the sort of thing that really might need to percolate before it can finally—"

Kori attempted to cut him off. "Cavanaugh—"

Good at being able to talk above a noisy crowd of relatives, Brodie didn't even seem to hear her. "Because I don't want you saying something that I'm going to regret hearing so maybe we should revisit this in six months or so—"

"Cavanaugh—"

"Or maybe I should leave," he said, throwing back the sheet, then stopping short of putting his feet on the floor. "Oh wait, this is my house, so then I guess that maybe you—"

"*Cavanaugh!*" Kori shouted, clamping her hand over his mouth to stop what promised to be an endless stream of words.

Her eyes on his, Kori slowly drew her hand away, ready to clamp it back down again if he insisted on talking again.

But all Brodie said this time was, "Yes?"

Kori inclined her head then repeated the word he had just said. "Yes."

The uncertain look in Brodie's eyes remained as he questioned, "Yes?"

This time she smiled at him, her mouth curving and the smile rising to her eyes as she repeated, "Yes."

And then, just like that, things fell into place. "Then you'll—?"

"Yes," she answered before he could finish forming the question. "Yes," Kori said again for emphasis, then followed it up with several more yeses in case there was any lingering doubt in his mind. "Now shut up and get back to making love to me. My body's getting cold," she told him.

Brodie drew her back into his arms, glorying in the way her body felt against his. "Certainly can't have that," he whispered.

"No," she agreed, "Can't have that. And with any luck, we never will again."

"I'm a great believer in luck," Brodie told her.

"Yes," she said, humor sparkling in her eyes, "Me, too." Her smile grew wider. "Thanks to you."

Any further conversation on the subject—or any subject—was tabled for the moment.

And for a long time after that as well.

Epilogue

"You would think that a man my age who's been through as much as I have wouldn't be so incredibly nervous about taking part in having his own dream come true," Bill Kennedy said, looking at his daughter in the reflection of the mirror that was before him.

He had been trying to tie a bow tie for the last ten minutes and failing miserably.

With a smile, Kori finally stepped in. Gently pushing her father's hands away, she made quick work in creating what in his estimation was the perfect bow tie. "Just proves you're human, that's all, Dad." She stepped back to admire her work. "There," she pronounced with a smile. "Done."

"Thank you," Bill exhaled. "I'm sure Maeve isn't nervous like this. That woman would be as calm as a cucumber in the middle of an earthquake." And then Bill looked at his daughter as fresh thoughts occurred to him. "She is here, isn't she?" he asked his daughter. "You don't think that she had a sudden change of heart and decided she could do better than—"

Kori framed her father's face with her hands, attempting to center him with her gentle touch. "Dad, take a deep breath. It's going to be fine."

He did as she directed, taking in a deep breath. And

then he slowly exhaled it. "Funny, you said the same thing to me that night in front of the convenience store," her father recalled.

"You heard me?" Kori asked, surprised. "You looked like you had passed out from the blood loss and were pretty much beyond hearing anything."

"I know. I was struggling to hang on. The sound of your voice was my lifeline, Korinna." He turned from the mirror to face his daughter again. "You've always been my lifeline, sweetheart."

"Well, your lifeline is telling you to get a grip, pull yourself together and go begin the rest of your life by marrying that wonderful woman who's waiting for you," Kori instructed, the smile on her lips lighting up the rest of her face.

Bill laughed, briefly giving his daughter a quick hug. "I make it a point never to disobey a beautiful woman."

"Yeah, yeah, save it for Maeve," Kori told him with a laugh. "Now let's get you to that altar before those very sturdy legs of yours buckle."

Bill nodded. "Good point."

At that moment, there was a knock on the door and Brian Cavanaugh, looking resplendent in a tuxedo, peered into the tiny room.

"Ready?" Brian asked his friend.

"He's more than ready," Kori told the chief. Gesturing toward her father, she said, "Take him."

Brian laughed. "You know, your daughter is bossy enough to be a Cavanaugh woman," he told Kori's father.

"Tell me about it." And then Bill looked at the man who had saved his life, a touch of anxiety in his voice. "Maeve is here, right?"

"I think she actually opened up the church," Brian told him.

"See, I told you so, Dad," Kori said. "Unlike you, the woman has nerves of steel. Don't make her come looking for you. Go on up there," she ordered.

Leaving her father and his best man in the small back room, Kori made her way into the front of the church. She slipped into the first row, taking a seat on the left side, the one that was reserved for the groom's family and friends.

She had just enough time to nod at several people before she heard the beginning strains of the "Wedding March" filling the air. Rising with the rest of the people in the pews, she turned around to watch Brodie, with Maeve on his arm, slowly make their way to the front of the altar. Her future stepmother was tastefully attired in a lacy, beige, street-length dress.

She looked perfect, Kori thought.

Maeve was beaming as she made her way toward the man who had won her heart.

Watching Brodie accompany his aunt and then step back after he brought the woman to her father, Kori could feel her heart swelling. Never in her wildest dreams had she ever thought that this was possible—that she would ever see her father *this* happy. It was obvious that she felt he had a totally new lease on life and something to look forward to: a life to build with a partner he loved beside him.

Kori held her breath as she listened to the chords from the "Wedding March" fade off.

Though tears had suddenly risen in her eyes, almost blinding her, Kori could still see Brodie smiling at his aunt, then squeezing her hand as he whispered something to the woman who had helped raise him and his siblings after his mother had passed away.

Maeve smiled up at him, beaming and obviously responding to what he had said just before she turned to her fiancé and husband-to-be.

Brodie stepped away and took his place right next to Kori. After a beat, he bent his head and whispered, "So, what do you think about us being the next ones to march up the aisle?"

Stunned, thrilled, Kori's heart was hammering wildly as the priest began the ceremony, addressing the congregation.

"Dearly beloved…"

"I'd like that very much," she whispered back to Brodie, the man she already envisioned as her partner in every sense of the word.

"Yeah," Brodie agreed. "Me, too."

Filled with anticipation of what was to come, Brodie and Kori grew silent so that they could hear the priest say the words that would join her father and his aunt for all eternity.

They knew that they would be standing like that before the priest as well as their family and friends soon enough.

They could hardly wait.

* * * * *

COMING SOON!

We really hope you enjoyed reading this book.
If you're looking for more romance, be sure to
head to the shops when new books are
available on

Thursday 3rd March

To see which titles are coming soon, please visit

millsandboon.co.uk/nextmonth

MILLS & BOON

THE HEART OF ROMANCE

A ROMANCE FOR EVERY READER

ODERN

Prepare to be swept off your feet by sophisticated, sexy and seductive heroes, in some of the world's most glamourous and romantic locations, where power and passion collide.

STORICAL

Escape with historical heroes from time gone by. Whether your passion is for wicked Regency Rakes, muscled Vikings or rugged Highlanders, awaken the romance of the past.

EDICAL

Set your pulse racing with dedicated, delectable doctors in the high-pressure world of medicine, where emotions run high and passion, comfort and love are the best medicine.

rue Love

Celebrate true love with tender stories of heartfelt romance, from the rush of falling in love to the joy a new baby can bring, and a focus on the emotional heart of a relationship.

Desire

Indulge in secrets and scandal, intense drama and plenty of sizzling hot action with powerful and passionate heroes who have it all: wealth, status, good looks…everything but the right woman.

EROES

Experience all the excitement of a gripping thriller, with an intense romance at its heart. Resourceful, true-to-life women and strong, fearless men face danger and desire - a killer combination!

To see which titles are coming soon, please visit

millsandboon.co.uk/nextmonth

LET'S TALK
Romance

For exclusive extracts, competitions
and special offers, find us online:

f facebook.com/millsandboon

🐦 @MillsandBoon

📷 @MillsandBoonUK

Get in touch on 01413 063232

For all the latest titles coming soon, visit
millsandboon.co.uk/nextmonth

JOIN US ON SOCIAL MEDIA!

Stay up to date with our latest releases, author news and gossip, special offers and discounts, and all the behind-the-scenes action from Mills & Boon...

 millsandboon

 millsandboonuk

 millsandboon

It might just be true love...

MILLS & BOON

MODERN

Power and Passion

Prepare to be swept off your feet by sophisticated, sexy and seductive heroes, in some of the world's most glamourous and romantic locations, where power and passion collide.

MILLS & BOON
MEDICAL
Pulse-Racing Passion

Set your pulse racing with dedicated, delectable doctors in the high-pressure world of medicine, where emotions run high and passion, comfort and love are the best medicine.